Close to Home

Neive Denis

Book 1 of the Merivale Retirement Village series

Copyright

Cataloguing-in-publication data
Creator: Denis, Neive, author

Cataloguing-in-Publication details are available from the National Library of Australia
www.trove.nla.gov.au

ISBN: 978-0-6489423-7-5 (paperback)
ISBN: 978-0-6489423-8-2 (digital)

Cover design: T A Marshall, Mackay, Australia

Disclaimer

This novel is a work of fiction. All characters and events are the product of the imagination of the author. While some of the characters might remind you of people you know, they are fictitious and any resemblance to anyone living or dead is purely coincidental. Although some locations also may seem real and familiar, most places referred to in this work constitute a collage of places the author has known. But they are fictitious, and any resemblance to an existing location is coincidental.

Contents

Chapter 1

"Here we are again… And I see one of us is missing. Is she lost to us forever, or just running late?"

The Activities Room at the Senior Citizens' Centre was abuzz with activity. Rod Maguire, hands buried deep in pockets, sauntered in and stopped. After scanning the room, he asked his question before continuing over to where our group had pushed two of the small tables together and now was busy setting up mahjong tiles.

"Looks like Alice isn't joining us today," he continued. "I assume she knows the place is open for business again."

"…Looks like she isn't joining us *again* today," Bernard Stuart-Parnell corrected him. "By the way, has anyone seen or heard anything of Alice lately?"

Without pausing what we were doing, there was a collective 'no', and a couple shook their heads for emphasis. Perhaps feeling a bit rude about the group's response to Bernard's question, Janet Furlong cleared her throat and volunteered a little more information.

"Well no, I don't think I've seen her since our last get-together here at the Senior Citizens' Centre."

Then Bernard turned to me. "What about you Marion?" Bernard demanded. "You're one of Alice's best friends. Have you heard what she is up to?"

"No. Like Janet, I haven't seen Alice since our last time here before they closed the place for refurbishment."

"*Refurbishment…,*" echoed Marjorie Bosworth. "It's a bit rich to call splashing a lick of paint here and there, and replacing the dead stove in the kitchen, a *refurbishment*. If you ask me, it's more like paying scant attention to a fraction of the long overdue maintenance the place requires."

"It's as well I didn't ask you, Marjorie. If I had, who knows what you might have had to say at the top of your voice so all and sundry could hear," Bernard added with an audible sniff.

I rushed in to avoid the all-too-often slanging match between Bernard and Marjorie. "I admit it's not like Alice not to make contact sometime during the last month. But, just after they gave us notice about this place closing down for a couple of weeks, Alice suggested she might make use of the time to visit her children. When I hadn't heard from her, and she didn't show-up last week, I assumed she must still be away visiting her kids."

"Why would she want to visit them?" Marjorie asked. "They never visit her; rarely even call her. The daughter doesn't have time for her mother. She is too busy being important at whatever it is she does. And, as for that son of Alice's... he's probably in gaol somewhere – again."

Janet Furlong shot her husband, Ted, a beseeching look. Message received, he attempted to intervene. "Now, now, Marjorie, not everyone in this world has the luxury of raising perfect children, and Alice is no exception. In spite of parents' efforts, offspring don't always turn out the way their parents hoped. Nevertheless, I agree someone as nice as Alice does deserve better than the way hers are."

"Do you think we might play mahjong sometime soon? I mean, like before they chuck us all out when they want to close up at the end of this morning's session?" Rod suggested.

"And that's another thing. It would be nice to have two sets of four players at least once in a while, instead of having to play two groups of three because people don't turn up," Marjorie grumbled. Nobody responded, as we all hurried to take our places and begin the games.

For the next few minutes, the only sound from the group was the clack of the tiles. At least it was, until something registered with Rod. "I've only just noticed, but isn't that a new group over there in the back corner. They aren't part of the regular line-up on a Tuesday morning are they?"

"No, they haven't been here on Tuesdays before. This is the start of the new season's offering by U3A (University of the Third Age). The group used to meet here on Wednesdays, but had to move to another day to make way for a new Learn-to-Paint class. I think today might have been the only spare slot for them to move into," Janet said.

"What is it they do anyway?" demanded Marjorie. "It looks like some sort of kindergarten group with so much coloured paper and cardboard, and stuff all over the tables."

"They make greeting cards, really fancy ones. I think what they do is called 'paper tole'. I've seen some of the work they produce, and it's beautiful, and so clever. I'd love to give it a go but, as I don't have a creative bone in my body, it would be a waste of time," Janet continued.

"Maybe that's what's happened to Alice," Ted suggested. "Maybe she's decided to give one of the new classes a go instead of playing mahjong. The line-up of courses U3A offered this term was extensive, and some of it was tempting. It's possible Alice also found it tempting and decided to try something new."

"Well, it's damned rude of her if it's what happened. The least she could have done is let us know she wouldn't be available for our Tuesday games." Bernard finished with one of his trademark sniffs for emphasis. "And, what about our Thursday games at the Village, is she planning to join us for those?"

"Those are questions to which we don't have answers as yet. Perhaps, if Marion can make contact with Alice, we might find out a little more about her intentions," Rod suggested.

"What if she's decided she is not coming back to mahjong? What are we going to do about finding additional people to allow us two sets of four players? Should we start contacting those other occasional players to try to persuade them to become regulars?" Marjorie asked.

"It might be a bit too soon just yet. Let's see if we can find out what Alice is doing before we do anything else," Rod replied.

Bernard drummed his fingers on the table as he thought about Marjorie's suggestion. "It would be pointless speaking to Brian Thomas. He spends more time out fishing than at home, and I doubt he's willing to give up any of his fishing time to help us out."

"Maria Lancini might be a possibility if we asked her. The last time I spoke to her, she was thinking of getting rid of her big house, and asked about vacant cottages at the Village," I told them.

"What about that Shirley woman?" Marjorie asked. "I grant you, she is pretty clueless, but she would give us one more player."

"I'm not so sure about Shirley Reardon. As Rod said, let's wait until we know what is happening with Alice before we do anything else." Not wanting to mention things I had seen in recent days, I rushed in to echo Rod's suggestion and quash any further mention of Shirley as a possible player.

The rest of the morning passed without comment, and with our mahjong mob hard at it right up to the last minute before the Centre closed its doors for the day. As we made our way out to our cars, we broke into two smaller groups according to the vehicles in which we would travel: Ted, Janet and Marjorie in one group, and Rod, Bernard and me in the other.

Our Mahjong group consists of seven regular players – when Alice is around – and with one of the two others who happens to be around on the day making up the eighth player to give us two groups of four. Six of us, Rod Maguire, Janet and Ted Furlong, Bernard Stuart-Parnell, Marjorie Bosworth, and me, Marion Dawson, live in the Merivale Retirement Village. Our seventh regular player, Alice Logan, lives across the park from the Village. While two of our occasional players, Maria Lancini and Brian Thomas, live close by in town.

"It strikes me as highly unlikely Maria Lancini will do anything about moving to Merivale Retirement Village until her husband finally does the right thing and drops off the twig," Bernard mused as we drove away from the Senior Citizens' Centre.

"That's an awful thing to say, Bernard," I exclaimed. "The poor man can't help being as ill as he is, and Maria is devoted to him."

"Now, now, children – let's not bicker about it. There's been enough already this morning." Rod, always the peacemaker, had found this morning's tit-for-tat episodes more tiresome than usual. It was obvious he longed to be home in his cottage at the Village, with a sandwich and a coffee for lunch, and the midday news on the TV. We two passengers took the hint, and spent the rest of the drive to the Village silently wrapped in our own thoughts.

Back in my cottage at the Village, while filling a kettle at the sink to make coffee, I looked out the window. The view from my kitchen window is across the park to the brick and glass monstrosity that is Alice's house. While the home is glorious inside, from my window, it appears more an impenetrable fortress than a place in which to live and bring up a family. After wrestling with the question of when might be the best time to make the trek across the park, I decided to try calling Alice as soon as I had settled down with my lunch. And, I would continue trying to call my friend until such time as someone answered.

Chapter 2

Thursday mornings the group spend playing mahjong in the Village's Recreation Room. The arrangement is for everyone to arrive by 9:30 for a quick coffee and chat, before being seated and ready to start playing by ten o'clock. By some unknown process, setting up for the morning and organising something for morning tea seems to have fallen to Rod and me. While neither of us minds the responsibility, I often find myself wondering by what process the two of us were allocated the jobs.

By the time I arrived with the morning coffee supplies and a batch of freshly baked scones, Rod, in his usual fashion, had arrived early and was busy organising tables and chairs. Within a few minutes, everything was ready. The tables and chairs were in place, and the urn was coming to the boil. It would be about another twenty minutes before the others arrived, so Rod and I dragged out a couple of chairs and sat down to chat while we waited.

"Rod, before the others arrive, and just so you know what's been happening, I've tried calling Alice a number of times since last Tuesday morning. There's been no answer. Although I've never used it, I happen to have her mobile phone number as well as her landline number. So, last night I tried calling her a couple of times on her mobile. It didn't get me anywhere either. I suppose, if anyone asks today, the bottom line remains the same as it was on Tuesday: I don't know what's happening with Alice, but I suspect she is not at home."

"We can't do any more than we've done already. After all, Alice is entitled to live her own life however she likes, and has no obligation to keep us informed. If the others start on about Alice again today, I'll try to quash it. By the way, I felt there was more to the way you dismissed further comment about Shirley Reardon the other day. Is there something I should know?"

7

"No-o, not really..."

"That sounds like a *yes, but I'm not going to tell you* sort of response. Look, I know Shirley is a bit different, but if there is something, please alert me to it."

"I'm not playing silly beggars, or being a bit coy about Shirley. It's just... Look, I'm not an expert but, in recent times, Shirley's 'different' seems to be 'more different'. Have you noticed anything?"

"No, I can't say I have. But, is this something we should mention to management? ... For Shirley's own sake I mean; not for any other reason."

"As I said, I'm no expert. Let's just leave it for now, but keep a bit of an eye on her whenever she is around."

There was no time to discuss Shirley further, or anything else. The others had arrived accompanied by all the usual banter and dragging of chairs across the floor. As usual, Bernard stood out in the crowd, and stand-out he certainly did – big time – when he stood next to Rod. A stranger might be forgiven for wondering just what type of gathering this was. Bernard, adhering to his usual dress code, wore a mustard-coloured, long sleeved shirt with vibrant blue and cerise-spotted bow tie. While Rod was in his standard 'uniform' of colourful board shorts, a tee shirt and sandals.

Within a couple of minutes, everyone was tucking into scones and coffee, and arguing about who would play on each of the tables today. When morning tea was almost finished, Bernard spotted a U3A brochure on one of the spare tables. After picking it up and glancing at it, he folded it in half, and was about to stuff it in his pocket.

"Oi, Bernard, no you don't. That's my brochure," I yelled across the room at him. "Put it back."

"Why should I? It was just lying there. I assumed management acquired a few copies for the benefit of residents, and this was the last one left. As it doesn't have your name on it, I don't see why I shouldn't take it."

"You can be such a prick, Bernard," Ted said.

Before the situation degenerated into another slanging match between Ted and Bernard, I jumped in to explain. "Rod brought it over for me this morning. I left it in his car after Senior Cits on Tuesday."

"Oh, thinking of taking on something new are we?"

"No, Bernard. But, what if I were? As tempting as it might be right now, I didn't take it for me. I wanted it for a friend who, following the death of her husband, needs to find an interest outside her home. I intend giving the brochure to her the next time she comes for coffee."

Before Bernard had a chance to say more, Rod cut in. "Even if all of us haven't finished our coffees, do you think we might get our games underway in the next few minutes – if not sooner?" His comment resulted in much embarrassed shuffling of feet, and included a fine display of huffing and sniffing by Bernard, as everyone hurried to finish their coffees and make their way to the tables to start their first game. While the other four rolled the dice to see who would play first in their game, Rod and I started clearing away our morning tea stuff before beginning our game.

As their game got underway, Ted, prompted by an earlier comment by Bernard, introduced a new topic of conversation.

"Mention of starting something new reminded me of something I've spoken to U3A about a few times in the past. I asked them about it again when they were putting together this season's list of courses. Just for something different, I wouldn't mind learning to play Bridge, but U3A say there isn't any interest, and they don't have anyone to teach it. What do the rest of you think about learning to play Bridge, or do any of you know how to play?"

After a shaking of heads all round, Janet said, "I suppose it would be good to be able to play something else besides mahjong, but I don't think I would be any good at Bridge. I think it's fairly complicated, and you have to keep scores, and all that sort of thing."

"Alice knows how to play Bridge," Rod said. "She used to be something of a gun player from what I've heard, but I don't think she's had a chance to play much lately. While I don't know much about the game, I agree with Janet. It might be worthwhile learning to play something else as well. Maybe we should put it to Alice the next time we see her."

"Huh, whenever that might be… and why would we want to learn something else when we can't even dredge up eight players for mahjong?" Marjorie demanded.

"It was just something I'd been thinking about for a while, Marjorie; nothing more," Ted replied.

Chairs were scraped out from the table as Rod and I, accompanied by our unfinished coffees, faffed about preparing for our first game for the morning. Just as our game seemed set to begin, a further delay occurred.

"Hello, may I come in? Is this a private get-together, or may I join you?" An unfamiliar woman hesitated in the doorway.

Rod sprang up and rushed over to the new arrival. Their mahjong games abandoned, in an instant, the other players' eyes followed Rod and me as we moved to welcome her.

"No, there is nothing private going on here. Come on in. You're the new resident who moved in across the way from my place a couple of days ago aren't you? I am Rod Maguire by the way. Welcome to Merivale Retirement Village. Let me introduce the others."

"Oh, yes, I noticed you out in your garden. I'm Cilla Longhurst. As Rod said, I only moved in a couple of days ago, and I'm still finding my way around the place. Today, I thought I'd check out this recreation room to see what goes on in here. Is there a regular schedule of things held here… maybe a program of coming events, or something similar?"

"Not as such," Rod replied. "It's mostly up to the residents to organise whatever they want to do but, apart from some sort of sewing group which meets here once a month, I think we're the only lot who uses the place on a regular basis."

"There is a small library of sorts in the bookcases along the wall over there." I volunteered. "It's not great, and the books aren't shelved in any particular order. Again, it's up to the residents to look after it. There is supposed to be a library committee, but I've no idea who is on it, and they certainly haven't done anything for a long while."

"Be good if they acquired a few new books for it," Janet added.

The next couple of minutes were taken up with Rod carrying out introductions and everybody shaking hands and welcoming the new resident to the Village. I extended the welcome a little further. "Come and join us. Would you like a coffee? And, help yourself to a scone."

"You don't happen to play mahjong do you?" Bernard asked as Cilla slathered jam and cream on a scone.

"Well, I have played a bit, but it was a while back. I'm no expert."

"Nor are we, My Dear, but it doesn't stop us playing twice a week," Bernard continued. "Why don't you pull up a chair and join us this morning? We play here every Thursday morning and, on Tuesday mornings, we go into the Senior Citizens Centre to play there."

"Thank you, but I wouldn't want to intrude."

"You wouldn't be intruding, Cilla," Janet said. "We could do with another player. So, you would be helping, not intruding."

"Yes, you are more than welcome to join us if you feel so inclined," Rod agreed. "You could play with Marion and me. It would be good to have a three-handed game again."

At last, the clack of the tiles resumed as the day's games got underway again. I noticed Marjorie frowning at the tiles. Deep furrows creased her forehead and her eyebrows were separated only by a couple of vertical furrows. I felt compelled to ask, "Is everything all right, Marjorie? You look as though something is bothering you."

"I was trying to remember what Ted was talking about just before Cilla arrived. I felt we might have left the conversation unfinished. What were we talking about, Ted?"

"Bridge… and how I thought I'd like to learn how to play it. Rod said Alice knew how to play, and suggested we might ask her to teach us."

"Yes, that's right. I remember now. There was something I wanted to add to the discussion." Ted steeled himself in readiness for an expected rubbishing by Marjorie, but he need not have bothered. She continued, "What's the point in talking about asking Alice anything? We don't even know if she is still on the face of this earth, or if she intends having anything more to do with us."

Rod's reply was sharper than he intended I suspect, but it probably was an accurate reflection of how he felt about Marjorie's comments.

"Those sorts of comment are uncalled for, Marjorie. Marion is endeavouring to find out what's happening with Alice, but without success so far. Alice is one of Marion' best friends. She doesn't need to hear such comments from you, or anyone else." His outburst caused a blanket of silence to cloak the recreation room. For the next hour or so, only the clack of the tiles punctuated by the occasional exclamation of victory or disappointment was heard.

When all the day's games were won and lost, Cilla stayed behind to help Rod and me clean and tidy up. Chores completed, the three of us then walked back to our respective cottages together. Part way along the street, Cilla asked, "Would it be out of order for me to ask what's going on with Bernard and Marjorie?"

"You wouldn't be out of order, Cilla, but what do you mean by 'going on'?" Rod asked.

"They both seem so angry about something. I couldn't work out whether it was with each other, or maybe with everything in general. It was hard to tell. Was it because I delayed the start of their game, or is it possible it was because of something I said?"

Both Rod and I dissolved into fits of laughter. "Oh no, Cilla, don't take their behaviour personally. It's how they are all the time," I replied. "They don't mean anything by it. It's just the way they are: aggressive and anti-everything. I do admit though, their negativity can become a bit wearing at times."

"What about the comments about Alice? Is there something there I should know about?"

By the time we reached my cottage, Rod was only part way through explaining the current situation regarding Alice. We waited outside my gate until Rod finished his story before the other two said goodbye and headed off to their own places.

As I cut a couple of thick slices from a Vienna loaf, it was Alice occupying my mind, not sandwich making. Although I tried to play it down in front of the others, I was worried about my friend. I paused and peered out the window, allowing my whole attention to focus on Alice's house on the other side of the park. It didn't matter what I tried telling myself, something was not right. It was not like Alice not to contact me in some way; even just a postcard. And, she hadn't even said goodbye before she left.

The last I heard from her, she thought she might take advantage of the Senior Citizens' Centre's shutdown to visit her kids. At the time, it sounded as though it was just a vague idea; not a definite plan. Then, after that last Tuesday at the Senior Cits'… nothing; no further contact at all. Had something happened to Alice, something serious? It would have to be serious for her to be out of contact with her friends … and not to have said goodbye, if she were going away. Perhaps something had happened to one of her children and she was called away at short notice.

That thought led my mind down a dark track. What if it hadn't been one of the kids? What if it was Alice something had happened to? Alice was about the same age as the rest of our group; in excellent health, and probably way fitter than the rest of us. Still, things can go wrong when least expected. Accidents do happen.

"Stop it!" I exclaimed. It was so loud in the silent house, I startled myself, but I continued my reprimand. "Stop this nonsense right now. Such thinking will do neither me nor Alice any good. If I keep it up, I will drive myself mad. Get on with lunch."

Having slapped slices of ham and tomato, and a leaf of lettuce on each slice of bread, I took my lunch through to the sitting room. As I ate it, I intended listening to the news channel on TV to allow the current woes of the world to ward off any further dark thoughts about Alice. It worked. I dozed off about five minutes after finishing my last sandwich.

It was gone three o'clock when I surfaced from what had been a deep sleep. Rubbing my now stiff neck and flexing my shoulders to encourage life back into them, I made my way to the kitchen. Coffee might boot some life back into me. As I waited for the stovetop mocha coffee pot to finish doing its thing, I once more looked across the park to Alice's house. For various reasons over the past couple of days, I had missed out on my regular afternoon walks. Today, I would walk – across the park to check out Alice's place.

At five o'clock, my usual hour for a stroll at this time of the year, I set off at a brisk pace out of the Village and into the park. Somehow, the park never seemed so wide when viewed from my kitchen window. No matter how often I make the trek to Alice's house, the park always seemed wider than expected, and the trek took longer than anticipated. The late afternoon sun shining through the trees, already dressed in their early autumn colours, created dappled patterns of light along the track. Coupled with a light, cool breeze, it made for a pleasant stroll.

While the walk was pleasant, its terminus proved disappointing. No amount of knocking aroused any interest from inside the house. In desperation, I called Alice's home phone. As I stood outside her front door, I heard it ringing… and ringing … until it went to voicemail. "No point in leaving a message, if no one is going to be there to listen to it," I told the universe. At least now I knew the phone was working and, no doubt, it had rung inside the empty house every time I tried the number over the last couple of days.

No point hanging around any longer, it was time to head back through the park. By then, the sun was well down, and the previous pleasant breeze now had a chill to it. Opting to avoid the trees in favour of open ground to make the most of the last warmth of the sun, I set a brisk pace for home. My return journey had me enter the Village at the opposite end of the street from where I set out.

As I strode along the street, I heard talking coming from somewhere up ahead. It became louder, and I realised it was coming from Shirley Reardon's front garden. Shirley never had visitors, and hadn't seemed to make any close friends since moving to the Village some years ago. Guilt flooded through me. I was guilty of not having made any effort to know Shirley better. The most I had ever done, if Shirley should happen to be out in her garden, was to say a few words as I passed by. Perhaps I had misjudged her situation. This evening, Shirley was having a long conversation with someone in her garden.

Curious, but determined not to intrude, my intention was to give Shirley a smile and a wave as I walked past. It didn't quite happen as intended. She was standing with her back to the street, and appeared to be in deep conversation with a rose bush, which she kept calling Vera. Mystified and a bit taken-aback by what I witnessed, I found my feet glued to the pavement in front of her house. As I stood there, she switched her attention from 'Vera' to a nearby shrub with purple flowers. I soon discovered it was called Dorothy. A few moments into Shirley's conversation with 'Dorothy', it dawned on me Shirley wasn't *talking to* the shrub. She was *responding to* something 'Dorothy' had said to her. Not wanting to be caught eavesdropping on Shirley's conversations, I persuaded my feet to start moving again.

Back in my own cottage, I poured myself a red wine and took it out into the back garden where I could sit in privacy to consider what I witnessed at Shirley's place. If I were honest, it tended to confirm something I already suspected. I had noticed Shirley do a few odd things over the last several months. Granted, they were insignificant but, when added to the strange things she said on occasion, it did tend to suggest something serious was amiss with our fellow resident.

Although I had intimated as much to Rod at the Rec Room this morning, he hadn't appeared concerned. Should I do something about it … but, if so, what? Shirley was free to live her own life. If she chose to have conversations with her plants, it was her business... Wasn't it? Who was I to judge? Her chats didn't harm anybody. And, if I thought about it, I was guilty of listening to something which was none of my business. Did I have the right to do anything which might interfere with one of a lonely old woman's few pleasures in life? Nevertheless, if Rod should happen to mention Shirley again, I know I won't be able to refrain from telling him about today's episode.

As I lay in bed that night, the vision of Shirley's conversation with her plants returned to unsettle me. "Why is it bothering me so?" I asked the night. "It was harmless. So, why should it concern me like this?" The night offered no answers. Come to think about it, Shirley might have conversations with her plants, while here I was talking to the night. Was there any difference?

Nevertheless, before sleep finally stilled the turmoil in my mind, I knew I would be making a major effort to spend time with Shirley in future. How to go about it was another question to which I had no answer... yet.

*****

Friday brought with it a feeling of something less than enthusiasm for the day. Concern for my friend, Alice, coupled with an uneasy feeling about fellow resident, Shirley, dogged me from the moment I opened my eyes. Concern was one thing, but how to do something about either of those issues was another matter. And, to add to my worries, was what I saw happening to Shirley, the same as might be in store for the rest of us before too much longer?

"Should I talk to Rod about my concerns?" I mused aloud as I waited for my coffee to brew. "What could I tell him? Anyway, it's not something I am able to deal with today."

With a visit to my chiropodist, lunch in town with a friend, and a visit to the city library, booked for today, there would be little time for anything else. Although, maybe I could ask my lunchtime friend, Lynn, if she knows anything of Alice's whereabouts. Lynn had been a close friend of Alice since her primary school days. After they lost touch for several decades, Fate brought them together again when Lynn moved back to the district. I knew she and Alice met frequently, so it was possible Lynn knew what Alice's plans were and where she might be now.

After my bad feeling at the start of the day, after breakfast, my Friday continued to go downhill. A call from a distant (in-law) family member to tell me of the death another even more distant (in-law) family member seemed to drag on and on. In the end, and with a certain degree of rudeness, I was forced to end the call. Time was running away from me and I didn't want to be late for my appointment with the chiropodist. But, seconds after I ended the first call, my phone rang again. It was some marketing mob wanting me to complete quick survey. This time, I had no hesitation in being rude and ending the call. Then, 'rush mode' was initiated in a bid to return the day to schedule.

Almost panting after rushing along the street, I entered the chiropractor's rooms right on time for my appointment. As it turns out, I needn't have bothered. He was running behind time, and I spent the twenty minutes of waiting time surreptitiously checking out my attire. I had been in such a rush to dress and leave home this morning, I wasn't sure I even managed to put on matching shoes. After checking I was fully and satisfactorily attired, I settled down to read the faded posters on the walls for the last few minutes before my name was called. But, somewhere during that time, I did make a mental note to do something about my fitness or lack thereof as evidenced by my panting arrival at the chiropractor's.

But, the rushed pace of my day didn't end with my arrival there. The 'domino effect' prevailed. Soon after he started with me, an urgent phone call took the chiropractor away the best part of ten minutes. By the time I stepped back out onto the street again, it was more than half an hour later than I expected. I had planned to visit a department store to pick up a few necessary items before heading to the bistro for lunch with Lynn. Now, I calculated I had just about enough time to drive across town to the bistro and arrive on time.

Deciding the things I wanted from the department store weren't so urgent or important after all, I hoofed it back to where I left my car in the shopping centre car park. As I walked towards my car, I noticed the number plate looked a bit strange. Up close, it was obvious why it looked strange. Someone had backed into the rear of my vehicle The other vehicle's point of contact was dead centre of the number plate, which now had the vague resemblance of a boomerang.

"Deal with it later," I told myself. There was no point wasting time fussing about it then and there. The car was driveable, and I had to be across town. As I climbed in behind the steering wheel, I hopefully checked the windscreen wipers for any note the culprit might have left. Of course they hadn't bothered with the niceties of leaving their name and contact details – probably didn't have a pencil and paper handy. Still fuming, I drove – carefully – across town to my luncheon appointment.

Lunch was a pleasant affair and stretched on longer than usual. Lynn had no information to offer regarding Alice as she also had been out of town for a few weeks before Alice pulled off her disappearing act. The one thing Lynn was certain about was, if Alice had gone to visit her children, she would not have been away from home for more than a few days. It's about as long as she could stand being with either of her kids, and Lynn didn't think they enjoyed Alice's company either.

The only thing left on my agenda for today was a visit to the city library. With a combination of factors working against me all day, and today being the library's early closing time, my rushing about continued. I received a frown from the librarian manning the desk when I rushed in at about ten minutes before closing time. In response to the frown, I was tempted to shout, 'it's all right; I know what I want and it will only take me a minute to get it'. Instead, I chose to ignore the frown. After rushing to the relevant section, grabbing the book I wanted, and checking it out at the self-service kiosk, I was out of the library before closing time.

My day out completed, and the rushing around over, I drove back to the Village at a sedate pace. The only thought of any consequence to enter my mind as I drove into the Village was whether Rod might be out in his front garden this afternoon. He wasn't. So, I drove home, poured a wine, and took it out onto my back patio to sip while I watched the sun go down.

Chapter 3

After dealing with a few domestic chores first thing on Saturday morning, I again strode resolutely out across the park. The only difference today was the spare key for Alice's house in my pocket. While any number of misgivings about the prospect of entering Alice's place when she wasn't there dogged me all the way, the little voice in my head kept asking the same question: what if something happened to her and she is lying injured, or even dead, on the floor in there?

Again, I tried knocking and calling out. And, again there was no response from inside. As I stood there on the doorstep, my resolve to check inside the house wavered. While arguing with my conscience, I wandered around the yard checking that, at least outside the house, everything looked okay. In reality, everything looked better than okay. None of Alice's precious plants had died or even wilted. How come? There hadn't been as much as a sprinkle of rain for at least two weeks.

Back on the doorstep, I slid my hand into my pocket and drew out my copy of Alice's front door key. Before attempting to insert the key, I tried the door knob. After all, I would look silly trying to use the key, if the door wasn't locked. Alice never left it unlocked if she wasn't home, so there was no surprise in finding it locked. Time to go in. As I studied the key lying in the palm of my hand, I drew in a couple of deep breaths to quieten my nerves. Then, just as I was about to insert the key, a voice called out.

"Can I help you with something?"

I spun around to face the direction of the voice. Alice's neighbour was watering her plants along the boundary fence. The neighbour might at least be able to tell me if Alice was away, and for how long. As I hurried over to the fence, my mind was a whirlpool of activity. What was the woman's name? … Winter? Weston? … Yeah, that's it, Weston.

"Mrs Weston, I've been trying to call Alice Logan for a while now, but she's not answering. I'm a bit worried about her."

"Oh hello; you're Alice's friend, Marion, aren't you? I thought I recognised you when you arrived, but my distance vision is not so good without my glasses. She's away on holidays at the moment. Have you tried her mobile number?"

"Yes, but she is not answering it either. Do you know when she left or how long she will be away?"

"Well now, that's the funny thing. When she first mentioned it, she thought she'd be away for maybe two weeks. Then, when she was leaving, she said it might be sixteen or seventeen days by the time she was home again. But, now it's four weeks she's been gone. I don't know what to think. She left Chester, her little dog, with me. He spends a lot of time over here with me even when Alice is home, so we didn't expect him to fret too much while she was away. So far, he's been really good, even though it's been a lot longer than we expected. He is no trouble, and he's good company. I'm happy to have him for as long as needs be. Although, I must admit, it's not like Alice to leave the poor little fellow for so long."

"Have you tried contacting her at all?"

"Gosh, no. I wouldn't want to intrude on her holiday – or for her to think Chester was wearing out his welcome."

"The last time I spoke to her, she suggested she might take a few days to visit her kids; but I doubt she would be visiting them for so long."

"She was going to see the kids, but only planned to overnight with each of them. The plan was for one night in Brisbane with her daughter, and then one night in Sydney with her son, before she left on her cruise. I think the plan might have been to repeat the one-night stopovers on her way back, but I'm not sure I've got it right."

"Cruise…? Tell me about this cruise she was taking."

"There isn't much I can tell you. She did mention the possibility of jumping on board a ship in Sydney for a cruise to Singapore, and then flying home from there. Then, a couple of days after she mentioned it over coffee, she came over to check if it would be all right to leave Chester with me while she was away. She had booked a thirteen-day cruise, but I don't remember her saying whether it was to Singapore or somewhere else. Maybe her daughter, Donna, would know details of the cruise and how long her mother was likely to be away. I don't have Donna's number, so I can't help you there."

"Don't worry about it, Mrs Weston. Now I know why Alice isn't home, I won't be so concerned – well, maybe not quite as concerned as I was before."

Mrs Weston invited me in for a coffee, but I refused, saying I had things to attend to at home. Moments later, I was on my way across the park again and, this time, if Rod wasn't in his front garden, I was going knock on his door to see if he was available for a chat. While I told Mrs Weston I wouldn't be so worried about Alice now, it was a long way from the truth. Knowing Alice as I did, this whole 'holiday' thing was way out of keeping with the woman I knew as my best friend.

Rod wasn't in the garden, so I marched up and rang the bell. This time I didn't refuse coffee, and we soon were seated on Rod's back patio with our coffees and blueberry muffins from the local supermarket. Taking my time, while being as succinct as possible, I recounted all I'd learned from Mrs Weston, and admitted to how it only increased my concern for my friend.

"What do you think, Rod? Am I just a silly old woman to be fussing so much about Alice's having gone away for a while?"

"No-o... But I suppose it depends on why you are so concerned. Is it because she didn't tell you about it before she left?"

"Of course not; it's just the whole thing is so unlike Alice … Even down to her leaving Chester with Mrs Weston for so long. She treats the dog like her baby. Granted, it's unlike her to leave him for more than a day or two but, on this occasion, it was supposed to be sixteen or seventeen days. And now it's developed into four weeks."

"What about her kids? Are they likely to know what's going on? I imagine, if it were possible, she would have called in to see them on her way to wherever she was going."

"According to Mrs Weston, Alice was going to overnight with each one of them before she went on the cruise. I suppose I could try calling her daughter, Donna, but I'm a bit reluctant to do so."

"Why? What would be so wrong in calling Alice's daughter to find out if Alice was all right?"

"You don't know Donna. She is a thoroughly unlikeable young woman with rampant ambition and little time for her mother. I have met her a couple of times in the past, and managed from the outset to develop an intense dislike for her. Still, I suppose it is worth a call. And, as it would be a short call, I suppose I could suffer it."

"You just said it would be a short call. So, any agony talking to her creates will be short lived. If you have her number, go and call her now. Get it over and done with, if you are so worried about it."

"Call her on a Saturday night...? Not likely; she is bound to be at some fancy dinner party, or about to go out to the opening night of the latest hit show. No, I'll leave it until tomorrow evening to try calling her."

As soon as I was home again, I checked the contacts list on my phone. I had a vague memory of Alice giving me Donna's number 'in case anything happened'. "Okay, so I do have her number," I confirmed aloud. "Tomorrow evening then..."

*****

So much for good intentions! All day I rehearsed my anticipated conversation with Alice's daughter. I would be to-the-point, but careful not to cause the young woman undue alarm. When Sunday evening rolled around, somehow the call didn't quite go as planned.

"Hello, Donna, I'm Marion Dawson. You might not…."

"Oh yes, I remember you. You're a friend of mother's. Has something happened for you to call me? Is mother okay?"

"Uhmm… actually … that was the question I was going to ask you."

"Why would you call me when you can walk across the park to ask her yourself? Has something happened I should know about? Please, tell me. I can be up there tomorrow if I need to be."

"No, there's no need. Look, I'm sorry, I'm not doing this well, and I don't want to alarm you. The reason I called is because I haven't been able to contact your mother for a while. When I spoke to her neighbour, Mrs Weston, she told me Alice had gone away for a couple of weeks, but had now been away for around four weeks. I just wondered if you knew what her plans were, so we could rest easy about her absence."

"I can tell you she wasn't planning on being away for so long. The last time I saw her was when she overnighted here before going on to Sydney to overnight with my brother, David, before joining her cruise to Singapore the next day. Although the cruise continues past Singapore to Japan and other places, Mum booked to leave the cruise at Singapore and fly back to Australia.

She would be on board for thirteen days. Then, the flight she booked would arrive in Sydney late in the afternoon the next day. If it were possible, she planned to spend the night with David again before coming here to spend another night with me. If it turned out it wasn't possible to spend the night with David on her return to Sydney, before leaving Sydney, she would change her return flight to one arriving in Australia in the early hours of the morning. In which case, she would fly straight home without calling in here again."

"Changing her flight meant she would arrive home a day earlier – if I understand you correctly."

"Yes, you're right. It's why, until she spoke to David, she wasn't sure what day she would arrive home. The arrangement

24

was, if she was going to overnight with me on her return journey, she would let me know. If I didn't hear from her, it meant she had booked a direct flight home. When I didn't hear from her, I assumed that's what she did. Now, you are telling me she never made it home ... not yet anyway. Have you checked with David to see if he knows anything?"

"I don't know David, and I don't have his contact details."

"That's probably not a bad thing... Long story; I won't bore you with it."

"Might something have happened when she returned to Sydney? Is it possible she stayed on with David for a while for whatever the reason?"

"It's more an improbability, than a possibility. A little bit of David goes a long way, even for Mother – and he wouldn't want his mother hanging around either. Anyway, he is only ever home for a few days at a time. I will try contacting David and will let you know what I find out. I don't know when you might hear from me though. David isn't easy to get hold of, but I'll keep trying until I do."

After the call ended, I sat for a few minutes analysing my conversation with Donna ... until my doorbell rang and saved me from myself.

"Rod, come on in. What brings you to my door at this time? Has something happened?"

"No-o, not as far as I know... but, it is Sunday evening. Last night, you weren't too convincing about giving Alice's daughter a call this evening. In fact, it sounded so much like you would wimp out on it, I thought I should come to remind you about it."

"I'm cut to the bone to know you would doubt me and sell me so short. Well, you've had a wasted walk. I've not long finished speaking with Donna." Rod made a show of peering at each side of my head. "What? ... What are you looking at?"

"You still have an ear on each side of you head."

"As far as I know, I've always had an ear on each side of my head ... as most people do."

"So, Alice's daughter didn't chew one off?"

25

"Ha ha, very droll... If you must know, I'm thinking I might have to reassess my opinion of the young woman. She seemed quite normal and polite this evening. Not at all the way she was when she was here with Alice. And, now I'm feeling guilty about having caused her possible unnecessary concern about her mother."

"Well, how about you tell me what you learned from the young woman – if anything."

I gave Rod an executive summary of my conversation with Donna, and admitted all I could do now was to wait until after Donna spoke to her brother. "It would be helpful if we at least knew if Alice arrived back in Australia, or if she remains stranded in Singapore ...Or, if something worse happened in Singapore to prevent her returning to Australia."

"Such thinking is not helpful. Don't let your mind start conjuring up fanciful ideas. Stay positive – at least until we have more information to work with. For all we know, Alice might have elected to stay with the cruise to see it through to its final destination. If she did, she still might be bobbing about on the high seas somewhere."

While I knew everything Rod said made sense, I didn't feel any easier because of it. As I considered his comments, my brief moment of introspection was interrupted by his voice.

"What...? Sorry; did you say something?"

"I asked you why you didn't contact the brother... David, was it? ...instead of having to wait for Donna to get back to you."

"I've never met David, so he wouldn't know who I was."

"That's probably a good thing."

"Why do you say that? It's the second time I've heard the same statement tonight."

Rod's only reply was to shrug and shake his head. I shot him a sceptical look, but continued with my explanation.

"Anyway, I doubt David would share information about his mother with a complete stranger, so I have to leave it to his sister to contact him. As it is, I only met Donna briefly on two occasions when she visited her mother, but I've never met David at all. Come to think of it, I don't think I've ever heard Alice mention a visit by her son."

After inviting me for coffee next morning, Rod took his leave. All of the Alice discussion accompanied me to bed. In spite of my best efforts to prevent negative thoughts developing, I knew I was in for a poor night's sleep. …And what about those veiled references to David which both Donna and Rod made? Was there something important about him I should know?

*****

As I dawdled over breakfast, I wondered why it was such a 'good thing' I didn't know Alice's son, David. What was there about him, and could whatever it was have something to do with Alice's non-return from her holiday? From way out of left field, another comment flashed across my thinking. It was a comment Marjorie made while we were at the Senior Citizens' Centre last Tuesday.

"What was it?" I asked the kitchen. "What did she say about David?" Slowly, the conversation from almost a week ago replayed in my mind. Then I remembered: *he's probably in gaol somewhere – again.* At the time, the comment hadn't registered with me as anything other than strange. I took it to be just another of Marjorie's negative, bitchy, comments. Now it hit me like a thunderbolt. And, it brought along with it another question: how much does Rod know about David? Well, I was damn well going to find out this morning when we had coffee together.

After those few moments of recollection, the morning seemed to drag on forever until ten o'clock finally arrived and it was time to walk to Rod's place. As soon as the clock ticked over to the appointed hour, I was out the door and striding along the street. Rod came to the open door as I started up the path.

"Good morning … and right on time as usual I see." His welcome did not fit with my mood, but I tried not to let it show. I was about to step up onto the doorstep, when a racket entered the far end of the street and came roaring in our direction.

"What the hell is making that noise," Rod asked. "Whatever it is, it will bring Bernard out of his unit to demand to know why it is disturbing the ambience of the Village."

"Good God, it's a motorbike. You're right. Bernard will not be happy about such a machine invading his territory. Why would a motorbike come in here?"

All questions about the bike and its rider were answered in the next few moments, when the bike came to a standstill next to the kerb in front of Rod's house. After pulling it up onto its centre stand, the rider, clad in once-green overalls, swung off the machine and rushed up the path to where Rod and I were standing.

As the rider unclipped and pulled off their helmet, a muffled female voice asked, "What do you think? Isn't she a beauty? What's up? You look as though you've seen a ghost or something."

Rod found his voice first. "Cilla, where did that machine come from, and why are you riding it? Whose is it?"

"She's mine. Meet 'Black Bess'. She's a Triumph Tiger, and an ex-police bike. I've had her since I finally started spending more than five minutes at a time in any one place, and that's been a for few years now. I had just finished doing her up when I moved here to the Village. It meant leaving her in storage down south until a bike transporter was available to bring her up for me. I didn't think it a good idea for the driver to bring his big rig in here, so I met him out at the highway first thing this morning and took delivery of her there. I'm stoked. There's not a scratch on her anywhere. They really did do a good job of looking after her."

"Does this mean the bike will live here with you from now on?" Rod asked.

"Oh, yes; I've missed having her around. As soon as she was unloaded and all the paperwork was done, I took her for a long run around the suburbs. It was so good to be back in the saddle again. But I don't think she's running quite as well as she should; still could do with a little more fine-tuning. I have a spare helmet. So, if you ever want to go for a ride…"

"I think I'm allergic to motorbikes." Still dumbfounded by the whole incident, I thought it best to quash from the outset any thoughts of taking me for a ride on the black machine. Cilla looked mystified by my comment, but didn't pursue it.

"Uhmm… Thanks. It might be worth giving it a go one day." Rod didn't sound sure he wanted to go for a ride on the bike either, but probably didn't want to close the door on a possible future opportunity. Nor would he want to insult Cilla with a point-blank refusal.

"Great… Anyway, I'd better take her home and dig out my tools ready to give her a tune-up."

"We're about to have coffee. You're welcome to join us if you can bear to tear yourself away from Bess," Rod called out as Cilla threw her leg over the bike.

"Right; thanks. I'll just put her away and I'll be over." Moments later, Cilla had executed a U-turn and was riding up her driveway across the street from where Rod and I still stood watching.

I leant in close and murmured, "It's a shame we don't have a mirror. We'd be able to see the pair of us standing here with our mouths still hanging open in shock. Oh look… Bernard has come out to investigate. It took him longer than I expected. He didn't make it out to the street until Cilla started the bike to go home."

"Probably took him a while to put on some clothes before venturing outside."

"What…? It's after ten o'clock. Surely he was up and about before now. I must admit, he doesn't look as immaculately dressed as he usually is."

Bernard looked decidedly dishevelled as he stood on the edge of the footpath expressing his disapproval His shirt, open at the neck was only partially tucked into his rumpled slacks, and the slip-on flip-flops on his feet were way out of character.

"He does like to lie-in unless there is something he needs to be up early for. And, as I said, it probably took him a while to find some clothes and throw them on before venturing out."

"Yes, I don't suppose he could have rushed out in his pyjamas."

"...No, not in his style of pyjamas." Rod gave me a meaningful look but I couldn't interpret it.

"Okay, I know that's supposed to mean something, but I have no idea what."

"Haven't you ever noticed anything … different … about what he hangs on the line?"

"Can't say I've ever felt the urge to inspect his washing."

"Let's just say you're never likely to find sleepwear – you know, night attire, PJs or whatever you want to call them – hanging amongst his washing."

"Wha…? You mean he sleeps in the….?"

"Well, I haven't actually been over in the middle of the night to confirm it, but so it would appear."

"God save us!"

"What's up? Surely it's not the first time you've heard of such behaviour. Anyway, I don't think you're likely to require God or anyone else to save you from Bernard."

I let his barb go by before responding. "No, it's not the first time I've heard of it… It was just the image which flashed before my eyes when I thought of what we might see in the middle of the night in the event of a fire in those units."

"Oh, I see … Or, perhaps I should say, 'I hope never to see'. If such an event were to occur, I don't know whether we should hope for a warm night or a freezing cold one to help improve the resultant vision which might confront us."

Rod was looking smug and I was still giggling, as Cilla, now minus her oil-stained overalls, started across the street to join us for coffee.

"Good to see there's another discerning resident who knows a good bike when he sees one," she quipped as she came up the path. "Although, I didn't expect it of Bernard, as I turned for home, he gave me an enthusiastic wave of appreciation."

"You're sure it was a wave he gave you?" I murmured as my memory replayed my earlier vision of Bernard standing at the side of the street. From my vantage point, it didn't look like a wave. It looked more like he was shaking his fist at Cilla... and was definitely more in keeping with any reaction I expected from Bernard.

Chapter 4

"Oh, I see our host is a man of many talents;" Cilla quipped as we sat down with our coffees, "cupcakes no less for morning tea. What a treat."

"Not as talented as you might think," I replied. "The local school's P&C held a cake stall on the High Street on Saturday. There are some good cooks amongst those women."

"Thank you, Marion. You might have allowed me at least a few moments of glory … even if they were ill attributed."

Cocking an eyebrow at Rod, Cilla asked, "…Nice dinner last night?" Then, before he could reply, Cilla, glancing from Rod to me, followed up with, "A good night was it?"

Rod looked confused, but I thought I picked up the inference in Cilla's questions. "Rod came to see how I got on with a call I made in a bid to discover Alice's whereabouts," I said, my tone more than a little indignant. "As for dinner, Sunday nights at my place involve something-on-toast for dinner."

"Oh, now I see where you were coming from, Cilla. It might disappoint you to know it was a quick visit and I was home by seven o'clock," Rod informed her.

"You're right. It is disappointing. I had hoped there was some life happening in this retirement village. After all, it is a retirement village; not a monastery – or a nunnery."

Chuckling, Rod replied, "Not to worry; between your sports car and Black Bess, I'm sure you'll manage to breathe some life into the place."

"So, remind me," Cilla began, "what's the story about Alice? Alice is the mahjong player who seems to have gone missing, isn't she?"

I gave her an abridged version of all we knew to date. "So there, now you know as much as we do so far. All we can do now is to wait until Alice's daughter comes back to me with whatever she has managed to find out."

"That's not strictly true," Rod began tentatively. "After I left your place last night, I called a friend, who has a friend. You know how the system goes. Anyway, while I hadn't expected any results for a day or so, my friend called me back a few minutes before you arrived for coffee. His friend did a bit of digging this morning and passed on what he found out about Alice. It seems she didn't change her return flight to return to Australia from Singapore, and arrived in Sydney as originally planned late in the afternoon."

"Well, that's a relief, even if we don't know anything else. At least she has returned to Australia. It has to be better than having her missing somewhere overseas," I suggested.

"But, it's not all he found out. It appears she might have planned to overnight in Sydney with her son. The moment she arrived in Sydney, she booked a flight home for the next day. It doesn't appear as though she intended visiting her daughter again on her way home." Rod took care in picking his words. While he wanted to pass on all he had learned, it was obvious he was trying to avoid increasing my concern for our missing friend.

"I wonder how Donna will react when she learns her mother was going to bypass her on the way home… or if it would worry her at all."

"Good question, but not one for us to worry about. The other piece of information my friend's friend managed to dig up was about Alice missing her flight home. She never checked in, or boarded, her flight from Sydney the next day as planned. On the off chance she'd been forced to delay her return due to unforeseen circumstances, the man checked flights for the following week. Alice did not rebook her flight during those days. He then looked for any flight she might have booked a seat on from the day after her missed flight and up until two weeks from now. There have been no bookings for Alice since the one for the flight she missed."

"While it is good to know what the situation is, I can't say any of it relieves my concerns in any way. If she is still in Sydney somewhere, why isn't she answering my calls to her mobile? And, it would take circumstances of monumental proportions to keep her from returning to Chester before now." I felt a headache developing, and almost wished Rod hadn't shared the information he had acquired.

"So, it looks as though we still need to hear from the son. Given all we know now, it appears he holds the next piece of the puzzle," Cilla observed. "Marion, you called the daughter last night to find out what she knew. Couldn't you call the son to see what he knows as well?"

"I've never met him and I don't have his contact information. Anyway, from what his sister said, I gathered he can be hard to contact because, whenever he is there, he is only home for a few days at a time. If she hasn't managed to contact him so far, I doubt I would do any better."

"In this day and age of extensive mobile phone coverage, he would have to be visiting some pretty obscure places not to have reception and be unable to receive calls. What's this bloke's name?" Cilla stared at some indeterminate spot on the table top as she spoke. It was obvious there was a lot of thinking happening behind her words.

"David … David Logan," I told her.

"Hmm … David Logan, eh? Er… what would be his approximate age?"

"Aw, I don't know much about him, Cilla, but I guess he might be in his late forties. He might be fifty, but I doubt it. Alice is one of my best friends, and I feel such a fool not knowing this stuff. But, Alice wasn't one to bore you with talk about her kids. Although she did mention Donna on occasion, it was rare. On the other hand, I might have heard her mention her son twice in the whole time I've known her. I wasn't sure I was remembering his name correctly until I spoke to his sister last night."

"What if…," Rod began. "What if, when she arrived in Sydney, she found her son was ill, or something had happened to him, and she decided to stay on to take care of him?" Rod suggested.

I shrugged. "It's a possibility I suppose. The only thing wrong with your assumption is Alice herself. She was one of those organised people. If something had come up – such as you suggested – she would have cancelled her flight, or at least rebooked it for another day. As your friend reported, she hasn't, although by now she would have a fair idea of how much longer she needed to remain in Sydney."

"Hmm… possibly," Cilla murmured. I spun around to face her, but Cilla offered nothing more, and her face was devoid of any tell-tale expression.

Easing himself up from the table, Rod went to a small desk in the sitting room and booted up his computer. A few moments later, he was interrogating Google. "Aha, yes, there is a listing for a David Logan in the Sydney area. He must be doing all right. It's in quite an upmarket inner-city area." He scribbled the phone number on a pad beside the computer before returning to the table. "Why don't you try the number? You never know: someone might answer. That someone might be Alice – if she is staying with David."

Reluctant, but not wanting to offend Rod after he went to the trouble of finding the number, I pulled my mobile phone out of my back pocket, and wandered outside as the number began dialling. It only seemed like moments later when, probably looking shattered and confused, I rushed back inside.

"What happened?" Rod barked when he saw the look on my face. "Did someone answer?"

"O-oh yes, someone answered. It was a woman … Not Alice. She sounded… Uhmm, I don't know how to describe it, but she sounded cheap, brassy – rough somehow. Anyway, she is a complete stranger to polite conversation. At first, she said, 'David isn't here'. I asked if Alice was there, or if she had been there. The woman said she didn't know any Alice – and she didn't know any David either. No one by that name lived there. And, then she suggested maybe I had the wrong number."

"Did you question her about the number," Cilla asked.

"No. That was it. After telling me I had the wrong number, she hung up in my ear. I promise you, I won't be trying the number again any time soon."

"Okay, so it appears the landline is a fizzer. Rod, you didn't happen to notice if there was a mobile number for David Logan?" Cilla seemed to have taken charge. No one objected. She might even come up with something else worth trying.

"I did check but, no, there was no mobile listing under his name."

"Well, as I'm confident he does have a mobile phone, and we don't know its number, it appears we are back at the same point we arrived at earlier: waiting for his sister to contact Marion." Cilla checked around the table as she finished speaking. She found her two companions nodding their agreement. Nevertheless, she did have another card up her sleeve, but she wasn't about to reveal it just yet. She suggested there was something she needed to do first.

For a few moments, I fiddled with my coffee mug, driving it in circles on the table, before I looked up at Rod. "Remember the comment Marjorie made at the Senior Citizens' Centre last Tuesday, the one about Alice's son being in gaol? Do you think it might be worth asking Marjorie what she knows about him?"

"I never realised you had such a masochistic streak," Rod said, shaking his head in mock disbelief. "No, it won't be necessary." He tapped the side of his nose. "I did pick up on her comment at the time, and couldn't let it go by without finding out more about it."

"Sometime in his dark distant past, Rod used to be a journo," I informed Cilla.

"Oh God, not one of those; I had you pegged as something of a more refine breed, Rod, like maybe an academic."

"Don't malign the profession keeping you informed about not only what's going on in your own backyard, but right across the globe. Now, do you want to know what I found out, or not?" There was no question about it, we both wanted to know.

"Right, well young David has an interesting track record as far as the law is concerned. From what I can make out, he was a spoiled, rich brat who wasted most of his teenage years and his early-twenties as well. After a couple of goes at finishing high school, he went on to university, had a lovely time there, and was chucked out after about eighteen months. He had a couple of scrapes with the law as a juvenile. While both were minor, they might have provided a clear indication of what lay ahead."

"Where were his parents while all this was going on," I demanded. "I can't believe Alice would just sit back and watch him waste his life."

"I don't know how much you know about Alice's husband, Roger Logan. At least, I don't know much about his beginnings, but he went on to become a wealthy man-about-town … And you can read into my comment whatever meaning you prefer. A liking for the high life saw him spend a lot of time in the major cities, both here and overseas. But his travels were always in the name of his various enterprises' operations, of course. At a time when I think both the kids were in high school, he built the home across the park here and settled Alice into it. My take on the situation is, he parked Alice here with the kids to manage as best they could, while he dashed around the world having a high old time." Rod paused and shrugged before continuing. "Although Roger was rarely home, I doubt Alice and the kids wanted for anything. They probably were well provided for, but I don't think Alice had an easy time of it."

For me, this was hard to hear. I had no idea what Alice's life had been like, but I suppose my thinking was influenced by the big house with all its wonderful furniture and appliances. Now, based on Rod's comments, it appears it was all just 'window-dressing' to hide a very different background. Poor Alice! Maybe it was just as well her husband didn't hang around into his old age. It sounds like she might have been well rid of him.

"What became of the husband?" Cilla asked. "Did they divorce, or is he still hanging around somewhere?"

"He died. It would be more than twenty years ago now, but he left everything to Alice. We never discuss it of course, but I think she is a wealthy woman. She is not one of those who flaunts it. I remember her saying once that her husband had died at an awkward time for the kids – when they were just becoming adults. His departure from this world doesn't seem to have affected his daughter in any way. She established a successful career for herself, and I suspect she is now a wealthy woman in her own right." Feeling a bit embarrassed, I glanced at both my companions in turn. "I'm sorry. I didn't mean to go on about it and bore you to death."

"Nothing boring about anything you said," Cilla replied. "It's all useful information; stuff that might inform our investigation into what's happened to Alice."

"Our investigation…? You make it sound as though we are bloodhounds on the trail of the missing Alice," I said.

"Well, aren't we? It is the situation, isn't it? Alice is missing and we are trying to locate her, or at least find out what has happened to her. To me, we are conducting an investigation. Whether you want to compare us to bloodhounds or not is up to you." Cilla ended with an emphatic nod, which I took to signal the end of that particular conversation.

Rod studied his hands tented on the table in front of him before making a tentative attempt to voice his thoughts. "I'm inclined to think it is safe to assume David has a mobile phone. Who doesn't these days? While there might be a few of the older generation who don't, I imagine you'd be hard-pressed to find anyone under sixty without one. On the other hand, people are doing away with their landlines these days. We don't know anything about the landline number I found, or the house to which it's connected.

David might have surrendered the number and it has been reallocated in recent times to someone else, but the directory hasn't been updated yet. Or, he might have sold or rented out his house, and the current tenants haven't bothered to change the number. None of this is helpful, I know, but I still think a mobile phone number for David is our best bet. Marion, do you think Donna might give you his number – perhaps if you asked really nicely?"

"No-o, I'm not sure she would. Call it a feeling – an impression – I gained from talking to her the other night. I think, if she were willing to give me his number, she might have done so at the time and without any hesitation. But, she seemed quite determined she should contact him, as opposed to giving me his number so I could try."

"Marion, do you know if Alice kept some sort of list of telephone numbers she used, like a private directory?" Cilla asked.

"Do you mean like the contacts list on her mobile phone, only a physical version?" Cilla nodded. "I'm not sure, but I remember seeing something on the desk in the office. It might have been some sort of directory."

"It would be worth a look. Now, all we have to do is work out how to get into Alice's house." As she finished speaking, Cilla raised her eyebrows in question and glanced from me to Rod and back again.

"Uhmm... Marion, don't you have a key to Alice's place?" Rod asked.

"We-ell, yes I do, but I wouldn't dream of using it unless it was in case of an emergency."

"For God's sake, Marion, how much of an emergency do you need before you decide it is a sufficiently serious situation to use the key? Is there sufficient reason for us to be concerned about Alice's welfare – yes or no? If you think the answer is yes, then let's use the bloody key to see if we can find a phone number." Cilla was right of course. There was cause for serious concern, but I remained hesitant.

"Yes, I know it makes sense, but I wouldn't feel right going into her home while she wasn't there. Perhaps I could ask Mrs Weston if she has David's number. It might be the way to go. I'll slip across later today to see if I can catch Mrs Weston at home."

"Right; well, if it's the best we can do for the moment, perhaps we should look at what other avenues of investigation are open to us." Cilla drummed her fingers on the table as she spoke. After a moment or two she stopped and fixed her eyes on Rod. "From the information your friend gave you, we know Alice arrived in Sydney as planned, but then failed to board her plane the next day for the flight home. Where did she stay overnight in Sydney? Was David home, and did she spend the night with him? What if she found he wasn't home when she arrived? Then where did she stay? If she stayed in a hotel, did something happen there to prevent her catching her flight the next day?"

"Thank you, Cilla. It's a wonderful list of questions. I don't suppose you have any answers to go with them?" Rod snapped. "We can sit here asking questions all day, but it's not going to get us anywhere is it? Argh, I'm sorry. I guess I'm just feeling overwhelmed and frustrated at not being able to do anything."

"Marion, do you know if Alice had a favourite hotel she might use in Sydney, or if she had one of those loyalty cards from one of the hotel chains?" Cilla asked.

"She didn't visit Sydney very often, only maybe once or twice a year to visit David. I doubt she would have had occasion to use a hotel while there. She would have stayed with her son."

"And, I suppose the same would have been true for Brisbane. If she had reason to visit that city, she probably stayed with her daughter," Rod added.

"Did you ever go anywhere with her, Marion, to see a show, go to a craft show, attend a mahjong festival... or anything, that didn't take you to Brisbane or Sydney?" Cilla persisted.

"Not really; neither of us went anywhere very much. Oh, wait a minute. There was an occasion when four of us travelled together to a literary festival up north. Alice got us a good price for our accommodation."

"Maybe she managed to wangle corporate rates for you," Rod suggested. "Do you remember what hotel chain you stayed with?"

"I don't think it was corporate rates as such. I'm trying to recall something which happened when we went to pay our bills before we left. Yes… Yes, Alice used some sort of card to verify our cheap rates. Just let me think about it for a while. I might be able to remember something about the card which might help us."

"Might it have been one of the Mantra Group hotels, or a Marriott Hotel for instance?" Cilla suggested.

"Wait a minute… yes, I remember now. It was a Marriott Hotel card. I remember Hazel, one of the other women with us, commented 'Marriott' was her maiden name."

"Well, it's a good start." Cilla ripped a page from Rod's notebook and scribbled the name with his pen.

"Oh yes, a very good start…" Rod's sarcastic tone wasn't lost on his two female companions. "It's unlikely we would have to check more than about a hundred Marriott hotels in the Sydney area to find the one she stayed at."

"Well, it's the best I have to offer," I bristled. "Do you have any better ideas?"

"Children … please … play nice. Arguing about things isn't going to help one bit," Cilla counselled.

"Now you've asked, Marion, I think I do have an idea." Rod spoke slowly, sorting out his half-developed idea as he did so. "Yes, it might be a possibility. If my memory hasn't failed me, I seem to remember a Marriott hotel located close to Sydney's international terminal. What if Alice was expecting David to collect her from the airport, and he wasn't there when she arrived? She would try contacting him to sort out what was happening and, when she couldn't reach him, she decided to book into the nearest hotel for the night?"

"I like your line of thinking," Cilla said. "It would be the most logical thing for her to do, if her arrangements with David fell through."

"We don't know it's what happened. It's only speculation on Rod's part. Why wouldn't David be there to collect her, if it's what their arrangement was?" I was far from convinced as, so far, we had nothing to suggest it was what happened. "So, what do we do now? Do we call that Marriott hotel and ask if Alice stayed there on the night of … the night of … Argh hell, we don't even know what night she might have been there."

"Mrs Weston would know when she left here. From that, we could work out the likely date of her return to Sydney. In fact, Mrs Weston might even know what date it was supposed to be." Rod looked pleased with himself for having thought of the possibility.

"Good point, Rod," Cilla acknowledged. "It's something else Marion can ask Mrs Weston about when she walks over there later today. Does anyone have any ideas about anything else we might be doing in the meantime? …No … okay, then I suggest we reconvene at 6.00pm this evening to review progress and share any further ideas we might have."

Although feeling hesitant, I posed my next question. "Rod, if your friend's friend found out when Alice arrived back in Australia, then there is a known date for Alice's first night back in the country. Wasn't there relevant dates along with the information he gave you?"

Rod looked sheepish as he flicked through his notebook. "Ah yes, here is where I scribbled down the details he gave me… and, yes, you are right. I do have the date of her arrival. Okay, now we know it was a Marriott and the date she stayed there. What do we do now?"

"Your friend doesn't have another friend does he, who could check on the hotel's registrations for us?" I asked.

"Worth asking I suppose," Rod conceded. He checked the time and then added, "I'll wait until about twelve o'clock before giving him a call."

"Right, it seems everyone has something to be going on with. So, when should we reconvene to discuss the outcomes of all those tasks?" Cilla asked, "At 6.00pm… or should we leave it until tomorrow?"

"Tomorrow might be best," Rod suggested.

"There is only one thing wrong with your statement, Cilla.

Not everyone has been allocated a task or two. You don't seem to have anything to do."

"Not true; I have a motorbike in need of tuning. It will keep me busy for at least the rest of today."

Rod walked us to the door. I held back for a moment, and we stood together on the doorstep watching Cilla make her way across the road to her house. "What the hell was that all about?" I murmured to Rod. "I feel as though I've been roped in to help with a police investigation." He shrugged, but didn't comment.

All the way home, I pondered what possible use Cilla might be in the search for Alice, and I held severe doubts about whether Cilla was genuinely interested in whatever Alice's present situation might be. Her comment about working on her bike when the rest of us was so concerned about Alice tended to reinforce my doubts.

Chapter 5

What time should I go? Would it be better to go early or later this morning? If I leave it until later, Mrs Weston might go out, or might have visitors over for coffee. And, she might expect me to have coffee with her. Then again, if I go early, Mrs Weston might be a late riser, and not be a morning person.

"Argh, it's too early in the morning for such decisions," I told the coffee maker as I set it on the stove. "Maybe after I have my first cup for the day, all will become clear." And, as if by some miracle, the situation did resolve itself as I rinsed my breakfast things and set them to drain on the side of the sink.

From my kitchen window, Alice's house on the other side of the park drew my eyes to it like iron filings to a magnet. Early or later...? Split the difference I told myself. Nine o'clock seems a sensible time to go. Mrs Weston will be up by then, but it might be too early for her to have gone out – or to insist I have coffee with her. "This isn't a social visit," I reminded myself. "I'm on a mission... on an investigation, as Cilla insists." The hard part then was to settle to do anything until it was time to go.

So, the decision having been made, at ten minutes before the appointed hour of nine o'clock, I set off across the park. It was a brisk morning with a weak sun, and last night's heavy dew lingered well into the morning. The bottom of my slacks became soaked before I was halfway across the park and, for the remainder of the journey, clung to my legs like wet leaves. Long before I reached Alice's house, I felt the cold wetness seep through my trainers and socks to chill my feet to the bone.

Although the concrete forecourt out front of Alice's house hadn't soaked up much of the early morning sunshine yet, it offered more warmth than the grassy park. After stamping my feet a few times in a bid to restore circulation and expel some of the dew I collected on the way over, I stood for a few moments in the hope of capturing some warmth from that same weak sun. It was during this exercise, I heard Mrs Weston talking to someone.

It sounded as though it was coming from the Weston's front yard. Maybe Mrs Weston was outside with a visitor. The thought only caused me more indecision. Should I be bold and intrude, or should I just go inside and check Alice's desk for David's phone number? Again, it seemed a good idea to find some 'middle ground'. My plan to cross the forecourt in silence so I could sneak a peek into the Weston's yard was scuttled by the squelching of my soggy footwear.

"Oh, hello dear. Marion isn't it? Back again then? Have you found out anything more about Alice? I am concerned about our wee Chester here. I think he might be starting to miss his home."

I had no sooner raised my head above the dividing fence, than Mrs Weston spotted me. Not surprising I suppose, I told myself. After all, she was standing only about a metre in front of the spot where I chose to peer over the fence. "Good morning, Mrs Weston. No, I've nothing new to report, and our concern for her continues to grow. Do you have a few minutes for a chat?"

"Come on over, dear. There's a gate in the fence just a bit further along from where you are. We can sit under the gazebo and watch Chester enjoying his morning exercise while we chat."

Okay, now I know, I told myself: Mrs Weston is not an early riser. The animal print short gumboots did not match her outfit of pale pink quilted housecoat, or the forest of red and blue rollers covering her head. A half-drunk mug of coffee sat on the table under the gazebo. She brushed aside my apology for such an early visit.

"Early...? Good heavens, this isn't early. I've been up for ages. It just takes me a while to get going in the morning. Now, I'm sure your visit is to talk about Alice, so how can I help?"

"Alice didn't happen to leave any phone numbers with you, did she? I don't mean just before she left, but at any time in the past. I'd like to contact her son, David, but I don't have his number, and I wondered if she might have given it to you at some time."

"No. No, the only number Alice ever gave me was for her mobile phone. She would never give me her son's number. I never heard her mention him, except on a couple of occasions, and that was a fair while ago. Do you think he might know what's going on? It's unlikely to be the case. I think he would be the last person she would contact if something went awry with her trip. She didn't seem to think too much of him. Although I've never met him, I formed the opinion he might be a bit of a waste of space on this earth."

"You might not be the only one to have formed a similar opinion. I knew it was a longshot you might have his number but, short of having a look in Alice's office, I don't know how else I might find it. My problem is, I hate the thought of going into her house when she is not here."

"Does it mean you have a key to her home?" I nodded and showed her the key. "Great…! Look, I don't think Alice would mind – given the circumstances and everything – and I need to go in there too. I've just about run out of the tablets I have to give Chester. I know Alice had another unopened bottle, but she said there was more than enough in the bottle she gave me to cover the time she would be away. Of course, at the time, she wasn't planning on being away for so long."

"Right… well, I suppose there is nothing for it but to see if this key works and gains us entry to the house."

"Perhaps, if you wouldn't mind watching Chester for a few minutes, I might change into something more respectable before we do anything."

Keeping an eye on Chester wasn't difficult. The moment Mrs Weston moved to go inside, Chester was at her heels and didn't re-emerge until Mrs Weston did when she was ready to go nextdoor to Alice's house.

As I expected, there was no problem with the key, and the two of us and Chester soon found ourselves in Alice's foyer. "Do you know where to look for Chester's tablets?" I asked – and hoped Mrs Weston did because I had no idea where Alice might keep Chester's pills.

"Yes, I think so. I think Alice keeps them with all Chester's other stuff in the laundry. Anyway, it's where I'll look first."

"Okay, while you check the laundry, I'm going to see if Alice has some sort of list of phone numbers on her desk. I'll be in the office if you need me."

The thing on the desk I thought might be a contacts list proved not to be. After searching the desk top for phone numbers, with some trepidation, I turned my attention to the desk's drawers. A small indexed notebook in the top drawer offered a brief glimmer of hope, but proved a disappointment. While it was what I was looking for, it contained no mention of David. A quick glance in the other two drawers discovered nothing of interest.

Slumped back in Alice's chair, I considered what other options might be available to me. I had been foolhardy enough to envisage myself announcing the successful completion of my mission to Rod and Cilla. Instead, now I would be admitting my failure. Mrs Weston's voice cut through my depressing thoughts.

"Did you find the number you were looking for, dear? You don't look too happy about it, if you did."

"No, Mrs Weston, I found nothing to do with David at all. It is almost as though he doesn't exist. Donna's contact information was there, but no mention of David. Did you find the tablets you were looking for?"

Mrs Weston rattled the bottle of Chester's pills at me. "Yes, thanks. They were in the laundry with all his other gear. So, what are you going to do now? Maybe, if you found one of Alice's phone bills, it would have David's number on it."

"There's no point in looking for a phone account. Apart from anything else, I would feel way out of line searching through Alice's files. Even if David's number did appear on a phone account, I wouldn't recognise it. The accounts just show numbers, and not who they belong to. No, I'm afraid I've drawn a blank, and the whole exercise was a waste of time. I'm sorry, I've wasted your time as well this morning."

"You haven't wasted my time. I'm glad things turned out as they have. I now have enough pills to keep Chester going for at least another month. It saves me a trip to the vet with him to get more medication ... and it also saves me the expense of the visit and the pills."

Back out in the forecourt, and with Alice's front door once more locked behind us, we parted company after I promised to keep Mrs Weston informed of anything we discovered about Alice's situation. As I made my way back to the Village, the park seemed twice as wide as it did earlier this morning. I hoped neither Rod nor Cilla were in their front yards when I returned, but it was just another disappointment for the morning. They were both outside; Cilla hosing down her driveway, and Rod watering his shrubs.

"Ahem, I don't think I'm game to ask how your morning has been," Rod said as I tried to march past his place. "By the look on your face, I think it's safe to assume your mission drew a blank."

"Well spotted, Sherlock…Total waste of time. It's as though she doesn't want anyone to know David even exists. So much for my part of the investigation."

"It always was a longshot." Cilla had crossed the road when she heard Rod speak to me. "It would have been all too easy, if you had walked in there and found David's number exactly where you thought it might be … And, it would have been nothing short of a miracle. It's not how investigations play out."

Cilla's comments seemed odd but, rather than respond to her, I settled for giving Rod a questioning look instead. His only reaction was a half-hearted shrug. Keen to put the whole event behind me and to do nothing more than go home and make a coffee, I turned to head for home… and then I remembered Rod also was given a mission to undertake.

"Okay, so I failed. What about your mission, Rod? As I recall, you were to endeavour to find out where Alice stayed on her return to Sydney. Did she stay at the Marriott hotel we discussed yesterday? Oh, and Cilla, how's your bike running after this morning? I suppose you have it perfect now." They were genuine questions, but my voice was tainted with a touch too much sarcasm for it to go unnoticed.

First of the two to find her voice, Cilla replied, "Not too bad now, thanks for asking. But, it still requires just a tad more tweaking."

I gave her a 'who-cares' look and half-hearted eye-roll, before sliding my gaze across to Rod. "Well, Rod, do you have anything to report?"

"If you stop barking at me long enough, I will tell you how I got on." I held my hands up in resignation before motioning for him to continue. "Okay, I contacted my friend as I said I would. His initial reaction was not encouraging, but he agreed to think about whom amongst his many contacts might be able to help with our query. So, as I wasn't feeling too confident about how it would turn out, I was surprised when he called about an hour ago to deliver the good news. The old-network-system came into play again, and a contact at the particular Marriott Hotel we were interested in came through for us."

"Alice stayed there…?" I blurted out, before a hasty apology for my interruption.

Rod continued. "The contact reported Alice did indeed stay at the hotel on the date in question, which was the night she returned to Australia. It seems she didn't have a prior booking, but called from the airport to arrange a room before registering at the hotel at about ten o'clock that evening."

"Hmm… she was a bit late," Cilla mused. "Maybe she hung around waiting for David to arrive, and only resorted to hotel accommodation for the night when he failed to appear after she waited a reasonable period for him to collect her."

"It would appear to be the case," Rod agreed. "The big question then is: why didn't he meet his mother's plane as arranged. Knowing Alice as we do, I am sure she gave him all the necessary details of her flight's arrival. I'm also confident, regardless of whatever else was happening at the time, Alice would have called him to find out why he wasn't there to meet her."

"Perhaps it also might be safe to assume she was unable to contact him and, in desperation, gave up waiting and called the hotel to arrange a bed for the night," I added.

"No, it is not safe to make such an assumption. Let's think about another possible scenario. What if she tried to contact David, but had difficulty reaching him for a while? Then, when she did manage to contact him, he gave her some reason why he was unable to collect her out of town or whatever and told her to make other arrangements as she wouldn't be able to spend the night with him. This is pure speculation on my part, as I don't know anything about Alice's son. But then, nor do either of you it seems." As Cilla finished speaking, she flicked her gaze between Rod and me a couple of times. "Do either of you have any argument with the possibility of such a scenario having occurred?"

We exchanged questioning looks before Rod replied. "No. No, I suppose it is quite possible it played out for Alice the way you suggested. I suppose such a scenario is one both Marion and I find difficult to think about our friend having found herself in when she arrived in Sydney. Although, there are likely to be other plausible scenarios which might apply, they too would be nothing more than speculation on our part. It doesn't matter how much speculation we apply, it won't resolve anything. Perhaps, at this stage, we would do better to review what we know to be fact, rather than indulging in hypotheses."

"You are right, Rod. We should concentrate on what we know. So far, as it amounts to not very much, where do we go from here?" I asked.

"Oh, I wouldn't say we don't know very much," Cilla responded. "We know Alice did arrive back in Australia, and the date of her arrival. We also know her original plan when she left home was to spend the night of her return with David. Now we know that did not occur, and she ended up spending the night at the Marriott hotel close to the airport. Further, we also know she was booked on a flight home from Sydney the following morning, but did not board the flight. At this point in time, that is all we *know*. Anything beyond those facts is speculation, and is not helpful to the investigation. The only way to move forward now, is to plan our next move based on what we know to be fact, and to ignore everything else we've been imagining."

With a defiant toss of my head to emphasise the point I wanted to make, I said, "So how is that helpful in any way? And, what makes you such an expert on 'investigations' anyway?" I stood glaring at Cilla. How could this woman who knew nothing of our friend Alice presume to tell us how to go about finding her?

"Marion, you are not being helpful," Rod said quietly. "Everything Cilla said is true and correct. Instead of getting your feathers ruffled, perhaps you might help by thinking about what else we might try in order to find Alice."

"Thanks, Rod, but I don't think Marion wants me involved in helping you find your friend. I might leave you to it. You know where to find me if you want to talk to me." With that, Cilla turned on her heel and start back across the road.

"Cilla, don't go… please stay and help. I'm sorry. I didn't mean to have a shot at you. We'd appreciate any input at the moment because, while I don't know about Rod, I'm all out of ideas. My problem is, I just feel so helpless to do anything about finding her. And, the longer she is missing, the more convinced I am something serious has happened to her. I wonder if… It probably sounds silly but, on TV, when a situation such as this exists, people ring the police and all the hospitals to see if they know anything. Should we try doing the same?"

"It's not a silly suggestion… And I am surprised you haven't done so already," Cilla said. "It's why I gave one of my contacts a call."

"It was good of you, given you've never even met Alice. How did it go?" Rod asked.

51

"There was nothing exceptional in what I did. Anyway, I don't have anything to report as yet, so we'll have to wait to see whether I've helped in any way. It's likely I will hear something later today, but I can't guarantee it."

"Well, it looks as though there is nothing more to be said or done for the moment," Rod said. "Let's touch base again this evening to see if we've discovered anything new, and to brainstorm our next move. My place at six o'clock for a glass of wine suit everyone?"

As it was lunchtime when I arrived home, after turning on the TV for the midday news, I went through to the kitchen to prepare something to eat. Since early in my conversation with Rod and Cilla, a half-formed thought remained lurking in the back of my mind. Now, as I stood at the sink and looked across the park to Alice's home, the thought began elbowing its way through to the front. With one slice of sourdough bread lying on the board and the serrated bread knife poised high above the loaf ready to slice off another, I froze. "Yes… That's it! That's what I'll do," I yelped. "What's the time? Ah, who cares? I'll do it now anyway."

With lunch temporarily suspended, I took my phone through to the lounge room, muted TV, and flicked through to the number I wanted. As the number was dialling, my resolve was evaporating. Just as I was about to swipe left on the red icon, the call was answered.

"Marion…! I wasn't expecting to hear from you so soon. Has something happened I need to be aware of?" Donna asked. "Has Mum turned up, or have you heard from her?"

"No, I'm sorry, Donna, I don't have any good news to share. Well, not much anyway. All I know so far is your mother did return to Sydney, but spent the night in a hotel near the airport. She did not board her plane home the next day. As yet, we don't know what happened beyond the first night she arrived back. I know how busy you are, and I wondered whether I might try contacting your brother, David, to save you the trouble. I would have contacted him anyway, except I don't have his number. If you were to trust me with his number, I would only use it to ask about his mother and what happened after her arrival. Can you see your way clear to give me his number?"

Hesitancy was apparent in the extended pause subsequent to my request. After a few moments, Donna explained David only gave her and her mother his phone number on the understanding they did not pass it on to anyone else, and they only called it when an absolute necessity.

"I understand my request puts you in a difficult position, but is there any way you might be able to give me his number?"

"While I know you wouldn't do the wrong thing, my problem with giving you his number is David would know who gave it to you. Not a good thing from my perspective. I can't risk it. I really am sorry, Marion, but I can't give it to you."

The call ended, I returned to my abandoned lunch making. The second slice of sourdough I cut reflected my mood following the call. "Damn! I can't even cut a decent slice of bread now." It had started okay, but ended about three times as thick.

I was desperate to achieve something positive. So far, Rod had discovered all we knew, and I had no doubts Cilla's call to her contact also would produce some amazing information. Of course it would. She was Cilla. "Good God, what is wrong with me?" I asked the empty house. "What have I got against Cilla? What has she ever done to me?"

No response was forthcoming from the house or anywhere else but, in reality, I knew I didn't need anyone to tell me what was wrong. I knew why I felt the way I did. It wasn't Cilla's fault … and it wasn't Rod's fault either, if I were honest with myself. It was about the new girl in the Village Cilla who seems so much larger than life; so much more accomplished and capable than I could ever hope to be. …And, it was about Rod seeming to have noticed all this about Cilla, and being smitten by what he saw.

That was it wasn't it? The crux of the matter was Rod's being so impressed by just about everything about Cilla. Although I knew such self-reflection would send my mood into a downward spiral, I couldn't help it. "We always got along so well, Rod and me," I told the universe. "And now, he takes her side all the time, and he takes me to task if I don't agree with their opinions."

Without a shadow of a doubt, I knew the other two would have more information to share when we gathered at Rod's place this evening, whereas I would have to admit yet again to having come up with nothing.

Chapter 6

My mood darkened as the afternoon sped towards evening and our meeting at Rod's place. Was there anything – anything at all – I might try before then. If I could just think of something … Something which might prove useful in locating Alice. Even just one last ditch effort I might try before having to admit my failure to the other two. In spite of how long and hard I thought about the issue, inspiration was not forthcoming. It seems my muse was off somewhere else this week… probably with Alice, wherever she was.

By the time I marched along the pavement to Rod's house, I knew I was feeling well and truly bitchy. My vitriol level had reached danger point. As I reached Rod's gate, Cilla pranced across the street to join me.

"Isn't it a glorious afternoon," Cilla chirped. "I hope Rod intends we should sit in his back garden. It's too nice to be cooped up inside. How's your day been, Marion? You look a bit tense. Is everything all right?"

"Fine, thank you. At least, everything is about as right as it can be given we still don't know what's happened to Alice."

Cilla, taken aback by my biting tone, seemed to spend a moment searching for some appropriate come-back. Rod intervened before she found one.

"Right on time as usual," he exclaimed after opening the door to the two of us as we strode in his direction. "It's one of the impressive things about you two: you know how to stick to a schedule. Come in, and come on through to the back patio. It's lovely out there this evening."

Of course it is, I thought as I trailed the other two out to the garden. Maybe Cilla is telepathic, and can mentally communicate with Rod. After all, a Happy Hour on his back patio is not Rod's usual mode of entertainment. He always preferred to entertain visitors in his cosy lounge room. But, now Cilla was here, she seems to be able to influence just about everything Rod does, says, or thinks.

Once we were seated with our drinks, Rod went into 'formal meeting' mode, and left no doubt about who was chairing the meeting. "Okay, another day has elapsed in our quest to find Alice Logan. What have we achieved today? Maybe the question should be: have we progressed at all? Who wants to go first? Anyone bursting to share their success story?" After a moment without a response, Rod continued. "No...? Right. Well, I might lead off then."

His audience of two women sat upright and eagerly awaited the news it was obvious he was bursting to share. "Well, I am afraid I have to confess to not much success. But, I have managed to confirm Alice has not been admitted to any hospital in the greater Sydney area. My friend organised for another check on airline bookings on my behalf. He reported no further airline bookings have been made in Alice's name."

"So, is it now reasonably safe to assume Alice is still somewhere in Sydney?" I asked. Expecting the other two to indicate their agreement, I glanced from one to the other of my companions when no such response was forthcoming. "What? Why isn't it a safe assumption? Rod's just told us she hasn't left Sydney."

"No. He told us she hadn't flown out of Sydney or made any bookings to do so in the near future. Rod, am I right?" Cilla asked.

"Yes, I think yours is a reasonable summation of the situation," Rod agreed, and nodded as he spoke.

"Okay," Cilla began again, "but it does not confirm Alice is still in Sydney. Think about it. She might have hopped on a bus or a train, and be somewhere else entirely by now. Or, she might have befriended someone – male or female – and they are touring the countryside by car. No, we cannot yet assume Alice remains in Sydney."

"Alice has *befriended* someone...? If you are suggesting she could be off having some sort of fling with someone, it just proves you don't know Alice. She wouldn't be interested in becoming involved in anything so sordid. She never has been." I couldn't believe anyone even would suggest Alice capable of such behaviour.

"Calm down, Marion," Rod said. "Cilla is right. Alice could have left Sydney by whatever other means, and possibly soon after her arrival. And, what would be so shocking if she went off with some bloke she met on the cruise? Alice has her own life to lead without concern or consideration about what we might think. If she found someone interesting, and fun, and romance was in the air, at our age, how can it be a bad thing?" Then Rod changed to a lighter note. "Anyway, my piece of information didn't contribute much to our investigation. Maybe someone else has something more exciting to share?"

As he finished speaking, Rod glanced around the table before allowing his eyes to settle on Cilla. After another sip of her drink, Cilla shuffled forward in her chair in readiness to speak in response to her cue to 'take the floor'. My scowl did not go unnoticed by Rod, but he chose to say nothing, at least not then. Anyway, Cilla had started delivering her report, so there was no opportunity to say anything without interrupting her.

"Well, my thoughts were along similar lines to yours, Rod," Cilla began slowly, "but my thinking was more along the lines of something happening to David. Maybe he was in an accident of some sort and Alice elected to stay to look after him. In the end, the results of my thinking mirrored yours. David wasn't in hospital anywhere and hadn't been an in-patient in recent times. So, I drew a blank with my accident/hospital line of thinking, but my contact came good on the other stuff I wanted to know about."

"Yeah, David in hospital was an angle I hadn't thought about," Rod said. "What was the other stuff you were interested in?"

"I asked him about the name David Logan. Perhaps we should be relieved if we find Alice isn't with him. Young Mr Logan has a wrap-sheet a mile long; all accumulated since he became an adult. God knows what else might exist but, as you told us, Rod, I suspect his juvenile record is just as interesting."

"Are you saying David has been in trouble with the police… has broken the law on occasion?" I asked. I'm sure the disbelief was so clear in my voice as I posed the question, the other two must have noticed.

"No, not really. What I'm saying is David Logan is a career criminal, and has been for at least all his adult life. Granted, it was petty stuff in the beginning but, as is so often the case, there was rapid progression to more serious criminal activity."

"Cilla, do you have any information on what his current situation might be?" Rod asked. "Your bombshell now has me wondering if he might be in gaol. It would explain why he wasn't able to meet Alice's plane when she returned."

"Oh, poor Alice," I exclaimed. "I now understand why she never talked about him. She doesn't deserve it. It seems all the wealth and opportunity lavished on her two children were wasted. Neither of them appears to have too much time or consideration for their mother. Is David in gaol?"

"Before we adversely judge their upbringing and their behaviour, we should remember those offspring also were a product of their father. And, over the last few days, I've heard tell how he wasn't the most honourable of men. Maybe the kids inherited more of him than of their mother. Anyway, getting back to David's current situation. No, he is not in gaol – at the moment – but should be." Cilla paused to gather her thoughts before continuing.

"Don't stop there," Rod demanded. "Tell us the rest of the story. Hang on a minute though. I'll refill our glasses before you do." Having topped up our glasses, Rod motioned Cilla to continue.

"Right… Well, a warrant for his arrest has been issued, but he seems to have disappeared. I'm not sure of the timeline for all this, but I understand it has happened during the last week or so."

Rod sounded hesitant – almost as if he didn't want to know – when he asked his next question. "Do we … happen to know … why they want to arrest him?"

As he asked the question, his eyes were fixed on me. He probably thought the details might be too much for me to handle. He seemed surprised when I appeared unmoved by Cilla's revelations. It appears I'm a better actress than I thought. But, the illusion was shattered later that evening, when he told me I hadn't looked unmoved. I looked stunned.

In response to Rod's query regarding David, after a couple of sips of her drink, Cilla resumed her report. "It appears he is an active player in the drug scene in the southern state. When I say he is an 'active player', I mean, while he might not be one of the big boys, he is fairly high up the ranks. Perhaps my next gem will help you gain a better picture of David Logan. At the moment, not only is there a warrant out for his arrest, but a couple of the *very* big boys in his field of endeavour are quite anxious to have a few words with him."

"You don't really mean they want to talk to him, do you?" I asked.

"Ah, no, not exactly. It's more like they want to prevent him talking … to anyone … ever again."

"Christ, this is not good news." Rod shook his head in disbelief as he spoke. "Did Alice know about all this? About what he was involved in, and how deep he was involved? I can't believe she did. She would have stayed away from him if she knew."

"But she didn't stay away from him," I said in a voice only slightly above a whisper. "Alice stayed *with* him the night before she joined her cruise, and she was supposed to stay with him again on her return. She too could be in danger now because of her recent association with him. I don't imagine the fact she is his mother means much to the people he is involved with.

In fact, her contact with him could be the reason she now is missing."

Without lifting her eyes from the spot on the table she had focused on for the last couple of minutes, Cilla murmured, "You might be right. It might well have something to do with why Alice is missing." She admitted she knew how upsetting for me her confirmation would be, but she couldn't think of anything to do, or say, to soften its impact. Having delivered her message, she looked beseechingly at Rod in the hope he might be able to rescue the situation.

Cilla's look didn't reach its intended recipient. Rod was staring at the glass of wine he was rotating slowly on the tabletop. He missed his cue to come to the rescue. A heavy silence ensued for a few moments before Rod became aware of its presence. Without looking at either of his companions, instead, he gazed at some indeterminate point beyond his fence, far across the neighbouring field, and off into the distance. After a long moment, he sighed, and returned his attention to his guests.

"God, I can't get my head around it. I know it's because my mind refuses to think about what might be happening – or have happened – to Alice. Marion, I know you are just as stunned as I am, and I wish I could shine even a glimmer of light on all this. But, I can't. Does either of you have any bright ideas on how we might go forward from here?"

The silence returned as both of us shook our heads before retreating into our own thoughts for a few moments. Finally, Cilla shifted uncomfortably in her chair, before clearing her throat.

"My contact will continue to monitor intel for me. The investigation has stepped up and is gaining momentum, so…"

Gaining momentum…? I don't know why you think so. Did I miss something? The only thing happening with our investigation is its descent into a dark place where none of us want to follow it. How can you say the investigation has 'stepped up'?" I snapped. My voice had risen to a level which allowed the neighbours clear coverage of the conversation.

"And, what's this *intel s*tuff you're on about?" I demanded. "This 'contact' of yours is sounding a bit iffy to me. How does he know so much about David Logan?"

"He is just a friend, who happens to be in the right situation to know these things, and can keep an eye on the situation as it develops." Cilla's condescending look and tone as she responded to my question did nothing to improve my sense of humour.

Rod cut in just as I was about to deliver my next barb to Cilla. "I don't think we need to know all the ins and outs of who is providing Cilla with information. The way things are at the moment, we should be grateful for anything we can get, and accept it without question."

Well and truly put in my place, I folded my arms across my chest and slumped down in my chair. If Cilla was being treated as the font of all knowledge, while I was being admonished for anything I said, I wouldn't say another bloody word. I was in desperate need of a plausible excuse to leave the meeting, and hoped it wouldn't take me too long to come up with one.

The sound of Cilla's voice cut through my sulk. While I hadn't heard what she said, my subconscious registered it was something I might be interested in, and I should start paying attention again – even if I wasn't going to join in. So, what had she said to stir my subconscious? Damn, the only way to find out was to ask.

"Sorry, Cilla, I was deep in thought and I missed what you said."

"I was explaining how I am not in a position to say too much about my contact. It's for his sake I can't disclose anything about him, not mine. All I can say is, he is the best bet we have for knowing what is happening as far as David Logan is concerned."

"Quite understandable," Rod assured her, "I wouldn't want to disclose anything which might help identify my contacts either."

"Well, I don't have a problem at all," I snarled. "After all, if you don't have any useful contacts, you don't have a problem protecting their identity. So, I don't have a problem."

This meeting had gone on long enough – maybe too long – for my liking. I sent my muse a strongly worded mental message to be forthcoming with an excuse for me to leave. It seems my muse might be stranded in an area of poor reception. There was no response. But, just as I was beginning to feel desperate about how I could remain civil for even a minute longer... my phone played its tune.

One glance at the screen had me pushing my chair back from the table to allow me to stand. "Excuse me, folks. I need to take this." I gave my companions a wide smile as I said it.

Then, with my phone still chirping loudly, I was heading through Rod's house on my way out to the street. I answered the call as soon as I was a few paces from where the other two remained seated. My challenge was to hide my excitement and maintain a neutral demeanour as I did so.

"Hello... Thanks for calling. I wasn't expecting to hear from you so soon."

"Marion, it's Donna. Are you not free to talk?"

"I am now. I was with a couple of other people, but your call gave me the perfect excuse to leave a boring meeting. By any stroke of good luck, do you have any good news to report?"

"If only... Since our first conversation, whenever I've had a few moments, I've been trying my brother's mobile phone. It's not unusual not to be able to get hold of him, but today was different."

"You spoke to him? Did he say anything about Alice?"

"That's just the point. After so many unanswered attempts to talk to him, a few minutes ago, my call was answered ... Not by David."

"Who was it? Has something happened to David?" My mind flashed back to Cilla's comments about David and the potential threats to his future existence.

"The male voice demanded to know who I was and why I was calling the number. Of course, I wasn't going to say anything until he told me who he was, and I said so. The bloke became rude and aggressive. It was obvious something had happened to David for some stranger to be answering his phone. I was so shocked, I didn't know what to do or what to say. In the end, all I could think to do was to demand to speak to David."

"Er… I suspect that didn't get you anywhere."

"No. He said he didn't think there was any David with them. And, then went on to tell me in no uncertain terms I had the wrong number and should stop ringing it. I gave him a mouthful. He seemed to settle down a bit then, and said he would check if there was anyone called David with them. If he should locate a David, who should he tell David had been trying to contact him? I told him I was his sister and I needed to speak to him urgently on a family matter."

"Did it do any good?"

"He just laughed and hung up in my ear. I just sat there in shock for a few minutes before I decided to try the number again. Now I get a message about the phone being switched off or out of service."

"Christ! I don't like the way this is shaping up … for David and for Alice too. Should we go to the police?"

"You don't know anything about David or you wouldn't waste your time on such wild ideas. Anyway, I don't think I have to talk to the police. I think they are keeping a close eye on me now."

"What do you mean? Are you in danger? Why do you think the police are watching you? For God's sake, Donna, tell me what is happening there."

"I'm fairly sure a vehicle, which parked in the street outside my house around the time I phoned you, has two police officers sitting in it. They drove in along my side of the street, carried on to the end, made a U-turn, and came back to park across the street from here. When it drove by, I got a reasonable look at the passenger. Earlier today, the same guy was sitting in the lobby of the building where my office is located. He seemed to have been there for quite a while, so I asked one of the receptionists about him. She didn't know why he was there, but she knew he was a copper. So, now it appears the cops are watching me. It's probably best if we don't contact each other for a while."

Her suggestion met with my approval, and we wasted no time in ending the call. As soon as it ended, I was on my way back to Rod's back patio ... and to have a word with Cilla. I rushed through the house and out the backdoor, letting the door slam closed behind me. Startled, the two still sitting at the table sat up straight in their chairs.

Rod sprung up off his chair and rushed towards me. "Marion, what has happened? Was your call bad news? You look a bit shell-shocked."

"Yes, I think it was bad news. But, I also think it's relevant to the conversation we had earlier – at least, to the information Cilla received from her contact."

"Come on, come and sit down. You look as though you are about to collapse." Rod rushed over, took me by the arm and walked me to my recently vacated chair.

"Here, take a couple of sips of this before you try telling us what happened." Cilla commanded as she refilled my glass and shoved it across the table to me.

She watched as I did as I was told. Then, I noticed she seemed to relax a little, and sat back in her chair before she spoke again. "The wine won't be as effective as something stronger would be, but it will have to do. Now, take a moment to gather your recollection of your phone call and, when you feel up to it, tell us what was so upsetting about it."

The next couple of minutes were taken up with my report on Donna's call, and how she sounded more than a little rattled. When I finished, Rod was sitting on the edge of his chair and looking most indignant. I had expected the most reaction to come from Cilla, but she appeared deeply engrossed in the circles she was creating on the table in the pool of condensate from her glass.

Although Cilla was silent, Rod's apparent deference to her indicated he had handed the meeting over to her. It came as a surprise to find I didn't mind. After all, I had intended my report of the call would be directed at Cilla. Both Rod and I sat watching Cilla drawing circles on the table, until she finally looked up and blinked at us a couple of times.

"I have to make a call. If you will excuse me for a few minutes, I'll make it from out in the front garden. I'll come back to talk to you when I finish."

Cilla didn't wait for our response. By the time she finished speaking, she was halfway to the backdoor. For what seemed like a very long few minutes, Rod and I sat sipping our drinks in silence.

Chapter 7

When Cilla returned, there was a definite set to her jaw, and she appeared preoccupied. As soon as I saw her coming through the backdoor, I cocked a questioning eyebrow at Rod. He shook his head and murmured, barely above a whisper, "Leave her until she is ready."

It was more than a minute later before Cilla was ready to speak to us. When she glanced around the table, a slight look of surprise flashed across her features. "Oh, sorry. Deep in thought..."

"Are you okay," Rod asked in a voice barely audible from where I was sitting. Cilla nodded, but didn't answer. "If my phone rings any time soon, I'm not going to answer it," he announced in a normal voice. "After the pair of you took phone calls, you came back looking as though you had been told to put your affairs in order as the end was nigh. I don't think I'm in need of any more bad news or surprises today. In fact, I'd rather not know. Cilla, by the look of you, your call was all bad news too. Is there anything we can help with?"

"No. No thanks. And I'm not sure at I would call it bad news, not yet anyway. I went to give my contact a heads-up about Alice's daughter, Donna, maybe being under surveillance by the police. He just about went ballistic. He might call me back soon. At least, I'm hoping he does."

"Why would he react that way?" I asked. "Does he know Donna, or something about why the cops are watching her house?"

"I can't go into details. Suffice to say, the cops should not be anywhere near Donna's place. Christ, I hope they haven't blown it."

Again, I gave Rod a questioning look – and received another shake of his head in response. It's all well and good for him to indicate I shouldn't ask questions, but my curiosity level is just about at explosion point. It can't be good for my blood pressure. Why did Cilla bother to come back after her phone call if she can't tell us anything about it? After all, it was what came out of my call which prompted her to call her contact.

Bugger Rod and his 'don't ask questions' routine, if this is about Alice, I want to know what is going on. I took a deep breath and sat forward on my chair ready to demand answers. Rod raised his hand to stop me but, at almost the same time, Cilla decided she had more to say.

"God knows how this will end up. They might have blown it. For Alice's sake, I hope not."

But, that was all she shared, before turning her attention to drinking a little more of her wine.

Sorry, Rod, but I want answers, and the only way I'm going to get them is to ask questions. "Cilla, from where I'm sitting, your comments suggest Alice's situation is precarious, to say the least. Could you at least explain who has blown what, and how it might impact on Alice?"

Surprise was plastered across Cilla's face when she looked up at me. She hesitated for a moment, and I half expected her to launch into an explanation. I was wrong. Instead, she just shook her head, and then returned her focus to what was left of her drink. I wasn't about to give up so easily. This was my friend, Alice, she was talking about and I wanted more details of whatever it was Cilla knew.

"I'm not asking you to disclose your contact, or to divulge any other top secret aspect of whatever it is you know. One of my best friends appears to be in serious danger. While another woman, whom I've just spoken to, seemed terrified by whatever is happening to her. I think I have a right to know more than you've shared with us so far. So, come on. What is going on? What is happening, and how does it relate to Alice?"

Cilla again started to shake her head but Rod, realising I was not going to let the matter lie, jumped in to avoid the situation becoming 'overheated'.

"Marion is right, Cilla. Although you don't know Alice, she is our friend and we are concerned for her safety. I understood this 'investigation' involved all three of us and, as such, it meant each of us taking on specific tasks and sharing the outcome of those tasks in a bid to progress the investigation. If you need to protect the source of your information, by all means do so. We understand you appear to have a need for secrecy. We don't want to know about your contact. We just want you to share – in broad terms if need be – the information you have received."

Rod's speech appeared to fail to achieve its intended outcome. As he finished speaking, Cilla already was shaking her head, and this became more emphatic at the end of his speech. I was through with playing Cilla's game. In fact, I was guilty of assessing her behaviour as a game of one-upmanship. Enough was enough. Who the Hell does she think she is? These are our people we are talking about, not hers.

"Right, if that's how you want to play it, you go right ahead. But, I have had enough of playing this game. My friend is missing and uncontactable, and I am worried about her safety and wellbeing. I am going to the police to report her as a missing person. And, if I gain the impression I'm being fobbed off – just as I am here now – I will go to my local Member of Parliament, and anyone else I figure might be able to make life difficult for the police and whoever else is involved. Of course, it could mean your contact will be uncovered, but so be it. Have I made myself clear enough, Cilla? If you don't understand any part of what I've said, now is the time to say so."

I slapped my hand down on the table to emphasise my closing statement. The noise it made caused even me to jump, and it set the wine sloshing about in the glasses. Then, sitting upright with my arms folded across my chest, I waited for whatever reaction might come my way. As I finished delivering my ultimatum, I stole a quick glance at Rod... and almost burst out laughing. The shocked look on his face was priceless. When I returned my focus to Cilla, her face looked much the same as

Rod's. Somehow, I managed to hold it all together and maintain my defiant glare at Cilla.

After a somewhat theatrical sigh from Cilla, she sat forward, placed her elbows on the table and held her head in her hands. After a further moment, and while continuing to maintain that position, she began speaking in a quiet, and perhaps a slightly croaky voice.

"I'm sorry. You're right. Of course you want to know the whole story, but it is a bit difficult … It's more than difficult in reality. I'll share what I can, but only on the proviso it does not go further than the three of us. In fact, it is imperative anything I tell you must go no further."

This was not what I had expected. I could feel Rod's eyes boring into me. I exchanged looks with him, before nodding my agreement to Cilla's demand. After securing Rod's agreement too, she took a few moments, presumably to organise her thoughts, before she began speaking.

"Before we go any further, please understand I am not privy to every detail of what is happening, but I will share all I can. Something is going down at the moment in regard to David Logan. I don't have the details, and don't know whether this is a police initiative, or something amongst players on the other side of the law. Regardless, it is believed David's situation at the moment is precarious. Please believe me when I say how much I regret sharing the next bit with you, but you insist on knowing. There is some suggestion, at least among some sections of the police force, that Alice's disappearance could be linked to the action involving David."

"What exactly do you mean by *something is going down* with David?" Rod asked.

"Good question, Rod," I said. "It's one I was going to ask, and I also want to know why the Brisbane police are watching Donna. Is Donna supposed to be involved in something with her brother? So, Cilla, a little more information would be useful."

"We are not sure… They – the police I mean – are not sure why Brisbane has gotten in on the act, but there is a fair chance they will end up stuffing up a Sydney-based initiative already under way."

At the risk of sounding naïve, I asked "Don't the two states' police forces talk to each other?"

"It's complicated. Under normal circumstances, there's little need for communication between the states. Each police service deals with whatever is happening in their own backyard. It's only if the crime looks like crossing state borders there is any need to discuss the situation with the other state. And then, everything is dependent on how it plays out: whether the whole show moves to the second state, or if the action continues in both states. In the latter case, there is a strong possibility the Federal Police would take over."

"Okay, I think I understand it so far," Rod said. "So, now Brisbane is in on the act, does it mean the action has moved to Queensland, or is it also continuing in the southern state as well? I suppose, it raises the question of whether the Feds are about to take over."

"All good questions, Rod, but ones I can't answer. No, Marion, don't look like that. I'm not fobbing off Rod's questions. I can't answer them because I don't know the answers. And, nor does my contact – or so it would seem."

"…Or it's what he is telling you anyway," I quipped.

Again, Rod came to Cilla's defence. "Be realistic, Marion. Cilla can't tell us what she doesn't know. Sometimes we just have to accept the disappointment life throws our way."

"Right, so what do you know, Cilla? If, as you claim, you don't know the answers, at least give us your thoughts on the situation. You seem well enough informed to be able to develop some ideas, and your call to your contact took long enough for you to have learned something."

Cilla sprang up off her chair and began pacing around. Rod shot me an angry look. He need not have bothered. I already was angry with myself for having blown what might have been our only opportunity to squeeze any further information out of Cilla. There was no mistaking how agitated she was. I expected at any moment she would rush for the door and disappear off to her own place. It would be no more than I deserved after pushing her the way I did. My assessment of the woman had been so wide of the mark as to be almost off the planet.

She stopped pacing and, in a low voice, delivered her next bombshell. "While I am worried about Alice, my main concern since my phone call is Donna. I can't help wondering if we haven't placed her in danger … and whether the danger might spread also to the Merivale Retirement Village."

Having stopped pacing, Cilla now stood with her hands buried deep in her pockets, her shoulders hunched forward, and her eyes focused on the ground beneath her boots. While Rod just sat there looking stunned, I struggled to work out what possible motivation there could be for Cilla's comments. The inference I drew from those comments was, maybe Donna's situation might be as a direct result of our investigating her mother's apparent disappearance. If this were the case, then I was directly responsible for putting her in danger. I was the only one who had contacted her … and I was the only one who might link whatever the danger was to our Village.

"Please, Cilla, can you provide a little more explanation about your comments, especially how they might relate to this village?" I asked in a quiet voice. I almost dreaded hearing whatever she might tell us.

"It's all about association – I think. You know how it goes. For whatever reason, when you add two and two, and you come up with five. I think, in Donna's case, it might be some such situation. At least, I'm hoping it is."

I'm sure my face reflected how confused I felt, but Cilla appeared to believe she had delivered a satisfactory explanation. I thought otherwise and let her know. With my hands extended, palms upwards, towards her, I gave her a questioning gesture. It seems I made myself clear. After a rather theatrical sigh of resignation, she began again.

"When you last spoke to Donna, I think you formed the opinion she had tried calling her brother a number of times. If

David's phone was being monitored, those responsible would be aware of Donna's calls. Whether they realised she was his sister or not is another matter. It may be Donna is now viewed as being complicit in whatever David has been up to and, hence, she is now under surveillance. As I'm sure you've realised, Donna probably has been trying her mother's phone, as you have as well, Marion. Any interested parties now have a link between Donna and Alice … and you, Marion."

"So, is it possible Alice's situation has worsened as a result of those calls?" I asked an obvious question, but there was no need for Cilla to confirm what I already knew.

"Possibly… We don't know where Alice is, or what her situation is now. And, we don't know what her situation was before our investigation began, and when you tried contacting her."

"…And, as a result of all those likely linkages, this place, Merivale Retirement Village, might now be on someone's radar as well?" Rod finally had found his voice again. I didn't need him to spell out so clearly how my efforts to contact Alice might have unpleasant implications for Merivale.

"Well, yes, it is the possibility I was alluding to, Rod. I admit, while it's a longshot, it remains a possibility. It strikes me there is little they could do as far as this place is concerned. Nevertheless, I think it prudent to follow Donna's advice and not try to contact her, or the other members of her family, again for a while."

Of course Cilla was right, and I had no intention of calling Donna again, but what about Alice. "How does any of this help us find Alice? If anything, all it has done is paint an even blacker picture of Alice's possible situation. Should we try to talk to those police watching Donna, or some other police, either in this state or in Sydney?"

"No," Cilla replied so emphatically, she stunned me until she went on to explain. "Ye-es, I admit sharing our concerns about Alice with the police would be the right thing to do under normal conditions. These are not normal conditions."

"Why aren't they? Alice is missing and we are concerned. Isn't it something the police should look into?" Cilla wasn't making any sense to me, so I had to ask.

"We only have the word of the receptionist at Donna's workplace about the bloke who seemed to be casing the building being a copper. The big question is why would the Queensland police be interested in what either of the Logan offspring was up to? With whatever David has been involved in occurring south of the border, he and his exploits should be of no interest to police in this state. But, there is a supposed copper sitting in a car across the street from Donna's home."

"Okay, I know all that, but…"

"But, there are two things we don't know for sure: are they really police, and more importantly, are they bent coppers?"

"Christ, Cilla, you are not exactly the bearer of good news, are you?" Rod murmured.

"Huh, it's probably because there is no good news to share so far. I'm afraid, for the next little while, all we can do is to play the waiting game."

"Play the waiting game…! How is that going to help anything? Alice already has been missing for far too long. God knows what might happen to her if we wait any longer to take action to find her – real action I mean." I couldn't believe Cilla was advocating we should do nothing. But, then again, Alice was my friend, and Cilla hadn't even met her.

What could I do anyway? There was no one – according to Cilla – to turn to for help, and I didn't have to be too bright to accept I shouldn't call Donna again. Still there had to be *something* we could do. As I pondered the imponderable, I pushed my empty glass around, creating crazy patterns in the heavy dew covering the table.

Dew…? When did that arrive? I sat up and viewed my surroundings. It was dark; very dark. Sometime, while I wasn't paying attention, night had cast its cloak over us. I shivered.

"Someone walk over your grave…?" Rod quipped, and

followed up with an immediate apology. "Sorry, poor choice of words, given our discussions."

"What time is it anyway?" I mumbled.

"It's gone seven o'clock," Cilla replied, as she checked her watch.

A stomach rumbled. "Was that mine, or someone else's," I asked.

There it was again, and this time there was no mistaking whose it was. My stomach was letting me know it was in need of feeding. I couldn't believe time had slipped away so fast, and we had gone from a pleasant evening on Rod's back patio to sitting in the soft glow of lights mounted high up under the eaves of his cottage. Everything around us wore a heavy blanket of dew, and I felt decidedly damp.

"Are they sensor lights which come on in response to movement in your backyard?" I asked.

"No, they are just ordinary lights. Why do you ask?" Rod asked.

"They seem to have come on of their own volition."

Both Rod and Cilla burst out laughing. "Have you been away with the pixies or something?" Cilla asked. I gave her a scathing look, which she ignored and continued. "Rod went and turned them on a while ago."

"Oh Hell, how much have I had to drink?" Before anyone could answer, my stomach let out a loud grumble. Feeling more than a little embarrassed about everything, I said, "Perhaps I should take it home and feed it before it starts attacking people."

"I should be going too," Cilla said, and pushed her chair away from the table. She was almost at the backdoor when she added, "I'm hoping to hear from my contact again sometime tonight. I'll let you know if I do."

As she disappeared through the backdoor, Rod and I stood up. He gathered up his glass and the wine bottle, as I picked up both Cilla's and my glasses. On my way out onto the street, I detoured through his kitchen to drop off the glasses and say good night. Then I was striding along the pavement to my cottage. I realised I was starving and chilled to the bone.

A warm shower was a necessity before doing anything about food. I had plenty to ponder as I stood under a steaming shower, and again later as I waited for a container of leftovers to reheat for dinner. Not the least of which was the identity of Cilla's 'contact'. Whoever he was, he seemed well-informed about what was happening in police circles in our neighbouring southern state.

And then, there was Cilla Longhurst herself, our most recent and enigmatic village resident. The more time I spend with her, the more I wonder what her story is. It is becoming increasingly obvious she is 'different'.

Chapter 8

I didn't have too much to drink last night. My mind remained clear and, in spite of staying up as late as I could, I spent a restless night, and woke this morning feeling like death warmed up – slightly. In part, the restless night might have been due to Cilla's promise to 'let us know' any new information her contact gave her when he called her later last night.

Did he call her? If he did, she passed nothing on to me before I went to bed. On the other hand, if he didn't call her... Why not? Had some new disaster developed to prevent it? Should we see his lack of contact as a bad sign?

"Stop it! Stop it at once," I told myself loud enough to cause the neighbours concern about my welfare. Torturing myself in this way was going to solve nothing, and I knew it. But, what could I do? By the end of last night, I gained the distinct impression I – and Rod too I suppose – was told to do nothing more; to abandon our 'investigation' in effect. While I wasn't about to comply with Cilla's instruction to do nothing, I couldn't think of anything I might do. And, a protracted breakfast and two huge mugs of coffee did nothing to change the situation. There was nothing I could do.

Today being Tuesday, in keeping with our long-established practice, our mahjong gang should be off to the Senior Citizens' Centre to spend the morning playing mahjong. If my outlook on life doesn't improve in double-quick time, I will not be pleasant company. No doubt Cilla, if she joins us, will be her usual positive, bright self. And, no doubt, Rod will be impressed. Maybe I should stay home today; give mahjong a miss.

The little voice in my head told me it would not be a wise move. You can't win the battle if you are not there to take part. I dragged myself off to shower and dress. There was half an hour yet before Rod collected me, during which I had to transform my outlook on life.

He is always on time for everything, and this morning was no different. I plastered a wide smile on my face and strode briskly out to his car. It seems I didn't hide my surprise when I opened the door to scramble in beside him.

Cilla wasn't in the car. "Are we waiting for one more," I asked.

"No," Bernard replied. "Who did you think we might be waiting for? The three of us are here, as in accord with our usual transport arrangement. I feel sure the other three will travel in Ted's vehicle as they always do."

Rod tried to stifle a laugh with a cough – or was he choking. I swung my gaze from Bernard in the rear seat to Rod, and received a strange look from the driver. Although I couldn't quite interpret it, I took it to mean 'shut-up-and-don't-say-any-more'. So, I didn't. In fact, Rod and I said little for the entire journey to the Senior Citizens' Centre. It proved not to be a problem, as Bernard had plenty to say today – and lots of opinions to share. Requiring nothing more than a brief 'yes' or 'no' from Rod and me at appropriate times, the Bernard-led conversation avoided my saying something I shouldn't in front of him.

Our mahjong morning was remarkable for its ordinariness. The other four of us from the Village played together while, as was becoming the usual practice, Rod and I were paired off and sat at a separate table. And, as usual, the six of us were all but the last to leave before the Centre closed for the day.

Again, Rod and I were a captive audience on the trip back to the Village as we listened to Bernard venting his spleen about how badly everyone else played this morning and how, in spite of his best efforts, he did not have a successful morning. Quite a bit of the blame was levelled at Marjorie, whom he claimed seemed to have some mental disturbance today, and couldn't seem to remember the rules at all. It wasn't until we turned into the Village, he realised he had monopolised conversation, while Rod and I remained mute for almost the entire trip home.

"Have I managed to hit a nerve of sorts?" Bernard asked

"No, not that I'm aware of," Rod replied. "Why do you ask?"

"I thought it must be something I said. The pair of you have uttered nary a word since we left the Senior Cits' place. What seems to be the problem?"

"Oh, I see. No, there's no problem, Bernard," Rod assured him. "I'm sure I can speak for Marion on this one as well. We listened to all your comments, and have been giving some thought to the matter of how to progress our group. I, for one, haven't come up with any solutions yet, but it is something requiring more thought."

"What about the new woman? You know, the one who invited herself along last Thursday … is she interested, or is she not? I know we were so much better players than she was, and we probably overwhelmed her. It shouldn't be a problem though. If she showed a bit more backbone, and came along regularly, she might have a chance for an eventual improvement – maybe even to a standard comparable to ours."

By this point in the conversation, we had arrived at my house. Rod eased to a stop out front. I dived out the moment it was safe to do so without injuring myself, and rushed inside. I did feel a tinge of guilt at abandoning Rod to deal with Bernard alone, but not enough to make me do anything about it. About ten minutes later, my phone chirped. It was Rod.

"I take it you survived this morning okay?" he said as an opening. "I thought I'd give you an update: Cilla went out early this morning and it doesn't appear she has returned home yet. I'm beginning to think something is not quite right, but I have no idea what to do about it – or, if there is anything we can or should do about it."

Lunch and the rest of the afternoon went by in a blur, lost in a whirlpool of worrying thoughts. At a little earlier than my usual hour for this time of the year, I decided a walk in the park might help clear some of those thoughts, and allow me to settle down a bit after having felt tense all day. The light breeze did not rob the lingering warmth of the day, but made for a pleasant hour or so taking in the beauty of the park and its birdlife. But, as time slipped away, I became aware of the evening chill sliding in early to extinguish the last of the sun's warmth. …Time to head home – and at a brisk pace to ward off the encroaching chill.

As I approached Rod's place, he came to the fence to talk to me. His face and demeanour suggested he was anxious about something. I felt my stomach tightening as I covered the last few metres to where he waited. Without any preamble he launched straight into what he wanted to say.

"I'm almost positive Cilla is still not home, and I don't think she has been there all day. The other night when you were here for drinks, you don't remember her saying anything about going away for a few days do you?"

"No, not that I remember. But then, I didn't even notice it was dark, and your having left the table to turn on the lights. So, it is possible she might have said something and I missed it. If it weren't for this damned 'investigation' as she calls it, we wouldn't be concerned about her absence. Perhaps we shouldn't be anyway. After all, she is an independent adult, the same as the rest of us and, as such, is free to do whatever she likes with her time."

"Yeah, I know all that, but it doesn't stop me feeling uneasy about it… especially after she talked about the possibility of our investigation triggering some unwelcome connection to this place. I don't suppose you've heard any more from Donna?"

"The only people I've spoken to today are you and Bernard – oh, and the others while we were at the Senior Cits'. Of course, it is possible she had planned to go away for a few days, or maybe some sort of family situation developed, and she needed to rush off to be with someone."

"Right; we don't know anything about her family do we? We don't even know if she was married, or if she had any children. I just wish I could convince myself her absence is due to something as innocuous as a family crisis or the likes. My problem is, I can't shake the feeling her absence is somehow connected to our investigation of Alice's disappearance."

"You will get no argument from me about your assumption. If we could just make ourselves step back and look at things for a few moments, what we would find is two of our friends are not where we think they should be at this time … and they haven't told us they weren't going to be there. Perhaps there are two factors we should consider: they don't have to tell us what they are doing, and it might be none of our business anyway. … And, if either of us believed any of what I just said, we would sleep easier."

"If only, eh…? Well, I suppose there is nothing we can do about any of it, except to sit tight and wait to see what happens. Somehow, the thought doesn't make me feel any better. Let's agree to continue to worry ourselves sick all night over our two missing friends, and then meet for coffee at my place tomorrow morning to see if we can come up with any bright ideas."

Rod was right. There was nothing we could do. You didn't need to be a genius to work that out. Nevertheless, I knew I would not sleep well tonight, and I suspected Rod would do no better. With nothing more to be said, I continued on to my place and a warm shower to ease the chill which had seeped into my bones while I stood chatting to Rod.

For the rest of the night, my mind focused on nothing else but Alice and Cilla. Although I remained a bit ambivalent about Cilla, she was one of us – one of the Village's residents – and it brought whatever was going on in her life close to home for the rest of us. With nothing riveting on TV to distract me, my mind kept coming up with possible scenarios for the situations involving each of our friends. My efforts to come up with ideas about how we might proceed drew a blank. Needless to say, the turmoil went to bed with me, but sleep seemed intent on avoiding me.

*****

Thunder woke me this morning. For it to wake me, I must have been asleep for at least some little while last night. Lightning rent a dark, threatening sky. The whole scenario provided for a depressing start to the day. A light drizzle began to fall while I dawdled over breakfast. As I lingered over my second mug of coffee, I became filled with foreboding about the rest of the day. In my mind, this morning was an advanced warning, a taste perhaps, of what was to come... And, by my reckoning, none of it looked good.

At a couple of minutes before ten o'clock, I set off for coffee with Rod. The drizzle had stopped. Was it a good sign? Maybe the day's outlook was about to improve. It was unlikely. Once I was outside, my hope was dashed when I realised the break in the weather was due to nothing more than Nature marshalling its forces in preparation for a deluge. Rod came out to welcome me and opened the gate. As he stood holding the gate open for me to enter, I noticed his attention was anchored across the road on Cilla's house.

"Is everything okay, Rod? Are we waiting for Cilla to join us?"

"Wouldn't it be a relief if we were? No, Cilla will not be joining us. I'm almost sure she still hasn't returned home. A few times last night, I looked over at her place to see if any lights were on. The place remained in darkness."

With nothing more to be gained from standing looking over the road, he ushered me into his lounge room where he already had laid out a plate of muffins, side plates, napkins, and mugs. A few minutes later, we were sipping our freshly brewed coffee and breathing-in its wonderful aroma. The arrival of our coffees brought with them the signal for today's 'real' discussions to begin.

The supposed reason for this morning's 'meeting' was to work out what to do about Alice, and maybe to think about Cilla's situation. Before we finished our first coffee, we had agreed we didn't have a clue if there was anything we could do about either of the missing women. Although, on his return from the kitchen with fresh coffees, Rod's comment did offer a glimmer of hope.

"I have to admit, in desperation, I called a Sydney-based journo I used to work with a few years ago. For some years now, he has been working the crime desk, and has a wide spread of contacts who keep him informed. I don't know the whole reason I called him, but I know a part of it was about Cilla."

"Are you saying you thought something had happened to her, and your friend on the crime desk might know about it?"

"No, my motivation was a whole lot of things. I asked him if he had heard anything about Alice, and if he had any recent info on David Logan. Before you ask, no, he hasn't heard anything about Alice. But he did suggest something to do with David might be afoot at the moment. He had heard a whisper about an operation happening, but even his best informants were keeping tight-lipped about it … if anything was happening, that is."

"So, we are no wiser about anything involving David, and maybe Donna as well. I can't help wondering if whatever is happening with David might have impacted on Alice. Did your mate have any more to say?"

"As a result of my call, and the fact everyone was being so tight-lipped about David, he decided to take a drive past the last known address he had for David Logan. His timing was perfect. He saw three people from the house being bundled into a police paddy wagon. He continued some distance along the street and waited a short while before driving back past the house again. The place was then wrapped in crime scene tape. Spurred on by what he had seen, he went back to his most trusted informant. My mate reported that, according to his informant, a couple of people might have been brought in for questioning last night. Although the informant didn't know what about, he didn't think it was anything major, and he told my mate they were always pulling someone in from that part of the city for one reason or another."

"It sounds like a load of rubbish to me. Do you believe the story? More importantly, did your mate believe what he was told?"

"No, of course not – on both accounts. We agreed it sounded like a major fob-off."

"You said something about asking him about Cilla. What did you ask him?"

"Cilla was something I threw in at the last minute, and I thought I might end up looking a fool for it. For some reason, the name Cilla Longhurst had bothered me all day. I felt as though it should ring a bell for me, but it didn't quite manage to do it. So, I asked my mate if he were familiar with the name, or if it meant anything to him."

"And…? Come on, don't leave me hanging in suspense."

"It seems his response to the name was similar to mine. Although there was something about it, he couldn't quite work out what that was."

"Well, having him react to the name might be something positive. I suppose we will just have to wait to see if he dredges up anything about it. So, until then, we remain at a stalemate."

"Yeah, it seems as though we are. He did promise to call me back if he found out anything about either of the people I'd asked him about."

Conversation seemed to die for lack of any other bright ideas to discuss. About ten minutes or so later, Rod was holding the gate open again for me to leave. I walked home feeling decidedly disappointed, in spite of telling myself I shouldn't be. After all, I hadn't gone to Rod's with the expectation of hearing some exciting good news. Nevertheless, the disappointment persisted for the remainder of the day.

While still sitting in my lounge after eating lunch, I let my mind replay this morning's conversation with Rod. After a while, an idea managed to battle its way through the fog to the forefront of my thoughts. In his earlier life, Rod had been a journalist. Had he encountered Cilla's name in some way in the course of his work back then? I gave the idea freedom to grow. Before too long, I was on my way to boot up my computer. If Cilla's name was ringing a bell for Rod, maybe it would do the same for Google. At any rate, it was worth a try. It wouldn't hurt to waste a few minutes looking into it … and what else was there I could try anyway?

It didn't matter how many variations on the name I suggested, Google appeared no wiser than I was on the subject of Cilla Longhurst. While my initial reaction was one of disbelief, after devoting a few moments' thought to the matter, I realised it was quite possible Google didn't know anything about Cilla. After all, I was sure, if I asked it to search on my name, it would come up with exactly the same result – nothing.

I accepted it stood to reason you had to have done something with your life, or been 'somebody' perhaps, to rate a mention anywhere except by family and friends. While I accepted the fact, a tiny part of me refused to believe it would apply to Cilla. There was something about the woman which made her stand out from the rest of us. I don't mean 'stand out' in the same way as Bernard did with his horrible bow ties. Although Cilla's customary oil-stained overalls might be seen to serve the same purpose.

No, in Cilla's case, there was something about the woman. Some elusive thing about her personality – the way she was; the way she acted – which suggested her background differed from those of ordinary folk like me. Having realised such was the case, I spent quite some time trying to analyse what I meant by it. While Cilla wasn't a ravishing beauty, she was quite attractive and spoke well. I assessed her as being well-educated, both in a worldly-wise sort of way, as well as academically.

Having frittered away most of the afternoon on fruitless endeavour, I decided it was too late in the day to begin anything significant. Instead, I decided to begin my afternoon walk a bit earlier than usual again today.

Chapter 9

Having set out on my regular (well, fairly regular) afternoon walk, instead of striding out on my usual set path, I wandered aimlessly around in the park adjoining Merivale Retirement Village. It was a lovely time of year with the trees all displaying their finest autumn plumage, and the small patches of Johnny-jump-up violas growing wild amongst the trees still flaunted a few late blooms. A couple of gabby willy-wagtails flitted from tree to tree keeping pace with me, and voicing their objections as I trespassed in their territory.

Lost in the solitude and beauty, I was startled back to reality when my phone played its tune far too loudly in such peaceful surroundings. It was Rod.

"I hope I haven't interrupted anything, but I thought you might like to know I've heard back from the journo mate we were discussing earlier this morning. If you're interested, perhaps we could meet up to discuss his report."

Although not the most astute person around, even I managed to sense a cautious approach in Rod's conversation. If I was right, his thinking echoed my own thoughts about not discussing too much over the phone. Given Cilla's comments the other night, anyone could be monitoring our phone conversations.

"I'm out walking at the moment, but why don't you come for dinner so we can discuss it then... say, seven o'clock or thereabouts?"

After delivering the dinner invitation and receiving an almost immediate acceptance, I went into a minor panic. What did I have in the house with which to produce a reasonable meal for a guest? What does Rod like – or not like – to eat? Does he have any allergies? Oh God, in spite of knowing him for a number of years, I knew so little about the man. And, I was so out of practice at having guests for dinner. I didn't have a clue what to cook, and in the time available.

In its usual fashion of contriving to make life as difficult as possible on occasion, luck had me at the furthest part of the park from home when Rod called. Now, all I wanted to do was to rush home to deal with the what-to-have-for-dinner problem. No longer fit enough to jog, I had to settle for striding towards home as fast as I could. By entering our street from the southern end today, I made it without having to pass Rod's place.

Sweating, out of breath, and with pulse thumping, my first priority was a shower. By the time I emerged from my steamed-up bathroom, I at least had decided we would be eating pasta tonight. All I had to do then was decide what sauce to make to go with it. By the time I had thrown on my 'house clothes', and was back in the kitchen, I had decided our main course would have a chicken-based sauce ... only because I had some leftover cooked chicken in the fridge.

Once I had the sauce under control and simmering happily, I needed to turn my attention to something for dessert. Oh, and we would need something to wash it all down. I still had one bottle of wine left from the few I bought last Christmas. It was by sheer good luck it was white wine and would be okay as an accompaniment to the chicken pasta. My problem was, the wine was in the cupboard and not cold, and I didn't have too much time before my guest arrived. I shoved the wine in the freezer and set a timer for half an hour.

Right, the pasta sauce and the wine were under control; now for dessert. Four granny smith apples in the fridge and a pack of store-bought puff pastry would have to do. The house filled with the delicious perfume of apples and cinnamon as the filling for the dessert sweated down on the stove. As soon as it was done, it went into the fridge to be cool enough soon enough, to assemble the apple turnovers I planned to make.

With everything under control in the kitchen, it was time to think about me. I threw open the wardrobe's doors and flicked through its contents. Nothing fitted. If it did fit, it was a squeeze and not at all becoming … and I did like to breathe. When had this happened? I go for a walk most days and I watch what I eat. While I seemed to still look much the same, a fair volume of my cargo seemed to have succumbed to the lure of gravity, and headed south. A rump of now considerable proportions just would not fit into some of my trouser collection.

Half an hour after my quest for an outfit began, a pile of clothes, tried on and then discarded, was spread over my bed. But, at last, I thought I looked respectable, but not overdressed for the occasion. It would take me a while to clear my bed before I could crawl into it later tonight, but it was getting late and I didn't have time to worry about such things now.

My newest pair of slacks still fitted and looked 'decent' on me, and teamed with a soft knit top, gave me a quite smart-looking outfit. I was happy with what I saw in the mirror, until I looked down at my feet again. The strappy sandals I had chosen were the perfect accessory for my outfit. The only problem was, in responding to the influence of gravity, some of my cargo had continued to move southward beyond my hips, and didn't stop until it reached my feet. My now chubby pedal attachments strained against the straps of my sandals and, in some places, managed to bulge out between them. I told myself it didn't matter, and he was unlikely to notice. Men never do notice such trivial things, do they?

Then it was back to the kitchen. In quick succession, the oven went on to preheat, the water for the pasta went on to boil, and the wine came out of the freezer and went into the coldest part of the fridge to finish cooling. I laid out a couple of sheets of the puff pastry now at room temperature and cut each sheet down the centre into two rectangles. After dolloping apple filling on half of each rectangle and folding the pastry over to enclose it, I tried my hand at a bit of fancy crimping around the edges. After a couple of quick jabs with a fork across the top of each parcel, the apple turnovers went into the oven. Only then did I check there was enough vanilla ice cream left to go with them. Thank God for small mercies, there was.

At last, everything was ready and under control – or so I thought until I glanced over at the table. While things had been simmering, I had dug out one of my 'good' tablecloths (with matching napkins) and a couple of placemats still in relatively pristine condition. The rose bush, now growing through the fence from my neighbour's garden, provided a couple of flowers for the centre of the table. I allowed myself a few moments to admire my handy work.

Candles! God, I forgot about candles. Now, which cupboard were they in? As I ferreted around in a cupboard for them, another thought flashed in from left field. Would candles be a bit 'over the top'? After all, tonight was just a couple of friends taking advantage of a meal, while they sat down to discuss mutual concerns. How would Rod react if, when I showed him in, he was confronted by low lighting and lit candles? It might be a scene I longed for, but I suspect Rod might turn on his heel and race back to the safety of his own place. Okay. Play it safe; forget the candles. The decision was a relief, as I couldn't find them anyway.

Christ, I am as nervous as a bride on her wedding day. I am just so out of practice at having guests over for a meal. I fussed with the table and tried doing fancy things with the napkins – unsuccessfully – and then had to try to flatten them out again. And, I seemed to be checking on the apple turnovers every ten seconds to be sure they didn't burn. I watched the time tick by. Rod always was on time, and I expected he would arrive right on the dot of seven o'clock. So, at a couple of minutes before the hour, I added the pasta to the boiling water.

Everything was in place for my first dinner party in a long, long time. I allowed myself the brief time until my doorbell rang to indulge in a nervous panic. Why was I behaving like this? It was just a friend coming for dinner, I told myself for the umpteenth time this evening. And yet, here I was behaving like a new bride with her in-laws about to descend on her for the first time for dinner. Tonight would be the first time Rod had come to *my* place. All there had ever been was coffee or drinks at his house. It felt like tonight was my big chance and, for some reason, it seemed important to make an impression.

I did know why I felt the way I did, but I wasn't about to admit it to myself or anyone else. Tonight was just about making the 'right' impression, indulging in interesting and pleasant conversation, and hopefully learning something more about Alice and Cilla, and nothing more... or so I told myself as the doorbell rang.

Dinner went well. We lingered at the table for a while before moving to more comfortable seating in the lounge. Our glasses were almost empty and, as soon as they were, I announced I would make us coffee. It was just as I stood up, Rod's phone demanded attention. He took the call out onto my back patio to answer it, while I retreated to the kitchen to brew coffee.

What to have with the coffee? God, I was so unprepared to be playing hostess tonight. I remembered a bottle of port purchased and opened a while back when I needed it for some new baking recipe I tried. Will it still be any good, the little voice in my head asked as I scrabbled around in the cupboard to find the bottle? About half a bottle remained. Cautious about its condition, I smelled it before tasting a tiny sip. While not an expert on such matters, it smelled and tasted okay to me. I retrieved a couple of liqueur glasses from the top shelf, filled them, and placed them on a tray.

Right, now we had something to sip with our coffee, but I knew something to nibble also was required. Some basic water crackers, a chunk of cheddar, and a lump of blue cheese went onto a plate, and was added to the tray. It was about then inspiration arrived to chastise me for my poor offering. Some chocolates... yes, they would be good. And, I just happened to have the remnants of a box of chocolates given to me for my birthday last week. As I tipped them into a small bowl and made room for it on the tray as well, I told myself they probably had something to do with none of my clothes fitting me at the moment.

As the coffee brewed, I took the tray through to the lounge and then returned to the kitchen to deal with the coffee. Just as I carried our coffees through to the lounge, Rod came back inside after finishing his phone call. I couldn't quite read the look on his face, but I didn't think it indicated his call had been good news. The way he flopped down into the lounge chair tended to support my conclusion. He made no move to say anything. I allowed him his silence, which lasted a couple of minutes, before he looked up. He seemed surprised by his surroundings, and to have me sitting across from him.

"Sorry… I was trying to make sense of the phone call I just had. By the way, this coffee is good. Oh yeah, the phone call…" He lapsed into silence again, and I could almost hear his mind working overtime as he tried to arrange his thoughts. After a few moments, he began again. "Yeah, the caller was my journo friend. The one who works the Sydney crime desk, and who checked out David Logan's house for us earlier."

He paused again, so I jumped in to prod things along. I was bursting with curiosity and all this stopping-and-starting was doing me no good at all. "So, did his call deliver good news or not? By the look of you, I'm guessing it wasn't too good."

"Well, to be honest, I don't know whether to call it good or bad. Let's just classify it as confusing and intriguing." I raised my eyebrows at him, but didn't interrupt. "If you remember, I asked him if the name Cilla Longhurst meant anything to him. He said it didn't, but later he had a vague recollection of the name from some time in the past. Long story short, he called someone else in the trade to see if the name rang any bells for him."

"This sounds like the old 'friend of a friend' network in operations again."

"Yep, it was a bit like that. Anyway, the 'friend' my journo mate contacted dropped a bombshell. The friend said he hadn't heard anything of, or thought about the woman in question in years … until a couple of days ago."

"What…? The bloke saw or heard something about Cilla?"

"No, it's not so simple. After 'cross examination' by my mate, the bloke admitted he wasn't sure. It seems he saw a woman at Sydney airport whom he thought vaguely reminded him of someone. Once my mate mentioned Cilla's name, it triggered the other bloke's memory. He reckons it was Cilla he saw at the airport."

"Can he be right? Why would she fly to Sydney at short notice and not tell anyone. I don't suppose she has to tell us where she is going or what she is doing, but it's a bit odd when we were talking to her only the night before we think she left. Did the bloke say when he saw the woman he thought was Cilla?"

"That's just it. I was prepared to dismiss the whole thing as a load of rubbish, until my mate mentioned the date this was supposed to have happened. It ties in with the morning I heard Cilla drive out – and not return. It's possible she caught the early flight to Sydney. It would have had her at the airport at about the right time to be seen by the bloke."

"Do you think it's possible it has something to do with our 'investigation' into Alice's disappearance?"

"I don't know what to think, but I have to admit to feeling a bit concerned about whatever is going on. Especially after my mate delivered his other piece of news. He is getting serious vibes about the situation involving David Logan. Although he still hasn't been able to confirm anything, he thinks it is big. While he can't dig up anything definite, he believes the Federal Police are involved now, and he thinks there has been some sort operation happening in Brisbane."

"We already knew about the Brisbane thing. So, you would have been able to tell him the police were watching Donna. Did it help him fit any pieces of the jigsaw together?"

"It didn't seem like it. When I told him what we knew about Donna, he was a bit excited for a moment or two. Then, he told me part of whatever was happening in Brisbane involved rounding up rogue cops. So, in effect, what I told him was old news to his ears. In the end, he did concede it was possible what was happening in Brisbane might be connected in some way with whatever was happening with David Logan in Sydney. Beyond that, it didn't help either of us piece anything more together."

"Rod, I have a bad feeling about what might be happening to Alice. Yes, I know there's nothing we can do from here, and I can almost accept the situation. This Cilla thing is a different matter. If she were the woman seen at the Sydney airport, I find her presence in that city intriguing, given what else might be going on there, and our recent conversations about David Logan. Is there any way we can find out whether it was Cilla who arrived at Sydney airport a couple of days ago? What about your friend who found out about Alice's flight booking? Would the same friend of your mate be able to check if Cilla had been on a flight from here to Sydney at the relevant date and time?"

"You're not the only one to think of that angle. I tried calling the bloke who could ask the right people the right questions to maybe find out for us, but he didn't answer. I left a message, so we'll have to wait to see if it gets us anywhere."

During our discussions, I had made a quick trip to the kitchen to refill our glasses with port. For a brief moment, I contemplated brewing yet another coffee, but decided my bladder couldn't deal with another cup. Ten o'clock had rolled around unnoticed, until we had exhausted all there was to discuss about the information from Rod's phone call. By 10.30, Rod was on his way home and I was stacking the dishwasher.

With an overload of coffee on board, and my mind buzzing with the information Rod received from Sydney, I expected to have difficulty falling asleep. I was wrong. Perhaps the wine and port managed to counteract the coffee's caffeine. After dumping the clothes piled up on my bed onto the floor, it was only minutes later before my eyes were refusing to stay open.

*****

Although not hungover, I woke with a thick head and no enthusiasm for anything much this morning. As it was just gone five o'clock when I opened my eyes, I was content to remain in bed for at least another couple of hours. In spite of my intentions, I was forced out of bed about twenty minutes later.

Then, as I was up and about, I decided I might as well get on with the day and went to make breakfast. My phone chirped when I was about halfway through filling the coffee pot. Why would Rod be calling me at this hour of the morning? It was only a few hours ago he went home. A possible answer to the question made my heart give a little flutter. Might our dinner last night have made a strong impression on my guest? So strong, he couldn't wait to call me this morning?

There's nothing quite like being brought down to earth with a thump before you've even had coffee.

"Are you right to go for a little drive?" Rod asked. The excitement in his voice was unmistakable.

"A drive...? Where would I want to drive to at this hour of the morning?"

"The airport... I'll pick you up in about ten minutes."

Ten minutes! I hadn't had coffee and I wasn't even dressed. The little voice in my head counselled me to forget coffee and get dressed – unless I wanted Rod to arrive and find me still in my less-than-glamourous night attire. In response, I seemed to develop six arms and legs all trying to go in different directions at once. In spite of the old adage about 'more haste...', somehow I managed to splash some water on my face, get dressed and comb my hair, by the time Rod pulled up out front.

An almost electric vibe seemed to fill the car. I scrambled into the passenger's seat, and was strapping myself in as we roared off along the street. Not a word was spoken until we were halfway across town. Not at my brightest, and still stunned by the whole exercise, I waited patiently for Rod to explain why we were on our way to the airport. But patience only stretches so far before it snaps.

"Uhmm..., Rod, is there any particular reason we are going to the airport at this time of the day? I mean, if you made bookings for us to fly somewhere, some advanced notice would have been good. I might have dressed differently, and maybe brought a small case."

"What are you on about, woman? You are dressed just fine. We are not going anywhere. Well, nowhere apart from the airport, I mean."

"Okay. Well, why are we going to the airport, or are those details classified?"

"Oh, didn't I say? No, maybe I didn't. Right; well, in the wee hours of this morning I had a thought about Cilla."

So much for my heart flutter earlier! He had been lying in bed thinking about Cilla – not about me or our dinner together last night. While I wanted to tell him how cruel his admission was, I managed to restrain myself, and avoided making a real goose of myself. But, I still didn't know why we were now almost at the airport.

"While I'm not about to pry into your private thoughts about Cilla, can you at least share with me what the airport has to do with your thoughts – or her?"

"What? Oh, I see. You're not at your brightest first thing in the morning, are you? Lots of people are the same. Okay, it's not a problem. I'll spell it out for you."

The cheek of him…! I might not be at my sparkling best this morning, but I am not incapable of understanding basic information. And, I told him so in no uncertain terms. He shot me a stunned look. Good.

"Now, Rod, if you can stop questioning my intelligence for long enough, do you think you might find your way clear to explain why we are now at the airport, and what we are going to do now we are here?"

"Keep your hair on, old girl. If you wanted to know what we were going to do, all you had to do was ask. Hang on until I find us a parking space, and then I will explain it all to you."

Chapter 10

Rod found what appeared to be the only free parking slot in the short-term carpark, and slid into it. I sat patient and quiet – until he killed the engine.

"It's amazing there are so many cars here already this morning. As it's about another hour before the first flight of the day departs, I expected this part of the carpark area to be almost empty, and with cars bringing passengers for the first flight just starting to trickle in."

"Yeah, it's remarkable the way some people interpret 'day-long parking'. They believe if they park here at eight o'clock one morning and return to collect their vehicle by about eight o'clock the next morning, they have complied with the 'day-long' criteria. Shall we go?"

"Go where … and why, or maybe I should be asking: for what? You still haven't told me why we are here at this hour of the morning."

"You do go on a bit, don't you? Okay; we are going to get out of the car and walk around the whole of the carpark area." I think I might have groaned. "No, don't interrupt until I'm finished. We will concentrate on the long-term parking area, particularly the undercover section. And, we will be keeping our eyes peeled for Cilla's distinctive-looking sports car. If it were Cilla the bloke saw at the Sydney airport … and I did hear her drive out in time to catch the early flight … it seems a safe assumption her car will be parked here somewhere."

"Oh, good thinking for so early in the morning." I hoped my comment carried at least a tinge of the sarcasm I intended "What prompted it? I don't recall your mentioning any such thoughts last night." I have to admit, my prevailing attitude didn't appear to be hitting its mark.

"No. It didn't occur to me until the wee hours of this morning. And, only after a call around midnight from my journo mate in Sydney. He dug up a vague recollection of something connected to the name Cilla Longhurst, but the name I gave him didn't quite fit. Anyway, the reason for his call was he vaguely remembered, the woman he was thinking of was maybe a solicitor, or a cop … something connected with crime in some way. He tried digging a bit deeper to find something on the woman, but found nothing. He came to the conclusion, if she had been a cop, she must have worked undercover, and had her identity well hidden."

"Wow, I had not expected anything like that. Mind you, the cop suggestion does sort of fit with some of what she has been saying in regard to finding Alice – the way she puts things, I mean. And, now I think about it, the 'contact' she had been talking to seems to have a close eye on what's happening with David Logan. Maybe he is a cop too, and still working as a cop. You know, now I think about it, sometimes her attitude does tend to suggest she would be more at home in such a predominantly male environment. You must have had mixed feeling about your journo friend waking you up around midnight."

"He didn't wake me up. After leaving your place, I sat and read for a while, and was just thinking about going to bed when he called. Now, shall we start walking – and looking?"

The morning air still carried last night's chill, and it hit me as I stepped out of the car. My lightweight jacket didn't feel adequate, but I told myself I would soon warm up once we started walking. And walk we did… I didn't know how much time, or how many steps later it was before I began developing serious doubts about our current line of 'investigation'. My shins were aching from striding around on the sealed parking area, and I was sweating under my jacket. While removing the jacket was an option, then what would I do with it? As someone once told me, the easiest way to carry a coat was to wear it.

Any enthusiasm I had for finding Cilla's car had all but evaporated. I might feel more committed if it had been a positive sighting of Cilla at Sydney airport, and not just someone *who might look a bit like her.* Nevertheless, Cilla was missing, and a flight to Sydney was as good as explanation as anything else we had at the moment. The fact she disappeared without as much as a hint about it in advance, does tend to add some credence to the 'flight to Sydney' assumption.

Tossing around all I knew to date about Cilla's absence from the Village occupied my thinking as I walked. And, to some extent, it took my mind off my aching shins. Regardless of what my thoughts were, I would not be sharing them with Rod, and I would not be voicing my objections to our pointless trudging around in the long-term parking area. My recently acquired bravado seems to have diminished, and I don't want to lose any ground I might have gained last night. Rod's focus at the moment seems much stronger on Cilla's current situation, than on any interest he might have in finding Alice. I would not do myself any favours by questioning his approach to finding Cilla.

Could that be a blister starting to form on my heel? Impossible; these are my most comfortable, faithful old sneakers. They never gave me blisters, and I've walked a lot of kilometres in them since I bought them a couple of years ago. But, the now very tender spot on my heel is telling me a different story. The little voice in my head told me not to limp, in case Rod interpreted it as nothing more than a ploy to give up looking for the car.

Still grumbling to myself about this whole exercise, I had reached the last row of cars in the section I was allocated to search. I was quite decided. As soon as I gave this last row of cars a cursory check, I would find Rod to tell him I'd had enough and I wanted to go home. Right, let's have a quick gallop along this line of vehicles and then go in search of Rod. Then it happened.

Soon after I started hobbling along the line of cars, I saw it. Just visible, peeping out from behind some sort of large four-wheel-drive vehicle, was a powder blue mudguard. Had I found it? Forgetting my blister and my aching shins, I rushed ahead… And there it was: a powder blue sports car. I was about to bellow for Rod when a niggardly thought made its presence felt. Was this Cilla's vehicle? To me, it looked the same, but I'm no expert on such matters. I checked the number plates... And, a fat lot of good it did me. I had no idea what Cilla's number plates were anyway.

Still, I thought it safer to allow Rod to make a decision about whether it might, or might not be, Cilla's vehicle. I yelled, "Rod, over here." And then waited.

Without moving from where I was standing, I swivelled around searching for Rod. He wasn't visible anywhere, but I knew he had to be in this parking lot somewhere. I tried my luck again and called out again. ...And then tried again. On all three occasions, my efforts gained me the same result: no response. If I'm honest, it wasn't because of a problem with Rod's hearing, but it might have had something to do with a plane coming in to land at the time. Regardless, I was over standing in a parking lot bellowing for my associate.

I dragged my phone out of my pocket and hit Rod's name on my contact list. It only dialled a couple of times before I heard him answer. By then, I was again aware of the painful blister on my heel, my aching shins, and of being totally over all this wandering round the car park. My response when he answered was a bit terse as I gave him instructions about where to find me. A few moments later, I saw him jogging in my direction.

So I would be easier to find, I walked back to the start of the line of vehicles and waved to him. I expected him to be out of breath when he arrived. He wasn't. I decided I had misjudged his fitness level. It was obvious he was a lot fitter than I am.

"What has you in such a tizzy now?" He demanded as he came to a halt in front of me. "I hadn't finished searching the area over there yet, so I hope whatever made you call me over here is worth the energy I expended coming to meet you."

"Well, I don't know. Perhaps you'll be able to judge for yourself when you see what I found."

Without waiting for a response, I turned on my heel and started back along the line of cars towards my 'jackpot' find. As

I reached the blue sports car, I stopped and demanded, "Well, is this the vehicle we are supposed to be looking for?"

"I would have thought the question unnecessary," he murmured.

"No, it's not unnecessary. I know the vehicle looks like Cilla's car but, as I don't know her registration number, I wasn't sure. And, I've never seen her vehicle with the top up. I've only ever seen her driving it with the top down. Seeing as how you've been taking a particular interest in all things Cilla, I felt sure you would be able to confirm whether or not this is the vehicle we've been looking for."

Rod shot me a dark look before turning his gaze to the number plate on the sports car. I waited for his comment, but none was forthcoming. Instead, he turned away, walked behind the vehicle and around to the other side. Having felt so superior up until then, my pride was about to take a dive as I watched Rod lean over to read the parking lot printout clearly displayed on the vehicle's dashboard. Of course, it hadn't occurred to me to check the dashboard … And now I've proved how useless at this 'investigation' lark I am.

In a bid to save some face, I called across to him, "Does the time and date this car entered the parking lot tally with when you think Cilla left home the other morning?"

"It matches to a tee. I don't know Cilla's registration number either, but I'm prepared to wager this is her vehicle. I haven't seen another one like it around here in recent times. Well, now we've found what we were looking for, I suppose we can go home again."

"That would be nice." And that earned me another dark look.

We scrambled into the car and Rod eased out of the car park and into the line of traffic heading into the city. Not a word had been exchanged since we decided to return home. Conversation didn't resume until we had crossed to the north side of the city, and I could no longer restrain the question I'd been dying to ask since we found Cilla's car.

"Okay, so we found Cilla's vehicle at the airport and confirmed, at least in our minds anyway, it is possible it was Cilla the bloke saw at the Sydney airport. So, where does it leave us and, perhaps more importantly, what do we do with the information we've gained this morning?"

"Maybe it's not just this morning's information we need to be thinking about. I'm now so confused by everything."

(HE's confused. Well, he is not the only one, I thought, but kept it to myself.)

Rod continued, "I need to try to put together all we know – and think we know – in a bid to obtain a better view of the whole picture. No doubt you will want to try to sort out things in your mind as well."

"You got that in one."

"Perhaps, if we both take the morning to reflect on everything and see what we can make something of it all..."

"Some quiet time alone might help me come to terms with things. How about we meet for lunch at my house at twelve o'clock?"

Rod didn't argue with the prospect of lunch at my place, so I settled back in my seat to think about what I might prepare for us. My relaxed moment lasted no more than a couple of seconds.

"Christ Rod, today is Thursday." He gave me a startled and somewhat confused look. "Mahjong... our Thursday morning mahjong in the Rec Room, and I haven't baked anything for morning tea. Anyway, we are not going to have any time to sort through our thoughts about our 'investigation' if we are playing mahjong all morning."

"Argh, Mahjong... Of course; I had forgotten about it being Thursday. Uhmm... how keen are you to play mahjong today?"

"Most of the time, I am keen. But, today, I would just as soon give it a miss."

"Right, then that's what we will do."

As he spoke, Rod pulled off onto the side of the road. I watched as he fished out his phone and made a call. It was a while before Rod could initiate a conversation. I assumed it had taken whoever he called some time to answer his phone. Then, I became an unintentional eavesdropper on one side of the conversation.

"Bernard, sorry old chap, I know it's a bit late notice, but there will only be the four of you for mahjong today. I have something on, and Marion tells me she has something to do as well. Oh, and I suppose it means you will have to organise something yourselves to have with your coffee ... Well, no, it shouldn't inconvenience anyone. The four of you will still be able to play as usual. The only difference today will be Marion and I will not be playing on the second table ... No, as I said, Bernard, I can't see how you can possibly think it will be an inconvenience to either you or the other three. Enjoy your morning. Talk to you soon ... Bye."

"Good thinking, Rod. But, I gather Bernard wasn't impressed."

"God, the man is unbelievable – and becoming worse I think. I doubt he could give a toss whether I was there or not. He probably was out of shape at the thought of missing out on your baking. It will do them good to manage by themselves today."

"The one thing you can say about Bernard is he is consistent. It doesn't matter what is happening or what the issue is, you know exactly how he will react."

As I scrambled out of the car in front of my place, Rod confirmed there would be a lunchtime 'council of War' at my house at midday. Before going inside, I watched him continue along the street to his house. *Council of War...?* I don't know what he was planning, but my thinking hadn't yet ventured beyond something with salad for lunch. And that created a few moments of panic. What did I have to put with salad?

My fridge would put Mother Hubbard's cupboard to shame. No cold meat of any descript lurked in there anywhere. Perhaps tinned tuna with salad would be nice I thought, and went to check on my supply. Well, yes, tuna would be nice – if I had more than one tiny tin to work with. My panic level was nudging into the red zone. I should consider the state of my larder before making such magnanimous offers in future.

It took me a while to remember I had a chicken in the freezer. It was soon out of the freezer and thawing out in the microwave oven. About an hour or so later, as I slid the chicken into my stove's oven to bake, I told the universe, "There, see, never a question of not having plenty of time to sort it out."

I had kicked my shoes off the moment I had come in but, in my panic to sort out lunch, I hadn't yet checked on the damage to my heels. I hobbled to the bathroom and dragged out the first-aid box in readiness to take action. Close inspection of the damaged areas revealed a massive burst blister on one heel, and another reasonably sized intact one on the other heel. Thank God for those packs of blister plasters available now, but I will think twice about wearing shoes for the next couple of days. And, I definitely will not be going for my afternoon walk in the park today.

With lunch sorted, and my heels dealt with, I sat down in the lounge with a mug of coffee to keep me company while I tried to make sense of everything going on with two of our friends. After examining all we had learned over the last few days, I still could think of no reason for Alice's disappearance, and was just plain confused by Cilla's behaviour. Although there were a couple of things I was certain about: we hadn't done enough about Alice's disappearance, and I was becoming more uncomfortable about Cilla's involvement in everything. If I were honest, I might have to admit to a touch of the 'green-eyed monster' colouring my judgement of the woman.

Nevertheless, if I were to translate the latter situation into plain English, I also would have to admit to becoming quite distrustful of the woman … and maybe even of her motives for becoming involved. What if she hadn't been a solicitor or a cop in the past as suggested by Rod's journo mate? What if she had been on the other side of the law, and the journo just was confused about how he came to remember her name?

Oh, God, if I keep up this 'thinking business' any longer, by the time Rod arrives for lunch, I will be checking for spies under the bed and barricading the doors against terrorist intrusion. Maybe I should stick to cooking chooks and making salads. With that thought uppermost in my mind, I heaved myself out of my lounge chair and took myself off to set the table for lunch.

In spite of everything else swirling around in my mind, there was one thing I would be doing over lunch, and Rod would have to hear me out, whether he liked it or not. I believe we must talk to the police about Alice, and I will be pushing Rod on the matter. It was amazing how, with one decision made – one clear course of action decided – the fog lifted and the world looked a bit brighter place. At least it did for a few minutes anyway ... until Rod arrived.

He was in a bad mood, and it was obvious from the moment I answered the door to him. I didn't know whether to ask about it, or pretend I hadn't noticed. I did neither. After a couple of snappy comments from the man, my self-restraint went out the window.

"For goodness sake, Rod, if you would rather not be here, then go home again. But, if you are going to stay here, and you can't bring yourself to be pleasant, at least be civil."

"Sorry, I'm just in a filthy mood. It's not your fault, and I can't blame anyone else for it either. It's just frustration getting the better of me. I've spent half the morning on the phone and have nothing to show for it. My efforts gained me nothing. Okay, the rant is over. I'm sure I can manage civil but, while I'm not sure about pleasant, I will try for it anyway."

"Right, thanks for that. And, in case you're wondering, you are not the only one suffering a major dose of frustration. Do you suppose lunch might improve our dispositions?"

There was consensus: lunch, and a glass of the wine he brought to go with it, might improve our outlook on life. We agreed to avoid any further discussion of our investigation until after lunch. I also made the additional decision to hold back on pushing for us to take Alice's disappearance to the police. Rod's prevailing mood would ensure a point-blank rejection of such a move.

As soon as we had eaten, Rod helped clear the table and stack the dishwasher. Then it was down to business. After I placed a couple of pads and pens on the table, we took our places ... and Rod assumed his customary position of in charge of proceedings. He had brought a length off a roll of butcher's paper and suggested we start by documenting everything we knew on the metre-long length of paper. I cast a sceptical eye in the direction of the paper. In my opinion, what we knew wouldn't fill a page of our pads.

In hindsight, only a complete optimist would have thought this afternoon's session would produce anything worthwhile. In line with my expectations, it didn't. Discussions ebbed and flowed for a couple of hours, and resulted in little scribbled on pads, and even less added to the butcher's paper. By the time we gave up and stopped for coffee, the only real conclusion we reached was, we hadn't managed to devise a possible way forward with investigating Alice's disappearance.

Over coffee and the last of my Anzac biscuits, I decided to try my luck. Rod had returned to being his usual self during lunch and had remained so afterwards. With us both sitting there with our coffees and openly admitting defeat, I decided to take a chance to suggest we take our concerns about Alice to the police.

"What good do you think talking to the police will do? Can you picture it? We rock up to the police station and announce we think something has happened to our friend because we haven't seen or heard from her in over a month... And then what?"

"Well, then they would take down particulars about the situation and begin an investigation. Isn't the procedure for registering a missing person something along those lines?"

"Yes, it probably does happen a bit like that ... and therein lies the problem. We would have to provide the particulars they need to ascertain whether or not to mount an investigation. And, as you can see from all the information we recorded this afternoon, we don't know anything. They won't want to hear our speculations. They need to know facts – and we have bugger all of those to offer."

Soon after his outburst, our Council of War dribbled to an end. After rolling up his butcher's paper and tucking it under his arm, Rod said he was going home to see if he received any better response to emails he sent out this morning. He would try calling a few people again tonight.

I stood at the door and watched him make his way along the street to his house. I won't say this afternoon was a complete waste of time, but I don't see where it achieved anything … other than I managed to avoid mentioning Cilla even once during the whole time. Come to think of it, neither did Rod.

Chapter 11

Somehow I had managed to create havoc with my diary for Friday. More appointments than I liked were added in without prior consideration of the commitments already booked-in. As a result, I would be spending most of Friday in town. It would start with taking my car in to have the dent in its rear end repaired. I was told a replacement bumper bar wouldn't take long to fit. I suspected it was another of life's lies, but I booked the car in anyway.

Then, as I was going to be stuck in town, I decided I might as well use the time to visit my hairdresser. It is so long since I'd seen her, she probably won't remember my name. A friend, the editor of the local newspaper, had suggested lunch, but it would have to be a bit early, say about 11.30, to fit in with her work schedule. Lunch with her would round out my morning perfectly. It would leave me only a visit to the supermarket to deal with in the afternoon.

Yes, I was labouring under the assumption my car would be well and truly finished by the time I was ready to visit the supermarket. At my age, you might think I would know better. Of course, the car wasn't finished by a bit after one o'clock when I went back to collect it. But they were ever so helpful:

No, it wasn't quite finished yet, but it would only be about another hour or so, and would I like a coffee while I waited?

My response was terse and more than a little rude, as I pointed out I had particularly asked for it to be available by lunchtime … and I had been assured it would be. After consulting the contents of a folder on a bench at the entrance to the workshop, the very sheepish man-in-charge agreed it was supposed to be finished by lunchtime – but no one had drawn their attention to the fact.

A further rude question about his literacy level sprang to mind, but I managed to bite my tongue. After all, I did want the car finished today, and upsetting the man might prove counterproductive. As it was, it was close to three o'clock when I finally headed for the supermarket. And, of course, by then it was crowded, and there were queues at the checkouts. It was the time when mothers collect their kids from school and then visit the supermarket on their way home. All manner of children, from screaming toddlers to scruffy, sulky teenagers, cluttered the aisles to hinder shoppers.

By the time I returned to the Village, I was tired and cranky. And one look in the mirror confirmed what I suspected all afternoon. My hairdresser had given me someone else's haircut. She must have, because it didn't suit me, and it wasn't the way she usually cut it. That's the trouble with hairdressing salons. The mirrors are so far away, and you can't wear your glasses while they are showering your face with clippings.

As a result, you can't tell how things are going until you're home and can inspect the damage. Well, if she thought today was a long time since she had seen me, it will be even longer before she sees me again. It will take me forever to grow it so there is enough hair there to do something decent with the next time. As I stood peering in the mirror to check out the damage inflicted on me today, I ran my fingers through what remained of my hair. A shower of hair clippings fell all over me.

Sometimes, living alone is a good thing. When you are alone, you don't need to worry about burdening someone else with your filthy mood. You are free to take out your mood on whatever else happens to be around at the time. Now, if I could just find something to kick, I'm sure what's left of my day would improve. My phone interrupted further thoughts about improving my day. It was Rod.

"I suspect you've had a big day and are contemplating what to have on toast for dinner," he said, sounding too cheerful for my liking.

"No, I hadn't even given dinner a thought until you mentioned it. At the moment, I'm collapsed in a big heap with my feet up in the lounge. As a first move before I think about what I might have for dinner, I have to persuade myself to get up out of this chair."

"Yep, I thought you might be a bit that way after a big day out. I'm going to throw a steak on the barbeque tonight. I have a spare one, if you would care to join me."

"Tempting thought, Rod, but I don't think my company is fit for human consumption right now."

"A steak would fix that … and, over dinner, we can talk about the responses I've had from people today."

"You're such a sweet talker. Okay; I'll bring a salad."

After having accepted the invitation, I dashed in for a shower as the first step in preparing to go out for dinner. Then I was confronted with the same problem I encountered a couple of nights ago: what to wear? There were no surprises. In the ensuing period, nothing had miraculously expanded to fit me. A repeat performance of the previous one occurred. Clothes came out of the cupboard, were tried on, and tossed in a pile on the bed.

At some point through the what-shall-I-wear performance, I remembered dinner would be steaks cooked on Rod's barbeque out on his back patio. Nights are still quite chilly and damp. My attention switched to warmer clothes more suited to the occasion. It only required a couple of failed attempts before I had my outfit sorted. Now, what to wear on my feet? I'm not wearing those strappy sandals again. My chubby feet bulging through the straps looked disgusting and, now with the blister plasters on both heels, they would look even worse. No, tonight I need something to keep my toes warm. Right, that's me dressed, and I have just enough time to make the salad.

A few minutes later I was tossing a colourful salad in my best salad bowl. After stretching a length of cling wrap over it, I went to find something to carry it in, and returned to the kitchen with a supermarket cooler bag. The bag gave me an idea. Two leftover apple turnovers from dinner the other night languished in the fridge. The new tub of vanilla ice cream in the freezer sealed the deal. The container with the apple turnovers and the ice cream tub went into the cooler bag, and the bowl of salad went in on top. Tonight, dinner would be a bit more upmarket than Rod might have intended.

Striding along the footpath to Rod's place, I congratulated myself on my choice of attire for my night out. Although it was still early, there was a decided nip in the air. As I strode along, my eyes insisted on focusing on Cilla's house. No surprise; there were no lights on inside. For a moment, my mood plummeted. While I am aware we don't have to know everything there is about our neighbours, Cilla was proving to be something of an enigma. I wanted to believe there would be a perfectly normal explanation for everything about her, but as the days slipped by, I found it increasingly difficult to convince myself it would be the case. But, then I was at Rod's gate and it was time to push such thoughts out of my mind, and summons my best sociable self for the occasion.

Rod already had the barbecue preheating, and had set out on the table a bowl of nuts, a couple of glasses, and a bottle of red wine which was being allowed to breathe. He appeared in no hurry to start cooking, so we sipped our wine, munched on nuts, and indulged in light conversation. As he stood up to busy himself with the steaks, he asked about my day.

"You were out and about for most of the day, so I expect you're feeling a bit the worse for wear tonight. If you're feeling too tired, don't feel you have to stay late. Did you have something particular to do today or was it just shopping and stuff?"

My report on my day's activities was hardly riveting listening and didn't take me long to present. As soon as I reached the end of it, the steaks went on the barbecue, and he brought out plates, cutlery, and napkins. While he finished fiddling with the steaks after applying chunks of some sort of herb butter to finish them off, I dished out the salad, while mentally willing my stomach not to rumble. I hadn't realised how hungry I was, but the smell of those steaks reminded my stomach about it.

While he had prodded and fiddled with the steaks, I sat sipping my wine and taking in the ambience of the evening. Good company, good wine, and a couple of very nice-looking steaks, all to be enjoyed outside on a pleasant evening. How very domesticated – and I couldn't help but think I could take a lot of this kind of life.

As soon as Rod and the steaks joined me at the table, I reminded him about his reference to the responses he received during the day. At the end of yesterday, he was both frustrated and dejected at the lack of response from anyone he contacted. But, I had to wait a bit longer. He wasn't about to discuss them with me yet.

"No, no. We are eating dinner. We are not going to talk about our investigation until dinner is over." He didn't make me wait just until we finished eating. Serious discussion remained on hold until after we cleared the table, loaded the dishwasher, and relocated to the lounge room with our coffees. By then, my patience had run out and my curiosity was in the red zone. But then, he was ready to talk 'investigation', and opened with something of a bombshell.

"My journo friend – the one working the crime desk – has picked up Intel that suggests David Logan has been on the run, but he thinks it's not from the police. Word has it, he took off because whatever he'd been up to didn't sit well with the mob he belongs to. The other interesting piece of information is, the police only became aware of what Logan was up to from information they picked up during another operation. At the time, they were closing in on the mob and were perfectly happy to include Logan in the roundup."

"It doesn't sound as though David Logan's chances are good one way or the other. As I see it, depending on who catches up with him first, he will either have a short life expectancy, or a long period behind bars. I'm sure neither of those prospects appeals to him. And appeal to his mother, Alice, a whole lot less. How has it all panned out?"

"We don't know. So far, that's as much as my mate has been able to pick up. You don't have to be too bright to work out why it's being kept so hushed-up, and why he is finding it such hard going to gain an inside running on whatever's happening."

"Well, while his information is interesting, I'm not sure it's helpful. The only way it might be helpful is if they roundup David, and he can shed some light on where his mother is, or what's happening with her. Did your mate have anything else to share?"

"Yeah… And sort of interesting too I suppose. Some of the vibes he's picked up suggest something might appear in our State's media in the next few days regarding a rogue cell of cops. He believes the cops in question are now behind bars."

"Oh, they might be the ones who were following Donna. She will be relieved if they have disappeared. We'll have to keep an eye on the media to find out a bit more about it."

"Hmm, well, we will keep an eye on the media, but there is a fair chance nothing will appear. I feel it's more likely it will be hushed-up. If the Feds have become involved, they'll definitely put a blanket over it, at least until their operation in New South Wales is complete. Even if the Feds aren't involved, the southern cops will lean on Queensland to keep it quiet until the southern cops have cleaned-up on their patch."

"I can see how, the minute Queensland mentions anything about rogue cops being behind bars, the media will dig into it as much as they can, and without a second thought about how it might impact on investigations elsewhere. What about Cilla? Have you heard anything else about her?"

"Just as we have been, my journo mate too was intrigued by Cilla's sudden appearance in Sydney. Having learnt about what was happening with David and the mob, my mate's first thoughts about Cilla centred on the possibility she might be a big player in the mob. The timing of her visit suggested she might have arrived in Sydney to 'sort things out' and save the day somehow."

"How did you react to that? Did you have any thoughts about the possibility of her belonging to the mob, and not to the police as we were beginning to suspect?"

"Hell no, nothing occurred to me along those lines at all. Anyway … My mate was so intrigued by her arrival in the southern city, he decided he needed to know more about Cilla in order to be able to understand what was happening. He decided to visit an old friend who now is 94 years old and living in a care facility. The old bloke is a former journo and was my mate's mentor when he first started in the business. He taught my mate everything he needed to know about running the crime desk. Although the old bloke has been retired for the long while now, my mate still visits him periodically; sneaks a dram or two of whiskey in with him."

"If the old bloke has been retired for so long, what did your mate hope to gain from visiting him?"

"It appears the old bloke has a few serious health problems, but his mind is as sharp as ever. He admitted he doesn't remember the Cilla Longhurst name from anywhere in the past, but he does remember someone called Gina Truman. She was an elusive sort of figure. Nobody ever saw or knew anything about her but, those whose business it was to know about such matters – like journos – knew she existed. Even after he retired, he continued to believe the mysterious Gina Truman had spent a lot of years working undercover (or something similar) in a task force they suspected, at the time, was set up to smash crime syndicates with strong overseas connections. During his time, and since then, nothing was ever found to prove it, or otherwise, but he believes it was true."

"Was he suggesting this Gina Truman he was talking about is one and the same as Cilla Longhurst? How would he develop such a connection between the two names? In spite of what's been happening, it's a bit of stretch even for me to think they might be the same person."

"I don't think it was quite so mysterious. The two men would have discussed the matter at some length, and my mate would have outlined any suspicions he had. All I received from my mate was the 'executive summary' of their meeting – just the outcome of their discussions, if you like."

"Of course, there had to be a process which led to their final thinking. Rod, what if they are right? What if Cilla is more than just another resident of this retirement village? If her background is as they suggest, are we safe with her living here? And, why has she gone to Sydney? Is she still involved in whatever used to be her world? Her dashing off as she did at just the time when things were hotting up down there suggests she is still involved in some way."

Rod's attempt to allay my concerns didn't do any good. He insisted, regardless of whether those two names belong to the same person or not, Cilla was now retired and, therefore, we had nothing to worry about.

In spite of his best efforts, I wasn't buying it. "And, Rod, the proof of this deduction of yours is…?" I demanded.

We ended up discussing the matter from every angle. After lengthy discussion of what we knew, there was agreement on a key point. Some of the things we saw or heard during discussions about our 'investigation' tended to back-up the suggestion Cilla had been a cop. We also almost agreed her 'retired' status probably was a good thing in terms of our safety, if she was going to be living here.

"You might be right, Rod, about her being retired and, therefore, nothing to worry about. How about you keep your 'positive flag' flying, while I keep a more open mind? For me the question remains whether she has retired or not."

He wasn't about agree with me, but couldn't come up with anything which went any way to alleviating my concerns about what Cilla might be bringing to our doorsteps – if she wasn't retired. Our discussion – argument – lasted a few minutes, but ended with neither of us changing our position on the subject. I decided to try refocusing our discussions on Alice.

"So, Rod, where are we now? To me, in spite of everything we've learned so far, it seems we are no closer to finding Alice, or learning anything about what her present situation might be. What can we do to maybe change that?"

"If you want an honest answer, I'd have to say I don't know what we can do, or if there is anything we can do. It appears there is too much going on in the immediate vicinity of our focus area at the moment, for us to see any clear openings we might pursue. Don't get me wrong, the thought of sitting here doing nothing doesn't appeal to me either. But, I just don't have any bright ideas about what we might do. I still have some feelers out there, which might bring us in some more information."

"The media is always full of information about what's going on in other parts of the country, stuff that wrecks people's lives and, in many instances, robs them of their lives. I've always felt a bit isolated from anything I see in the media, but now I just feel nervous about it. Now, it feels just a bit too close to home."

With little more to be said about what was going on elsewhere, or what we might do to progress our investigation, we turned our attention to something more mundane and settled down with a nightcap before I headed home. At least, we believed we had discussed everything possible, but it seems I couldn't leave it alone.

"Do you think we should hold out any hope we might learn something in the next day or two? If the cops catch David, is it likely he might know something about his mother and be prepared to share it? Somehow, I'm not tempted to put money on it. Are you convinced we would be wasting our time reporting Alice as a missing person?"

"Let's leave it for another day or so, until we see what happens down south – or some of my other contacts come back with information. In the meantime, I share your concern, but don't have any ideas on what else we can do. And, I am reluctant to go to the police at this time, particularly given what might be happening elsewhere. Something else to keep in mind: if Cilla belongs to the 'good guys', the police are likely to know about Alice by now anyway."

Now, there was nothing more to say, but Rod poured us another small glass of port, which we both drank in almost meditative silence. Then, with our glasses empty and in the dishwasher, we returned my empty containers to the supermarket cooler bag, and we were saying our good nights as we headed for the door. My departure came to an abrupt halt when we heard a car coming along our street.

"Hang on a minute. Let's see where it goes. It might be Cilla coming home after returning on the late flight," Rod said. We moved to the front window to watch for the approaching car. After a moment Rod commented, "Hmm… Something is not quite right. The car is going much too slowly. It almost feels like its casing the area; looking for something; an address maybe." In a flash we had turned out the only lights on in the house, and moved to stand beside the window to watch for the car.

A strange car crawled past. It went to the end of the street, before turning and travelling back along the way it had come. It disappeared from view from our vantage point, and we heard the sound of its engine fading into the distance before disappearing altogether.

"Has it left the village, do you think?" I asked. The nervousness in my voice would have been obvious to even someone hard of hearing.

"I'd say so," Rod replied, but didn't attempt to move away from his watching position at the front window.

"They had to be up to no good, whoever was in the car. You don't come into a place like this and check it out at this hour of the night for no good reason. Should we report it to the police?"

Rod shook his head without answering. He looked as though he was grappling with thoughts of his own, and I decided to remain silent while he did so. But, one thing I wasn't going to do right now, was to go outside and walk home. What if the car came back? I doubted they would be happy to see an old lady walking on the footpath when they were cruising the area with ill intent in mind. The next time I looked over at Rod, he was turning his phone over in his hands while keeping his eyes focused on the street. Whatever was troubling him persisted, and I thought I detected a degree of agitation in his actions.

Then, as if he had reached some critical decision, he flicked open his phone and stabbed in a number. Although there was only a weak moon tonight, it provided enough light for me to see everything Rod did. I maintained a silent vigil as he stood with the phone to his ear. It appeared whoever he called was taking their time about answering. Just as I was beginning to lose interest, Rod started impatient pacing.

At last, somebody must've answered. Almost under his breath, he barked one word into the phone and headed to the back door. He had moved too far away for me to catch what he said, but it sounded like a strange word – and just the one word. It wasn't the response I expected when someone answered his call. He didn't say his name, or identify himself in any other way, to the person he called.

As he then went out onto the back patio to make the call, I didn't hear any of it. I returned my attention to the street and kept an eye out in case the strange car paid us another visit. Moments after he left, Rod returned. His call had involved only a brief conversation.

Chapter 12

While Rod's phone call had me curious, the grim look on his face when he returned made me nervous. My misgivings increased when he refused to be drawn on who he had called, or what his call had been about. We stood in the dark, both of us watching the road in an awkward silence, which lasted at least a minute or so. Then, Rod regained the power of speech.

"It's quite likely the car we saw was just a load of young hoons who were out joy-riding, and decided it might be a hoot to check out the oldies; perhaps even give them a bit of a scare."

"Yeah, it probably was something like that. Well, now they've gone, I should be off home."

Why were we both lying? I felt sure neither of us believed it was a carload of hoons looking for something to do. At least, I didn't believe it to be the case. And, it's probably why I felt a little uneasy about the short walk along the footpath back to my place. While I knew I was being silly, I couldn't ignore the flock of butterflies tap dancing in my stomach as I tried to avoid asking myself the big question: What if it comes back while I'm out there? The only thing I was sure about, as I picked up my cooler bag and started for the door, was my determination not to mention to Rod my nervousness about walking home.

As I brushed past him on my way to the door, he grabbed me by the arm and held me back. "Look, Marion, while the strange car has gone, and I believe it probably won't be back, I would prefer you didn't walk home alone. No doubt, you will think I'm making too much of this, but I'd be a lot happier if you let me walk you home."

"Although I am quite sure I would be all right on my own, I don't have a problem with your walking me home if it eases your concerns – and you're okay with the neighbourhood gossip it might generate. So, shall we go?" I was quite pleased with my show of bravado, delivered with not even a hint of nervousness in my voice.

Who were we kidding? The pace we set suggested we both were as nervous as the flock of butterflies in my stomach. We were about halfway along when we heard it: the sound of a car crunching through the newly laid gravel at the entrance to the Village. Our pace stepped up a couple of notches. It only took a moment for us to realise the vehicle was coming our way, and it was drawing closer. My house was just ahead of us, but I doubted we could reach it, and be inside behind closed doors, before the car was on our street.

Rod appeared to be of a similar mind. We were in front of my neighbour's house when he grabbed me by the arm and hauled me towards the front fence. "Come on, jump over the fence. We can hide behind those shrubs."

Jump over the fence…! I can step over it. Fences around here are token structures. When the Village first opened, there were no fences; nothing to mark the separation of one house from the next. It didn't take the operators long to realise they had gotten it wrong… And to accept they didn't know much about human nature.

The equivalent of range warfare broke out between keen gardeners and their neighbours who were less enthusiastic about mowing grass and eradicating weeds. In addition, the exact location of the boundary between one yard and the next became subject to interpretation, and a source of constant friction. Then, there was the other misguided 'benefit' offered when the Village opened: pets were allowed.

These days, even some motels allow guests to have their pets stay with them, so the Village's operators might be considered to be forward thinkers – even enlightened for the time – in allowing those early residents to have pets … and without any criteria defining what those pets might be. Perhaps it was fortunate, the first intake of a handful of residents arrived pet-free. A little later, a gorgeous little fur-ball of a dog named

Cindy arrived with its owners. And, that's when the problems with pets began.

Cindy liked the open space the Village provided and took it upon herself to roam free wherever and whenever she wanted. For some residents, that was okay. But Cindy had a few bad habits, which placed her off-side with some residents. Foremost amongst those bad habits was her preference for fouling somebody else's yard, rather than her owner's. Fences arrived with some haste, along with other restrictions relating to the size of dogs and the types of other pets allowed.

Rather than have the place resembling a jail with high fences everywhere, and with aesthetics in mind, the operators settled for 450 millimetre high 'token' models, which would contain only the smallest breed of dog or a cat. The downside of such low fences is, while they are easy to jump over, they are useless to hide behind if a strange car happens to be cruising your street.

Tonight, it's fortunate for us, my current neighbours are not of the keen gardener variety. They do manage to cut the grass when it needs it, but do little else in the yard. Hence, a clump of shrubs in the front corner of the fence adjoining my yard hasn't been trimmed since the current residents moved in. The untamed gardenia and camellia bushes provided the dense cover needed by two people anxious not to be seen on the street. While I had silently objected to the untidy look they gave the place, right now, I was thankful they were as they were.

We were no sooner huddled behind the shrubs, than a vehicle turned onto our street. My stomach tightened, and I scored a face full of dust and cobwebs as I became up close and personal with a camellia bush. I'm almost positive I stopped breathing as I peered at the street through the foliage.

The vehicle cruised past in a repeat of its previous visit, before again driving out of the Village. When it reached the far end of the street and was turning to run back past us, I whispered to Rod, "Is it the same vehicle we saw before?"

"Looks like it, but I can't be sure. Sssh, be quiet. It's coming back now."

As soon as the car left out street, it was time for us to move. "Let's play it safe and go in through your back door," Rod whispered.

Almost on tiptoes, I followed Rod as we ran along the side fence to almost the back corner of my neighbour's yard. Thank God they don't have a dog, I thought as we scrambled over the fence and into my yard. Then, it was a short sprint to my backdoor, followed by a few moments wait while fumbled about in the cooler bag for my keys. Without turning on any lights, once we were inside, we rushed through to the front window in my lounge room. As in the case of its previous visit, the car was nowhere to be seen, and appeared to have left the Village.

Although I was now in my own home, my concern was for Rod. I didn't want him to be out on the street again.

"Rod, we don't know whether they will come back again or not. The fact they made a second visit suggests they are not just hoons having a night out. They crawled along our street as though they were looking for something – or someone. As they don't appear to have found whatever they are looking for, I think we might see them again. It's not safe for you to be out there, if they do come back. It would be safer for you to stay here tonight and go home in the morning."

"Nice thought, but I'm sure the neighbours would take a dim view of it. I can just picture them lining up outside the director's office in the morning to complain about such unsavoury behaviour right under their noses. No, I'm going home, but I'll take the back route.

A couple of minutes later, I let Rod out the backdoor and watched him step over my back fence. Created by walkers over the years, a rough, overgrown track ran along the back fences of houses on this side of the street. This was Rod's chosen path back to his own back fence, and the safety of his own yard. As arranged, a tense few minutes later, he called to confirm he was home and safe. He also suggested I not turn on any lights, and should just take myself off to bed.

While he was speaking, I heard the sound of a vehicle away off in the distance. "Rod, I can hear a vehicle again."

"Yeah, I hear it too. Let's see what it does, although I'm sure it will be the same car and will do exactly as it did previously."

Our call ended without further comment. With my phone still in my hand, I moved to resume my watching position at the lounge room window. A short time later, as anticipated, a vehicle, with only its parking lights on, oozed out of the darkness and onto our street. As before, it crawled to the far end of the street, turned and then made its way back out towards the entrance to the Village.

It wasn't just checking out the scenery. Whoever was in the car was looking for something or someone, and it did not bode well for someone living here. I'd had enough of this nonsense, and there was no way I could go to bed while I thought the vehicle might be cruising the neighbourhood. I flicked open my phone and dialled 000.

After going through the usual rigmarole about what service I wanted to speak to and where I was located, I found myself speaking to a police officer. It wasn't until I was explaining my concerns to him, I realised how much like some dotty old woman I must sound. His comments when I concluded my story suggested it was exactly how he saw me. "Not to worry, Love, a couple of our boys will check it out. You leave it all to us. Just you go back to bed, and have yourself a good night's sleep. It's the best thing you can do."

I was too slow off the mark, and he had hung up by the time I was ready to deliver my rude response. But, going to bed, and the possibility of a good night's sleep, were not high on my to-do list until morning was making an appearance. As I dragged one of the dining room chairs over to the window, I assured myself the same car would be back again tonight, and I would be watching for it … So I might as well make myself as comfortable as possible while I was about it.

Sure enough, there it was again, and only about fifteen minutes after its last visit. It seemed like yet another encore performance. The vehicle crawled past on its way to the end of the street and then turned to return. But, that's where this performance varied from the previous ones. While still travelling at a crawl, the car started back in my direction. This time, it slowed even further – until it came to a stop in the middle of the street. I was out of my chair and had my face pushed up against the window as I tried to see what was happening further along the street.

My mind took a few seconds to assess the situation. Yes, the car had stopped in the middle-of-the-road ... But it had stopped at a point immediately between Rod's and Cilla's houses.

"They are targeting Rod," I hissed at the universe. It had to be Rod they were interested in. After all, there was no one home at Cilla's place, so why would they be checking out her house.

I jumped, startled as the silence of the night was shattered by the wail of a siren. At the same time, the street lit up with red and blue flashing lights. The occupants of the car also took on board what was happening at the far end of the street where, only moments before, they had turned around. The driver of the car gunned the motor. Its tyres screamed as its wheels spun. Then, having gained traction, the vehicle shot forward and roared along the street towards the exit from the Village ... with the cop car close on its tail.

As I took in the scene playing out in the street in front of me, I saw lights come on in the block of units beyond Rod's house. Not surprising perhaps, given none of the occupants would have been able to sleep through the racket happening outside. I identified Bernard's windows as some of those lit up and, as I cast my eyes over the rest of the units, I saw what I believed to be Marjorie's lights come on too. While I knew some of the units were unoccupied at the moment, I didn't know how many. Judging by the number of windows lit up, maybe only Bernard and Marjorie were in residence.

Something moving on the street caught my eye. It was a person. I caught my breath. Had the vehicle left someone behind to finish off whatever they came to do? With the vehicle and its pursuing cop car now gone from the street, it was difficult to make out too much about the person on the street. Christ, now he's coming down the street towards here. I raced over to check the front door was locked, and then dithered on the spot for a moment while I tried to work out what else to do.

Apart from locking doors and windows, there was nothing else I could do to ensure my safety. I raced back to the lounge room window to see where the person was now. He had gone past. Whoever it was out there wasn't coming to my house after all. A strangled sob escaped in response to my discovery. Then, as I watched the man running along the street, the reality of the situation hit me. It was Rod. Rod was running along the street in pursuit of the two vehicles.

What the Hell did he hope to achieve. A dog chasing a car came to mind. I wanted to scream at him to go back inside where he would be safe, but I decided it wasn't the wisest thing to do. It could put him in even more danger. Instead, I kept silent, and let the tension slowly turn my stomach into a solid lead ball.

At the apex of the corner at the end of our street, after which the street widens to become the main road in and out of the Village, Rod came to a halt. I don't know how long I stood and watched – maybe as long as five minutes. Then, I became aware of more sirens. I couldn't judge how many there were but, collectively, their discordant wails blocked out all other sounds, and just about all cohesive thought.

For just a fleeting moment, a loud bang almost drowned out the sirens. Then everything was silent, except for the mournful wail of one lone siren hanging in the heavy night air. At least, I thought it sounded like a loud bang. It was a bit hard to tell what it was, but it was loud enough to be heard above everything else going on out there. Another loud noise followed. It sounded like some type of explosion. And, it in turn was followed by a bright orange glow in the sky. It took me a while to realise it was a fire. By then, the pall of black smoke billowing up into the air to blot out the sky left little doubt. A serious fire was close by.

Mesmerised by the scene unfolding close by, but out of sight, I remained by my window. A knock on my front door startled me. After rushing to the door, I hesitated. Who could it be at this hour of the night, and should I open it? Then Rod called out for me to open the door. I hadn't seen him walk back from the corner where he was standing the last time I noticed him.

"How did you know I wasn't asleep?" I demanded.

"I didn't need to be too bright to work it out. If Bernard and Marjorie are awake, I wouldn't expect you to be asleep. May I come in? I won't stay long, but I thought you might like an update on what happened." He wasn't wrong. Of course, I wanted to know.

"Come in, come in. Could I interest you in a coffee, or perhaps a drink of something?"

"A mug of hot chocolate would go down well, if you have any."

"Hot chocolate I can manage. You must be almost frozen to the bone after being out there for so long. Come and sit at the breakfast bar and tell me about tonight's drama while I make our drinks."

In fact, little conversation occurred until I had filled our mugs and tossed a couple of marshmallows in on top. By then, I was dying of curiosity and couldn't wait to hear his story. So, I prompted the conversation I wanted to hear.

"Okay, Rod. Now, start talking. You gave me quite a start when I saw you running down the street after those cars. Have you any idea why the strange car stopped in front of your place? I have to admit to being surprised and a bit relieved when the police car appeared. I don't know where they came from, or when they arrived. I didn't even know they were in the Village until they were tearing along the street with siren and lights going flat out."

"While I have no way of knowing what their intent was, from what I saw, our visitors' interest was in Cilla's place. Even a blind man could see no one was at home, but it didn't lessen their interest in her house."

"Do you think they might have planned to break in or something, if the police hadn't arrived when they did?"

"As I said, I don't know. Nobody got out of the car. I didn't even see a car door opened before the cops spoiled their party. Then, it was all pretty straight forward. It was like a classic cops-and-robbers scene on TV. In spite of all the noise they were making, I could hear an extra siren somewhere in the distance. I figured it was heading here as well, and I decided I wanted to see how the performance ended. The only way to do so was to find a vantage point at the corner of our street where I had a clear view of the start of the Village's entrance driveway."

"Oh, yeah, I had forgotten, once you start to turn the corner, you can see clear out to the main road. From what I could see from my window, something quite dramatic happened out there. I wasn't game to go outside to see what was going on. And, when you were so long coming back, and I couldn't see you at the corner any longer, I didn't know what to think. I couldn't call you to see if you were all right. What if you had been forced to hide somewhere, and I gave away your location by calling your phone?"

"You didn't have to worry. Relax and listen, while I try to tell you about everything I witnessed out there. Right; you saw the two cars pass here going flat out with all the attendant drama of siren and flashing lights. Then, both cars reached the road works happening for almost the length of the entrance road. It's a bit like an obstacle course at the moment, and includes a considerable drop-off about halfway along.

While the two cars were crawling along the entrance road towards the main road, a second police car arrived and positioned itself across the main road just beyond the Village's gates, cutting off traffic in the direction of the harbour. When it arrived, our visitors' car hadn't quite reached the new patch of gravel at the start of our entrance road. Then, another police car – a third one – sped up and positioned itself across the main road just prior our entrance to cut off travel in the direction of the city. As the third police car was taking up its position, the visitors' car had cleared the torn-up entrance road. The driver pushed the accelerator to the floor.

The visitors' car had just about reached top speed when it hit all the loose gravel at the gate. I think, realising the hopelessness of the situation they were in, the visitors' driver jumped on the brakes … and had a lock-up. The car kept going flat out, sending gravel out in all directions on to the main road. It couldn't stop. The gravel helped it slide across the road and career into the brick wall on the other side of the road – the brick wall which separates the road from the golf course. From the little bit of the brick wall I could see after the collision, it will require major repairs.

Anyway, the impact of the crash compacted the car to about half its length. Fuel lines, and maybe the fuel tank, must have been ruptured, and the whole vehicle went up in a ball of flames."

"What about the occupants, what happened to them? Were they still in the car when it went up?"

"Uhmm … I don't know how many were in the car, but no one got out. It's likely those in the front seats were crushed along with the front of the vehicle. Anyone who hadn't jumped out beforehand didn't stand a chance once it caught fire."

"So, now we are never going to know who they were or what their game was." After I said it, I realised how crass it sounded, but it was the first thing to come into my mind.

We finished our hot chocolate in silence. I had nothing to say. My mind was fully occupied with coming to terms with what had happened at the entrance to the Village. As soon as we drained our mugs, Rod insisted I should go to bed and try to catch some sleep during what was left of the night. I didn't think sleep even a remote possibility, but I didn't argue and, a few moments later, I watched him heading along the footpath back to his place.

Then, by dawdling over dealing with the empty mugs and preparing for bed, I managed to stave off my inevitable restless night for a few minutes longer.

Chapter 13

The acrid smell of smoke hung heavy in the air this morning. It wasn't so noticeable until I opened the door. I decided the door could remain closed until after I'd had breakfast, and then I would go out to investigate. About fifteen minutes later, I wandered out into my front garden and sniffed the air. Rod's story of what happened at the entrance to the village last night came back to me in an instant, as did my memories of the plumes of black smoke and the orange glow lighting up the sky.

My wandering mode took me out onto the street. With no particular purpose in mind, I began a languid stroll towards the corner. The closer I was to the corner, the stronger was the smell of smoke. Once I rounded the corner and was walking directly into the breeze, I imagined the smell would become almost overpowering. I was saved from finding out. When I was still about one hundred metres away from the corner, Rod Maguire came running around to meet me. He was a lather of sweat, but his breathing remained normal.

"Good morning, Rod. You are up early after our disturbed night. Have you been to bed at all?"

"Of course I've been to bed. But, yes, I was up at my usual early time so I went for my run. Were you going somewhere in particular, or just going for a walk in general?"

"I wasn't going anywhere, I thought I'd come outside to investigate the smell of smoke still hanging around. Is it coming from what happened out there on the main road last night?"

"Yep, the smoke and the smell from the vehicle as it was completely burnt out became almost overpowering last night, and it is still hanging around this morning, particularly the smell of burning rubber from the tyres. But, the crash itself wasn't the end of the story. It managed to start a grass fire which burnt along the side of the road before jumping the boundary onto the golf course. They managed to stop it going any further than the clump of trees adjacent to the ninth green. While the fire itself is under control now, the trees and other material in that area continue to smoulder."

"Well, I don't think I will go any further. The smell is bad enough here. I was about to go back inside to make a coffee. Would you care to join me?"

"Thanks. I had breakfast before I went for a run but I haven't had a coffee this morning."

We took our coffees out and settled down on my back patio after we discovered the air out there seemed less contaminated. As soon as we were settled, and I felt the time was appropriate, I started on the long list of questions I wanted to ask.

"Rod, at the risk of sounding daft, I have to ask, what do you think last night was all about? They weren't just hoons having a lark were they? It was about something else altogether, wasn't it? I'll bet it was about Cilla."

"No, I think it's safe to say our visitors last night were not hoons out for a good time. I'm fairly sure their focus each time they came was on Cilla's house, although I'm sure it was as obvious to them, as it was to everyone else, there was no one home. While I don't know what their game was, I now am a bit concerned for Cilla. I think she may be in danger."

"My thinking was along much the same lines, but I would be a lot happier if I knew why I felt that was the case. I can't help wondering what might've happened if she were at home. After all, the Village isn't exactly deserted at night, even though there aren't too many people out and about. Anything going on anywhere in the residential area was bound to have some of us out of our beds, no matter what time of night it was. I can't help thinking, for the sake of our own safety, we might have to consider distancing ourselves from Cilla." Rod chose to ignore my Cilla comment when he responded.

"I've no doubt last night is bound to have caused a few residents to develop a nervous twitch, and I suspect people will be paying more attention to locking doors and windows for the next little while."

"Is there any way we can find out who they were… Or why they were here … Or, the big one: are they likely to come back again? Rod, there is another thought I almost don't want to give oxygen to: are we sure it was Cilla they were interested in? Could it have been you, or even me, they were looking for?"

"I also suffered a similar thought sometime this morning. All I can say is, there is no evidence to support such thinking. Though, why they would be targeting Cilla here, and not in Sydney, doesn't compute for me.'

"Maybe if we knew who they were would help make sense of it."

"Early this morning I called a mate I play the occasional game of golf with. He is one of the local cops. He wasn't on duty last night, but he was able to tell me they were at a bit of a loss as to what it was all about. He did say someone from the crash investigation team was likely to interview me today about what I saw last night. They will want to speak to you as well. Don't be too concerned about it. They just will want you to tell them what you saw."

"Anything I can tell them isn't going to be much help, but I will tell them as much as I know. Is it appropriate to mention Alice when we are being interviewed about last night? I mean, should we tell them Alice seems to have disappeared, and also should we mention whatever's going on with Cilla?"

"The best I can suggest is to play it by ear, but I'm inclined to think it's not wise to mention Alice or Cilla, or our investigation into what's going on with those women. By the way, as for your concerns about last night's episode, I can put your mind at rest on one count. On my run this morning, I stopped to talk to one of the police officers on duty at the crash site. He confirmed what I thought I already knew. There were no survivors. At this time, they don't know any more, and will have to wait for the bodies to be identified by their dental records. He did say the vehicle had interstate plates, and they suspected it's where the deceased were from, and they weren't local."

"We're coming back to Sydney again, aren't we? It seems like Sydney is where it's all centred. It's where Alice disappeared; it's where Cilla rushed off to without telling anyone; it's where David Logan is being hunted by the police. And, now it's quite possible those who were staking out Cilla's house last night might well be from Sydney as well. I know Sydney is a long way from here, but there is something about the whole mess which makes it feel as though it's too close to home for comfort."

"Don't get too concerned about it. We have to wait until the police find out about the people in the vehicle last night."

"Yes, I know. But what are we going to do about finding Alice? We keep talking about finding her, but we don't seem to be doing anything about it."

"Here's a short answer to your question: we wait. I know, in your opinion, we've waited too long already, and have nothing to show for it. It might be hard to accept, but we do have to wait, until at least after we are interviewed by the police, before we can devise any strategies. In the meantime, I will continue harassing my Sydney contacts. Even the tiniest snippet of information might prove useful."

It was around lunchtime before the police arrived. They interviewed Rod first. Then, he brought them to my place when they were finished with him. I became a bit short with Rod when he first arrived. He was treating me like some doddery old woman; kept telling me there was no need for me to be nervous, and just to answer the questions the police asked me. I was about to tell him off for treating me like a fool when, just in time, I realised he was trying to give me a signal. While I wasn't sure what it was, or what it meant, I assumed it to mean not to mention Alice unless they asked me about her.

In the end, the police interview was almost a non-event. While I was happy enough to follow Rod's instructions and just answer their questions, I did want answers to a couple of my own about last night. After tossing it around in my mind for a while, I decided it would look strange if I didn't appear curious about last night's events, and ask questions about it. So I did. My main question was why the Village had been targeted, and should we, the residents, read something into it? My second question was about what to expect in the future: are those unwelcome visitors, or others like them, likely to come again? I made sure the police knew there were only old people residing in the Village, and no one would feel safe if repeats of last night happen.

Perhaps I shouldn't have been surprised by their response to my questions. The cops did not offer much in the way of reassurance. After all, they were still trying to piece basic information together. Nevertheless, by the time my interview was over, the cops had agreed to keep us informed so we would know we were safe.

Soon after the police left, a friend dropped by. She had been at her market stall all morning and brought some unsold vegetables with her. She already had more than enough for own needs at home so, rather than take the leftovers from the markets home, she thought I would appreciate them. Any I didn't want, I could share with the other residents. Free fresh vegetables are always welcome, so I was more than happy to accept them. The problem was, she requested a coffee in return, and then settled down in the lounge room. She wasn't showing any signs of wanting to go home, and I was becoming anxious for her to leave. I was grateful for the vegetables, but I wanted go to talk to Rod about the police interviews.

At last she was on her way, and was barely out of the street before Rod called with an invitation to join him for an afternoon coffee. I'm not sure I needed another coffee, but I sure as hell needed to talk to Rod. A few minutes later, we were perched at his breakfast bar with freshly brewed coffee and muffins from the local bakery. I managed to hold off on the questions I wanted to ask, until I'd eaten at least half my muffin.

Then our discussion of the police interviews began in earnest, and it didn't take too long for us to agree, the police were just going through the motions of exploring every avenue. The little we told them wasn't going to be much use in their investigation, and they had nothing useful to tell us. With our review of the police interviews completed, I was about to launch into the subject of finding Alice, when a knock at Rod's front door interrupted proceedings.

Bernard and Marjorie stood on the doorstep. From Bernard's flushed face, I knew he was agitated about something… And I didn't have to think too hard to work out what it was. His opening line was to demand we join 'the protest'. Rod, more tactful and patient than I felt, invited them in and offered them coffee. Of course they didn't want coffee. They were on a mission and, instead of sitting around drinking coffee, we should be joining them.

"Well, Bernard, if we knew something about this 'mission' of yours, we might be interested in joining your protest," Rod told him. "Perhaps you might like to tell us what you're protesting about, so we can judge whether we want to be involved or not."

"What do you think it's about," Bernard barked. "It's about the nonsense that went on in the Village last night. Hooning, that's what it was, and it has to be nipped in the bud before it becomes established."

Bernard's face had darkened to an alarming shade of red. I was beginning to feel anxious about being too close in case his head exploded. With his agitation level on the rise, he had sprung up out of his chair and was now pacing around Rod's lounge room. I saw Rod gather himself up as if readying to say something, but he didn't get a chance. Bernard continued his rant.

"Solidarity – that's what we need. We all had our sleep disturbed last night, so we all need to gather outside the director's office to let her know this is not good enough. At our age, being subjected to such goings-on in the middle of the night is not in our best interest."

"You might well be right, Bernard, but what is it you expect the director to do about it? I hardly think she had any control over what happened here last night, or would have if it happened again in the future. I'm sorry, I don't quite see what your protest is hoping to achieve." I marvelled at Rod's patience. His voice was so calm and friendly, whereas I wanted to shout at Bernard to stop being such a brainless prick. But, I surprised myself by managing to keep my mouth shut and letting Rod do all the talking.

"Don't reject the mission until you know what our demands are," Bernard told Rod. "We have discussed the situation and have reached a consensus on what is required. Our aim is to take our complaint to the director, and to present her with our list of demands."

"Oh, right, so there is a list of demands. Would you mind sharing it with us?" Rod almost looked enthusiastic as he asked the question… And it seemed to encourage Bernard to even greater oratory.

"We want gates at the entrance to the village, located right at the beginning of our driveway where it comes off the main road. And, they have to be locked every night. It's not safe with hoons coming into the Village. Now one mob has come in, others will follow just as soon as they hear about it. They will consider it their mission in life – a real lark – to come in here and terrify the oldies." Bernard added one of his trademark sniffs for emphasis as he finished his delivery.

Rod appeared to take a few moments to consider all Bernard had said before offering his thoughts on the subject. "My concern, Bernard, is for those of us who go out at night. I know most people here don't. But some of us do go out at night. And, there are those who have been away and return on the late plane to consider. How do those people get back in, if the gates are locked?"

Demonstrating he was still capable of quick thinking, Bernard took no more than a moment to respond. "Keys… every one of the residents is to be given a key. That way, everyone has their own key and can go out and return whenever they want."

133

"Hmm… Keys get lost, Bernard. As you pointed out, all of us in here are getting on a bit, and lost keys are likely to become a common situation. Apart from losing your key, think about the process of coming into the Village late at night. Nobody wants to have to climb out of their car, and stand on the side of the main road while they are faffing about unlocking the gates. Then, once you drive through the gate, you have to climb out of the car again to lock them behind you. Unlocking the gates won't be too bad because you would have the car's headlights illuminating what you are trying to do. But, you will need a torch to see what you are doing when you have to lock the gates again behind you. And, what do you do if you forgot to take your key with you? How do you get back in? Who do you call to come to let you in?"

I felt compelled to add something to the conversation. "What about those of us who rely on taxis to get around? I can't see the cab driver being impressed with the whole process. The resident could use his key to open the gates and let the taxi in, but how does the taxi exit the Village after dropping off his fare?"

Bernard came straight back. "You don't lock the gate after the taxi drives in. The gates are left open until it leaves."

"And then what happens? Who has to go and lock the gates again after the cab departs? Maybe it could become your job, Bernard."

I was feeling quite pleased with my contribution. Bernard now had something to think about for a few moments and, while he was about it, he provided Rod and me with a short reprieve from his attack. When Bernard was taking too long to consider my comments, Rod stepped in to reignite the conversation and keep it flowing … probably in the hope of distracting Bernard from the notion of holding a residents' protest march.

"Bernard, we're not trying to be difficult, or putting a negative slant on everything just for the sake of an argument. Let's be honest for a moment shall we? You will have only one chance to present your demands to the director and have her listen to you. And, when you do talk to her, you will need to identify not only the problem, but also the most acceptable solution. If you give her too many opportunities to pick holes in your demands, you will end up with nothing. What Marion and I have done over the last few minutes is exactly what our esteemed director will do when you go to her. It might be better to delay descending on the director's office for an hour or so while you regroup to rethink some of the potential pitfalls in your presentation."

"Right, yes, I see where you are coming from. The idea of keys for every resident is problematic for all the reasons you have outlined – and probably was doomed to failure. But, you do have to admit there is a need for something to be in place to prevent unwelcome night time intruders gaining access to the Village." Bernard stroked his moustache and fiddled with his bow tie as, deep in thought, he paced the length of the lounge room before turning to face us. He cleared his throat. We knew we were about to receive another of his pearls of wisdom.

"Of course…! yes, of course," he muttered to himself rather than to anyone else. "There is another solution to the problem; a much better solution. I don't know why it took me so long to think of it. *The gate should be manned,*" he announce with a degree of triumph in his voice. "Yes, it should be manned by a security guard. It would need to be manned only at night, say, from eight o'clock to six o'clock in the morning – or for some similar period of time."

After a quick glance at Rod, I struggled to suppress a giggle as I tried to imitate the intent look on his face. To any observer, Rod was giving Bernard's suggestion thorough consideration… and he appeared to nod his approval as he did so. I knew Rod better than to believe it for one moment. I also knew, if the performance was maintained for much longer, I wouldn't be able to control myself, and would burst out laughing. Preventative action called for on my part.

"A gatekeeper on duty every night is an interesting proposition, Bernard. What sorts of costs are likely to be involved in employing one?" I hoped my demeanour as I asked the question indicated I was giving the suggestion meaningful consideration.

"Whatever costs were involved would have to be passed on to the residents," Rod said. "Might be a good idea to have at least a rough idea of the cost of the complete package before taking the idea to the director. For a start, I can think of wages and superannuation. And, there's bound to be some sort of insurance involved –and the cost of a uniform and any equipment necessary to carry out the job. Of course, those costs would come after a guard was employed. Now I think on it, we probably would need at least two guards to work shifts. And, guards couldn't be employed until a facility was constructed at the entrance to house the guards and the necessary equipment."

If it were possible, Marjorie's alabaster skin seemed to have taken on a whiter shade of pale. "It sounds like an expensive proposition. Do you have even a rough idea of what it might cost all up?" she asked. "And, how might the cost be distributed across the residents?"

Rod and I exchanged exaggerated looks and shrugs. "Bernard dear…," she asked, "do you have any ideas about any of this?"

"Not off the top of my head, no, but I'm sure it can be worked out. When you think about how many residents there are to spread the costs across, I don't think it will work out too bad. Of course, once the initiative is in place, there will be the ongoing annual costs of employing the guards to consider."

Bernard's bravado was showing signs of cracks, which opened up into chasms under further questioning by Marjorie, who could clearly see her hard earned savings being drained away by Bernard's latest brainwave. Careful not to openly suggest a manned gate might create something of a financial dilemma for her, Marjorie did manage to convince Bernard, an estimate of costs for a gatekeeper needed to be taken to the residents for approval before discussing it with the director.

By the time Marjorie had finished with him, both Bernard and Marjorie were not happy with the way Bernard's initiative was shaping up. He announced they were going back to work on some figures, before calling a meeting of the residents. I suspect both Rod and I heaved a silent sigh of relief as we waved them off on the doorstep.

Ted and Janet Furlong were hurrying along the footpath as Bernard and Marjorie were taking their leave of us. "Thank goodness…," Ted exclaimed when he saw Bernard and Marjorie. "We thought we were running late, and were rushing to be at the director's office before it was all over and we'd missed out on the fun."

"Perhaps it is well you've caught up with this pair when you did," Rod suggested to Ted. "Bernard is having second thoughts about a few things. It might be best if all of you went home to discuss the matter further."

"Oh, I see," Janet said. "But, shouldn't we go to the director's office anyway, in case some of the other residents are already there? They might have started discussing things with her. Are you coming with us Rod?" Rod and I shook our heads in unison. "Why not? Aren't you interested in our safety?"

"Ye-es, the safety of everyone in the village is a concern for both Marion and me. But, so far, we haven't heard any suggestions with which we would want to be associated. Besides, today is Saturday … And the director isn't in her office on Saturdays. So, you have until Monday to go away and reassess the situation. Catch you all later…" With that, Rod grabbed me around the waist, spun me around and propelled me back inside the house.

"I think we need something to drink, and it needs to be a bit stiffer than coffee," he announced as he headed to the kitchen … and I collapsed into the nearest lounge chair.

Chapter 14

Although I wasn't sure the day had reached a decent hour to be indulging in a glass of wine, it was most welcome after our long session with Bernard and Marjorie. We sat in silence sipping our wine until my glass was about half empty. The wine was working some kind of magic. My brain was starting to function again, and it brought forward a whole host of thoughts and questions. I shared what I considered the most relevant question with Rod.

"Have you heard anything from any of your contacts? It seems those who were incinerated last night are likely to be tied up with something happening in Sydney. I wondered whether any scuttlebutt was doing the rounds down there about what happened up here."

"With everything else going on around here today, I haven't checked my emails, but nobody has tried to call or text me. My journo friend in Sydney called early this morning to say he thought something big had happened there last night. He had picked up only a slight whisper, but didn't have any details. But, he suspected it might be to do with David Logan. He promised to email me if he found out anything. Sit tight and finish your wine while I check my emails to see if anything has come in yet."

I think I might have been starting to doze off when Rod's yelp startled me back to life. "Wha…? What happened? Rod, is everything okay?"

"My journo mate has sent me a short message. From the whispers he's picked up, he believes Logan is in custody, but is being kept under tight wraps. He hasn't been able to confirm anything so far, but thinks it's being kept quiet because it might be part of some bigger operation."

"How does that suit us, Rod? I mean, if David is in custody, will we stand a better chance of finding out about Alice, or will it ruin any chance we had?"

"It's a valid question, but I don't have an answer for you. Maybe we will be in a better position to judge when – if – we find out more about what's going on down there, and why David is in custody. I suppose it means no change for us. We need to continue to be patient and wait."

"Hmm, maybe... but something just occurred to me. How are we going to find out if David knows anything about where his mother is, or what is happening to her? Nobody knows there is a problem with her. Nobody knows she is missing, so nobody is going to be asking David anything about her."

Rod's hurry-up-and-wait approach to our 'investigation' wasn't doing my frustration levels any good at all. God knows what might be happening to Alice while we sat around on our hands. I decided to give Rod another push.

"Alice has been my friend for quite a while now. If I continue to sit around here doing nothing, I will feel I have let her down; deserted her when she needs me. I'm not suggesting you don't care about her but, if you can't come up with anything more positive to do than sit and wait, I'm going to the police to report her missing." Rod heaved a sigh and shot forward in his chair. I knew the signs: he was about to argue with me. "No, Rod, don't waste your breath trying to argue with me. I already feel bad about not having done something about her before this. So, unless you have some other suggested course of action, I'm going to talk to the police."

"Alice was my friend too, Marion, I understand how you feel, but..."

"No, you don't. Yes, you were friends, but you weren't close. You were more like acquaintances who played mahjong together. I'm sorry, Rod, but this waiting around is getting us nowhere, and I've had enough of it."

"Okay, okay. Just give me a moment to think about things before you go rushing off to do anything. Perhaps another glass of wine while I'm thinking...?"

"Ooh, no you don't… You know damn well, if I have another glass of wine, I won't be able to drive to the police station to report Alice is missing. If you need another glass of wine to help you think, you go right ahead and have one. I'll settle for a glass of water, thanks."

He sipped his wine, and I sipped the glass of water I didn't really want – and we spent the next couple of minutes in complete silence, during which he supposedly applied some mental gymnastics to the problem of our missing friend. When he finally looked up at me, there was something of a defeated appearance about him. I smiled – encouragingly I hoped – and asked if he had come up with any bright ideas.

"Short answer: I don't know. Perhaps you are right. If nobody knows Alice is missing, no one is going to ask David – or anyone they might bring in – the right questions to give us answers."

"Alleluia…! Are you suggesting I might have been right for once?"

"Not exactly, no. I don't think we should go to the police. Hang on, wait until I finish before you start arguing. But, I do think we should get the word out there about Alice's disappearance. My thinking is to tell my journo mate on the crime desk the story of Alice's failure to return from Sydney after her cruise. He could then drop a few words in the right ears."

"What do you mean by 'the right ears'? Either he lets the police know about Alice, or we are no better off than we are now."

"It's all about the way journos work, crime journos anyway. He goes to all the official press conferences held by the police… usually because they want a story out there to encourage the public to come forward with information to help with a case. But, at other times, the press conference is an attempt by the police to have the story they want out there in the public arena – and to avoid the one they don't want becoming public. So, my mate does all the 'official' things, but he also spends a lot of time talking to his contacts. If we think about our southern neighbours at the moment, we know something big *might* be happening down there, and David Logan *might* be involved somehow.

I almost can guarantee my mate will be talking to his contacts just about every five minutes in the hope they might let something more slip than they should. One of his casual conversations with a contact might be the ideal time to suggest Alice might somehow have become involved in whatever is going on."

"So, what happens if one of contacts lets something slip that he shouldn't? Does your mate then rush out and print it so everyone who reads the paper knows about it? I'm surprised the contact doesn't become an ex-contact the moment the paper hits the street, and would never speak to your mate again."

"Of course not, that's not how it works. Whatever his contact tells him would only be a little nugget of information; not a whole exposé. It would be just a suggestion – a hint – to lead him to where he might dig up more details. In that way, whatever he eventually writes can't be laid at the feet of any one individual, and can't be traced back to his contact."

"How does telling his contact about Alice's disappearance fit with the scenario you just outlined? And, how does he do it without it sounding contrived?"

"Sometimes it is contrived, such as when it is used as a bribe to extract a bit more information. You know the sort of situation: you tell me X and I might share Y with you. In Alice's case, for the last few days, he has been making enquiries about David and whatever else is going on. The next time he is talking to his contact, he might just happen to mention he recently heard something about David Logan's mother, Alice, disappearing from somewhere in the Sydney area. He would then ask the contact if he had heard anything about her disappearance."

"And the contact then mentions it to his superiors and they decide whether it is relevant and if they should follow-up on it. Perfect networking opportunities… Do you think the system might help us with finding Alice?"

"Well, I don't know, and we might never know whether it played any part or not. But, it does achieve something you have been going on about: letting the police know Alice is missing."

"Your mate has already helped you find out some information about Alice – where she stayed when she arrived back in Sydney, and her missed flight home – so he already knows she is missing. Why do you need to go through this other rigmarole in order to have him drop a word to his contact?"

"As you say, my journo mate was aware something had gone amiss with Alice's return home, but he would never mention it to anyone without my prior approval. For a start, he doesn't know the whole story about Alice, or her family. So, he wouldn't risk trying to drop a hint to one of his contacts only to end up looking a right fool."

"I don't understand how he could end up looking a right fool by mentioning Alice is missing."

"It's not mentioning Alice is missing that's the problem. Yes, he knows I am concerned about her disappearance, but he doesn't know why. For all he knows, I might be trying to locate her for personal reasons, and if it is the matter for the police at all. Think about it. What if Alice and I had been in a relationship and it turned sour for some reason? Perhaps she went on a cruise to get away from me and sort herself out. Maybe she is staying away from me now because she still is trying to do that. Imagine how my friend would look if the police got involved, and then they found out I was the reason Alice didn't come home. Come to think of it, if it were the situation, it wouldn't be only my journo mate who'd end up with egg on his face. Both Alice and I would end up embarrassed as well. So, no, he would not mention Alice to anyone unless I encouraged him to do so. And, it is exactly what I'm going to try to do as soon as I can get hold of him this evening."

Right; now it was my turn to feel a bit embarrassed about how thick I have been about how such things work in the real world. As we didn't have anything else to discuss, I headed home. By the time I had reached my front door, I had decided I was going for a long walk this afternoon; blisters or no blisters. If nothing else, it might help clear my head after everything that's happened over the last twenty-four hours.

Today, I decided I didn't want to walk in the park. To appease my curiosity, I would follow our driveway along to the main road to see the scene of last night's accident. This wasn't some ghoulish desire on my part. It was more about helping put all the pieces together; helping make some sense of everything going on around me at the moment.

A few minutes after I arrived home from Rod's place, I was striding along our street in the direction of the entrance driveway. The Village is always quiet by 'town' standards, but this afternoon it seemed quieter than usual. Then again, some Saturdays are so quiet you might think we all had died, whereas on other Saturdays, people seem to be coming and going all day. After those involved with Bernard's protest march gave up and went home, the place was as quiet as a morgue.

The smell of burnt rubber and smoke still hung heavy in the air as I approached our entranceway. Last night's burnt-out wreck, and the many metres of crime scene tape flapping in the breeze were visible for quite some distance before I reached the main road. As I drew closer, I could see the gravel sprayed everywhere as the driver tried to brake when he realised he was hemmed in. The deep ruts in the newly repaired piece of roadway helped tell the story of the vehicle's occupants' tragic end.

Somehow, standing there on the side of the road beside the crime scene, felt disrespectful, and I was aware of how conspicuous I would look to any passers-by. I turned on my heel and headed back along the driveway and into the Village. If there were any intent involved, it was to go home but, at the end of our street, I realised I needed to walk off more baggage before I went home. A detour into the park and a walk through the trees might help settle me.

While a part of me accepted Rod's approach to finding Alice made sense, a glance across the park at Alice's home fanned my frustration at how dependent on others we were, and at how long Rod's way of doing things would take. I seemed incapable of accepting the fact there was nothing more direct we could do – and it did not sit comfortably with me. For the remainder of my walk home, I wrestled with a question of my own making, and the temptation accompanying it: should I risk calling Donna Logan this evening?

If those who were watching her were rounded up and taken off the street, would it be safe to call her again? But, what if someone else is still monitoring her phone, might I be putting me in danger as well as Donna? Now I have created another question for myself: should I ask Rod what he thinks about my giving her a call? At least the answer to that one is simple: NO. He would veto it straight off, and then give me at least a dozen reasons why I shouldn't call her.

So far, my search for something I could do to help find Alice was going nowhere. I resolved to devote thought to the matter after dinner. It was Saturday night, and there is nothing worth watching on TV tonight … except for sport, if you are interested in it, and I'm not. When I think back, I still have vivid memories of all those years when the TV set in our house had nothing but sport on it; for the whole weekend, every weekend, and nothing but sport – except for the occasional break for a news broadcast.

Invoking those memories took me back, not just to weekend TV, but to a whole previous life. I was reminded how 'all those years' were in fact not many at all, and they were a long time gone now. Was my 'other' life a happy one? I've never really thought about it. While I wasn't unhappy, I'm not sure I would describe it as happy either. Life was just as it was, and I don't remember questioning it. And then, after almost eight years, that life was over.

For a few months afterwards, my days were dogged by recriminations; not actual regrets, just things I knew we could have done differently. We put off starting a family until we were a bit settled and on our feet. Then, when we thought the time was right, it wasn't to be. The question of whether we had been happy took centre stage again. If not being unhappy means you are happy then, I suppose we were happy. But, I don't remember it as romantic, or of us being particularly close as a couple.

Our families had been friends for years before we were born, so we had known each other all our lives. Somehow, we just seemed to fall into marriage – almost as if it was the ordained thing and everyone expected us to marry. But then, after only those few years, I was free again, free to make my own life. I liked it, and was happy for it to remain so, despite the many efforts of family and friends to pair me off with someone again.

And yes, weekend sport on TV was a regular and constant part of those eight years. These days, I can't even tell you what season it is. Are they playing one form or other of football, or maybe it's cricket, or hockey, or tennis? Maybe it is the season for all those blokes on bicycles to be doing a *Tour de somewhere*. No, there will be no watching sport on TV this Saturday night. And, yes, it is a good time for me to look at everything we know about Alice's disappearance, and give some thought to how I might make some positive contribution to finding her.

Everything went according to plan. The dishwasher was doing its thing, the TV was switched off after the news, and I was comfortable in the lounge with my notebook and pencil. Then, I heard a car driving along our street. It was just after ten o'clock. My notebook was on the floor, my pencil was nowhere to be seen… and I had a stiff neck. I have to admit no planning or inspirational thoughts had occurred during the almost three hours I had been asleep in my chair.

A number of thoughts now collided. Was this to be a repeat of last night's performance? It couldn't be the same people as last night. They were incinerated. Might it be the police patrolling the Village just in case there were others out there with the same intentions as last night's visitors? The only way to know what was going on was to rush over to the window.

While the intent was keen, the body was less so. I discovered other parts of me also were either stiff or had gone to sleep. So, instead of rushing to the window, it was a slow and undignified scramble out of the chair. As the lounge room lights were still on, I would stand out like the proverbial, if I stood at the window. Instead of the lounge room window, I hobbled through to the bedroom and peered out of the window there.

Before I made it to the bedroom, I heard the car slowing down. "Come on, hurry up … or it will be all over and you will have missed it," I muttered as I tried to step it up a gear. It is not such a long trek from my lounge chair to the bedroom window, and at last I reached my destination … just in time to see tail lights disappearing into Cilla's garage.

Moments later, the roller door came down and the house across the road from Rod's was in complete darkness again. Had Cilla returned, or was there something else going on over there? As I pondered the question, a light came on inside the house, and others joined it in quick succession. Either Cilla had come home, or there were some pretty brazen intruders in her house.

As I stood watching lights being switched on across the road, a new question slammed in from left field: should we do something to confirm it is Cilla moving about in her house? If there's damage or stuff is stolen, we will be guilty of not having taken any action. If only I had seen the vehicle before it disappeared into the garage, I would know if it was Cilla or not. Even in the dim street lighting, her sports car would be easy to identify. In the midst of beating myself up about being too slow off the mark, my phone chirped.

"I noticed your lights were still on, so I assumed you hadn't gone to bed and it was okay to call you," Rod said by way of an opening statement. "Can I also assume you saw the car arriving?"

"Well, no, that would be a bit much of an assumption. I did see its tail lights in Cilla's garage before the roller door came down, but I can't say I saw the car. Did you see it arrive? Do we have a problem with something happening over the road?"

"No, no problem as far as I know. It was Cilla's car I saw drive in, so I assume she arrived back on the late flight, and

146

then came straight to the Village. I've sent my journo mate a message to ask his friend to check if Cilla was booked on tonight's flight."

"Now she appears to be back, how do you think we should play it the next time we talk to her? Should we pretend we hadn't noticed she wasn't here, or should we act concerned and curious about her taking off so suddenly, and without a word to anyone?"

"Perhaps we should leave it to Cilla to set the tone. Let's not make any decisions and just play it by ear. After we see how she behaves the next time we meet up with her, we'll know how to handle it."

With nothing else to be said, it was a short phone call. Of course Rod was right about us having to play it by ear, but Cilla would have to be from another planet if for one moment she thought we hadn't noticed her absence. And, if we don't comment on having noticed she was gone, will she feel slighted about her friends not having missed her? Argh, it was all too complicated for this time of night.

As I took myself off for a shower, I rued my earlier decision not to have a shower until I was ready for bed. I knew having a shower at almost eleven o'clock was not the best way to ensure a good night's sleep. In fact, it was almost certain to wake me up, and make sleep more difficult to come by.

Chapter 15

Sundays in the Village are usually quiet; a day when many of the residents subscribe to the notion of a day of rest. While some choose to leave the tranquillity of Merivale to go off to play golf or bowls, most are to be found 'at home', and with some dealing with a visit from family. For me, Sundays have no set routine. It's a time for pottering about in the garden, dealing with overdue correspondence or, if I'm bored and desperate, doing a bit of housework.

Today was to be an exception. I'm still at a loss as to why they decided it had to be today – as opposed to one of the other five week days – but today the Fundraising Committee had scheduled a meeting. In case you're thinking it would make this Sunday a good day to get stuck into some much neglected housework or other domestic chores, you would be wrong.

A meeting of the Fundraising Committee is a command performance. Failure to attend could have you blackballed by all and sundry, and excluded from everything henceforth. Tempting as it might sound, I do intend to continue living here, and compliance makes for an easier life. I shouldn't complain. Residents' vigour and enthusiasm for fundraising has dropped over the last few years to average only about one meeting a year in recent times. Perhaps it's down to the fact there has been no equipment or facility identified as required for the place to motivate raising funds to purchase it.

As I had nothing better planned for today, at the appointed hour, I headed for the Recreation Room, having carefully planned my arrival for after the actual meeting had started, and to miss the fifteen minutes of pre-meeting socialising over coffee and a dry biscuit. Rod caught up with me as I cut across the lawn to shorten the journey.

"It's as well they are all inside and can't see us," Rod said as he caught up with me. "We would never hear the end of our total disregard for all things, from nature, to beauty, to respect for the work it takes to keep the lawn looking good. I noticed you weren't in a hurry to be here too early. Anyone would think your interest level was subpar."

"They would be wrong. My interest level is at absolute zero. I admit to being here only in the interests of maintaining a quiet life, and to find out what harebrained ideas they've come up with this time. I don't suppose you have any advanced warning of what they're planning?"

"Not a clue… But, whatever it is, I'm sure I'm going to be away somewhere on the day."

"Somewhere nice I hope. I know I'm going to be sick that day, so I won't volunteer to do anything. I wouldn't want to let them down at the last minute."

Rod chuckled. "God, what a sad pair we are. I suppose it's too much to hope it will be a short meeting and will finish well before lunch." I nodded my agreement but there was no chance for further comment. We had arrived at our destination.

"Oh look," I whispered to Rod, "they reserved two seats for us right at the back."

"And you will note they are the only two unoccupied seats in the room. Just try pretending you were there when you weren't."

Clarice Smethurst, the self-appointed organiser of the fundraising committee, was partway through her opening spiel when we clattered in to take our seats. It earned us a filthy look from the speaker, and from several others in the room, who we guessed were committee members. The rest of those present already looked half comatose. The sad part about it all was, we would soon join their ranks.

Today was Sunday, and residents obliged to attend the meeting turned up in whatever they were wearing at the time. Some wore smart casual clothes, while most of us arrived in our 'house clothes' of the day. On the other hand, Clarice, no doubt in response to her self-appointed importance, wore a severely tailored beige business suit. The only other person who appeared to have devoted some effort to his attire for the occasion was Bernard. He ensured he stood out in the crowd by choosing to wear a lime green long sleeved shirt finished off with a large, equally fluorescent pink bow tie with black pinstripes. Where does he find those ties? The sales assistants must see an opportunity to have a real giggle when they see him coming.

Amidst others in similar attire, for once, Rod didn't look out of place in his board shorts, tee shirt and sandals. As a few others had worn track pants, my baggy slacks didn't standout too badly either. I spent the first few minutes, until Clarice reached the 'serious' part of the meeting, checking out who was there and what they wore.

After a long welcoming speech and a heap of other rubbish, Clarice finally came to the part where she was going to tell us the reason we needed to raise funds. Rod and I exchanged glances, but we kept our heads down and tried not to draw attention to ourselves.

The assembly was assured the Rec Room was in need of new curtains. Did the room have curtains? I did a quick check, because I couldn't recall having noticed any here before Clarice mentioned them. Oh yeah, there were curtains; didn't seem to be too much wrong with them. In fact, they looked perfectly okay to me. But, Clarice had still more items on her shopping list.

It seems we needed a couple of those fancy chairs that elevate your feet and help you stand up when you want to get out of them. The existing chairs don't suit a couple of the frailer women who attend the Craft and Conversation sessions held in the room every week. And, there should be a computer station and internet kiosk set up in a corner somewhere, so residents could access modern technology without the expense of having to purchase their own equipment.

I suppose she had identified valid needs within the Village's community, but I wondered about the internet kiosk. To the best of my knowledge, anyone who is interested already had set themselves up in their own home. Who would use such a facility? Perhaps the question is not so much who, as how many would use such a facility to warrant the expense in the first place?

Bernard appeared to have thoughts along similar lines and, never one to hold back, he was quick to voice his questions. "It is all very well to say we need these things, but whom did you envisage would maintain them? When they break down, or are rendered inoperable through operator incompetence, who will fix them, and how will they be paid for their services?"

Someone should tell Bernard that's not how these meetings are supposed to run. We, the plebs in attendance, are not supposed to ask difficult questions. In fact, it's almost a mortal sin for us to ask questions at all. After all, any questions will be seen as a direct attack on the organiser and her integrity.

"You've got to marvel at his temerity," Rod whispered. I struggled not to giggle.

Until then, I hadn't noticed Cilla was at the meeting, but I spotted her the moment she spoke. Someone had made quick work of letting her know the meeting was on and, more importantly, had dragged her along to it. Whoever it was obviously forgot to acquaint her with the conduct of proceedings at such meetings, and she echoed Bernard's questions regarding the need for the computer and Internet kiosk.

Clarice made the serious mistake of suggesting the pair of them were only asking questions because they had no understanding or appreciation of today's world of information technology. Oh dear; judging by the colour of Bernard's face his blood pressure went up quite a lot of points on the strength of her comments. Unlike him, he spluttered a bit as he tried to issue a response to Clarice's barb. While he spluttered, Cilla proved she was up to the task.

"On what basis have you identified this so-called need? Were the residents surveyed? If they were, I wasn't asked for my opinion. Nevertheless, perhaps there has been an identified need, and the potential outlay for any such relatively expensive purchases needs to be assessed in terms of cost-effective use of funds raised across the whole of the Village's population. I'm sure you're aware of that, and no doubt you have conducted such an assessment. But, so everyone here becomes aware of the justification for such purchases... *Hands up all those who would be interested in using such equipment if it were installed here in this room.*

Not one hand was raised. Cilla made a great show of scanning the room to be sure no one was overlooked. Then, she slowly turned back to Clarice and, abandoning her previous formal approach, Cilla announced, "Right, just as I thought. It seems no one else wants it, except you. I can't speak for anyone else, but I don't feel inclined to raise funds to accommodate your personal whims and fancies. Perhaps you might achieve more support by asking us what we think should be acquired – if anything."

Murmuring filled the room for a few moments. Clarice banged her empty coffee mug on the table as a makeshift gavel in the hope of regaining control of the meeting. It didn't work. Cilla stood up again and let out a shrill whistle. The place fell silent.

"Right, that's better. Now you've all had a chat about it, what are your suggestions? What do you think we need to purchase? Come on, this is your one chance to have your say. Speak now, or forever hold your peace." Attendees were shrugging and shaking their heads. "Well, it seems we have a blank shopping list. Madam Organiser, you appear to be the only one who thinks we need anything. I think you've been outvoted."

With that, Cilla sat down again. But, Bernard had found his voice at last – and he had a score to settle with Clarice.

"As the business of this meeting was presented and discussed, and is now resolved, I move we declare the meeting closed, and we all go home."

A few 'ayes' were heard from amongst those in attendance, but they were all but drowned out by the scraping of chairs as the mad rush to evacuate the room began. Rod and I stayed in our seats to watch the stampede.

"She's wearing heels!" I hissed as I watched Clarice's retreating rear view. "Clarice is wearing heels… *and stockings!*"

Rod coughed to stifle a laugh. Within seconds, we were the only ones still in the room.

"I don't know about you, but I find it too early for lunch yet. Would you care to join me for a coffee?" Rod asked, as he flexed his legs and prepared to stand.

"What a welcome invitation. I didn't have my mid-morning coffee before I came to the meeting, and I could more than do with one now."

Just as we climbed out of our chairs, Cilla, behaving furtively, returned to the Rec Room. "Oh good, I thought you might still be here, so I decided to sneak away from the pack and return." She flopped down onto a chair recently vacated by Shirley. "God save us from fundraising committees. What a waste of a Sunday morning. I intended taking Black Bess for a run this morning … until Bernard came knocking on his way here; insisted it was a requirement for all residents to attend. I will be having a word to him about that porky sometime in the near future. Anyway, do we really need new curtains in here? I don't understand why we are bothering with curtains at all."

Rod's chuckle developed in a belly laugh. "You sound like you need a coffee. We had just decided we were in need of caffeine. Would you care to join us?"

"Ooh, yes please. Shall we go somewhere, or were you planning to have it here?"

"Here…? Not a chance. If the mob got a whiff of coffee brewing, they all would be back here in a flash – and would expect something to go with it. No, I invited Marion to my place for a cup. Let's walk back together, shall we?"

Apart from the occasional comment, conversation as such didn't resume until we were seated with our coffees around the table on Rod's back patio. Cilla initiated it with an outburst which startled me and almost made me spill my coffee.

"Books…! That's what we need. We need some decent books for our so-called library. When was the library set up, and how is the supply of books managed?"

"Well, it's a residents' initiative, and it's more of a book-swap than a proper library. There is no librarian. No one checks the books out or in. Anyone of the residents can come in and take a book," Rod explained

"Why would you bother?" Cilla continued. "Some of those books are ancient. I saw one there with a release date of 1939. You might want to argue it's a classic and other such rubbish, but I had a look at it. It would be painful to read, and would take you forever to finish it – if you could stick it through to the end. And, some of the others look so dog-eared, they should have been pensioned off long ago. There are no recent releases amongst them. I thought someone would have complained to management by now."

"Now there's the crux of it all." Rod gave Cilla an emphatic nod. "The 'library' has nothing to do with management … or maybe, I should say, management has nothing to do with the library. When the early residents moved-in, some brought their collection of books with them. They soon found they didn't have room for all of them and, as they had read the paperbacks, they wanted to get rid of them … but couldn't bring themselves to throw them out. So, they persuaded management to provide some shelving – and a library was born."

"So, people could dump their unwanted books on the shelving provided in the Rec Room, and others, regardless of whether they were contributing to the library or not, could take a book to read. Is that how it works?" Cilla was shaking her head in disbelief as she spoke.

Rod shrugged and nodded his confirmation. "That's pretty much how it works. Of course, in no time flat, it became a terrible jumble of stuff on the shelves. There was no catalogue and, as I mentioned, no record of what was happening with the books. A couple of years ago, a resident – a foolhardy but good intentioned soul – tried to establish a library committee to manage the books. The first task he envisaged for the new committee was cataloguing the books."

My self-restraint deserted me and I laughed out loud. "Oh, Cilla, you are still so new to the ways of this place. There was no problem getting people to be on the committee. There never is in this place. People have so little to do and are so bored, a committee sounds like a great way of filling in time. And so it was with establishing a library committee. Then the rot set in. Every one of them thought somebody else should be responsible for the cataloguing, with many of them arguing, as they didn't understand the Dewey system, they would only make a mess of things."

Cilla sat forward in response to my comments, and almost seemed a little excited. "So, there was a library catalogue created. Who would know where it was now? Is the bloke who started the committee still around?"

Both Rod and I put on our best sad faces and shook our heads before Rod explained. "No. He had only been here about six months when he passed away suddenly. I think he did try to make a start on a catalogue, but I don't know how far he got with it. As far as I know, it doesn't exist. At least, I'm not aware anyone has seen it. Anyway, it would be pretty useless after all this time and, if there was to be a catalogue, it would be a case of start again from scratch."

"I see the purchase of books for the library as something the Fundraising Committee might see as a worthwhile project. And, if they are interested in things the residents want, they might think about some new jigsaw puzzles. It seems the existing ones have been here for a century, and those who work on them have completed the same ones at least a hundred times. They tell me that all of them have at least one missing piece by now, and some have so many pieces missing, they are left to Rest In Peace." Cilla seemed deep in thought as she spoke. When she finished speaking, she sat staring off into the distance while drumming her fingers on the table.

"Forgive me if I'm wrong, Cilla, but I have the feeling you haven't completed your address to the plebs yet. Do you have more pearls of wisdom to share with us?" Rod asked.

"Actually, I do. Soon after I arrived, I had a brief look at the gym, and was surprised. Given the nature of Merivale Village, I was surprised by the types of equipment I *didn't* see in the gym. While I don't know much about them, there are various devices designed to assist the elderly to develop and maintain strength and mobility. None of those devices are in this gym. And, if I'm honest, what is available is pretty basic.

Now there's something a Fundraising Committee might get its teeth into: raising money to buy some more elderly-dedicated equipment for the gym. Of course, in a perfect world, such equipment would be provided by the management. Obviously, it hasn't been, and I suspect it's not likely to be. If we were to raise the funds to purchase such equipment, we would need expert advice on what to buy before we spent any money. Is there a physio or an occupational therapist who visits the Village on a regular basis?"

"There used to be one came occasionally, but only for a resident whose doctor had prescribed specific physio treatment. You remember her Rod; Pam Browne, wasn't that her name?" I asked.

"Yeah, Pam came a few times. She was only supposed to treat that one resident. But, if you happened to be in the gym when she came, she would spend some time with anyone who was there. Once the bloke's doctor said he didn't need any further physio, she stopped coming. I also have a vague recollection of an occupational therapist.

She came a few times just after I moved here. I think she was doing basketry, or something equally non-essential, with a few residents – mainly women I think … something to do with keeping their hands and arms working properly. Anyway, it's been a long while now since anyone of that nature has visited the Village."

"Okay, then it's really quite straightforward. Any funds raised should be spent on the purchase of books, jigsaws, or specialty equipment for the gym. Forget about bloody curtains for the Rec Room." Cilla gave an emphatic nodded as she finished speaking.

"So, we should reconvene the Fundraising Committee meeting. Hang on while I look up Clarice's number and give her a call." Rod made as though he was about to get up from the table.

"Don't be daft, Rod. You know it's not what I was suggesting. All I was saying is, if we are to have such an animal as a Fundraising Committee, it should direct its energies to providing what the residents need, instead of pandering to one person's fanciful ideas."

"You're right of course. The situation calls for stronger action. And, I think I feel a coup coming on. Clarice should watch her back. There is about to be a takeover bid for control of the Fundraising Committee, and Cilla Longhurst will be installed as its new organiser," Rod announced in mock excitement.

"What…? You do talk such a lot of rubbish, Rod Maguire. Nobody said anything to suggest that either. I am not a committee person, so there's no way I would be getting involved."

"You know, Rod, what Cilla said makes a lot of sense. Some of the fundraising events we've had in the past have been fun … And, yes, some of them were absolute rubbish. But, we could do with some new books for the library, and I can understand the jigsaw mob's frustration. I don't know how we make it happen, but I was wondering if coming at it from a different angle might work."

"Right, what sort of different angle did you have in mind?"

"Cilla talked about specialty equipment designed to assist the elderly maintain mobility. I don't know if you're aware, Cilla, but from time to time we have 'experts' from out there in the community come in to give us a talk on various things which might be useful for us oldies to know.

The community liaison police officer comes every so often to talk about security, there's been a financial planner came to tell us what to do with our money – as if we have enough to worry about what to do with it – and I remember a dietician or a chef, or some such, came to tell us about what we should eat. Perhaps we should try to arrange for a physio or occupational therapist to come to give us a talk about what we should be doing to look after ourselves. With any luck, it would create an awareness of the equipment we should purchase for the gym.

Yes, I realise it should be a management responsibility, but we all know how that works around here. So, if we believe we need these things, it's up to us to make it happen."

Silence reigned for a few moments after I finished delivering my speech, until Cilla posed the question.

"This residents' community consists of people who were something or other in a former life. Do we have anyone here who was a former librarian, or worked in a library in some capacity?"

"Uhmm... ye-es, I think so. Marion, wasn't Marjorie a librarian before she retired?" Rod asked.

"Yeah, I believe so. And wasn't Bernard a professor of something to do with books?"

"There's your answer, Cilla. Why did you want to know?"

"Ah well, Marjorie might be the person we need to work on. If we could persuade the Fundraising Committee to buy some books and, if we could persuade Marjorie to head up a new library committee to get the library up and running properly, we might have achieved something. What you think, is any of it possible?"

"Quite possible," Rod replied. "Now, all we have to do is work out how to achieve it."

As none of us could suggest a reasonable strategy, it was agreed we should devote some thought to the matter over the next day or so, and then hold another brainstorming meeting.

My stomach wasn't the only one rumbling as we dispersed for lunch. I felt I had a renewed spring in my step as I walked home. It wasn't until I sat down to eat lunch I realised not a word had been said about Cilla's recent mysterious absence.

Chapter 16

Sunday afternoons are a time for doing not much, and I made the most of it by doing just that. Then, having frittered away a few hours, I forced myself to put my trainers on and take myself off for a walk. All those clothes in my cupboard are never going to fit me if I sit around all day, I told myself as I dragged my reluctant body out the door. I couldn't even use the recently sustained blisters as an excuse not to go, they were all but healed.

Once I got going, I was right. It was pleasant striding through the park. The warmth of the sun lingered in spite of the light breeze which had the trees whispering as I passed beneath them. An angry plover let me know it wasn't too happy about my being so close to its nest – wherever she had hidden it. Yes, I was pleased I had forced myself to take a walk this evening. I was relaxed and everything felt aright with the world... until a thought from yesterday returned to annoy me.

Should I call Donna Logan? Although I knew what his answer would be, I had intended to ask Rod Maguire for his opinion. As it tumbled around in my mind today, a new possibility occurred to me. What if Cilla knows something about what is happening in Sydney? She might not know about Alice specifically but, at least if we knew what was going on down there, we might feel more confident about Alice's current status. She might know what the story is with David Logan. Even that would be more than we know so far.

It is strange none of us mentioned Cilla's absence while we were at Rod's place this morning. Are Rod and I supposed to continue pretending we hadn't noticed she was missing? It might prove difficult. I'm still concerned I'm bound to slip up and say something I shouldn't. Yep, best I talk to Rod about how we are going to play this in future. If he is at home – and alone – I'll stop for a chat on my way past.

Sometimes I'm lucky. I could see he was pruning shrubs in his front garden, but the prospect of interrupting him didn't deter me. "Rod, I can see you're busy, and as much as I hate to interrupt you, do you think you might spare me a couple of minutes for a chat?"

"Only a couple of minutes? I hope you can spare more than that. I've been hoping for an excuse to stop with the horticultural stuff. Come on through to the back patio. Would you prefer coffee or a cold drink?"

We both opted for an orange juice, and I wasted no time getting down to business. "I'm sure you're also aware, but I noticed, during our time here this morning, there was no mention of Cilla's absence over the last few days. Was it by design, or was it just the way it worked out? Or, has she said something to you in private about it?"

"As you say, I was aware, and no, she hasn't told me anything about it. When she came back to find us after the meeting broke up, I thought she might have wanted to talk to us then. On the walk back to here from the Rec Room, I more or less decided to let her make the running. I wouldn't mention anything, and would wait for her to tell us. And, as you observed, it didn't play out as I hoped."

"So, are we going to continue as though we hadn't noticed she was away, or what are we going to do?"

"The difficulty is, she doesn't have to tell us anything if she doesn't want to. I intend sticking to my original decision, and will wait until she brings up the subject before I say anything. It won't be easy, and I'm not sure how long I'll be able to hold out before I say something."

"Maybe the next time we are together, we should start talking about the hoons who visited here the other night, and then barbequed themselves out on the main road. We know she wasn't here when it happened, and already had been away for days. Talking about it might ignite her curiosity and she could be tempted to ask about it. If she did, it would give us an opening to be surprised she wasn't kept awake like the rest of the Village.

Some answers might be forthcoming. I don't suppose you've had any more news from Sydney."

"My journo mate contacted me earlier this afternoon. If you remember, I asked him to see if his mate would check if Cilla was booked on a flight home the other night. It seems she wasn't. But, Gina Truman was on the last flight last night."

"Gina Truman…? Isn't she the…."

"Yes, it's the alternate name we think Cilla uses on occasion – but we don't know why. Now, if someone could tell us her reason for doing so, it would make me a happy chap."

"Rod, is it possible it's because she is mixed up in something … 'unsavoury'. I can't get past the fact she chose to sneak off to Sydney just when the situation regarding David Logan and his associates was starting to blow up. It seems a convenient coincidence for her to be in Sydney at such a moment. I find it suspicious. And, she appears quite relaxed about our concerns over Alice."

"Taken on face value, I admit is does look a bit 'iffy'. Still, apart from asking her point blank what her game is, there isn't much else we can do, except to sit and wait for her to enlighten us."

"Fine for you maybe, but the ability to sit on my rear end and wait for enlightenment doesn't seem to be in my genes. But, there is one other thing I would like your opinion about. Do you think it would be safe now for me to call Donna Logan to see if she knows anything new?"

"I don't think it would be wise. We still don't know what the situation is in Brisbane. Sure, those we understood to be rogue cops shadowing her were rounded up. But it doesn't mean they haven't been replaced. The danger might still be there. Anyway, it would be a waste of time trying to call her. She knows how concerned you are about her mother. If she knew anything more than when you last spoke to her, she would have let you know somehow. And, the way things have been in Sydney, I doubt she's been able to talk to her brother at all."

While I knew he made sense, his comments weren't what I wanted to hear. As there wasn't much else to be said, I wandered off home and felt twice as frustrated than before I left for my walk. And, just to round off a less than pleasing afternoon, I decided I really had to do something about again being able to fit into all those clothes hanging in my cupboard. I might have no chance of ever being as sleek and streamlined as Cilla, but I could at least try to do something about the way I look.

Make a start, I told myself. The pasta dish you were planning to have for dinner is a good place to begin. Replace it with a salad. A salad wasn't exactly appealing on a cool evening but, with nothing equally low-calorific coming to mind, it would be salad. Later, as I sat munching my way through my bowl of 'rabbit food', I thought about other changes to my menu I might make. What a depressing exercise it proved to be.

Casting my mind over the things I liked to eat, and did eat on a regular basis, was an eye-opener. It felt as though just about all the food in my house would need to be eliminated from my eating regime for some time to come. And, its possible replacements were not an exciting prospect. What about if I went to Rod's place for coffee or a drink, would I have to say no to everything offered ... and avoid morning tea at mahjong in the Rec Room? The latter wasn't so hard to contemplate. If I wasn't to eat morning tea, I wouldn't prepare anything to take for it.

By this stage of consideration of my dieting initiative, I was about ready to throw the whole idea out the window, and find comfort in the new tub of ice cream in the freezer. Anyway, how strict does this diet need to be? I'm not so overweight as to need to lose a heap of kilos. Well, I don't think I am. Perhaps I need to pay a visit to my dreaded – and long-ignored – bathroom scales before I give any more thought to dieting. After all, if it's only a few grams I need to lose, I might need to cut out only a couple of things... like ice cream and cake. God, it is so depressing just thinking about it. First things first; go and jump on the scales.

"That can't be right!" I sprang off the scales in shock. How did that happen? Nah, I can't be THAT heavy. The scales must need adjusting. Ye-es...; because they haven't been used for so long, their settings must be out of whack. I fetched an unopened two kilogram packet of flour from the kitchen, waited until the scales showed 00.00, and plonked the flour on them. Damn, two kilograms exactly... Maybe they are working okay for lighter weights. I added a couple of one kilogram packets each of icing sugar and cooking salt to the packet of flour on the scales. Yep, just as I expected – only a whisker over six kilograms ... and that would be due to the packaging.

Having returned the foodstuffs to the kitchen, I marched up to the scales – and then hesitated. I was developing a sneaking suspicion there was nothing wrong with them. Was I about to prove it? "Get on with it," I snarled aloud. Before taking a deep breath and stepping onto the scales again. Ooh, yes, that's exactly the same as it told me the last time. Bugger! "How did this happen?" I demanded of the universe. Twelve kilos – how could I have put on so much extra weight in such a short time? This dieting lark is going to require a bit more dedication than I was counting on.

I flopped down in a lounge chair to consider the situation – and sulk – for a bit. If I was honest with myself, it was more like fifteen kilos I needed to lose. No wonder nothing fits me, and it's why my feet look like miniature footballs. But, there was something positive about all this dieting preparation: I now had lost all interest in having anything for dinner tonight... and that should help get things started. The next couple of hours were spent carrying out a stocktake of all the food I had in the house and working out the meals I needed to make, and would be able to make with the food I already had on hand. I even consulted a Weight Watchers' recipe book I picked up at a car boot sale years ago – in the days when I paid a bit more attention to how I looked.

By the time I went to bed, I believed I had my head around this dieting stuff and was determined to make it work. The first challenge to my resolve came at a little before two o'clock when I woke with a gnawing pain in my stomach. At first, I thought it was my ribs rubbing together but, after lying there thinking about it for a couple of minutes, I realised I was hungry. Lesson 1: don't skip meals... especially at night.

*****

Monday morning found me feeling less than sociable. I started the morning early with a long walk through a still dewy park. In keeping with my new 'get fit/lose weight' regime, my usual stroll was to be replaced by a power walk. The required 'power' component ran out before I had gone too far, and I was back to strolling again. I finally arrived home with sodden shoes and socks, and frozen feet. This getting-fit nonsense, especially early in the morning, is likely to lose its appeal fast.

First thing after breakfast, I indulged in a brief frenzy of cleaning and tidying – just in the living area – as a friend had threatened to visit me this morning. I don't see her as often as I would like, so I'm looking forward to her visit. Of course, it might not happen – again. It's often the case. Whenever she plans anything, you can almost bet your socks on the grandchildren being dumped on her at short notice. I half expected a phone call at any minute to tell me she won't be coming because her daughter is bringing the grandkids over.

There should be a law against unfair treatment of old people ... maybe it would be more politically correct to say 'older generations', or even 'senior family members'. It's disgusting to see so many quite elderly women at the supermarket trying to cope with young children, some no more than toddlers. It's what childminding centres are for, isn't it? But, I'll be keeping those thoughts to myself.

If I mention anything along those lines around here, someone will want to establish a committee to fight for it... and all of us would be expected to be involved. Taking up a hobby as soon as you move into places like this should be mandatory. It would ensure residents were too busy to be running around forming committees and annoying the rest of us. I'd be okay. I could claim mahjong as a hobby to fill in my time. I could let my allergy to committees become common knowledge too. Maybe it would help exempt me from any such memberships.

Still, if I don't get a visitor today, at least the living area will be liveable again. But, if I don't end up with a visitor this morning, I'm at a loss as to what else to do to fill in my time. I've resisted the temptation to bake something to go with our coffee. Baked stuff is not allowed on my diet, so we will have to settle for crackers with tomato and cheese – if she comes. If she doesn't come – perish the thought – I might have to do more housework to entertain myself for the rest of the day.

My fears were confirmed soon after nine o'clock, when my friend called to say she couldn't make it today. One of the grandkids was sick and couldn't go to school, so she was babysitting all day. It just goes to prove my point: something should be done to prevent grandparent exploitation.

Just as I was contemplating a solitary morning coffee, Rod called. "Come for coffee. I have news."

Salvation! I was saved from housework. It took me no more than about five minutes to freshen up and be on my way to Rod's place. The big question occupying my mind as I strode along the footpath was whether Cilla also had been invited. The answer was forthcoming as I reached Rod's gate. Of course she was… Cilla called out 'good morning' as she strode across the street to join me.

A few minutes later, we were seated around the table on Rod's back patio. No muffins today. Instead, a plate of TimTams occupied the centre of the table. I tried hard, but the temptation was too great. Damn Rod! All the rubbish I eat at his place probably is responsible for the excess weight I'm carrying. Although, I suppose a lack of self-control might have something to do with it as well.

As usual, we had to follow Rod's preferred protocol for such occasions: nothing should interfere with partaking of food and drink. The business of the day had to wait until we finished our coffees. Today, it meant waiting an agonising ten minutes or so, before Rod began sharing his 'news'.

"My journo mate in Sydney contacted me earlier. It seems he is starting to pick up a few whispers. The big news he was able to confirm via his contacts is, it is definite David Logan has been taken into custody and, so far, he is being uncooperative. He also reported the consensus among his contacts was, questioning of Logan was part of a bigger plan. While Logan has been charged with various offences, he was given home detention until he is required to appear in court in about six weeks' time."

"Home detention seems a bit generous doesn't it? While I don't know what he has been charged with, I understood the outstanding warrants for his arrest were for serious drug-related offences. If that is the case, why would they let him go home, even with an ankle bracelet, or whatever device, to monitor his whereabouts?" I had to ask, as it didn't make any sense at all to me, unless there was something else going on I didn't know about.

"The official line appears to be it's for his own protection – or so I'm told," Rod explained. "If he were incarcerated, even in one of our better prisons, Logan's 'employers' might arrange for him to meet with a little accident, or a fairly major one perhaps."

I was having trouble following the logic in everything Rod was telling us. "I realise 'accidents' do happen in prison, but wouldn't he be safer there than locked up in his own home?"

Cilla cleared her throat and then murmured, "Not if he was intended as bait."

"Eh? What do you mean by 'bait'? Are you suggesting the police have deliberately stashed him at home where he has no protection and would be easy to get at?" I was almost sure the police could not do that, not lawfully anyway.

"No, it's not what I'm saying. While it is likely he has been set as the bait in the trap, he would not be left unprotected. The police would be quite keen to nab anyone sent to dispatch Logan to prevent him talking to the police." The tone Cilla used reminded me of a frustrated teacher trying to explain something to a not too bright student.

The red mist started to descend, but I bit my tongue, smiled sweetly, and thanked her for her thoughts. Something about her behaviour suggested she was holding something back. But, what do I know about such things? I'm probably just miffed because of the patronising way she spoke to me, or the fact she was there at all... Or so I thought, until Rod's next comment.

"I see. Maybe you're right. My contact suggested something along those lines could be behind the whole idea of Logan's home detention. I admit, I thought it a strange move when he first mentioned it but, once he explained what he thought was going on, it made sense."

"Rod, did your mate have any other snippets of information you'd care to share?" I demanded.

"Well, he had picked up another whisper, but hasn't been able to confirm it yet. He suspects Logan was on the run from his 'employers', as well as from the police. When he found himself running out of places to hide, he decided the police were his safest option. It's possible his home detention is part of some deal between Logan and the police."

"Why were his employers looking for him? I know we discussed it previously, but please refresh my memory." This was a world I did not understand.

"It seems David was an enterprising young man who decided to set up a little business of his own – a sideline enterprise. The only problem was, he sought to operate in competition with the big boys, and he acquired the wherewithal to run his business by skimming from his employers. For some reason, they were offended by it, and..."

"...And, hence David found himself on the run from them as well as the police." In an exasperated tone, Cilla finished Rod's explanation for him.

After a moment or two to consider all I'd been told, I asked the question I'd wanted to ask since the discussion started.

"What about Alice? Has your mate picked up anything on David's mother, Alice?"

"No, not so far anyway," Rod replied.

"Hardly surprising," Cilla chimed in. "David isn't likely to say anything about his mother, even if he does know where she is, and does know what's going on. It's logical to expect he would want to keep her out of everything, if he knew anything about what was happening. I think it likely he doesn't know much, if anything, not even about Alice being missing."

"Well, at least we now know where David is, despite his future looking a bit bleak. It is something we've learned today, although I can't see how it will help us find Alice. In fact, given what we have learned, rather than feeling relieved, I think I'm now even more worried about her." As I finished speaking, I looked over at Rod. He gave a hint of a nod of agreement, but didn't comment.

Cilla heaved a theatrical sigh before adding to the conversation. "I wouldn't work myself into a state over Alice if...."

"That's because she is not your friend, and you have never met her, and you couldn't care less about where she is, or what's happening to her."

Regardless of whatever else Cilla intended saying, I wasn't going to listen to it. She had brought a sharp edge to my tongue. Just as my temper reached explosion point, and I was all set to allow my vitriol to pour forth, a filthy look from Rod took the wind out of my sails. I lost traction and, for a moment, I sat in stunned silence while I tried to regroup. Cilla took advantage of the situation.

"If I might be allowed to finish…"

She could if she wished, but I wasn't going to sit there and listen to anymore of her rubbish. I sprang up off my chair and began striding towards the door.

"Christ, Marion, stop carrying on like a four-year-old, and at least listen to what Cilla has to say. Then, if you still want to hare off home in a huff, you're welcome to do so." Rod's voice was sharper than I had ever heard it before. It brought me to a sudden halt.

You would like that, Rod, wouldn't you, I thought as I glared at him. You'd like me to go home and leave you here alone with her, wouldn't you? Well, you've changed my mind for me. I'm not going anywhere. I'm staying right here for as long as she is here, and you both can suffer the consequences of it. Instead of heading for the door, I changed course and began pacing about in an area off to the side of the table.

"Oh, I wasn't going home, Rod. I felt a cramp coming in my leg and needed to move about before it grabbed me properly. Of course, I want to hear whatever Cilla has to tell us." I gave him my sweetest smile as I headed back to my chair. I tried sending one to Cilla too, but I'm sure what I managed was more of a grimace than a smile. As I lowered myself back onto my chair, I said, "Apologies for the interruption, Cilla. What were you going to say?"

"Right… well, I was going to say, I don't think it will be too much longer before we are in a better position to gauge what Alice's situation might be. It seems as though there is quite a bit happening, or about to happen, in Sydney. When that sorts itself out, we should know what we can rule out in regard to Alice's whereabouts. When the dust settles in Sydney, it's a possibility our investigation will be over, and we will be able to move on to welcoming her home again."

Rod ran a hand across his face as he considered Cilla's words for a moment before asking a question. "Okay, I admit it would be a great outcome, and the sooner it happens the better, but what if it is not how it plays out? When the police or whoever have sorted out the Sydney situation, what happens if Alice is still missing and her whereabouts remain a mystery to everyone?"

"I would be surprised if such a situation eventuated but, if it does, we will deal with it when it occurs." If Cilla had more to add, we didn't hear it, as her phone's chirp brought our discussions to an end.

"I need to take this. I might head home now, and will catch up with you again soon," she said over her shoulder on her way to the door.

Chapter 17

In complete silence, we watched Cilla make her way through the house and out onto the street. Even after she had disappeared from view, the silence continued until Rod cleared his throat.

"Ahem, I'm almost not game to ask, but did you have a bad night or climb out the wrong side of the bed this morning? I've never seen you so antagonistic. What's wrong?"

"Nothing... Well, nothing you will understand."

"Try me. You might be surprised."

"Truth is, I'm not sure how to put it into words." He made a 'give me' gesture, and I felt compelled to try. "It's about a feeling I have. I just feel Cilla knows more than she is telling us. The bit she does tell us suggests to me she knows a lot more detail of what's happening in Sydney. Does she know more, or is she just big-noting herself by trying to look knowledgeable? And, if she does know more than she is saying, why isn't she telling us the whole story?"

"Yeah, I agree with you. I did get the feeling she knew more than she said, especially when she suggested the situation in Sydney could be resolved any time soon."

"While I know she didn't say anything definite, her comments regarding Alice, in relation to the Sydney situation, clinched it for me. She seemed so definite that, once the situation in Sydney was wrapped up, we wouldn't have to worry about Alice any longer. We would know where she was and what was happening. How could she make such a comment, if she didn't have a reasonable understanding of what was happening, and of the likelihood of the whole mess being sorted out soon?"

"Hmm... While we share the same thoughts, I'm convinced we won't get anything more out of her at present. Maybe it would be best if we left it for a day or so before we mentioned it again. Whatever her reasons for withholding information from us, upsetting her won't change anything. If she can't, or won't, tell us anything more, we will probably gain more by being patient than by ruffling her feathers too much."

I didn't want to agree with him, but I knew he made sense. And besides, Cilla appeared to have gone home, so there was nothing more I could do or say to upset her today. A few minutes later, I too was on my way home, and wondering what lunch on my new diet might look like. I don't think I could cope with the sort of regime which allows only a lettuce leaf and cottage cheese.

The rest of the day seemed to evaporate with nothing of any consequence to report other than I decided to go for my afternoon walk a little earlier than usual. Once again, I tried power-walking. This time, the 'power' lasted about thirty seconds longer than it did this morning, before I was forced to revert to strolling again. Nevertheless, by the time I arrived home, I was exhausted ... and starving. The latter condition, in spite of a light but reasonable dinner, persisted until I went to bed.

Sleep proved difficult to come by. A terrible storm woke me around midnight. The weather forecast had rabbited on about troughs and cold fronts and some sort of convergence, none of which meant anything to me. The only bit I understood was the part of the forecast which mentioned showers for this area. It said nothing about a violent storm. I would have remembered any such comment.

Wind gusts were so strong, rubbish bins were blown over, and the noise of the rain on the roof was deafening. Sleeping through the thunder and lightning was impossible. By two o'clock, it had rumbled its way further along the coast, leaving us with lovely steady rain. At last, sleep was a possibility once more, as the storm had provided pleasant sleeping conditions by lowering the temperature a bit.

*****

I slept late this morning and woke to glorious sunshine and the temperature a bit nippier than over the last few days… and every clock and device with a timer was blinking at me. At some point, presumably during the storm, we lost power, and the only things now not blinking at me were those with battery back-up.

After setting the time on everything, I went outside to stand my rubbish bin upright again. A strong breeze leftover from the storm whistled up our street – and it wasn't just nippy. It was cold. Abandoning my morning walk was a no-brainer today I decided as I scurried back inside. Then it registered with me. Today was Tuesday, and Tuesday meant a morning of mahjong at the Senior Citizens' Centre.

With nothing much to do until it was time to get ready for mahjong, I took my time organising a breakfast of not much. Although I was only a couple of days into it, this dieting regime was fast losing its appeal, and with little else to do this morning, creating a more substantial breakfast was a temptation. It was while I sat at the breakfast bar with my meagre rations, Rod called.

"The Senior Cits' secretary called. There is a power outage, courtesy of last night's storm. It seems the whole of the city heart area is affected. So, we will not be playing mahjong there today. I have called the others. Everyone now is aware."

"Thanks, Rod. I suppose I'll just have to find some other way to amuse myself this morning."

"We could change the venue and still be able to play. We could set up in the Rec Room as we do on Thursdays."

"I don't think it's available. Doesn't the Crochet-and-Chat group use it on Tuesday mornings… or does the jigsaw mob have it booked? I'm almost sure some group has a permanent Tuesday morning booking."

"Damn. I had forgotten about them. I don't think we could set up here at my place. We would have to play out on the back patio and it's a bit cool to be out there today. Besides, I only have one table out there, and not enough room to add another one. Right… Well, it looks like we aren't playing mahjong today. I'll check if the others have any bright ideas about a suitable venue, and I'll let you know if the situation changes."

Although I did give it some thought after his call, I knew his chances of finding somewhere else in the Village today were non-existent. There's a Pilates class – or is it Tai Chi? – happens in the gym this morning. Plenty of stuff happens on Tuesday mornings in the Village, Apart from whatever is scheduled in the gym, the hairdresser visits and the doctor has a clinic … and the director often has a staff meeting in the main admin building's meeting room. Come to think of it, the main building seems to be busy most days, and has all its various sections being utilised. The Recreation Room is a more recent addition to the Village. Whoever thought of locating it as a separate structure from the main admin building should be congratulated.

A few domestic chores took me through to ten o'clock. When I stopped to make a coffee, I noticed the wind had abated to be nothing more than a light breeze. By the time I finished my coffee, I had decided. It was now a glorious day outside. I would go for the walk I didn't have this morning.

Forget the power-walking nonsense. I kicked my stroll up another gear, so it was a bit faster, while still nowhere near as fast as a power-walk. This morning I opted for what I call my long route, which brings me back to the wooded area of the park towards the end of my walk. I usually enjoy wandering through the trees while being accompanied by the resident birdlife, but it was freezing under the trees this morning. Once I stepped out of the sun, I felt goose bumps come up all over me. A short power-walk brought me out into the sunshine again, and close to the end of my route.

This last stage took me out of the park and brought me back into the Village at a point close to the admin building. The arbour just off to one side of the Village's main ring road was a riot of colour. At this time of the year, the roses climbing over the arbour as well as the sweet peas were in bloom. I just had to detour via the arbour to breathe in its perfume before heading home. More than the flowers' perfume was there to greet me.

Shirley Reardon, with her handbag beside her, sat demurely beneath the arbour. She was too well-dressed to be just having a rest while out walking. Come to think of it, I had never seen Shirley out walking. Remembering the conversation I eavesdropped on between her and her plants, I thought a bit of company might be good for her. I flopped down on the wooden bench beside her, and found it was snug under the arbour.

"Good morning, Shirley. Do you mind if I sit with you for a few minutes?"

"Of course not, make yourself comfortable."

"Are you going somewhere this morning... shopping perhaps?" Making a conversation happen already felt like hard work.

"No, no. I had an appointment to see Doctor Anthony this morning. He had a lot of patients to see today."

"So, are you on your way home now?" She gave me a confused look, so I clarified my reason for asking. "If you are on your way home, I could walk with you as far as your place."

"Walk with me...? I'm not walking anywhere, and it is much too far for me to walk home. I'm waiting here for Henry to collect me and drive me home. He won't be long, but you can sit here and wait with me if you wish."

Oh God, now what do I do. We sat in silence for a few minutes, until I saw her check her watch. It gave me an idea. "Is Henry running a bit late, Shirley?"

"Uhmm... yes, a little, but he probably has been held up in traffic. He'll be here soon."

"It's nearly lunchtime, Shirley. Would you like to come home with me to wait at my place rather than sitting out here?"

"No, thank you, dear. But you go on home. I like sitting here. It's so peaceful. Anyway, Henry expects to find me here. He would worry if I weren't here when he arrived."

Going home seemed like a good thing to do – the only thing to do. But, I wouldn't be going home. I needed to talk to someone about this. After checking again if she would be all right if I left her there alone (and being told yet again that Henry would be along soon), I took my leave. If I'm honest, I think my intention always was to stop at Rod's place on my way home. It didn't occur to me he might in the middle of having lunch, or doing something else important. I needed to talk to someone, and Rod was exactly the person with whom to discuss my problem.

He wasn't having lunch; only preparing it, but still was gracious enough to invite me in. Unsure about how to tell him my problem, I just dived straight in and hoped for the best.

"I've just come across Shirley Reardon sitting alone under the arbour beside the ring road."

"She has a nice day for it. So, what's your problem with it?"

"After what I'd seen at her place a little while ago, I had decided to try to spend a bit of time with her. Today presented as an ideal opportunity to do so. She had been to see the doctor and, afterwards, went to wait at the arbour. So, I sat and started chatting to her."

"Well, it's a nice place to sit and wait, but what was she waiting for?"

"Henry… She was waiting for Henry to come to pick her up and take her home."

"Who is Henry… a son?"

"No… her husband."

"Ah, right…Ooh, I didn't realise she had a husband. I don't think I've ever seen him around here."

"Probably not – he's been dead for at least ten years."

"What? Shirley's sitting there waiting for her dead husband to come and collect her. Hmm, now I think I see the problem. What happened? Is she still sitting there?"

"Yeah, I tried to persuade her to walk home with me, but she was having none of it. What are we going to do? We can't just let her sit there."

"Is the doctor likely still to be at the clinic? I'll give him a call."

"Sometimes Doctor Anthony stays on until one o'clock if he has had a busy day. Otherwise, he leaves around midday. Shirley said he was busy today, so he might still be there."

No such luck... today, Anthony had left by the time Rod called the clinic. "So, what's our next move, Rod? I suppose we should advise the director she might have a problem, but I'm reluctant to tell her. If Tanya Jellicoe handles this the way she usually does, it would only make matters worse. So, what else is there we can try?"

"Give me a chance to think about it." Rod indulged in mental gymnastics for what felt like ages, but probably was only a minute or so, before sharing his thoughts. "I don't know if this will work, but I don't know what else to try."

"I'm listening. Whatever it is, it's all we have at the moment."

"Right... I will drive around the ring road to the arbour and tell Shirley her husband has called me. Something has come up and Henry would be delayed for a while. He knew Shirley would be waiting for him, so he asked me to pick her up and take her home. How does that sound?"

"Yeah, it might just do the trick."

"The only tricky part is the bit about 'taking her home'. Where will she expect me to take her, and what happens when I don't take her to wherever that is? Do you know where she used to live with Henry? Although, I wouldn't be taking her there anyway?"

"Nah, I don't know anything about them before they moved in here. It must have been about twelve years ago and then, only a couple of years later, Henry died."

"So, if I took her back to her house here, she might remember it as 'home'?"

"There is a chance she would think so. After Henry died, management tried to persuade her to move into one of the units..."

"Probably because they had a surplus of units available and no unoccupied cottages ... and prospective new clients all wanted houses."

"I suspect that about sums it up. Anyway, there was no way Shirley was going to move into a unit. The cottage was the home she shared with Henry and she wasn't moving. They tried telling her the smaller unit would easier to look after, and there would be the other unit residents around her for company, but she wasn't having any of it."

"Quite right too; the unit residents – in the same block as Marjorie and Bernard – never come outside. They don't have roses to prune or gardens to water, so they stay indoors ... and some install clothes dryers so they don't have to come out into the real world even to hang out their washing."

He made a compelling argument for giving his idea a try. It wasn't a hard argument to win, given we were fresh out of other ideas. So, while he went to collect Shirley, I waited at her gate for her to arrive home.

It was a good fifteen minutes later before Rod pulled-up in front of Shirley's house. I had almost given up on waiting for them, and was sure his attempted 'rescue' hadn't worked. So, I was more than a little surprised to watch him help a smiling Shirley out of his car and escort to her front door. As she passed by me standing near her gate, she paused to say hello and tell me how she hadn't seen me around for a while, and had wondered if I were okay. Then, behind Shirley's back, I signalled Rod I would meet him back at his house ... where we later arrived at almost the same time.

"How did it go?" I demanded as soon as he was out of the car. "I can see it was a successful operation. She is home again. But, were there any problems achieving it?"

"No, not really... At first, she had trouble remembering who I was. Once we sorted it out, and I convinced her Henry was okay and he would see her later, she hopped in the car and was happy to be brought back here to her house. I don't feel guilty about telling her she would see Henry later. If there is any truth in all that fairy dust about what happens after you drop off the twig, then they will be together later."

"Okay, she is home safe and sound for the moment, but it's obvious something needs to be done about her worsening condition. She didn't seem to remember I had been talking to her less than half an hour before she saw me at her gate. So far,

I suspect we are the only ones who know about it. What's our next move? What do we do? Who do we talk to?"

"Well, as you have already said, probably not Tanya Jellicoe in the first instance. She might be all right at business management, but has zero people skills. Doctor Anthony is our best bet. He might already be aware of the problem, and might need just a little more evidence to initiate appropriate action – whatever it might entail."

"Yeah, I suppose you're right, but his next clinic here won't be until next Thursday morning. Do you think Shirley will be all right left on her own until then?"

"Not being an expert in such matters, I don't know – but I am concerned. I suspect it might need more immediate intervention, rather than a 'wait and see' approach."

"I feel concerned for her and what her future might be. She might no longer be able to live alone, and they will put her into care. I'm not sure how she would cope with it."

"Perhaps, I might try giving Doctor Anthony a call. Do you have his number or know where his practice is?"

A couple of minutes later, Rod was on hold and listening to orchestral music while he waited for Doctor Anthony to speak to him. I decided not to hang around, as I suspected trying to talk to the doctor could become a protracted undertaking. After asking Rod to let me know how his discussions went with the doctor, I headed home and was soon sitting in my lounge and nibbling my lunch (slices of tomato on water crackers today).

Rod called when I was hallway through my first cracker. "I finally spoke to Doctor Anthony about Shirley. He's going to come to see me on his way home this afternoon, and he would like you to be there too when we discuss what's happening with her. Are you available? He said it might be around six o'clock before he arrives."

"Yep, I'll be there. Isn't his coming to talk to us a bit of a strange move on his part?"

"Maybe, but I think there might be more to it. While it was more of an impression than anything he said, I felt he already had some concerns about Shirley. I don't imagine he will be able to share too much with us – patient confidentiality and all that – but we might pick up something from talking to him. If it suits you, perhaps come to my place any time after, say, 5.30p.m."

After Rod's call ended, it didn't take me long to finish my now soggy crackers, but I remained bogged in my lounge chair for quite a while afterwards. What else might be going on with Shirley to cause the doctor concern? Or, had he too noticed her worsening dementia? Regardless of what it was, one way or another, Shirley occupied my mind for the rest of the afternoon.

After freshening up and changing, I was at Rod's by 5.45p.m. Doctor Anthony arrived a few minutes after six o'clock. Once we were seated in the lounge with our coffees, Anthony wanted a detailed report on my morning's encounter with Shirley. When I finished, he then asked if I had encountered any other similar episodes involving the woman. Although reluctant at first, I told him about eavesdropping on Shirley's conversations with the plants in her garden.

He looked as though he was deep in thought for a few moments before asking his next question.

"Did those incidents concern you?"

"Uhmm… her conversation with the plants struck me as odd, but I wouldn't say it concerned me. Although, as a result of it, I did promise myself I would try to spend more time with the obviously lonely woman. But, today's incident really did trouble me. It's why I came to discuss with Rod what to do, after I had left her still sitting there waiting for Henry. I'm not asking you to break patient confidentiality, but is there something happening we should know about, or something we should do to assist with whatever it is?"

"In the course of a normal week, would you see much of Shirley, either about the Village or even just in her garden?"

The question made me uncomfortable. I had to admit to not having paid any attention to the woman, but it also made me realise she had been almost invisible over recent months.

While I always said hello to her if she was out in her garden when I walked past, I couldn't recall having seen her anywhere else around the Village – not since Henry's death. While he was alive, they were always out and about, and involved in almost everything happening here.

Then the questions ended, it was his turn to speak. By the time Anthony left, I felt utterly depressed – and guilty. And, it was likely he would be recommending to management for Shirley to be moved into a care facility. Both Rod and I were shell-shocked and, after seeing Anthony off, we returned to the lounge with glasses of something stronger than coffee. We sat sipping our drinks for a couple of minutes without exchanging a word, until I broke the heavy silence.

"God, I feel so guilty … and so selfish about completely ignoring someone so in need of friendship and support."

"You weren't to know what was going on in her life. And, sometimes any overtures by an outsider are not welcomed. As Anthony said, he can't be sure about the extent of her condition, because she has rebuffed his attempts to have his diagnosis confirmed. Anyway, he did say he thought she was aware of what was happening to her, and seemed determined to just let it run its course."

"If he is right, she only has a few months at most to live. Perhaps the upside to it is his belief that, by sometime within in the next month, she won't know anything about what is happening to her. Is it possible to know you have a brain tumour, without its being diagnosed, and to just go on ignoring it?"

"Perhaps in Shirley's case, she sees it as her ticket to again being with Henry."

The drinks and chat with Rod after Doctor Anthony departed did nothing to improve my outlook, and I went home in a dark hole of depression.

Chapter 18

Wednesday morning found me confused about everything including what day of the week it was. Having to forego our morning of mahjong yesterday seems to have thrown my whole routine off kilter. It seems I'm now too old to have anything alter my routine without my whole life being thrown into chaos.

The bit of fog still hanging around when I scrambled out of bed probably didn't help get me going. So, after a later start than usual and dawdling over my meagre breakfast, it was later than normal when I headed off on my morning walk. Nothing creative this morning, I decided as I exited my front yard. Just the basic route along the street, through the park and home again. After passing Rod's place and a couple more houses, I was approaching Shirley's home.

As I neared her gate, the little voice in my head told me I should see if Shirley would have coffee with me this morning. So she had a reason to leave her house today, coffee should be at my place. If she accepted my invitation, I will have to rush home from my walk to whip up a batch of scones or something to go with our coffees.

With my hand on her gate and about to push it open, I froze. A veritable river cascaded down the path running along the side of her house, and it had an adjacent garden bed running a banker. A broken pipe was my first thought, followed almost immediately by the thought she might have left a hose turned on after watering her plants last evening. The latter seemed the most likely explanation given the current state of her faculties. I pushed open the gate and went in search of the source of the problem.

I found the source of the flood, and my assumption about a hose being left turned on was correct. But, I also found something else far more disturbing … and it explained the flood. Shirley was lying prone on the grass beside the path. Judging by how cold and wet she was, I guessed she had been there all night. As she was barely conscious, there were two things I needed to do. First, I called an ambulance, and then I called Rod to tell him about the situation I'd discovered.

"Rod, it might be worth letting Doctor Anthony know what has happened. Could you try calling him, please?"

A few minutes later, Rod joined me in Shirley's garden, and an ambulance arrived a couple of minutes after Rod. No time was wasted getting her strapped onto a gurney and loaded into the van. We both stood in silence as we watched it drive away.

"What do you think happened?" Rod asked.

"I'd be guessing, but I suspect she tripped while watering her garden last evening. It was either that, or she suffered a turn of some sort while she was out there. Did you manage to talk to Doctor Anthony?"

"Yes. He was going to call the hospital to let them know he would be there soon after the ambulance dropped her off. He didn't say much, and didn't offer any suggestion about what might have happened."

"No surprises there, but I guess we both know this might be the end of Shirley's life in Merivale Retirement Village. If her medical condition is as serious as Anthony suggested, it's probably all downhill for her from here." Just talking about it was depressing and somehow, going for a walk lost its appeal. Going home again seemed a better option. Rod interrupted my thoughts.

"Perhaps the only good thing to take away from this morning is Shirley might not have to wait too much longer to see Henry again … if you happen to subscribe to such belief. I don't know about you, but I need a coffee. Shall we go to contemplate what a bastard life can be over a coffee on my patio?"

Instead of our usual lively conversation, this morning we both were quite subdued. A knock at the front door interrupted our reflective period. Cilla's voice calling out to us didn't improve my outlook either. Rod showed Cilla through to the patio before retreating to the kitchen to make her a coffee. Her chirpy arrival was too much. I wanted to get up and leave.

"Good morning, Marion. I saw you and Rod come back from somewhere, and it occurred to me we hadn't spoken in a couple of days. Well, I spoke to Rod on the phone when he called me yesterday about mahjong being cancelled at the Senior Cits' Centre. So, has anything interesting been happening?"

Bite your tongue, the little voice in my head warned me – and I tried to comply. "Interesting…? Here in the Village…? I must have missed it, if something interesting did happen." Before I could say anything more (or do any damage perhaps) Rod arrived with Cilla's coffee and picked-up on our conversation.

"No, Cilla, you soon will come to realise the Village is not a place where 'interesting' things occur. All sorts of things happen here, but 'interesting' is not a word I often use to describe them. Just so you are aware, the only thing of note to happen over the last couple of days, is the lady from a couple of doors further along the street was carted off to hospital this morning."

Cilla looked more confused than interested. "Do I know the woman in question?"

"Maybe not…," Rod replied.

"Oh good; then I don't need to be concerned for her. What happened anyway? Was it a heart attack, or a stroke? It's what you expect in a place like this … I mean, with so many old people living here, it's bound to be something like that, isn't it?"

I was about to acquaint her with the reality of living in 'a place like this', but Rod sensed it, and jumped in before me.

"Perhaps it is not as common as you might think. In this case, the woman became tangled up in her hose while watering her garden and fell; might have damaged a hip or leg as a result." As he finished speaking, he shot me a hard look. I interpreted his look as a warning to behave.

"Well, whatever she has done, it seems to have taken your mind off your missing friend for at least a little while. By the way, what's your latest news on the lady?"

"Neither of the subjects you've broached this morning are matters for light-hearted conversation." I avoided looking at Rod as I spoke. I knew he would be glaring at me, but I'd had enough of this insensitive woman.

If Rod wanted to sit here and listen to Cilla prattle on, he was welcome to do so, but I was going home. Her insensitive comments had fuelled my already dark outlook. Perhaps Cilla needs to look in the mirror. She will find, like the rest of us in the Village, she too is old ... and quite possibly a contender for all those things she thinks only happen to 'old people in a place like this'. I sprang up off my chair ready to take my leave.

"Sit back down, Marion ...please," Rod asked in a voice barely above a whisper. Then he turned to speak directly to Cilla. "Cilla, neither of us is in the mood for light-hearted banter this morning. So, was there a purpose for your visit this morning?"

"Oh, I see. I'm sorry. I saw you both come back together from somewhere with your faces as long as a wet weekend, and I thought you might need some cheering up. I didn't come to upset you. I was just trying to be sociable, and perhaps help lift the atmosphere here. If you would prefer I left..."

"Of course not... besides, you haven't finished your coffee yet. But, as you are here, I have to ask, have you heard anything more from your contacts in relation to what might be happening Sydney?"

"I can't give you any details, but I heard the operation they had running along in the background for a few days might have produced some results over the weekend. I guess we will have to wait to find out what they might be. At this stage, I can't say if it had anything to do with David Logan or his mother. Rod, maybe your contacts will have more information by now about what went down. Have you heard anything from them?"

"Not yet; but I haven't been able to reach my main Sydney contact. I assumed it was because he was a bit too busy to talk to me at the moment, and your comments tend to confirm my assumption. Who knows? Maybe tonight I'll hear something."

"By the way, what happens with mahjong for the rest of this week?" Cilla asked in a skilful segue to move the conversation away from Sydney.

"Tomorrow will be business as usual. We will be back in the Rec Room in the morning for our usual game. Are you planning to join us?"

"Yeah, I think I will. Apart from the fact I feel I should become involved in whatever is on offer here in the Village, it's a pleasant enough way to fill in a morning. And, you never know, with a bit of practice, I might even improve my skill level. So, look out, Rod, I might be aiming to take the champion's mantle from your shoulders."

"Champion's mantle…? I've never heard such rubbish. Mahjong is not a championship sport. Well, not for us it isn't. Like you, for us, it's a pleasant way to fill in a couple of hours with friends."

Cilla's phone brought the discussion to an end. "I have to take this. It's about a part for Black Bess I've been chasing," she said as she headed for home.

After Cilla's departure, and unsure about Rod's view of the world at the moment (at least in regard to Cilla's place in it), I thought it best to allow him to initiate any new conversation. Besides, the thoughts foremost in my mind were likely to cause an argument, or at least earn me a reprimand. So, there I was doing my best to exercise my utmost self-control, when he asked me the absolute wrong question.

"Well, Marion, what did you make of Cilla's comments about Sydney? An honest answer please."

"Honest, eh…? Okay, I don't doubt the truth in what she told us, but I would have liked to hear the rest of the story, so I could form a more accurate assessment."

"You don't think she told us all she knew?"

"Of course she didn't. It's the impression I formed anyway. What bothers me is why she would behave the way she did. And, she would never make a good actress or poker player, if that's the best demonstration she can manage of trying to be convincing."

"Yep, I agree. I don't think she told us all she knows. In fact, I'm certain of it. As you said, the big question is: why? Why does she feel it necessary to withhold information she knows we are desperate to receive? Is it all an act? Does she actually know anything? What do you think? Have you any ideas about why she is behaving as she is?"

"My first thoughts were, it was about one-upmanship, and she was going to drip feed information to us to keep us begging for more. Now, I'm not so sure. What I mean is, I'm quite sure she does know more than she is saying, but I can't work out why she is holding back. Do you have any thoughts on the subject?"

"Argh, I must be getting old, too old for guessing games. There was a time when it was a big part of a journo's job to be able to guess what was going on behind the words you were hearing. In Cilla's case, my antenna is not working at all. I suspect it all comes down to who her contact is. Perhaps there is a need to be cagey about what she tells us in case it points the finger at whoever is providing her with the information."

"As I have no idea about how to uncover her contact, and your contact is not talking to you at the moment, what else can we do? I have a strong gut feeling whatever happened in Sydney over the weekend is important to us; important to finding Alice."

"We can sit here wondering about it all day, but I doubt it will get us any closer to finding Alice. As much as I hate to say it, I think the best we can do is to wait until my journo mate gets back to me. I will keep trying to contact him. If the crime desk is busy, as it might well be if a big operation went down on the weekend, he will have no time to talk to the likes of me. So, patience is the keyword I'm afraid."

I walked home feeling just as depressed as I had done when I arrived at Rod's. He was right of course. There was nothing else we could do except be patient and wait for others to feed us information. I had meant to ask him about risking giving Donna a call to see if she'd heard anything about David but, once again, I had forgotten to ask him. So far, today had been a disaster: no walk this morning, Shirley's being carted off to hospital, and Cilla playing games about sharing information.

The rest of the day developed into a sulk of sorts until it was time for my afternoon walk. And then, as if the gods were well and truly offside with me, a heavy shower came over just as I was about to step out the door. So, instead of going for a walk, I fell asleep reading a magazine in my favourite lounge chair. The whole house was in darkness – just as the rest of the Village was outside – when my phone woke me. I managed to coax my thick tongue to slur 'hello' to the caller.

It was Rod. My tone caused him concern about whether I was okay. After reassuring him I was fine – and lying about being preoccupied with something else when I answered his call – he moved on to explain the reason for disturbing me. Could he see me after dinner to discuss it?

"You could come here, and we could have a post-dinner coffee or drink while we discuss whatever it is you want to talk about. What time would suit you?"

He suggested in about half an hour's time. It gave me just about long enough to reheat some leftovers and scoff them before he arrived. I surprised myself by having accomplished that, and having splashed water on my face to freshen up, by the time he rang my doorbell. As he came in, he announced coffee and a port would go well. He settled in the lounge room while I retreated to the kitchen to deal with the coffee and glasses of port. (Mental note to self: buy another bottle of port.)

"Right, you have the floor. Come on, share whatever it is you've come to discuss," I said as soon as I joined him in the lounge room.

"Okay… the first thing is, my journo mate in Sydney returned my calls. As I suspected, he barely has had time to breathe, let alone call me. He did confirm what scant information Cilla gave us this morning. Something big – real big! – did go down in Sydney on the weekend. It seems it all started at the house where they had stashed David."

"Where we thought he was held as bait to lure out others the police were interested in?"

"That's the one... And, it worked. Three heavyweights paid the house a visit the other night. The police waited until all three were inside, before taking them down. In the meantime, a separate action went on out front of the house. The driver of the getaway van was also taken into custody."

"Hmm... it's a start, but does it help us find Alice at all?"

"No, not of itself it doesn't, but there is more to the story. The police recognised those they rounded up as belonging to a mob they'd been keeping an eye on for some time. While they were keen to make a move on the rest of the mob, they were hesitant because there was a real possibility of denial by everyone involved. It seems the police might have struck a bit of luck. One of those they'd rounded up at the house where David was 'bait' decided to be cooperative. He gave the police the confirmation they needed to make a move on the mob's headquarters."

"This is sounding better by the moment. Don't stop there. What happened next?"

"A successful raid was what happened next. An unknown number of people were rounded up and taken into custody, including the person they believed to head the mob. My mate doesn't know all of the finer details yet. But, it appears there were a number of splinter organisations – satellite operations connected to the mob – dotted around the state. By keeping a lid on what they'd already achieved, the police were able to mount successful raids on some of those other locations."

"Is it believed the mob has been put out of operation as a result of the police's weekend operation, or are there likely to be more episodes in the saga?"

"Difficult to tell at this stage, or so I'm told. Nevertheless, my mate has detected quite an upbeat atmosphere throughout the police service following the weekend's operation."

"I'm having trouble trying to work out how to feel about all of this. If it helps us find Alice, I will be excited by what's happened. But, I've noticed you've made no mention of Alice so far, and I suspect it's because your mate hasn't mentioned her either."

"You're right about Alice. My mate hasn't picked up any whispers about her, not even vague whispers about a woman being found at any of the raided locations. There is something you should be aware of though. This morning, Cilla said a major operation happened over the weekend. She wasn't quite accurate. It seems there was a buzz around police circles on Sunday which alerted my mate to something which might be happening in the next day or so. As it turns out, nothing happened until Monday night, and the first action on Monday night took place at the house where they had stashed David."

"It doesn't matter how you look at it, Monday night is not the weekend. Does it suggest Cilla was only fishing around in her old environment for crumbs of information she could share, or she has made assumptions about? Regardless, when did the rest of the action happen?"

"The main raid on the mob's headquarters happened at about four o'clock on Tuesday morning. Raids on some of the satellite locations happened around the same time, while others continued through yesterday. So, it was late last night or early this morning, before the operation was over. Of course, now there will be the usual long period spent questioning everyone. My mate believes the investigators, along with the forensic team, started work on the mob's headquarters sometime this morning."

"What are they hoping to achieve? What would they be looking for at the headquarters? They seem to have the main players under lock and key now, so what more do they need?"

"For a start, they need to find evidence – good solid evidence – to support the charges they bring against those they rounded up. In the first instance, we're talking about drug trafficking. But, there is always a chance they might find evidence of other illegal activities being carried on at the same time. This would then strengthen the case against those rounded up, and would help ensure those involved stayed behind bars for even longer. I know it sounds like a long shot, but we will have to wait to see what the forensic gang digs up before we make any assumptions about whether Alice was there or not."

"I wish you hadn't used the words 'dig up'. If she is not found there, I don't want to think about what might have happened to her."

"We can't allow ourselves to think along those lines. If she isn't found at any of the locations raided, or no evidence of her is found, it doesn't mean it's the end of the story. It just means we were following the wrong trail. What was happening with David and the mob might have had nothing to do with why Alice hasn't come home. We might have to turn our attention to other options – like her having gone off on some sort of romantic interlude."

While I know such things happen, in Alice's case, I doubt it. She would have let someone know what she was doing – even if she didn't share all the details. Knowing Alice as I do, she would have told her kids she would be away for a while. At least she would let Donna know, even if she didn't tell David. And, she would have contacted Mrs Weston about being away from Chester for so long. No, I'm convinced the reason she hasn't come home is because something happened to her, something which prevented her coming home."

"If I were planning to disappear for a romantic getaway, I wouldn't be telling my son about it. It's not something parents share with their kids."

"How close are you and your son? If you were close, and spoke to one another on a regular basis, wouldn't you expect him to be worried if you suddenly disappeared?"

"You might have a point. I do speak to my son every couple of weeks or so, but is not a scheduled thing. Did Alice call her kids on some regular basis?"

"Okay; I'll concede you have a good point as well. No, I don't think their contact was a regular thing. Look, I know you are trying to be helpful, and everything you've said makes sense, but I still think something happened to Alice in Sydney and, somehow, her disappearance is tied in with the mess David is in."

Rod heaved a sigh of resignation before commenting further. "For what it's worth, I share your thinking on this one. And, like you, I don't want to think about what not finding her at the mob's headquarters, or their other locations, might mean. But, all we can do is to wait for more information to filter through."

Having delivered his news and discussed it at length, there was little else to say. After promising to let me know the moment he heard anything more, he was about to head home when I stopped him at the door, with what I thought would be one last question.

"Do you think – believe – Cilla knew all of this when she spoke to us this morning?"

"I've no way of knowing – and she wasn't about to tell us. At the time, I suspected she did but, given her misinformation about when the raids happened, now I'm not sure."

"Right … Well, one last question then: do we let her know what you have discovered through your contact, or do we pretend we don't know any more than she told us this morning?

"Let's play dumb. I think it might be the best approach for the moment. Let's see what she comes up with, before we mention knowing anything other than what she shared with us."

As I rinsed our mugs and glasses, I thought about his parting comments. In some strange way, the fact he didn't appear to trust Cilla any more than I did, seemed to lift my spirits a bit.

Chapter 19

It was Thursday and, with mahjong the highlight of the today's agenda, I hit the floor running this morning.

Straight after breakfast, a batch of cupcakes went into the oven. Welcome to another day when my diet goes out the window. I know I won't have enough willpower to ignore the cakes when we have coffee before we begin playing. Still, if I tried for two long walks today, it might help offset the cake I eat later this morning.

So, as soon as the cakes were out of the oven, I headed off for my walk – and kept one eye on the time. Discretion dictated I shorten my intended walk to allow me to be home again in time to put frosting on the cakes and have it set before I took them to the Rec Room. But, in spite of what I thought was careful time management, I was almost hyperventilating by the time I joined Rod in the Rec Room. Arriving a little later than I usually do, I found he already had dragged the tables and chairs into position for the day's games.

The question which had hung around in my mind all morning was about how many players we might have today. I felt confident our usual six (Marjorie, Bernard, the Furlongs and Rod and I) would be there, and yesterday Cilla sounded as though she would come as well. …So, one table of four players, and one with three. Pity we can't recruit one more player from somewhere. I have to admit to being a bit surprised Cilla wasn't there when I arrived. I felt sure, if she were joining us today, she would come with Rod.

When she still hadn't turned up by the time the others arrived, I was beginning to think I misread the situation yesterday. Or, maybe it was just so much hot air on Cilla's part when she indicated she would be joining us. I queried Rod on the subject.

He shrugged and said he hadn't heard from her this morning. He confirmed Cilla was aware of the time we started, and confessed he had expected her to walk to the Rec Room with him.

"Well, by the look of things, it will be just you and I occupying the second table again today, Marion," he said.

"With Alice still missing, and with Cilla showing some interest in playing, I was thinking I might contact Maria Lancini again to see if I could persuade her to play with us. I don't imagine she would consider playing twice a week, but once a week would work well for us. But, if Cilla doesn't join our ranks, talking to Maria won't help much."

Then, just as we were about to take our places at the tables, Cilla arrived – in her customary greasy overalls. "This week seems to be right out of whack for me. This morning, I even forgot today was Thursday, and I was supposed to be here, and not taking my bike for a long ride around the neighbourhood. Still, I'm here now – and I see you are ready to start. I'll just make a coffee first, and then I'll be right with you. Who am I playing with today?"

Rod had just sat down at our table. He raised his hand and waved at her. "You're over here with us. We will be playing three-handed games today."

"Those cakes aren't half bad," she remarked as she sat down. "I'll have to watch such temptations or I end up wrecking my figure."

Bernard issued his usual sniff of contempt at Cilla's comment. "There are more important things in life than retaining one's figure and, at our time of life, there are many other more significant issues to consider."

"Too true," chimed in Marjorie. "Like looking after your health and making every day count."

"Shall we play?" Rod called out.

His not-so-subtle intervention did the trick. It brought everyone's head down to concentrate on the tiles – and prevented any further debate on the subject of preserving Cilla's figure. From under a raised eyebrow, I glanced sideways at him. He gave me a hint of a shrug before becoming busy with his tiles. Within moments, the only sound in the room was the clack of the tile, and the gurgle and hiss of the urn as it continued to maintain boiling water for anyone who might want another coffee. The rest of the morning passed without incident and in almost complete silence, broken only by cries of frustration or exhilaration depending on whether the person won or lost.

It was a few minutes after midday when we packed up and the others went home. Cilla walked out with them, leaving Rod and me to put away and clean up as usual. As I was putting the last of the crockery away, Rod came and leaned on the bench beside me.

"Doctor Anthony called me as I was about to leave this morning. He wanted to update me on Shirley's condition. She spent last night in hospital. Today they will be moving her to the nursing facility here at the Village. He indicated she would not be returning to her house here, and he expected her to spend the rest of her days in the nursing facility. Should we want to visit her, he suggested we do so as soon as possible. It won't be long before she won't recognise us or be able to communicate."

"Although the woman who runs the nursing facility is an absolute dragon, I'll make a point of going to see Shirley as often as possible. Did Anthony give you any other indications of what was wrong with her? He seems to have firmed up his opinion of her future since Shirley last went to see him."

"Yes. As they now have determined she has no family, and we were the only ones who seemed interested in what happened to her, he felt it was okay to discuss her condition with us. His comments about a brain tumour still hold but, while she was in hospital – and couldn't argue about it – they did a whole lot of scans. It seems she is riddled with cancer. Once she regained consciousness, he sat down to discuss her situation with her."

"God, you wouldn't want his job, would you? I know it's hard for the patient to get bad news, but it must be difficult for doctors to have to deliver it. Did he say how she reacted?"

"At first, he thought she must be so heavily medicated she didn't understand what he was saying, but she proved she did understand what he was telling her. She told him she knew she was in a bad way, and that it wouldn't be long before she was with Henry again. As there was no other family, or even close connections, she didn't want to do anything about it. From the moment she realised something was not right, she just wanted it to run its course, and for it to be over and done with so she could join Henry."

"I don't know whether to say 'how sweet' or 'how sad'. Either way, it's bloody depressing. While none of us knows how we might react if we found ourselves in a similar situation, I doubt I would see things in quite the same way as Shirley does. Well, I will front the dragon in her den and visit Shirley as often as I can while it still counts. You don't happen to know what the visiting hours are, do you?"

"No idea, but there used to be a period in the morning, another one in the afternoon, but I don't think there was one in the evening. I don't recall the times for those visits, and they might have changed since I did know."

"Has there been anything more on the Sydney situation?"

"Ah yes, I was waiting until the others were gone to share the latest with you. Do you want to sit here and talk, or should we talk over lunch? I have cold chicken and salad if you're interested."

Here we go: more ruination of the diet. But, chicken and salad sounded way better than slices of tomato on crackers. We were halfway to Rod's place when an unpleasant thought occurred to me.

"If Cilla sees us going back to your place at lunchtime, she won't have to be too bright to work out we're having lunch together. I don't mind, except she probably will wander over to join us. Do you want her there while you share what your contact had to say?"

"Probably not; don't interpret that as snubbing Cilla, but I think just the two of us should discuss it first. Then, if we feel it's warranted, we can share it with her later."

While I went along with the sentiment, I still couldn't see how we were going to achieve it. Cilla never seems shy about inviting herself over to Rod's if she sees me going there, and I told Rod I couldn't see how we were going to pull it off.

"How are your stealth skills, and how do you feel about being furtive?"

"As I've no idea what you're talking about, I don't know how to answer."

"Well, the container with the leftover cakes needs to be dropped off at your place when we leave here, so why don't we go to your place first. Then, we can go out your back door, over the back fence, and along the track running along outside the fence. Once we get to my place, we climb over my back fence again and go in through my back door. Are you up for a bit of furtive behaviour?"

"I'll feel like a teenager escaping from boarding school, but it's probably going to be the most exciting thing to happen to me today. Do you really think we can pull it off?"

"We are about to find out. Here is your gate. Shall we go into your house?"

After dumping the container with the leftover cakes on the kitchen bench, I led Rod through to my back patio. "Right, let's just run through this again before we go any further, just to make sure I don't get any of it wrong."

He laughed and told me there wasn't anything to get wrong. Then he grabbed me by the arm and led me to the back fence. "It's not a high fence. Are you going to be able to scramble over it okay ... I mean, without damaging yourself in some way?"

"While I admit to getting on a bit in age, I am not yet a doddery old woman. I am more than capable of scrambling over a low fence." I hoped it wasn't false bravado, but I had scrambled over a front fence recently, so I should be all right – or so I told myself.

It might sound silly but, from the moment I climbed over the fence, I felt an enormous adrenaline rush. I doubt a resistance fighter in any of the wars would have felt more excited or tense than I did then. To avoid drawing attention to ourselves, we didn't run along the track, but confined ourselves to a power walk instead. Then, we were at Rod's back fence. An onlooker might have thought we were about to try breaking into Fort Knox. While trying to look nonchalant, we stood at Rod's fence and scanned the area around us for anyone who might be watching. Deciding we were in the clear, we were over the fence in a flash and racing up onto Rod's back patio. Laughing, we both collapsed onto the chairs there.

Rod giggled. "Go on, tell me you didn't enjoy our few moments of dangerous endeavour. Now I need food to quell the adrenaline rush. Come on through to the kitchen, and let's make lunch."

We took our lunch and long glasses of iced tea out to the patio. In keeping with Rod's strict code of behaviour at such times, we ate lunch before there was any mention of the matter we were to discuss. As soon as our plates were empty, I stacked them and took them through to the kitchen. On my return, as soon as I sat down, I wanted to get down to the real business. "Okay, Rod, what have you been discussing with your journo mate in Sydney?"

"Right… Well, he called late last night and again this morning. Don't get too excited. Wait until you hear the whole story. Okay, as a result of all that happened on Tuesday night, quite a number of people are now behind bars, including David Logan. But, in David's case, he is not locked up with the rest of them. It seems he's been squirrelled away somewhere else, probably for his protection. My mate gave me a fair bit of information on the mob's headquarters. I had figured it must've been a building in either the business district, or out in the industrial area. It turns out my thinking was way off the mark."

"I suppose, if I gave it any thought at all, I guess I would have imagined it as a seedy-looking place in a less salubrious area of Sydney. Do the details or the location of the headquarters matter?"

"Yep, they do – and we both were wrong. According to my mate, the mob's headquarters are on a significant estate of quite a lot of acres just outside the city. In case you weren't aware, it seems there is money – plenty of money – to be made from the drug trade. 'Headquarters' consists of a large mansion, complete with pool and poolside guests' cabana. There is a whole collection of various outbuildings, some of which are substantial and look as though they might be accommodation for the 'workers'. And, all of this is set in the midst of rolling manicured lawns, trees and garden beds."

"Sounds luxurious... You have me wondering what it was like to live there, and exactly what 'work' went on. If so many have been rounded up, what's the situation at the headquarters at the moment?"

"It seems the place is deserted, apart from the forensic people who are pulling it apart. I asked if there were any whispers about an unknown woman being found on the premises. There has been nothing so far. He has dropped the hint to all his contacts in the police service to keep an eye out for Alice."

"If they find her, they might think she belongs to the mob in some way."

"He says such a scenario is unlikely. I asked if any of the buildings had a cellar, or if the forensic blokes had found any hidden rooms or spaces of any sort. It seems he had alerted everyone he could think of, to look for possible hiding places for a woman."

"I feel sure they would have found her by now if she had been kept at the headquarters complex."

"Perhaps... My mate reminded me to think of the other possibility. He said he also suggested to the police they look for recently established garden beds or the likes. I told him such a possibility hadn't escaped my thinking, but I was trying hard not to dwell on what that alternative scenario might look like."

"Why would he tell them to pay attention to new garden beds? Alice wasn't a gardener and she wouldn't... Oh, you don't mean...?"

"Yeah, I'm afraid we can't discount the possibility we won't see Alice alive again. While I intend to go on hoping it won't be the case, I do know it is possible we might have to accept a horrible truth sometime soon."

"Well, I won't entertain any such thoughts. Why wouldn't they keep her alive? She wouldn't be much use to them if she were dead. No, I won't accept the possibility she might not be coming home."

For the next half hour, we talked over and around everything we knew, which might be connected in anyway with Alice's disappearance, and it included a lot of speculating. But, there is only so much of it you can do before it loses its appeal, and all you end up doing is depressing yourselves. It was time for me to go home. As I stood up to leave, a question occurred to me.

"By the way, which route do I take to go home: along the street, or over the back fence?"

"Do it in comfort. Take a stroll along the street."

"You do realise don't you, we could have simplified the whole thing by having lunch at my place. If we had, there wouldn't have been any need for all the cloak and dagger stuff of climbing over fences. I'm pleased we didn't decide to stop at my place though. Apart from the fact I didn't have much to offer you for lunch, the trip to your place was the most exciting thing to happen to me since the night the hoons visited the Village."

"Then we should do it more often. The next time we decide to have a meeting or a meal together, we should use the same route. If nothing else it will give us a certain smug sense of achievement; of having done something without the whole Village knowing about it."

There was no 'strolling' involved in my journey home along the footpath. Instead, a feeling of light-heartedness had me almost skipping along. In fact, if there had been empty cans lying about, I probably would have been kicking them down the street as I went.

My 'high' continued and had me tackling all kinds of domestic chores for the rest of the afternoon until it was time to go for my evening walk. Although I hadn't noticed it until I stepped outside the door, the wind had come up sometime during the afternoon. It was about to usher in a storm to accompany it. Maybe just a short walk today, I told myself as I strode out with determination. The first big spots of rain fell as I reached the end of our street.

With no one around to hear me, "Bugger," I swore aloud. The world seemed determined to break my resolve today: cake for morning tea, more lunch than I needed at Rod's place, and now no evening walk. Maybe life would be a whole lot simpler if I just told myself it was okay to be overweight. What's wrong with being cuddly anyway? ...And, I knew the answer to that without having to think about it: Cilla wasn't.

There is no way Cilla might be considered 'cuddly'. She was a lean streak of womanhood, and somehow to me, it gave her a definite advantage. When you are old, showing your age and overweight, how do you compete against someone who looks like Cilla? In spite of Rod's doubting her truthfulness at the moment, the man is not blind. No, the odds definitely are stacked against me.

I reached this conclusion as I arrived back at my front door. The rain was bucketing down now and formed a heavy grey curtain over the Village ... And I was soaked through to the skin and shivering. "Well, I suppose it was an appropriate end to a less than wonderful day," I told my steamy bathroom as I stepped out of the shower. But, it seemed Fate wasn't done with me today. As I stood there dripping water everywhere, my phone played its tune out in the lounge where I had left it. With a towel wrapped around me, I left wet footprints on the carpet as I raced to answer it.

"Apologies if I've interrupted your dinner, but I thought you might want to hear the latest," Rod said.

Whatever the 'latest' was, it was obvious from his voice, he had something exciting to share. "Do we need to meet up?" I asked. ...And then wondered why I would ask such an inane question. Of course we are going to meet, regardless of whether he thinks it necessary or not.

"It mightn't be a bad idea to get together – but a bit later would be better. There could be more to come on what I've just been told. Have your dinner in peace and I'll call you as soon as I hear anything. Will it matter how late I call you?"

So, he is capable of inane questions too.

He need not have asked. With my excitement running full-throttle, it would be pointless for me to go to bed until I heard from him again. I wouldn't be able to sleep. The little voice in my head broke in to ask me another unnecessary question: what if it is after midnight and he still hasn't called? Perhaps, I had better find something on TV worth watching – preferably a movie or something else which runs for a couple of hours – because I suspect I could be in for a long night of not much sleep.

In spite of a couple of cups of coffee, it was after several catnaps in my lounge chair in front of TV before my phone again demanded attention. In my haste to answer it, I managed to knock it off the side table. But, it kept chirping, and I finally managed to bark 'hello' before it gave up in disgust and adopted a silent sulk.

"Did I wake you?" Rod asked. "I wasn't sure whether I should call or not at this hour."

What hour was it anyway? I checked my watch. Christ, it was a few minutes after midnight already. Maybe I had more catnaps than I thought. Either that, or time is moving particularly fast tonight.

"No one here was asleep," I assured him. "It took me so long to answer because I dropped my phone and it ended up under my chair. Now, tell me about what's happening."

"Will it be okay if I come to your place to tell you about it?"

Yet another silly question to add to the day's tally, and I told him so.

"Okay, I'll be right there. Coffee would be good, and I'll bring a bottle of something to go with it. I'm sure you haven't had a chance to buy another bottle of port."

It felt as though he appeared on my doorstep almost the moment the call ended. When I opened the door, I found him standing there with an excited grin on his face, and a bottle of Tia Maria in hand. Of course nothing was going to be discussed or even hinted at until we were seated in the lounge with our coffees and glasses of liqueur… and my frustration and curiosity levels were almost off the chart. At last, after a couple of sips of coffee, he was ready to talk.

"My journo mate had a big day, and is having an even bigger night. He has called me twice tonight. During his first call, I thought he was almost as excited as we are about the way things were shaping up. Then, when he called me a few minutes ago, he was so excited, he was shouting down the phone at me."

"Well, if it is not too much to ask – I know it's been a long day and we are both tired – but do you think you might share at least some of his news, so I might become excited too?"

"Oh, sorry… okay, take a long slurp of your drink and fasten your seatbelt for the ride. Do I have some news for you!"

"…And if you don't start tell me soon what it is, I'm likely to get up and belt you one in the ear."

Chapter 20

"Okay, okay… here is the story. Prior to when my mate called earlier this evening, he had heard a whisper about a possible interesting discovery at the mob's headquarters. He called in a few favours or whatever, and then called me. One of his contacts thought the 'interesting discovery' might have been a cellar, or some similar hidden space. While there was nothing definite by then, he thought the information might be close to the mark. So, he called me, but went to great pains to remind me, if they had found such a space, there was nothing so far to suggest it contained anything of interest to us."

"He's right of course. But, it doesn't help us at all, if no more to the story develops. I'd like to think it does give us some hope at least. It does, doesn't it?"

"Only time will tell, but we can keep hoping."

I didn't know whether to feel excited or depressed. Part of me wanted to be excited about their finding a hidden space, but the pessimistic side of me was convinced the space wouldn't contain anything, and we would be no wiser about Alice's whereabouts. More for something to say than out of any real enthusiasm, I asked an important question we had overlooked in our discussions.

"How long do you think it will take them to check out the hidden space? I suppose I really mean, how long do you think it might be before you hear anything more from your journo mate?"

"Good question… but I don't have an answer. Both aspects could take quite a while. It seems they discovered the hidden space when they were checking the physical dimensions of the building. Something didn't seem quite right – not quite normal, even for such a large building. So, they called in some special bit of technology to do some scanning, and discovered the space. At first they thought it might be a 'panic room', but…"

"A panic room…? What's that?"

"Sometimes people who tend to live dangerous lives create a special room where they and their family can be safe if their lives are threatened. Such a room usually is reinforced and virtually impenetrable from the outside once the occupants lock themselves in it. As with typical panic rooms, the space they found doesn't exactly have a door with a doorbell. They suspect there is a concealed mechanism which opens an entry to the space, but they haven't been able to locate anything yet."

"Are you saying they haven't been able to explore the space?"

"Yes, that about sums it up. When my mate last called, the police were still trying to find an entrance to it. There was some talk they might bring in a jackhammer to remove a few bricks from one of the walls, if all else fails to find anything."

"Removing a few bricks sounds like it might take a while. They might decide to wait until morning to even make a start on it."

"You might be right. There even might be some health and safety regulation regarding jackhammering a hole in a wall in the middle of the night. From our point of view, there is nought else we can do except to wait for the next instalment of the story."

"However long it might take… and then we will have to wait for your mate to find out about the outcome and find time to call you. We might be lucky to hear anything more by the end of tomorrow. Ah ha, correction required: tomorrow is now well and truly today."

It was three o'clock by the time I said goodnight to Rod. I fell into bed as soon as he was gone and remained there until about eight o'clock, after which it took me several more minutes to feel human enough to climb out of bed.

*****

Should I go for a walk this morning or not? This losing weight project was proving more difficult than I anticipated. The last thing I felt inclined to do this morning was to go for a walk but, as everything seemed determined to scuttle my diet, I suppose I should try to maintain the exercise part of the project.

The cool early morning already was replaced by a glaring too warm sun, which assaulted me the moment I stepped outside. I know I *need* to, but do I really *want* to go for a walk this morning? The short, but definitive, answer was 'no'. The warmth of the sun seemed to evaporate my willpower as I stood on my doorstep. No, I do not want to go for a walk. I'll stay home and do some housework instead. Housework counts as exercise, doesn't it? It requires energy and burns up calories. Within moments, I was back inside and had my walking shoes unlaced and ready for removal. ...And then Rod called.

"Are you out walking or are you home again by now?"

"Home again..." How easy it rolled off the tongue. But, it wasn't a complete lie. Only the 'again' bit wasn't quite true.

"If you still have some energy left in reserve, how about joining me for a coffee?"

"Okay, thanks. What time suits you?"

"I meant *now*. I have news. "

"I'll be right there as soon as I put my boots back on. Oh, do I have to go over the back fence again?"

"Uhmm... Might be just as well to use the back route again this morning. I don't think either of us will want a third party involved in the conversation we are about to have."

No further encouragement required. I laced up my boots and was out the backdoor within moments of the call ending. While I didn't jog (I don't think me jogging would be the most dignified sight), I did make the legs work as fast as they could. Rod welcomed me onto his back patio by handing me a glass of water.

"When I saw you stepping it out on your way here, I thought you might need this by the time you arrived," he said as he handed me the glass. "Take a seat. I have coffee brewing. I'll bring it out as soon as it's made."

Cheeky sod. How dare he suggest I was so unfit as to need a glass of water when I arrived? He was right though, but I wasn't about to give him the satisfaction of knowing he was. After only drinking about a third of the water, I pushed the glass away from me across the table. I wanted to give the impression I didn't need the water at all.

An almost overwhelming temptation was to tell him not to bother with coffee. If it wasn't already well on the way to being made, I might have done so. I wanted to hear his latest news, not sit here drinking coffee. And, no doubt, he would insist we drank our coffee before discussing anything.

Moments later, the coffee arrived. And I was right... Well, almost right. He flopped onto the chair opposite me, lifted his mug to me, and said, "Let's top up our caffeine levels before we deal with any serious stuff."

As it turns out, he was only teasing. After a couple of sips, he sat forward in his chair, plonked his mug down on the table and said, "That's enough of sitting around drinking coffee. I have serious business to discuss." The twinkle in his eyes told me he was aware of how my curiosity was almost killing me.

"Ah well, if you are sure you don't want to finish your coffee first, I suppose we could move straight to business." I gave him a sweet smile – and a 'trumped you' kind of nod.

"Okay, you win. My journo mate in Sydney called just before I invited you over. There has been a major development in the main house at the mob's headquarters. They were waiting until this morning to bring the necessary equipment to bust a hole through into the hidden space, but it turns out it is not needed. A couple of the blokes pulling apart the cabana near the pool as part of the investigation came across what looked like a trapdoor in the floor under the bed in the main bedroom there."

"Does the cabana have a cellar after all? I thought all the buildings were single storey and built on slabs – except the main mansion, which was a two-storey construction."

"Your thinking is correct, and even the mansion's ground floor sits on a slab. The hidden space they found is part of the ground floor of the main building. Anyway, back to the trapdoor in the floor of the cabana…. When the two investigators lifted the trapdoor, they expected to find a cellar. What they found was a set of stairs leading down into some subterranean construction. Turns out the stairs led down into a tunnel. They called the lead investigator and his crew, who were still messing about in the main building, to come and investigate the tunnel."

"How far away is the cabana from the main house? As I haven't seen the place, I don't have my head around the space and size of the place. Regardless of wherever the tunnel led, it must have been a major engineering project."

"According to my mate, it is. He didn't say how far apart those two buildings are, but I looked it up on Google Maps. I think the distance must be at least 70 or 80 metres. So, yes, it was a major piece of engineering."

"So, you're saying the tunnel runs between the cabana and the main building?"

"Yep. One of my mate's contacts was one of the two blokes who explored the length of it and found it ran under the main building. More than that, it appears the tunnel is an escape route from the hidden space to the outside world, via the cabana. It's a way into the space too I suppose."

"Okay, so they were able to enter the hidden space, what did they find?"

"Don't go getting ahead of the story. No. When the contact called my mate, all they had found was a matching set of stairs and trapdoor at the other end of the tunnel. At the time, they still were trying to work out how to lift the trapdoor."

"How can it be so difficult to open a trapdoor? They wouldn't want it to be too hard to open if they were in a hurry to be safe inside the space. I mean, you wouldn't want to find yourself stuck at the top of the stairs trying to open the damned door, when the Hound of the Baskervilles is snapping at your heels."

"True; but you also wouldn't want how to open it to be too easy or too obvious. If it were, it would sort of defeat the purpose of the whole exercise. I imagine there might be some hidden mechanism which opens it. Even a fingerprint, or specific code, might be required."

"Maybe the investigators should bring in some type of heavy-duty equipment and just bust their way in."

"Yeah, that might be all right – as long as there was nobody in the space at the time. The object of the exercise would be to rescue the person inside, not to kill or maim them."

"I know, I know. But, it's so frustrating to be so close to finding out something, and then having to wait for goodness knows how long before you do find out. I suppose I shouldn't let myself become too excited about what they might find once they open the trapdoor. There might be nothing in there – or worse."

Having discussed all we had received about the Sydney situation, conversation moved sideways to Shirley Reardon... and led to another guilt trip for me. I still hadn't done anything about going to see her, or even made enquiries after her condition. A stray thought slid in, but I figured it was just my way of lessening the guilt I felt.

"Do you think they would let me in to see Shirley if I fronted up at the nursing facility? Would she be allowed visitors?"

"Doctor Anthony said we could visit her, so he didn't think there would be a problem. Even if they did let us in to see her, I'm not sure what her response might be. I mean, I don't know if she would recognise us, or how her basic faculties are. Is she even able to speak after all she's been through?"

"God, is there no good news to be had today? The way things are going at the moment, it's enough to make you take to drink."

As Rod was about to answer, his phone played its tune. He started to walk away as he answered it. I took the hint and stood up to leave – via the back fence again. I wasn't in the mood to risk running into Cilla. I turned to wave goodbye to him, and then stopped dead in my tracks. Everything about him screamed 'excited'. He motioned for me to sit down again. Either his excitement was contagious, or I was allowing hope to override common sense. Could this be another call from his journo mate? A phone call from who else could have him so excited at the moment?

I did as he indicated and sat back at the table … and fiddled with everything within reach while I waited for his call to end. It seemed to go on forever. Was it a good sign, or not? I don't know how long the call lasted, but I don't think I took a proper breath the whole time. Then, at last, it ended.

"They think they have found her," he shouted as he shoved his phone in his pocket.

"How is she? Is she okay?"

"Calm down, calm down and I will tell you. I'll give you the bottom line first: they have found her and she is alive. No more information is available at the moment. The investigators still haven't worked out how to open the trapdoor, but they have spoken to Alice. It seems she is weak, and probably not in good shape. Since the police rounded up everyone at the headquarters, she has had no food or water."

"If they still haven't entered the hidden space, how do they know all this? How did they find out someone was in there in the first place?"

"It seems the investigators' frustration was on a par with the way ours is at the moment. After fiddling with the trapdoor for a while, one of them vented his frustration by banging on the door. Someone knocked back in response."

"How simple was that? So, then what happened?"

"As I understand the sequence of events, the investigator demanded to know who was inside. At first, the person didn't answer. Then, when the investigator identified himself as a police officer, he received an answer. It was a woman. She said her name was Alice, and she had been kept captive in the room for weeks, but she had lost track of exactly how long. The woman had difficulty speaking as she had run out of the little water she had, and her mouth and throat were now so dry."

"Well, come on... What are they going to do? They have to get her out of there before it is too late."

"The last thing my mate told me was about how they were going to try to break into the space. It seems Alice was able to give them some clues about opening the trapdoor but, if they still couldn't open it, they would tell her to stand well away from it while they busted their way in."

"So, we still have to wait for the next episode to know how she is."

"Unless I'm misjudging the situation, I doubt we will have to wait long. The investigators now are aware of the situation inside the hidden space, and how critical it is to remove the woman – I mean Alice – from in there as soon as possible. I would be surprised if such an operation wasn't under way at the moment."

"Rod, I need a glass of water. Is it all right if I go through to the kitchen to fetch one?"

"No, it is not. I'll bring you one. Sit down again while I fetch it. How do you feel about cold chicken and salad again for lunch?"

"I think it must be just about my turn to provide lunch, but I want to stay close by in case your mate calls again. Let's give him half an hour. If he hasn't called by then, we can go back to my place and have lunch while we wait for his call."

There are only 30 minutes in half an hour as far as I am aware but, today, it felt as though there were at least 130. But, according to my watch, only 29 minutes had elapsed when Rod's phone demanded attention again. Already on my feet and ready to leave when the call came in, I glanced over at Rod to assess his reaction to whatever the caller was telling him. I had hoped for excitement again.

On this occasion, there wasn't a hint of excitement. He seemed to be listening so intently, it could have been his bank manager asking him how he managed to become so far overdrawn. Then the call ended. Rod made a beeline for the chair he so recently vacated, and collapsed onto it. I still wasn't sure the caller hadn't been his bank manager.

A couple of heartbeats later he was thumping the table and shouting, "They've done it. They've done it. Alice is safe. They got her out okay." ...And then we both were cheering and shouting and carrying on like a pair of lunatics. Tears of relief streamed down my cheeks.

Rod recovered first. "If we are going to your place for lunch, let's go now, so I can tell you all about how it happened."

While the location might have changed, the menu remained the same; we sat down to cold chicken and salad – and, to help us celebrate, a glass of chilled white wine from the bottle Rod grabbed from his fridge before we left his place. I had waited long enough, and had no intention of waiting until we cleaned our plates before hearing the story of Alice's rescue. When I told Rod, he laughed.

"Okay, but might we at least eat a couple of mouthfuls before I launch into the details?"

Permission granted, we both attacked our plates with more enthusiasm than usually generated by cold chicken and salad. A couple of minutes later, I demanded "Now, please..."

"Right... well, as the story was relayed to me, it appears they still couldn't work out how to open the trapdoor, so ended up battering their way in. Once they were in the hidden space, they could see how the damned door was supposed to open, and opened it properly to make it easier to move Alice out. One of the investigators carried Alice out and down the stairs to where the paramedics were waiting with a gurney to wheel her out of the tunnel. At the exit from the tunnel, the two investigators and the two paramedics were assisted by other police officers to carry the gurney up the stairs and into the cabana."

"I don't suppose the tunnel was constructed with such an operation in mind, so they were lucky they could get a gurney in and out of it. After Alice was back above ground, I assume she was taken to a hospital somewhere."

"A fairly new private hospital is situated not far from the mob's headquarters complex. I'm told it boasts all the up-to-the-minute facilities and equipment. So, I think it's safe to assume she will receive the best of treatment, and the police will be guarding her around the clock while she is there."

"Although it's a relief to know she has been rescued and is safe, now I want to know about her condition. How bad was her treatment over all those weeks, and how has it affected her? What's her recovery going to involve?"

"The space is quite small and she couldn't walk about much. It has left her legs quite weak. The investigators think she received regular food and water, but don't know about the quantity or quality of what she was given. Nevertheless, they say she is in much better condition than might be expected. The worst period was the last few days when there was no one to bring her anything."

"I want to go to Sydney to be with her. Do you think they would let me see her?"

"Not yet I shouldn't think. You have to remember, as you're not family, they might not let you near her for a while; not until they are sure she is safe and has recovered a bit."

"Yes, I know what you are saying is true, but I still want to go to Sydney to be with her. If I knew which hospital she was admitted to, I would give them a call to see if I might be able to speak to her over the phone, and to ask about the possibility of visitors."

"Even if you do find out which hospital she is in, good luck getting them to admit she is a patient, let alone telling you anything else about her."

"Right... but I will do some digging to see if I can locate the hospital. By the way, do you think Cilla's contact has kept her informed about Alice? I mean, if she knows Alice has been found, why hasn't Cilla rushed over to tell us the good news? It's not as though she doesn't know how concerned we've been about Alice's disappearance."

"It's a good question. I wish I knew the answer. Perhaps her contact isn't someone with direct knowledge of what's going on down there, and there is some delay until information filters through for them to pass it on to Cilla. Our best bet might be to wait a day or so to see what happens, before we pass judgement on her."

"Yeah, you might be right, but I think there is more to the story; something deeper perhaps. All along, I've felt she was holding back whenever she shared any information with us. But, anything she did share seemed to be up to the minute and from a source close to the action. I'm not saying she has a police informant, but whoever it is must have at least the same access to information as your journo mate does."

"As I said, let's give her a day or so to see what happens before judging her."

Lunch was over and there wasn't much more we could discuss about Alice, so I wasn't disappointed when Rod made noises about going home. I was keen for some time alone. Time to sit and think on all we've learned today, and about Alice. About everything she might have endured for so many weeks, and what her recovery might be like. Will she be left physically or mentally damaged in some way? Would it be better if she recovered here at home with friends and Chester for company, and to keep an eye on her? And then there was Cilla...

In spite of Rod's comments about not judging her too soon, I am convinced something is going on there. I just wish I knew what it was. The only thing I feel sure about is that Cilla knows more than she has said, and I'm confident – well, reasonably confident – she already knows as much as we do about what happened in Sydney over the last few hours... including details of Alice's rescue. So, why hasn't she rushed to tell us about it?

Chapter 21

Weekends are much the same as any other day around here, with the exception of Tuesdays and Thursdays when we play mahjong, and this weekend was shaping up to be no different from any other.

Yesterday afternoon, no more was heard about Alice, or regarding any other aspect of the Sydney operation. In spite of my best efforts to locate a possible hospital where Alice might be a patient, I drew a blank. All up, yesterday afternoon produced a whole lot of nothing of any use. By the time I fell into bed last night, I was a bag of mixed emotions: frustration at having wasted the whole afternoon for no result, elation over Alice's rescue, and a general shell-shocked response to everything we had learned about Sydney.

An attempt last night to contact Alice's daughter, Donna, produced much the same result as everything else I tried yesterday afternoon. After dithering about whether it was foolhardy to call her or not, I finally decided to risk it at about eight o'clock last night. She didn't answer, and I admit to being a bit surprised at not encountering an answering machine telling me to leave a message. I still find it strange someone, who is as busy as Donna, doesn't have an answering machine or some other voicemail arrangement.

So, what do I do today? My calendar for the weekend was empty apart from a couple of long walks pencilled in for both days. I kept promising myself to make these walks a regular feature of my day, but the world kept putting obstacles in the way. Well, apart from the walks, the only other thing I might try today is to visit Shirley in the nursing facility.

There's another of my resolutions which hadn't taken long to fall by the wayside. How many days has she been in the nursing facility now, and I still haven't been to see her? Right then, let's get fair dinkum about what I'm going to do today at least. First, right now, put my boots on and go for a walk. Then, after a walk and a shower, call the nursing facility to check on visiting hours and ask if Shirley is allowed visitors. Okay, now my morning is organised. All I need to do is add in a morning coffee break and lunch, and my schedule is complete until this afternoon.

With something less than enthusiasm, I laced up my shoes and headed off on what I call my 'long route'. While in the first instance, my resolve was strong, I soon found myself strolling instead of power walking. It hadn't been a conscious decision, but more like a lack of concentration. My mind was preoccupied with everything I knew about Alice and what happened in Sydney. Strolling seem to fit better with my state of mind, so I shed any guilt feelings about not power walking.

It was a beautiful early morning. The air was so clear and the birds were in fine voice. But the warmth already present promised a hot day to follow. It wouldn't be long before we were cursing the heat of summer days, but at least the nights will remain cool and pleasant for sleeping for a bit longer yet. After wandering across wet grass and through the trees, my walk brought me back onto the ring road and the arbour where I'd found Shirley waiting for Henry to collect her.

As if compelled by some invisible force, I plonked down on the seat under the arbour. The bees were busy working over the blooms, and a brightly plumed bird was dining out in style. It was a languid sort of day and, somehow, it matched my mood. But, while I sat there with no particular intent, other thoughts snuck in. Sure, finding Shirley here the other day probably was the trigger for those thoughts, but they went deeper than Shirley.

Before I knew it, dwelling on Shirley's current situation had me thinking *there, but for the grace of God...* It could happen to any of us, at any time, on any day. Shirley didn't expect to lose her grip on reality. Even if she knew she was seriously ill and wouldn't be long for this world, I doubt she envisioned the current situation. It made me stop and think about the Village and its community.

We all were ancient. It's what this place is all about. You have to be old… Well, over a certain age and retired… And, to all intents and purposes, that means OLD. None of us knows how much longer we have to spend in this place with our friends or, as with Shirley now, before we are forced to spend the last of our days in care. It amounts to a waste of a life, or what's left of a life, if you don't make something of every last moment you're given. At last, reality and the world around me managed to wriggle its way back in.

Christ, Marion, where is all this rubbish coming from, and why have you suddenly developed a masochistic streak, I asked myself. I realised I'd never really thought about how much time I had left. Of course, I realised I was getting old, and common sense told me I didn't have too many more years left, but I hadn't put a possible date to any such thoughts. Now there's a conundrum. What does 'not wasting a moment I have left' mean for me, Marion Dawson?

For a start, it means I have to get up off this bench, go home, and call the nursing home about Shirley. It also means I need to spend time giving some thought to how I might contribute more productively, both to this Village, and to my own life. I don't even have a hobby – apart from mahjong. A hobby: that's a good place to start. What hobby, craft, or other way of relaxing have I considered over the years? There was nothing filed away on that topic, not even in the darkest corner of my mind.

I was meant to be a housewife, or so I had been brought up to believe. Okay, I did deviate a little by being a working wife, but wives with full-time jobs had become the norm by then. Of course, many of them 'retired' to stay home and raise a family once kids started arriving. In my case, I didn't fit the mould. There were no children, and my husband died early in the marriage. So, I suppose, once again, I then became another single, working woman. In retrospect, my life makes for a pretty uninteresting story so far. How do I make what's left of it count for something?

As I trudged home, I was startled when someone called my name.

"Wha…? Oh, Rod, did you say something? I was deep in thought?" I didn't realise where I was, until I looked up and saw him watching me from his front garden.

"Not happy thoughts by the look on your face as you came down the street. What have you been up to? You haven't encountered another demented old woman on your walk, have you?"

"No not today; no lost dogs or demented old women (other than me) out and about today. I must say, your garden is looking good. It's a pity spring is almost over and it's about to be replaced by summer's heat. I probably should do something about some plants to brighten up my place, but I don't think I have any room left on my patio for more dead plants."

"They don't have to be dead – not if you water them occasionally. Find some which don't require much looking after. Try succulents. They seem happy to be left to their own devices. I have some we could use to get you started."

"Thanks, but it would be too cruel. By the way, what are you doing for dinner tonight? Would you care to join me?"

"I would love to join you. Is it a special occasion of some sort?"

"No. I just thought it would be nice to have company for dinner. Mind you, I have no idea yet what will be on the menu. But, I guarantee you will be fed. Shall we say seven o'clock?"

"Lovely morning isn't it?" Cilla's voice boomed out above the sound of Black Bess. "Such a beautiful time for a ride, I just couldn't waste it. I don't suppose either of you would care to come for a ride with me. I have a spare helmet."

"No thanks," we chorused together.

"You don't know what you're missing. I take it neither of you is a fan of motorbikes?"

While I just shook my head, Rod opted to reply. "Not really, no, but you will probably have Bernard out waving at you again when he hears you riding off this morning."

"Is he a fan of motorbikes? Do you think he might like to go for a ride?"

"Perhaps you should ask him."

"Well, if he came out to wave at me, I would ask him."

I felt it was cruel to let her go on labouring under some misapprehension about Bernard and motorbikes. "Cilla, does Bernard strike you as a sort of bloke who might be interested in motorbikes?"

"If I'm honest, no, not really. But looks can be deceiving, and people do surprise you at times, don't they?"

Rod almost collapsed with laughter. I continued my 'educating-Cilla' program. "People do surprise you on occasion but, Bernard out on the kerb waving at you, is not one of them. He wasn't waving. He was shaking his fist at you. And, I'm surprised he is not out here again now repeating his performance."

"Why would he be out here shaking his fist at me this morning?"

Somehow, Rod managed to stop laughing long enough to gasp out an answer. "It's your noisy bike, you see. You've probably woken him long before he intended waking up this morning."

"It's after eight o'clock. He wouldn't still be asleep at this hour, would he?" We both nodded and Cilla looked genuinely shocked. "What does the old rogue get up to at night, to require him to sleep so late in the morning?"

"Perhaps you should ask him," Rod managed between bouts of laughter.

"You've already delivered that line of the script, thanks Rod. I think I'll be off before he does come out – and I am tempted to ask him." With a toss of her head, she kicked Black Bess into gear and roared off down the street.

"You were mean, Rod Maguire," I reprimanded him.

"Perhaps… but wasn't it fun?" I left him standing in his garden and still chuckling about it.

For the rest of my walk home, the little voice in my head kept repeating the same question: Whatever possessed you to invite Rod for dinner? It wasn't until later in the day, I realised the invitation was a result of my new philosophy on life: make the most of the time you have left. Of course, if I were genuine about making a better person of myself, I would have invited Cilla also to join us for dinner tonight. …And, both me and My Maker knew there was Buckley's and no chance of that happening; not tonight anyway.

But, now I was home, there were two tasks demanding my attention: to call the nursing facility, and to find something for dinner tonight. Perhaps dinner warrants more urgency. There is a small leg of lamb in the freezer but, if we are going to have it tonight, it had better come out now to be thawed in time. With the decision about dinner dealt with, it only left the call to the nursing facility to deal with before I stopped for a coffee.

There was no surprise when the director's voice barked the name of the facility at me when she answered the phone. I was hoping they might have employed a polite young receptionist, who was tasked with dealing with incoming calls. But, no such luck – at least not today anyway. I went to great lengths to dredge up and engage my best non-confrontational attitude before telling her the reason for my call. Her response had me wondering whether the facility had embraced the current 'no waste' philosophy. Her response did not waste words.

"It doesn't matter what time visiting hours are, Shirley Reardon is not allowed visitors."

The clatter of the phone being slammed down was deafening. But, she had answered my questions – in a manner of speaking – so I don't suppose there was much else she needed to say. I didn't have to be a genius to work out calling the nursing home again tomorrow would gain the same response as today. I resolved to wait until Monday to try again. Perhaps there is a proper receptionist, but she doesn't work weekends.

While I had crossed both tasks off my To-Do list, I realised I had completed only part of one of them: what to have for dinner tonight. The leg of lamb was locked in and thawing out, but what about dessert? My initial thought was along the lines of apple pie and custard. After giving it a little more thought, I decided apple pie added to roast lamb would make for a heavy meal. Nevertheless, there had to be dessert, and it had to be something to satisfy Rod's sweet tooth. It didn't take too much thought to scrap the apple pie in favour of a cheesecake with a dollop of fruit salad on the side. But, a cheesecake needed to be assembled and in the fridge now if it were to be set in time for dinner.

Today, lunch such as it was, ended up being a little late but, by the time I sat down to munch my crackers with slices of tomato, I felt relaxed in the knowledge everything was under control for this evening. I allowed myself the luxury of putting my feet up to read a book … and promptly fell asleep in the lounge chair. There must be something wrong with these chairs. Every time I've sat in one of them of late, it sent me to sleep.

"No," I told the little voice in my ear, the universe and anyone else who might be listening, "No, it does not have anything to do with growing old. And, I refuse to revisit that line of thinking again, not after the fit of depression it brought on this morning." On reflection, it was as well there were no bridges between the arbour and Rod's place. The way my mood was after my time in the arbour this morning, I might have been tempted to throw myself off one. Now there's a thought. Perhaps it was something to do with the influence of the same rotten arbour which affected Shirley's behaviour after I found her sitting there.

I am now quite certain Fate is conspiring against me. My diet and fitness campaign are about to be torpedoed again. Not only is tonight's meal more substantial than my diet allows, but I will have to forego this afternoon's walk, if I'm to have dinner prepared on time. Is this some subliminal message telling me I just should accept the way I am and get on with life? …Nice thought, and it would be the easy way out, but I'm not sure it would be in my best interest.

In keeping with what I know of Rod, he arrived on my doorstep right on the dot of seven o'clock, and was armed with two expensive looking bottles of wine; one red and one white. As he came in, he waved the bottles of wine at me and said, "I didn't know what was on the menu, so I came prepared for whatever it happened to be."

To give us crudités to nibble before dinner, just before he arrived, I had cut up a selection of raw vegetables and piled them on a platter, along with a small bowl of aioli. Rod opened his bottle of white wine, and we nibbled raw vegetables and drank white wine while we waited for the roast vegetables to finish cooking. Conversation was light and inconsequential; very relaxed and comfortable. I mentally congratulated myself on my streak of bravado this morning, which led to my invitation to Rod for dinner. So far, it was shaping up to be a pleasant evening.

The evening was progressing well, and we had retired to the lounge with coffee and glasses of port after our meal, when Rod's phone played its tune. One glance at it and he was out of his seat and on his way out to the patio. Although I hadn't heard a word, my alarm bells were ringing. His reaction suggested the call was not a mate looking for a friendly chat. I was relieved when he returned after only a few minutes.

"Apologies for my rude departure, but the call was from my journo mate in Sydney. As I wasn't expecting to hear from him, it took me by surprise."

"From the look on your face when you checked the caller, I figured it would be bad news."

"No, it wasn't. He called to give me an update on Alice. It appears they put her in ICU when she arrived at the hospital so she could be monitored while they checked her over. This evening, they moved her out of ICU and into a private room. He checked with both the hospital and the police on guard duty. She is allowed visitors within certain conditions, and they think she will remain in hospital for up to a week."

"Thank God for some good news at last. I'll try calling her tomorrow… at least I would, if I knew which hospital to call."

"Ah well, I might be able to help you with that one. My mate gave me those details. Grab a pencil and paper and I'll give them to you."

I looked at the details I had scribbled in the notebook I keep on the end of the kitchen bench. Now I had not only the name of the hospital, but also its phone number. As I sat looking at what I had written, my mind was in overdrive. At last some clarity emerged.

"Rod, I was thinking… If Alice is allowed visitors and she is only going to be in hospital for about a week, I might take a trip to Sydney. I'll give her a call tomorrow to see if she is okay with my coming down to see her, and to ask if there is anything she would like me to fetch from home for her – anything except Chester I mean. Then, when she is ready to be discharged and, depending on what her travel arrangements are, I could travel home with her. What do you think?"

"It seems our thoughts are in sync. You go ahead and talk to her tomorrow if possible. After you've spoken with her, we can decide what we are going to do. I also had decided I would go to Sydney to travel home with her. If everything works out, we could fly down in the next day or so, and stay there until she is allowed to leave hospital. Then the three of us could travel back together."

"The area where the hospital is located is somewhere I'm not familiar with at all. Do you know the area? We might have trouble finding accommodation somewhere close to the hospital."

"Nah, I don't imagine it will be a problem. I haven't been anywhere near the area for quite a while, but I'm sure there will be at least one motel somewhere close to where we want to be. While you talk to Alice tomorrow, I'll chase up possible accommodation. After you've had a chat with her, we should be able to book our flights tomorrow after we have decided when we want to go."

After discussing our possible trip to Sydney at some length, it was about ten o'clock when Rod went home by way of the back fence – to avoid ruining my reputation, or so he claimed. For a fleeting moment, I did wonder if it were my reputation, or his, he was worried about.

Alone with my thoughts at last, I knew it was pointless to go to bed. My mind was far too active for sleep. For something positive to do, I decided to check on flights to Sydney next week. There were no apparent problems with the airlines. The usual two flights each day to Sydney were operating. I preferred the early morning one. It didn't require having to wait a couple of hours or so in Brisbane for the connecting flight to Sydney. A decision about when to leave didn't take much thought. Monday, tomorrow, was out of the question as I would have to wait until a civilised hour before trying to call Alice. So, Tuesday would be the first opportunity, if seats were still available after I spoke to Alice.

With potential flights sorted out in my mind, I decided I probably would sleep, if I went to bed… so I did. It took a while, with a myriad of thoughts about Alice keeping my mind busy but, once sleep arrived, it stayed with me until seven o'clock next morning.

*****

As I dawdled over breakfast, the only thing on my mind was when might be a sufficiently civilised hour to call the hospital to ask to speak to Alice. While Alice is, by habit, an early riser, they might be keeping her sedated, and she wouldn't wake too early. My initial thought was to try at nine o'clock. Would a receptionist be on duty by then? If I called too early, and received much the same reception as I did from the director of the local nursing facility, I might cruel my chance for a second try later. I did not want to fall at the first hurdle by upsetting people. Maybe ten o'clock would be a safer bet.

Having decided I would try calling Alice at ten o'clock, I only had three hours to wait. So, what was I going to do to help fill in those hours? I almost had to drag myself by the scruff of the neck out the door to go for a walk – a long walk preferably. There was nothing preventing my striding off through the park, and I knew I should do so. But, a part of me wanted to stay home to try helping the clock run faster.

A long stroll, a chat to a couple of people I encountered along the way, and a shower when I returned home, only managed to eat up about an hour and a half of my waiting time and it was not quite nine o'clock. When all else fails, have another coffee, I told myself and headed for the kitchen. The fact it was far earlier than my normal morning coffee break didn't deter me. And, the half of last night's cheesecake sitting in the fridge was too much temptation. Coffee and cheesecake so early in the morning came with a hefty serving of guilt. But, the cheesecake was so good, the guilt was short lived, and I survived the ordeal.

The hands on the kitchen clock had barely made it to ten o'clock, when I picked up the phone and keyed the number scribbled in my notebook. Alleluia! A pleasant young woman's voice asked how she might help me. The pause I encountered after I asked to speak to Alice Logan suggested she might be checking with someone first. I think I must have been holding my breath while I waited because, the moment she spoke to me again, I gulped a huge lungful of air in relief. *I'm connecting you now* were the most wonderful words I've ever heard.

Chapter 22

Her voice was thin and hesitant. "Hello… this is Alice Logan," was all she said… And I almost burst into tears with relief.

"Alice, it's me, Marion Dawson, your neighbour – sort of neighbour – from the Merivale Retirement Village. Do you feel up to having a bit of a chat?"

"Oh, Marion, it is so good to hear your voice." Alice was back. This is how I remembered her voice. "Did you get a parcel?"

"What parcel…? I haven't received any parcels? Why do you ask?"

"I sent you a parcel from Singapore just before I left to come home. I sent you all one, and I thought you would have received them by now."

"How did you send it? If you sent it by ordinary mail, it will probably come by ship, and everything has been delayed due to protests and industrial disputes on the wharves. It was kind of you to think of sending me anything … and so unnecessary. I'm sure it will turn up, so don't worry about it."

"Do you know if any of the others received a parcel?"

Perhaps whatever happened to Alice over the several weeks has affected her more than anyone thought, affected her mentally that is. Why else would she be fixating on some parcels she thinks she sent from Singapore?

"Which 'others' do you think you sent parcels to?"

"All of the mahjong mob… All of you at the Village who I play mahjong with. And, I don't *think* I sent parcels. I *know* I sent five of them to Village residents."

"Well, your absence was mentioned often enough for anyone who received a parcel from you to have said so. I think it is safe to say none of us has received anything from you. But, don't go worrying yourself about it. I'm sure they will turn up in due course."

"As you say, they probably will arrive at some point. Now listen, Marion, this is important. When anyone receives one of those parcels from me, they …must …not …open …it. Under no circumstances are they to open the parcel. They should just hang on to it and tell me they have it. Or, if it arrives before I'm home again, and they don't want to hang on to it, they should take it to the police. Whatever happens, don't open those parcels."

"Okay, okay. Don't go distressing yourself about a few parcels. I'll make sure everyone knows not to open them when they arrive."

"Thank you. I'll explain later. Now, how is Chester? Have you seen him, and how is Gwen Weston managing to put up with him?"

"Chester is fine. I stopped by to say hello to him again on the way home from my walk this morning. Mrs Weston says there are days when he frets for you, but most of the time he is okay. None of us doubts how happy he will be to have you home."

"And I can't wait to be home with him again too."

"If talking becomes too much for you, Alice, just say so. I can call you again some other time."

"I'm fine to talk all day if you wish. It is just so good to be able to talk to someone again."

"Okay, here is the big question: how are you? Don't give me the 'official version'. I want the truth. How are you?"

"I really am fine. I've had a couple of hot showers, good food and coffee, and they gave me the most comfortable bed to sleep in. But, I do miss being amongst my own things and sleeping in my own bed. They are still monitoring me – whatever that means – to confirm I am as okay as I keep telling them I am. The best I've been able to extract from anyone so far suggests I'll be here for a 'few' days. No one seems prepared to put a number to the word 'few'. I did overhear part of a conversation when they thought I was asleep.

227

There appears to be some concern about when the time comes for me to leave the hospital to go home. As far as I can work out, finding someone to travel with me to make sure I'm all right on the trip home is the issue causing concern. I keep telling them I will be fine, but nobody believes me."

"Well, this is your lucky day. Rod Maguire and I might have just the solution to the problem. We are planning to come to Sydney to be with you for as long as you are in hospital, and then plan to travel home with you. I don't know if we would meet the police's requirements, but you wouldn't be travelling home alone."

"Are you sure? I wouldn't dream of asking you to go to so much trouble on my behalf, but it sounds to me like a great solution to the problem. Are you both sure you want to do this?"

"Of course we are sure. We discussed it last night and decided we would book our flights after I spoke to you today. So, if there is anything you want brought down with us, tell me so I can arrange with Mrs Weston to collect it for you."

"You have a key. Mrs Weston doesn't need to be involved. I would like some fresh clothes. If I describe them to you, do you think you will be able to find them in my wardrobe? Oh, and when do you think you might come down?"

"We had thought to book on tomorrow's flight if seats are available, otherwise we will try for the next day. Don't worry about the clothes. Just tell me what you want, and I will try to collect the right pieces for you." She described the clothes she wanted while I scribbled a list of the various outfits.

Then a doctor came to check on her and it ended our conversation. As soon as the call ended, I called Rod.

"Don't tell me over the phone. Come and tell me over a coffee," he said, before adding, "I bought a fresh pack of blueberry muffins first thing this morning. How about those as an added enticement?"

"I'll be right there. Put the coffee on. I'll be knocking on your door before it's ready."

Forget the diet… today is for celebrating, not worrying about kilos, I told myself as I closed my front door behind me. And that's another thing. I am over this sneaking over the back fence lark. I don't care who knows I'm going to Rod's place, or if he is on his way to visit me. With my head held high and jaw set, I strode out along the footpath.

Over the promised coffee and blueberry muffins, I gave Rod all the details of my conversation with Alice. He had a few questions, most of which I could answer, because I too had thought to ask them of Alice. As soon as we had dispatched our late morning tea, Rod jumped on his computer to check the availability of seats on tomorrow's flights to Sydney. There weren't many but, if we were quick to book, we could secure two seats on tomorrow's early flight.

Aware of the urgency in booking my flight, especially as Rod was booking his now, I stood to leave. "Where are you going? Hang about," he demanded.

"No, I need to go home and book my seat too."

"I've booked your seat. Sit down and wait a couple of minutes."

"You can't book mine. I don't have my credit card with me to pay for it."

He didn't respond, and just kept tapping on his keyboard. When his printer finished spitting out numerous pages, he gathered them up, sorted and stapled them, before bringing them to the table with him.

"Okay, now here is your flight information. Now what's all this nonsense about a credit card? I've paid for them. If it bothers you, you can pay for the accommodation. Aha, and accommodation is the next thing we need to organise. After I came home last night, I checked on motels near Alice's hospital. There is a reasonable looking one about a block away. After we arrive in Sydney, we'll need to catch a train to take us out to the station nearest the motel, and then we will have a short cab ride to book in. Should I go ahead and book us in?"

"No, just give me the motel's details and I will make the booking – and pay for them. How long do you think we need to book for?"

"Let's say three nights. But, when you make the bookings, check if we can stay on for a bit longer if we need to."

Forget lunch. You've just had an enormous blueberry muffin I reminded myself as I rushed home. As soon as our rooms were booked, I grabbed the key to Alice's home and, armed with a large tote bag, I set off across the park. I saw Mrs Weston drive in and I decided to share today's good news with her before I went in search of the clothes Alice wanted.

She had been to the supermarket, and as she attempted to unload bags of groceries from the boot of her car, an excited Chester danced around her legs, making it almost impossible for her to do anything without tripping over him.

"How do you think he would react if he knew his mistress would be home in a few days?" I called to her over the fence.

"Have you heard something? What do you know? Come on, don't keep me in suspense. As for this little bloke," she said as she shoved Chester out of the way gently with her foot, "I think he will be a happy little chap. Now, come on tell me about Alice."

Without going into all the details, I told her Alice had been found, and might be home by the end of the week. I asked her if she wished to come and give me a hand to find the clothes Alice wanted, but she declined, citing the groceries still in her car. Why I did it is a mystery, but I made a point of not mentioning anything about Rod and me going to Sydney, or about Alice being in hospital. And, I was relieved she didn't ask why I was collecting clothes for Alice, if she were going to be home by the end of the week.

I left Mrs Weston dealing with her groceries – and Chester – and let myself into Alice's house. From the outset, I knew it wasn't going to be easy, but finding the outfits Alice requested proved more difficult than I imagined. For a start, her description of colours varied from my idea of what the colours looked like. Details of the styles of the outfits were sketchy enough to have me wondering if I was in the right wardrobe in the right house. Needless to say, the task took at least twice as long as I thought it would but, in the end, I walked home with a bag bulging with clothes, and a definite lack of confidence about the outfits I had chosen.

As I emerged from the park onto our street, Cilla came along after a day out on her bike. She eased to an idle beside me.

"You look as though you're on your way home from a dirty night out," she said as she eyed off the bag of clothes.

"At my age, I don't know if I could handle a life which included dirty nights away from home, but it might be fun to give it a go sometime."

She laughed, and threw me a wave as she roared off home. A tide of relief swept over me. I had dreaded the thought I might have to share our news of Alice, or the plans Rod and I had for tomorrow. Thinking about tomorrow raised another question: how would we travel to the airport in the morning? Was Rod planning to take us in his car, or would we call a taxi? Another quick call to Rod was required as soon as I was inside, and had relieved myself of the bag of clothes.

The part of my conversation with Alice about the parcels she says she sent us from Singapore came flooding back. I hadn't mentioned the parcels to Rod earlier and now I wondered whether I should have. Alice seemed quite adamant about having sent them to us, so I suppose it is true. But, a shadow of doubt remained in my mind. Did she intend sending us something but, for whatever reason, didn't do so? Maybe thoughts about sending us gifts have stuck in her mind somehow, and she now thinks she has sent parcels. Yes, I do need to discuss it with Rod. He might have some other ideas which explain the situation better than I can.

Packing for the Sydney trip proved more complicated than I imagined. My original intention was to take one smallish suitcase, but Alice's clothes filled the case and left no room for anything of mine. There was nothing for it but to take a larger case. I then spent the whole night worrying about whether the larger case would complicate matters at check-in for our flight in the morning.

Although I set the alarm, and I always wake up early, I didn't seem to sleep properly all night. It felt as though I was awake and checking the time every five minutes.

*****

As expected, Rod pulled up outside my door right on time. I had to check it was the right which had come to collect me. The driver was a stranger to me. He wore a grey business suit, pale blue shirt, and a patterned tie in mainly a midnight blue colour. Where was the Rod who lived in board shorts and tee shirts? But, this was Rod. The Rod I hadn't known. This was the journalist who had lived and worked in Sydney for a large slab of his life. And, I had to admit he looked just as at home in his suit as he always did in board shorts and tee shirts.

Rod shot me a look as he manhandled my case into the car.

"Don't look at me like that. Most of the stuff in the case is Alice's. My things would have fitted in a much smaller bag."

The airport was quiet when we arrived, and Rod had no problem finding a parking space under cover in the long-term carpark. Check-in was smooth and swift. My case didn't even raise an eyebrow. Then, it was onto the cafeteria for a coffee and something we might call breakfast. The requirement to check-in at least an hour before your flight ensured the cafeteria had a solid flow of customers for most of the day. Eating and drinking was one way of filling in the waiting time.

After our breakfast, we were on our way to our departure lounge – via the newsagents stand. Then, with Rod armed with today's newspaper and me with a magazine, we made ourselves as comfortable as possible in uncomfortable seats to wait out the remaining time before our flight. There was only one other couple in the lounge, and they chose to sit as far away from us as possible. It seemed an ideal time and place to tell Rod about Alice's preoccupation with parcels she believed she sent us from Singapore.

It took him a few moments to answer after I finished telling him about them. "I'm inclined to believe she did send parcels, but now has learned something about their contents which is causing her serious concern."

"What... drugs maybe? I suppose you do hear all the time these days of instances of drugs being slipped into people's bags ... and it seems as though it is almost impossible to prove you knew nothing about the drugs before they were found by customs or whoever. Given her concern, I don't think any of us need those parcels Alice says she sent us from Singapore. What do we do if – when – they arrive?"

"I think we do as Alice told you to do: either to take them to her or the police but, under no circumstances are we to open them. Regardless of whatever is in the parcels, all this intrigue makes them all the more interesting – and makes us all the more curious."

His thoughts on the subject of the parcels were not in line with what I wanted to hear. I needed something to reassure me, if the parcels did exist, there would be nothing illicit or concerning about them. But, the lounge was filling with passengers and we were to board our flight in a few minutes. Conversation ceased and remained that way for most of our flight. But, I couldn't resist the occasional surreptitious sidelong glance and the handsome bloke in the suit travelling with me.

On our arrival in Sydney, I let Rod be 'the man'. He is more familiar with the city than I am, and knows how to find his way about in it. While I've visited Sydney on several occasions during my life, it's quite a few years since I was last there. I knew we would have to catch a train for the next leg of our travel, but I didn't know which train, where to catch it, or where I would need to get off. Yes, it would be much better if Rod took care of such matters.

In no time we were we were on a train to an area outside the main city precinct. Then a taxi took us to our motel to check in. We agreed to freshen up before walking the block to the hospital to see Alice. After splashing water on my face and neck, I opened my suitcase and extracted Alice's clothes. I had packed two large plastic bags: one contained my things, while the other one contained the clothing Alice asked me to bring for her. Her bag of clothes went into a large cloth shopping bag I brought with me especially for the purpose. A couple of minutes later we were striding along the street to the hospital, me with my handbag over one shoulder, and the bag of Alice's clothes slung over the other.

The hospital was expecting us and, after identifying ourselves to the police officer on duty outside her room, Rod stepped back to allow me to go in first to see Alice. She was sitting on the side of the bed. The moment she saw me coming through the door, she sprang off the bed and raced to wrap me in an embrace. The tears already were flowing by the time she reached me, and her hug had me in danger of having the life squeezed out of me. But Rod saved me.

Alice relinquished her hold on me, and rushed over and hugged Rod, albeit in a more refined and restrained way than she did me. He escaped her clutches by asking, "Should you be out of bed? We don't want to be chucked out of here for encouraging you to break the rules."

"I am not ill. I am not infirm in any way. In fact, I don't know why I am still here, and why they haven't let me go home before this."

We tried placating her as best we could, but had little success. After we exchanged a few of the usual pleasantries, and she asked every imaginable question about Chester, the conversation turned serious when she demanded, "How long are you staying in Sydney? When are your return flights?"

Rod chose to answer. "We intend staying here until such time as we are allowed to take you home. Because we were uncertain when that might be, we have not booked our return flight."

"Oh, that is good news. They told me because you would be travelling with me, they would arrange for me to be discharged tomorrow. I don't have all the details yet, but officers from the... oh, I don't know what it's called... but two police officers will be coming to talk to us in about half an hour's time."

"Is there a problem of some sort they want to speak to us about?" I asked. An uneasy feeling was beginning to develop in my stomach.

"No; not as far as I'm aware. I understood they wanted to talk about releasing me from this place, and my travel home afterwards."

"This is a nice room, and you have it to yourself. So, it's not as though they stuck you in a ward with a herd of other patients. And, you are being fed and looked after. Stop whinging and enjoy it while you can," I told her, and managed to make her giggle.

It was only about twenty minutes later when the two police officers – one male and one female – arrived to speak to the three of us. The male officer took charge and, without wasting time, launched into what they had come to tell us.

"Now you have arrived and have the intention of travelling home with Mrs Logan, we are able to release her from here. It hasn't been possible until now because our resources are stretched at the moment, and we don't have the manpower available to allocate an officer to travel with her. An added issue was our desire to avoid using a commercial airline if at all possible. Your arrival has allowed us to put in place a number of things which will allow Mrs Logan to fly home tomorrow, Wednesday, first thing in the morning. How does such an arrangement sit with the pair of you?"

Again Rod opted to answer on our behalf. "We are available, and able to fly home as soon as everything is in place for Alice to leave. You said you wished to avoid using commercial airlines. What alternative do you have in mind?"

At last, it was the female officer's turn to speak. "Here's a brief run-down on how things will work. At eight o'clock tomorrow morning, a police vehicle will collect you from your motel, and then continue to the hospital to collect Mrs Logan. At a private airfield about half an hour from here, a non-commercial plane will await your arrival. Once you are on board, it will fly you direct to your destination. There will be no stops along the way for refuelling or anything else. When you arrive at your destination, an ambulance will meet the plane. It will transport Mrs Logan to hospital, where she will be admitted." She turned her attention to Alice before continuing. "Mrs Logan, it is likely you will be in hospital for a couple of days or so, before you will be free to be discharged."

But she wasn't done yet, and returned to addressing Rod and me. "I trust the pair of you will be able to make your own way home from the airport." We assured her we had a vehicle parked at the airport in readiness for our return.

"Good; then everything is in place, and the operation will be live from eight o'clock on Wednesday morning. In the meantime, feel free to visit and spend as much time as you wish with Mrs Logan whenever it suits you."

The male officer stepped up to have what he thought would be the final words. "Well, now we all are aware of how things will play out, we will leave the three of you to catch up on lost time."

"No you won't," Alice snarled, "not until you explain a few things to me." Both officers looked stunned for a moment before exchanging looks and shrugs of confusion. Alice ignored them and continued. "Why am I to be taken to hospital again? There is nothing wrong with me. I feel as though you are treating me as you might some criminal; like one of those you rounded up over the weekend. I can tell you now, I won't stand for it, and any attempt to curtail my freedom is likely to see us all meet again in court to discuss my deprivation of liberty."

Both officers looked genuinely surprised by Alice's outburst. The female officer recovered her power of speech first. "I don't know why you feel you are being held against your will. I understood the doctors had explained some of the effects of your recent experience might not manifest until around the end of this week. While we understand your desire to go home, our duty of care requires us to take every precaution to ensure you are monitored and cared for until the period of concern for your welfare has passed."

Alice looked ready to prolong her argument until Rod stepped into the breach. "I'm sure Alice's reaction is nothing more than her disappointment talking. Please don't let us detain you any longer. We will take some time after you leave to discuss the plan you have in place."

Needing no further encouragement, they said their goodbyes and left. Alice glowered at Rod. "I wasn't finished with them," she barked.

"Yes, you were. I assume you do want to be out of here and back home?" Alice cocked and eyebrow at him and then nodded her agreement. "Good; then don't carry on like that. If you do, people will think you still are suffering the effects of what you have been through in the last few weeks. Bite your tongue and be nice, instead of arguing with the very people who are making it possible for you to go home. We can work out what to do after we all are back on home soil. Do you understand what I'm saying is in your best interest?"

She nodded, and I stepped in to move the conversation back to Chester. About half an hour later we left when Alice's evening meal arrived. Rod ducked out first and was finishing a phone call when I joined him outside Alice's room.

"How would you like to go out somewhere for dinner tonight?" he asked. I raised my eyebrows at him and shrugged. If I was honest, I didn't feel like going anywhere. "My journo mate is picking me up later and we will go somewhere around here for dinner. He has invited you to come too."

"Thank him for me, but I'm more interested in a hot shower, a meal in my room, and an early night. Please put in your breakfast order before you go out tonight. I will go over to the office later to settle the account and tell them the bad news about us checking out early tomorrow."

I let myself into my room, and Rod carried on to his, a couple of doors down from mine. I hoped his plans for the night went well, because mine sure did. After a room service meal, and settling our bill in preparation for an early check-out tomorrow, I was in bed before nine o'clock.

Chapter 23

Everything went to plan this morning. The police car arrived on the dot of eight o'clock. At the hospital, Alice already was waiting out front on the pavement, with her police minder keeping a close eye on her. Our run to the private airfield took only twenty minutes instead of the promised half hour presumably because, as the driver kept commenting, of the exceptional lack of traffic this morning.

As promised, a sleek-looking plane had its engines warmed up and ready to go when we arrived. The transfer from car to plane took no more than a handful of minutes to complete. And then we were in the air and on our way home again. Almost as soon as we levelled off after take-off, I noticed Alice nodding off. By the time, I nudged Rod in the ribs and nodded towards her. She was sound asleep with her head against the window.

He grinned and said, "I'd bet my boots she hardly slept a wink last night. She would have been so keyed up about going home today, it would have been a long night for her."

The pilot was in the cabin to welcome us as we came aboard, and pointed out our 'provisions' for the trip. Our refreshments included a couple of large thermos flasks of coffee, bottled water, a supply of sandwiches, and half a dozen individual packets, each containing two biscuits. And, for our comfort during the flight, a toilet was located at the rear of the cabin. As I sat scanning the interior of the cabin, I realised this probably wasn't the most expensively outfitted plane, but it had a touch of class, and was more comfortable than some commercial airliners I'd flown in.

For the flight, Rod had equipped himself with the section of yesterday's paper he hadn't yet read and a paperback novel. I still had to read a couple of the least interesting articles in the magazine I bought yesterday. And, if needed to help fill in time on our flight home, I would tackle its crossword. I warned Rod I wanted his newspaper when he finished reading it, as I didn't think my magazine could keep me entertained for long, and the crossword would be a last resort.

Again, according to plan, an ambulance was parked at the side of the runway when we touched down at an airfield adjacent to the airport. The strip mainly is used by private planes, and the local aero club flies out of it as well. The place looked deserted. There was no one around and no planes, other than ours, were moving about.

In a major show of independence, Alice rebuffed all offers of assistance, and insisted on descending the stairs to the tarmac unaided. She also was not the most co-operative or polite patient the paramedics ever had to deal with, as she was less than gracious about being strapped to a gurney for her trip to hospital.

"I'll come to see you either this evening or tomorrow, depending on how soon they will allow you visitors," I told her as they loaded her into the ambulance.

As soon as the ambulance drove away, our plane taxied over to a refuelling set-up, and the pilot went about preparing his plane for the return flight to Sydney. Rod and I found ourselves standing alone with all the luggage beside the runway. Not only did we have our luggage, but we had Alice's suitcases as well. She had not travelled light, when she went on her cruise.

"Rod, it's a fair hike back to where your car is parked in the long-term parking area at the airport, and a pack horse would be handy to cope with this luggage."

"Never fear... it is not an insurmountable problem. This is what taxis are for." He already had his phone out and was scrolling through his contacts as he spoke.

In keeping with what appears to be the local taxi company's practice of not rushing to pick-up fares, it was about twenty minutes later before a cab appeared. Then, at the airport, he refused to drive into the carpark area because of the hassle of having to collect a ticket on the way in and pay for it on the way out. Rod suggested the cab would be in the carpark no more than five minutes and he was prepared to pay the cost. But, the driver refused to entertain any suggestion which involved his entering the area.

As a last resort, Rod negotiated a different arrangement. The driver would let Rod off at the entrance to the carpark and then drive, with me and the luggage still on board, to a grassy area near the airport's boundary where we would wait for Rod to join us. It was about ten minutes later when Rod met us, and the cab's cargo, including me, was transhipped to Rod's vehicle. As I had escaped lightly so far in terms of expenses for the trip, I paid the cabdriver – and no, he did not receive a tip.

It was an almost silent drive home to the Village. While I couldn't see steam escaping from Rod's ears, I knew there should have been. He was not at all impressed with the taxi company's performance … and nor was I. But, it was dealt with and we would be home in a few minutes. "Rod, don't let it upset you. We both know what the local taxi mob is like. We shouldn't have expected anything other than what we experienced."

"True… but, today they annoyed a journalist…"

"An ex-journalist – or a retired journalist, if you would prefer..."

"No. I am still a journalist. And, if you want to split hairs about it, okay, I'll admit to be semi-retired. But, I still do articles and opinion pieces for some of the major tabloids."

"Oh, I see. Okay, but how does anything you write impact locally?"

"Well, the local taxi mob is no longer 'local', and hasn't been for about four months now. They were taken over by one of the larger country-wide companies. An article in the major tabloids will alert executives and others to the company's poor management, and the article could suggest using other companies' cabs might be a wiser move. And, an article in the local paper will warn local business people they too might be well advised to use Uber or some other transport arrangement."

"So, the moral of this story is: don't ruffle a journo's feathers. He could turn around and bite you where it really hurts."

Rod chuckled. At least my comment had lightened the atmosphere in the car for the remainder of the drive home. "Are you sure you want to go to see Alice in hospital tonight?" he asked. "She'll have had little time to be admitted and settle in before tonight's visiting hours."

"No, I don't think so. The most I think I'll do is call the hospital to see if they will let me speak to her for a few minutes."

My plan was scuttled. When I called the hospital, and after waiting on the line for some time, I was informed I couldn't speak to Alice, as they were in the process of moving her into another room. But, I was assured I would be able to visit her tomorrow, and I was given her new room number and directions on how to find it. Far from being disappointed, I was relieved not having to find something to talk to Alice about tonight.

It wasn't because I didn't want to talk to her. It was more a case of feeling wrung out. The trip to Sydney had been a whirlwind affair and, coming so soon after the episode with Shirley, it left my resilience at a bit of a low ebb. If truth be told, after the episode with the cab driver and Alice's embarrassing performance earlier, I was over 'precious people' for today. I had no doubts, after a good night's sleep in my own bed, and a return to something more akin to normalcy, I would bounce back to being myself again. Tomorrow would be different.

Thinking about tomorrow brought back to mind Rod's reminder as we drove home from the airport. Tomorrow is Thursday, and Thursday morning meant mahjong in the Rec Room. Damn! Up until I remembered mahjong just now, I had decided I would go to the nursing facility tomorrow morning and demand to see Shirley. If I went to see Shirley early enough, I might still be back in time for mahjong. But it wouldn't allow me time to make anything for morning tea.

After procrastinating for a bit longer, and swearing about the way Fate works against you, I decided if I got on with it, I could make something this evening. It didn't take too long to come up with the idea of a cheesecake. If I made one now, it could stay in the fridge overnight to set and be ready to take with me in the morning. Although morning tea was usually single-serve fare – often cupcakes or scones – it wouldn't hurt tomorrow to have something to slice for a change.

Once I got stuck into it, in no time a cheesecake was in the fridge and ready for tomorrow. Then, it was time to crawl into my own bed for a good night's sleep.

*****

A solid walk this morning to rid me of the sluggishness brought on by the events of the last few days, and then finding something to do to fill in time until I called the nursing home to enquire about seeing Shirley, before dashing off to mahjong in the Rec Room – that's how my morning was looking today. Then, this afternoon, I would be off to the hospital to see how Alice is behaving. If nothing else, it looks as though I will have little time today to sit around being bored.

My call to the nursing home to enquire about visiting Shirley brought a surprise. I was told to come any time and stay as long as I liked, and they suggested I should talk or read to her while I was there. But, the catch was, she was unresponsive… no, they didn't mean comatose, just unresponsive. They didn't know whether she could hear or not, but talking to her was the best thing I good do. It did not sound like a fun visit, but I set off for the nursing home as soon as my call ended.

They were right about her not responding to anything or anyone. Nevertheless, I did as was suggested and prattled on about anything and everything I could think of. Carrying on a one-sided conversation for any length of time is hard work I soon discovered.

At first, I tried to think of things Shirley might be interested in, and chatted about Alice, our trip to Sydney, missing mahjong on Tuesday, and how I had made a cheesecake for morning tea at mahjong today. None of it caused even a flicker of an eyelid. Then, in desperation, I reverted to talking about the weather, my diet, and Cilla and her bike. Again, no indication any of it had registered with her. After about twenty minutes, I gave up. I apologised for having to rush off so soon, and cited having to set up for mahjong as the reason for my early departure.

On my way out, a doctor lurking in the reception area stopped me for a chat. "Are you a relative of Mrs Reardon?"

Ah, here it comes. As I'm not family, I'm about to be told I can't visit her. "No, I'm not related. We were sort of neighbours in the Village. As far as I know, she doesn't have any family."

"It's good of you to spend time with her. I know how hard it must be for you. My reason for asking about family is, sometime in the near future, we are going to need to contact them. If possible, we would prefer to prepare them for the bad news before it happens. So, you don't know of any offspring or siblings anywhere?"

"No. I remember her telling me she was an only child. She and her parents emigrated from England when she was about three, and her father died in some sort of accident a couple of years later. Henry, her husband, died about ten years ago. They didn't have any children."

"Well, if you have the time, and can cope with it, please feel free to visit whenever you wish. Bring a book and read to her if you like. We don't know whether she can hear or not, but on the off-chance she can…"

"Thanks… you mentioned 'bad news', should I prepare myself for it too?"

"I know you are aware of Mrs Reardon's medical situation. Her prognosis is not good and her deteriorating condition indicates she is unlikely to last much longer. If you leave your contact details with the receptionist, we will contact you when the inevitable happens. It will avoid your having to learn about it when you come to visit her."

This is not the way I prefer to start my days, but I knew the doctor wasn't telling me anything I didn't already know. It wouldn't be long before Shirley would be with her Henry again. After giving the receptionist my contact details, I power-walked all the way home. It wasn't about my diet or getting fit. It was about trying to walk off the feelings of sadness and depression before joining the empty-headed mob for mahjong.

Again, Rod had set up by the time I arrived at the Rec Room. "Apologies, Rod, I don't intend this to become a habit. I went to see Shirley this morning, and was a bit later than intended leaving the nursing home."

"How is she? I was going to see if I could give her a call."

"Don't bother. She is unresponsive and, according to the doctor who spoke to me as I was leaving, she won't last much longer. As much as I'm not looking forward to it, I'll probably go to see her again tomorrow – but I'll take a book to read to her next time."

We abandoned discussing Shirley when we heard the other four players approaching. There was time for just one last word of warning from Rod. "I haven't mentioned anything about Alice, not even when I told them we wouldn't be at mahjong on Tuesday. I think it best they are kept in the dark until Alice is home and ready to face the world again." He received no argument from me.

Bernard led the small contingent into the Rec Room. Today he was resplendent in a purple shirt … well not really purple. It was more of a mauve colour I suppose … and he teamed it with a bright lemon bow tie. The only good thing about his attire today was that the tie was one of those understated, neat flat bow ties instead of the huge, puffy ones he seems to prefer. The usual bickering and moaning already had begun. When barely in the room, Bernard's eyes fell on the cheesecake amid the coffee mugs on the table near the urn.

"What's the idea of this? Our morning tea is supposed to be single-serve, not something to be carved up, and its slices distributed."

"Oh, my apologies, Bernard, I was unaware there was a rule about morning tea." I tried to sound normal, but speaking through clenched teeth is not easy, and the sarcasm came through.

245

Marjorie jumped in before Bernard could respond. "I wouldn't call it a 'rule', Marion. It's more about the way things always are done; a bit like a historical tradition, if you see what I mean."

"And, exactly when and how did this 'tradition' originate?" Rod asked. His interest even sounded genuine.

"It has been in place ever since we started gathering here in this Rec Room to play mahjong, and tradition – or common practice, if you prefer –should not be altered without the consent of the others involved," Bernard stated in his most superior, condescending way.

Before Rod could retaliate, as I saw him prepare to do, I had a mouthful to deliver first. "Who the hell do you think you are, Bernard? You and your cosy friend here [I gestured at Marjorie] presume to have some right to come in here and complain about the morning tea, and bang on about 'tradition'. Who do you think established what you are now calling tradition? How do you think morning tea arrives here every week? Well, when you work it out, you then can forget about it … *because morning tea will not be provided in future.* Is that clear to everyone? … Anyone need clarification? No? Good.

Now, are you going to partake of morning tea, play mahjong, or go home again? At this point in time, I don't much care which you decide to do."

By the time I finished delivering my broadside, Bernard's face was deep crimson, and Marjorie was twittering beside him about minding his blood pressure. Behind me, I heard Rod cough as he tried to stifle a laugh. All of a sudden, loud clapping thundered through the room as Cilla stepped around the door and came in.

"Well done, Marion, well done. What a pompous, ungrateful turd you are, Bernard… and it also applies to any of the rest of you who share his views on the supply of morning tea." Cilla fixed her eye on Marjorie as she ended her speech.

"I'm sure no one meant to upset anyone this morning," Janet Furlong spluttered. "We didn't did we, Ted?" Ted, looking uncomfortable about the whole performance, simply shook his head in reply. Janet continued. "Perhaps, if changes to the morning tea provided does upset people for whatever the reason, whoever provides it should be made aware of our preferences … and the whole thing would be sorted out."

"Good thinking, Janet, if a little late in proceedings," Cilla began. "The person who provides morning tea – free of charge, every week – has been told… And you have been advised of the solution, which has been put in place as of about five minutes ago."

"No one has spoken to anyone yet," Bernard barked, "but a discussion…"

"Wrong, Bernard," Cilla cut in. "You have told Marion just now what you think of her morning tea, and delivered your demands regarding what is supplied in the future … AND … Marion has given you her reply: *there will be no morning tea in future.* Congratulations on a job well done."

Then Rod tried resurrecting what was left of the morning. "So, what are we going to do today? Are we going to play mahjong, or are we all going home again?"

No one spoke.

After a couple of seconds, Rod continued. "In all fairness, I would point out at this juncture, if we all go home now, this mahjong group is disbanded. Of course, you will be free to make your own arrangements about playing in the future… but this group arrangement will no longer exist. So, I ask again: what are we doing this morning?"

Ted Furlong, who had remained silent so far, at last found his voice. "I can't speak for the rest of them, but I do apologise to Marion on behalf of me and my wife. We were guilty of never giving a thought to how morning tea miraculously arrived here every week, but I can tell you, we do appreciate it and are grateful for it. Regardless of what others choose to do, Janet and I would welcome a game or two of mahjong this morning … right after we sample Marion's delicious looking cheesecake."

Marjorie was undecided. She started to move towards Ted and Janet, who were helping themselves to morning tea, and then stopped and looked back at Bernard. He hadn't moved, and I didn't discern any reduction in the colour of his face.

"Come on, Bernard. No point in cutting off your nose. What's done is done and all that. Let's move on shall we?" she suggested.

For a while, Bernard appeared to have become the proverbial immovable object. He just stood there glaring at everyone, but especially at Cilla – who had her back to him and was unaware.

By the time everyone had coffee and had loaded up their plate, I sensed Bernard was beginning to relent. The others had taken their customary seats at their table, when Bernard made himself a coffee and went to join them there.

Cilla, Rod and I were arranging ourselves around the other table, when I heard Marjorie tell Bernard, "It really is delicious." I heard a chair scrape across the floor and looked up to see Marjorie move to the table and load a slice of cheesecake onto a plate.

She slapped it down on the table in front of Bernard and hissed, "Don't waste it."

Still angry from this morning's events, I played worse than a raw beginner, and was never as pleased as when the morning ended and the others took their leave. Today, Cilla stayed behind to help Rod and me clean up and put things away.

"I can't believe the unmitigated gall of that arrogant sod," Cilla exclaimed out of the blue. "Who the hell does he think he is?"

"He's always been a bit that way," Rod said, "but today he was worse than usual."

"… And, as for that empty-headed Marjorie, what is she all about?" Cilla asked. "She just about drools over Bernard. Does he respond? I mean, what's going on there between those two?"

"Ah well, that's something else you'd have to ask him about," Rod said as he tried not to laugh.

"You won't stop making morning tea for us, will you, Marion?" Cilla asked.

"Of course she won't," Rod replied. "She might feel like telling the lot of us we can starve, but she will be here next week with morning tea as usual."

The cheek of the man! So he thinks I'm such a pushover, does he? Well, I've a bloody good mind to turn up with no morning tea next week – just to prove a point. Who was I kidding? Rod knew me better than I thought he did."

"I have a bucketful of leftover spaghetti I could reheat for lunch if you'd care to join me," Cilla said.

"We would love to," Rod responded as he gave me a hard look.

I took the hint. "Thank you. It would be lovely. I won't be able to stay long though, as I have somewhere else to be this afternoon."

"I won't mind if you eat and run," Cilla told me. "I'll slip home now and put our lunch on to heat up. Come over when you are ready."

"Do you think you might need another cup of coffee before we leave?" Rod asked.

"Oh, yes please. I don't know if I really need the coffee, but I do need to just sit and enjoy a few minutes of peace and quiet before we head to Cilla's place."

"Does it mean I'm not allowed to talk to you?" Rod asked in mock horror.

My anger must've subsided, or maybe it was just Rod's company, but I found myself laughing at him. We had another coffee, locked up, and then headed for Cilla's house, stopping for a few minutes along the way to drop off the container with the leftover cheesecake at my place.

Lunch was a pleasant affair involving good food, excellent wine, and light conversation. After we dispatched our meals, we refilled our glasses and took them out onto Cilla's back patio. We were still settling at the table out there when Cilla dropped her bombshell.

"I hear your Sydney trip was a success. How is Alice?"

Before I had time to engage my brain, I blurted out, "How the Hell do you know anything about that?" I swung around to glare at Rod. "I thought you said you hadn't told anyone."

"And he hasn't," Cilla murmured, "But Rod is not the only one with contacts on the ground in Sydney."

"But, you are more secretive about yours, or so I've noticed," he replied.

This was frustrating, getting us nowhere, and in danger of ruining what had been a thoroughly pleasant lunch up until then. "Perhaps it might help if we all stopped playing cat-and-mouse, and laid our cards on the table – so to speak – so we all know where each of us is coming from."

"Well, there never has been any secret about where my information was coming from: my journo mates in Sydney," Rod retorted.

"Aah, ye-es … I suppose it is time I shared something with both of you." Cilla's comment caused Rod and me to shuffle to the front edge of our chairs.

"Please, do," Rod said. "It would help ease our minds, I'm sure."

"Before I do, I must say I was most impressed with your performance this morning, Marion. I didn't think you had it in you."

"Thank you; and I rather liked yours."

Rod rapped on the table to get out attention. "Now we've established how wonderful you both were this morning, could we please return to whatever it was Cilla was about to share with us?"

"Uhmm… Yes, of course. Well, my contacts are a little closer to the action. You see… no, just a minute… Look, what I'm about to tell you must never go any further. Can you both give me your assurance of that?"

We both did the 'scout's honour' thing and promised never to breathe a word to anyone.

Chapter 24

After taking yet another few moments to gather her thoughts, and fidget on her chair a bit, Cilla cleared her throat and launched into her 'explanation'.

"In a former life, my job had me close to the action. Then, I reached an age when the rules said I must retire. Retirement didn't suit me or my employers – not right at that particular time anyway – but, according to the rules, retire I must. In the true style of Baldrick, we devised a 'fiendishly devilish plan'. Yes, I had to retire, but they could continue to use me as a consultant. The new arrangement suited all parties well.

So, every so often, when a major operation is being planned or about to go down, I disappear off to Sydney to oversee planning and logistics. There is a set team of specialists who work with me when we have something happening, but work as a specialist team within the Service the rest of the time. The head of the team happens to be my son."

Too stunned to say anything, for a few heartbeats after Cilla finished speaking, I sat blinking at Rod. He didn't appear to be coping with the revelation any better than I was, but Rod found his voice first.

"You had a hand in the major round-up in Sydney at the start of this week?" Cilla nodded.

"Although you didn't notice I was missing for a couple of days, I flew to Sydney, did what needed to be done, and flew home again."

"Actually… We did notice you were absent, and we also knew Cilla Longhurst didn't fly to Sydney … but Gina Truman did." It was going so well, I decided to let Rod run our side of the conversation.

"Aaah…," was her only response.

"Well, the question now is: which is it, Cilla or Gina?"

"Aah well… Now, that is something for me to know, and you to wonder about. But, you still haven't answered my question."

Rod and I exchanged a look, shrugged and shook our heads. What question…?I had no idea about the question she was referring to, and neither of us offered an answer. She could see we didn't have a clue, and helped us out.

"I asked you how Alice was, and I'm still waiting for an answer."

"Oh, Alice is okay I guess. She's not happy about the way things turned out after she arrived back here, and I guess she has let everyone know she is not happy by now," I said.

"Why she would be unhappy about it is a mystery to me. People are going to a lot of trouble to ensure she stays safe," Cilla responded.

"Perhaps they could ensure she stayed safe in her own home, rather than in hospital," Rod suggested.

"What's she still doing in hospital…?" Cilla's surprise sounded genuine. "Her initial medical assessment after she was rescued did mention some possibility of after effects not appearing for several days. But her recovery soon quashed those concerns. She should have been fine to go straight to her own home after the flight. Did she have a relapse – a turn of some sort – for them to think she needed to be kept in hospital a bit longer?"

"No. She is fine – and has told everyone within earshot she is. I suspect the local coppers are complying with some instruction they received from your mob in Sydney. Anyway, the bottom line is, there is one cranky, unhappy Alice Logan in hospital at the moment … and I don't doubt she is making some people's lives a misery because of it," Rod said.

A glance at my watch spurred me into action. "God, look at the time. I have to go." Without further ado, I took my leave and rushed home to grab my bag and jump into my car. Given Alice's current frame of mind (I didn't doubt it hadn't improved), she would not be impressed if I wasn't at the hospital when visiting hours arrived. In spite of my best efforts, in the end I arrived about ten minutes after visitors were allowed in.

Once the lift deposited me on the right floor, I rushed along the corridor to where I could see a copper sitting outside one of the rooms. After identifying myself to him, I took a deep breath and pushed open the door to Alice's room. Oh, this does not look good I told myself but, with a wide smile plastered across my face, I marched towards her bedside.

There was no warm welcome today. The look she gave me was angry and menacing. "I didn't think you were coming… especially after you didn't even call me last night."

"As a matter of fact, I did try calling you, but I couldn't speak to you. At the time, you were being transferred from wherever you had been, to this room. So, how are you feeling?" I figured ignoring the rest of her barb might be the wisest approach.

"How do you think I'm feeling? I'm fine. Every bit as fine as I was when I left Sydney yesterday. So, what other inane questions do you have for me today? Come on; roll them out, so we can have done with them. And, don't waste time on platitudes. I am not in the mood for any more of such crap."

"Right… okay then … It is good to see you are well and being kept safe. And now I have established those facts, I will leave you to vent your spleen on other people. I can do without such treatment. Maybe we'll catch-up sometime after you're home again." I stood up and turned to the door in readiness to leave her.

"No, Marion, don't go – please. I'm sorry. I didn't mean to take it out on you. It's not your fault I'm stuck here. In fact, I haven't been able to establish whose fault it is, I'm locked up in here like some criminal who is likely to abscond if left unattended."

"That is rubbish, and you know it. I'll grant you, this room is not as nice as the one you had in Sydney, but it is not bad. What have the doctors told you since you arrived here?"

"...Several days... That's all they've said. I don't know what that means, and I don't think they do either. I don't suppose you could smuggle Chester in to see me?"

"Not a hope; I don't think I would be allowed through the front door with him. Anyway, it wouldn't be fair to the poor little bloke. He would be all excited at seeing you, and then I would have to take him away again. While he might have coped okay with your absence up until now, I don't think he could handle just a brief visit."

"Yeah, I know, but I do miss him. And, you're right; this room isn't too bad – as far as hospital rooms go. It's a vast improvement on the one they put me in when I first arrived. I had to share it with an elderly woman, an elderly woman with dementia. She had 'an episode', or so they called it, soon after I arrived."

"I understand how it would have been upsetting."

"Upsetting...! It was terrifying. She kept going on about a cat in the room... how she hated cats... shouted at me to get rid of it. One minute the cat was under my bed, and then it was on top of her bedside locker. When it started crawling up her bed, she really lost it and started screaming the place down. The copper posted outside the door brought nurses and doctors running to deal with it. I think he – or his superiors – insisted I be given a different room, and one I didn't share with anyone else."

"How did a cat get in there?"

"There was no cat. It was all in her mind. But, in her befuddled state of mind, there was a real cat in there."

As Alice was now in a more affable frame of mind, I tried moving the conversation away from the hospital for a while. I had no doubt it would return soon enough to the hospital and her 'incarceration' as she called it.

"Do you know if your daughter has been advised of what has happened, and she knows where you are?"

"Donna hasn't tried to contact me, not while I was in hospital in Sydney nor here. She does live a busy life, so who knows whether she has been informed or not?" A look of sadness crept over her face as she spoke.

"Would you like me to contact Donna to let her know you are okay? I'd be happy to give her a call."

"Yes… No; maybe not. While I remain under 'house arrest', maybe we're not supposed to tell anyone anything. I'm sure, if it was okay for her to know about me, someone would have let her know by now."

Okay, mentioning Donna wasn't the cleverest move I've ever made. Try a different tack. "How was your cruise? I didn't know whether you had gone ahead with the idea or not, until I spoke to Mrs Weston about your absence."

"It turned into a last-minute decision in the end. I hadn't given it more than a passing thought, until I saw an advertisement for a cruise which was just the one I had in mind. But it sailed four days after I made the decision to book for it. I think I must have taken the last cabin. In the end, it was quite a rush, but I did manage to overnight with Donna and David on my way to catch the boat. I left the ship at Singapore, spent a few days there, and then flew home. It was a pleasant break away … until I arrived back in Sydney."

"Alice, when I called you in the hospital in Sydney, you seemed anxious about some parcels you had sent. You asked several times if they had arrived, and were quite insistent they should not be opened when they did. What's that all about?"

"I went shopping in Singapore. Well, everyone does, don't they? Amongst other things, I bought a gift for each of our mahjong team. I mean one each for all the single members, and one between Janet and Ted Furlong. When the salesman realised I was buying them as gifts for friends in Australia, he told me the store offered free gift wrapping, and asked if I would like them wrapped. After I said yes, I had to wait while he took them out the back somewhere for them to be wrapped.

As I left the store, I realised they were quite heavy, and the wrapping and packaging might be too fragile to survive the journey home in my bulging suitcases. I decided to send them home rather than to try squeezing them into my luggage. So, then I had to buy postage boxes, and tape and stuff to be able to post them. I found a post office and managed to send them off before I left for the airport to fly home.

Trying to post them was an exercise in confusion. There were so many different ways of sending them, all taking different lengths of time, and costing different amounts. In the end, the young man serving me realised I didn't have a clue about it, and he suggested the best way for me to send them. I was running out of time to get to the airport and, in my rush, I forgot to ask him how long it would take for them to arrive."

"Well, it seems they are coming on a slow boat, or maybe by carrier pigeon. But, why were you so concerned we should not open them. I'm sure, in the normal course of events, all of us would have opened them as soon as they arrived."

"Uhmm… look, I don't want to go into details here and now. I don't think it would be a good idea yet. I will tell you the whole story once I'm home again. In the meantime, please make sure the others know not to open them."

Our conversation moved to Chester. I spent the next few minutes telling her about how Mrs Weston and Chester were getting along, and how Mrs Weston and I had gone into her house to find the extra bottle of Chester's pills. But, visiting time was about to end and, as if to remind me, a nurse arrived to take the usual patient observations. I used her arrival as an excuse to leave. So, I told Alice I would see her tomorrow, picked up my bag and was on my way home, all within the space of a few minutes.

As I drove into my street, I felt my stomach start to tighten. A removalist's van was parked out front of Shirley Reardon's house. "Surely not…," I murmured. "She was alive and okay this morning." As the universe didn't provide any answers, as soon as I closed the garage roller door, I hurried along the footpath to Rod's place. If anyone knew what was happening in our street, Rod would.

He was trimming shrubs in his front garden... shrubs he only trimmed last week. As I approached, he rushed to open the gate and invite me in. "You look as though you could use a glass of wine – or two. Let's sit on my back patio while we watch the afternoon fade away."

After a couple of swigs of my wine, I felt it was time to ask my question. "What's going on at Shirley's place. I can't say the sight of a removalist's van parked out front went down well with my nerves."

"It came here first. It seems the driver confused the numbers, and I had to direct them to the house two doors further along."

"But, why are they there? It's obvious they are moving all her stuff out, but why? She hasn't died, has she?"

"Not since you saw her this morning ... no, I don't think so. I think management has been given the bad word about Shirley's condition, including the news she will not be returning to the house ever again. Management is moving all her belongings into storage so they can prepare the cottage for a new resident. I know. It sounds a bit cold-hearted, but it is a sound business move. Shirley could be in the nursing facility for weeks, months, even years. We all know she will not be coming out of there – except in a box. The house and everything in it would deteriorate if left to sit there as it was. So, the bottom line is, we will have a new neighbour in the near future."

With nothing much else to discuss, after giving him a rundown on my visit with Alice, I went home still feeling more than a little unsettled by the presence of the removalist's van and what it meant. Depression over the fragility of life kept me company all evening. It threatened to encroach on an area I stay clear away from: What will my end of life be like, and who will care?

I stayed up as late as possible and had a nightcap in a bid to ensure dark thoughts did not accompany me to bed and keep sleep at bay.

*****

With the decision made last evening to visit Alice this morning, and to leave seeing Shirley until this afternoon, I had plenty of time for a long walk before doing anything else.

My long walk took me close to Alice's home, so I detoured to take a quick look over her fence into Mrs Weston's yard. Chester was chasing a lizard across the grass while Mrs Weston sat under the pergola drinking her coffee and reading a book. She didn't look up, so remained unaware of my presence. Even Chester was too engrossed in his lizard to notice me, but I would be able to tell Alice I had checked on him again today.

In the end, I didn't have too much time to spare before I had to leave for the hospital, and it was right on the start of visiting time when I arrived. As I rushed along the corridor to Alice's room, I fished around in my bag for ID to show the officer on duty. Then it hit me. Something was not right. There was no police officer sitting outside her door. I felt my stomach tightening as I raced the last few metres to her door … And almost collided with Alice as she came out of the room.

"Where are you going?" I demanded. "And, where is the police officer who is supposed to be outside your door?"

"Oh, the copper… no, they called off guarding me at about eight o'clock last night. There's been no one sitting out there since then. I'm pleased you're here, and your timing is perfect."

"Perfect for what? … And, you still haven't told me where you were going when I arrived."

"You saved me having to call for a cab. You can take me home. I'll just get my bag and we can go."

"Hang on; who said you could leave?"

"When the doctor did his rounds this morning he said, although I no longer needed a police guard, he would be keeping me in for at least another day. He might see his way clear to discharge me tomorrow."

"So, why are you packed, and asking me to drive you home?"

"I told him it wasn't going to happen that way. I was going home today. He argued. I asked if I was under arrest or something. He said no. I told him, if he was finished my check-up for this morning, he could go and leave me in peace. As soon as he left, I went downstairs and discharged myself. They called the doctor to confirm I could leave. He arrived and started reading me the riot act. Basically, I told him to piss off, or I would call the police and have him arrested for trying to hold me against my will."

"Then what happened?"

"I came back up here and packed, and was on my way down to the taxi company's free phone in the hospital's lobby, when you arrived. So, are you okay to take me home, or do you have something else to do?"

About fifteen minutes later, I delivered her to her front door, and then helped her inside with her luggage. "Please agree to stay and have a coffee with me," she begged. I agreed. "Good; and after we have a coffee, I'll go nextdoor to reclaim my dog."

While I sat at the breakfast bar and waited for her complicated-looking coffee machine to be filled and do its thing, I asked her about discharging herself from hospital. I was concerned about possible repercussions, given all she had been through in Sydney and the subsequent police involvement.

"There won't be any. And, before you ask again, I am fine and there was no need for me to be in hospital since our return from Sydney. I know the local coppers were relieved when they didn't have to post a guard outside my door any longer. I think they are short staffed, and there's been a bit going on around here keeping them busy.

Apart from it being unnecessary for me to be in hospital, I was not spending another day in the room they had me in. Last night, Deidre from the beauty salon was at the hospital to visit someone else and, when she saw I was there, she popped in for a few minutes. She was quite concerned about my health and what was wrong with me. I kept telling her I was fine, until she finally explained why she was so concerned. She told me:

Nobody who is fine is put in this room. If they are telling you there is nothing wrong with you, but they have put you in this room, you should start asking them how long they think you have left to go. It's kind of the last-stop-hotel."

"What was she suggesting? Was she saying the room you were in was reserved for the critically ill and dying?"

"Deidre's mother was put in the same room when she was admitted a couple of months ago. It seems one of the domestic staff, when they brought her meal, said she hated having to bring meals to that particular room because it was 'God's waiting room'. Deidre's mother quizzed her about the 'waiting room' comment and was told, everyone they put in there isn't long for this world. Deidre claims it so upset her mother, over the subsequent few days, her mother slowly lost her mind, and it necessitated transfer to a nursing home somewhere."

"You didn't buy all that rubbish about God's waiting room, did you?"

"No, of course not, but a couple of other things Deidre said did make me wonder for a few moments. She claimed to know of at least three other people who had died after spending only a short time in that room, and rattled off their details for me. Even her comments didn't worry me too much. It was what happened afterwards which convinced me I was out of there as soon as possible."

"I can't quite picture such talk upsetting you to such an extent. What else happened to convince you to get out of there?"

"Someone with a clipboard came and wanted to know my 'wishes'. I didn't have a clue what she was on about, but it turned out she need to record, on some form or other, whether I wished to be revived or not, if I was... well you know what I mean, and she wanted to know who to contact, and if they had authority to turn-off life support. Then, a bit later, and while I was still recovering from that interesting conversation, a young female doctor came to see me. Her visit was just as upsetting. She wanted to know if I had an EPA in place, and if my will was in order, *should something happen to me.*"

"Oh, dear...," was the only response I could manage as I tried not to giggle. It wasn't funny, but picturing Alice's indignation at the time was funny.

"Yes, oh dear… Anyway, I demanded to know what they were planning to do to me, if they thought I was going to die, and for them to need all the paperwork in order beforehand. She appeared to become quite upset with me, and left in a bit of a state – and without any of her questions answered I might add. I'd had enough of being in a place which seemed to expect their patients to die. Then, when the doctor came this morning and insisted they needed to keep me a bit longer, it was the last straw. Well, it wasn't going to happen. I was out of there."

Picturing Alice being subjected to such treatment was too much for me, and I ended up almost rolling on the floor with laughter. But, at last, she saw the funny side of it too and could laugh about it.

"Now things are on a much better footing here, it's time I left … and you went nextdoor to tell Chester you are home again. I suspect it will be a reunion worth seeing." I could picture how excited Chester would be the moment he saw Alice again.

"Then, stay and help me welcome Chester home."

While it was tempting, it didn't feel the right thing to do, so I climbed into my car and drove home. Rod saw me arrive, and was waiting at the gate when I closed the garage. I thought I detected a hint of tension about him as I invited him to come in with me. Although it was closer to lunchtime than morning teatime, I asked if he would like a coffee. I needed one.

"Yes, please, but I didn't come for coffee. I'm afraid I'm the bearer of bad news."

I took a deep breath, and then gestured for him to get on with it.

"Doctor Anthony called about an hour ago to tell me Shirley Reardon had passed away earlier this morning. He said it wasn't unexpected. Yesterday, they thought she only had 24 to 48 hours left. As I knew you planned to visit Shirley this afternoon, I thought I should tell you as soon as you came home. Oh, and they already must have someone interested in moving into Shirley's place. The cleaners were working flat-out in there this morning."

"Life's a bitch isn't it? I've just delivered Alice home from hospital and had a laugh with her about her experiences over the last day or so, and now I learn I won't be visiting Shirley this afternoon. I suppose it's all about checks-and-balances but, would it be so terrible, if it got out of whack, swung to the upside, and stayed there for a while? Thanks, Rod, for coming to tell me about Shirley. Now I do need a coffee – and perhaps something a little stronger."

Chapter 25

While my intention was to give housework a bit of attention this afternoon, I fell asleep in my lounge chair while watching the lunchtime news. It took me ages to get going again once I woke from what was a heavy sleep. Any inclination to indulge in housework had well and truly evaporated. After a few minutes of wondering what to do with myself, I decided to wander along the street to where a cluster of vehicles was parked in front of Shirley's house.

The signage on the side of the closest vehicle announced it belonged to the Merivale Retirement Village. So, I didn't need to be too bright to work out our director, Tanya Jellicoe, might be showing a potential new resident the house. No guesses about the second vehicle; it was the cleaners' van. But the third vehicle looked familiar, although I couldn't think why.

There was a definite feeling of familiarity about the small, bright red hatchback. And, just to make me feel worse about it, the little voice in my head kept telling me I did know whose car it was. I stopped beside the vehicle and stood looking at it. Nothing... it didn't seem to matter how hard or long I looked at it, I couldn't associate it with anyone I knew. Then a familiar voice calling out to me threw me into a real state of confusion. The voice had said *hello neighbour.* But, I didn't recognise the voice as belonging to anyone on this street.

I turned to face Shirley's house, the direction the voice had come from, in the hope of recognising its owner. Standing on the doorstep and waving frantically at me was Maria Lancini.

"Maria... Goodness, what are you doing here?"

"Didn't you hear? I'm moving in. It probably will be sometime next week before it happens. There are a couple of things I want done to the place beforehand. It will be better to wait until they are done, rather than trying to move in with work going on around me. Isn't it great? Now I'll be playing mahjong with you twice a week."

"Yep, it will be good to have you as a regular player, but I'm a bit confused by how this all came about. Won't you still be needed at home to look after your husband?"

"Ooh, you haven't heard that either. He passed away early last week. We knew it was coming. It was a relief really – for both of us. A couple of days before then, I came to see if there was any likelihood of a house becoming vacant in the near future. You know I always said, as soon as I was free, I wanted to move into Merivale Village. I couldn't believe my luck when I received a call a couple of days ago about this place becoming available."

"What about your house in town, what's happening with it?"

"About two weeks ago, I spoke to a real estate agent about putting it on the market. He said the market was quiet at the moment and it would take a while to sell. It didn't matter. I wanted it listed. My husband and I knew he only had a week or two left, and I had been clearing stuff out ready to move as soon as I could after he went. So, the agent listed it, and an unconditional contract was signed yesterday. They asked for a shortened settlement period, so it settles in two weeks' time."

"It sounds like the gods were in your corner over the last little while. It will be great to have you here."

"Everything just fell into place. I think I'm still in shock. Anyway, I will be playing mahjong next Tuesday and, as soon as I'm settled in, there will be a house-warming party."

"Well, when you are finished here, come to my place for a coffee – or stay for dinner if you like."

As she wasn't sure how long she would be at her house, coffee was out of the question, but she accepted the dinner invitation … which meant I had to hurry home to work out what we might have … and to think about whether I should invite others to join us. I tried hard to ignore the little voice in my head saying 'aw, come on, do the right thing'.

Rod said 'yes' without a moment's hesitation. Then, I had to deal with the big question: whether to invite Cilla or not. There was the little voice in my head again repeating its "aw, come on...' message. "Okay, okay I'll call her," I barked, and reached for my phone. Wouldn't you know it? She had to be home by 8.30pm but she would love to come.

Dinner for four gave me something to do for the rest of the day. By the time everything was ready, I had just enough time for a shower before guests started arriving. Maria came first, followed soon after by Rod, who arrived again with two bottles of wine. Cilla came a couple of minutes later, and also was accompanied by a bottle of wine. With introductions all round completed, I was surprised at how fast a sense of fun and relaxed friendship developed and continued through the evening.

It was a great night with lots of laughs all round. Cilla left first to be home just in time for the 8.30 call she was expecting. Maria, who was beginning to look a bit weary, took advantage of Cilla's departure to follow her example. Rod stayed on, in spite of stating earlier he had an article to finish writing.

After everything was stacked in the dishwasher, we shared a nightcap before he made a move to leave. I took advantage of the situation to point out Fate had delivered us a new problem. "With Alice and Maria both now available for mahjong, we have gone from not having enough for two full tables, to one too many. How are we going to deal with it?"

"Right... I hadn't thought about it until you mentioned it. Let's not worry too much about it yet. Life has a way of sorting itself out." I wished I felt as confident as he did, but there wasn't time to discuss it further as he was on his feet ready to leave.

As I walked him to the door, he said, "The food won't be as good, but our next dinner together will be at my place." I felt a little flutter, but just smiled and nodded.

*****

How we were going to manage so many players proved not to be a problem at our next mahjong get-together. Maria was tied up with various solicitors in trying to finalise her husband's estate, and with the sale of the house, which it seems is in her name, and not part of her husband's estate. Then, just before I was about to leave home, Alice called. Chester had been off his food a little since she came home. She had an appointment for the vet to take a look at him. But, she had forgotten about mahjong when she made the appointment, and now realised she would not be able to play today. I shared the news with Rod.

"See; I told you life had a way or sorting things out," he said.

"Okay, but it probably only sorted it out for today; just delayed the problem for a couple of days." As it turned out, I was wrong.

Bernard dropped his bombshell at the end of the morning's games. "I've been engaged as a supervisor and tutor by my former university. My contract is for an hour per week as a supervisor for a postgraduate student, and an hour per week as a tutor for a couple of promising undergraduates. I've discussed the situations with all the students involved, and we have arranged things to better suit our needs. In both cases, we agreed to meet only every second week.

So, from next week, I will not be available for mahjong on Thursdays. Every second Thursday, I will have a two-hour session with my postgraduate student. Then, on the Thursday of the alternate week, I will be tutoring my undergraduate students for two hours. I realise these arrangements will make mahjong difficult but, if you are keen enough, I'm sure you will find a way around the problem."

I watched Marjorie's face fall as Bernard delivered his news. Obviously, the arrogant sod hadn't bothered to share it with her first. I couldn't let the moment go by; couldn't let Bernard go on thinking he had the upper hand in some way.

"Actually, Bernard, your news doesn't create a problem for us. In fact, it helps solve one we were about to encounter. With both Alice Logan and Maria Lancini joining our ranks again in the next week or so, we were facing going from not quite enough players to one too many. So, thanks for helping provide at least part of the solution."

My tone had been a bit tart. The look Rod gave me suggested he didn't approve. Too bad! This is the new me, Rod, and I intend telling things as I see them in future. Later, on our way home, and while we were still digesting Bernard's news, Cilla decided it was the appropriate time to share her news as well.

"The others don't need to know the details of this but, as you are aware of my other part-time life as a consultant, I can tell you about it. My role as a consultant has changed to encompass a bit wider range of operations than it did previously. As a result, it will necessitate my meeting with my teams once a week. While the day isn't confirmed yet, and as no other days seem to suit, meetings look like being on Tuesdays. So, there is a fair chance I'll compromise our mahjong days as well."

Rod didn't hesitate to respond. "Congratulations... that is, if congratulations and not commiserations are in order. Don't worry about mahjong. It will sort itself out as we go along. In the meantime, just continue to join us whenever you are able. Do these meetings mean you have to hare off to Sydney every week?"

"Oh, God, no. Our meetings won't be face-to-face... except on the odd occasion, I mean. We'll meet in cyberspace via Zoom or something similar."

*****

At our Thursday mahjong session, both Maria and Alice dropped in as we were wrapping up our last games for the morning. Everyone lingered a bit longer to catch-up with them, before drifting off home for lunch. It left only Rod, Cilla and me with the newcomers. Alice's eyes drifted to our so-called library. I had noticed her glance at it a couple of times while we chatted. It finally got the better of her.

"I see nothing has been done about that bloody atrocity," she commented as she pointed to the 'library'. What are we going to do about it? There is no point in having it, if it can't be improved."

"Many attempts have been made to squeeze some funds out of management, but the requests have fallen on deaf ears. Short of robbing a bank, we have to come up with some other clever way of raising the dollars to buy some decent books," I told her.

Our discussions adjourned for the ten minutes or so it took us as a group to walk across the park to Alice's house. She had invited us for lunch. The 'library conversation' resumed over our meal. Then, after much discussion, Cilla shared her thoughts.

"Bingo…! Yes, we could run bingo nights. Those who come, buy cards to play."

"Ye-es, but then the money raised by selling the cards is paid out in prize money," I said.

"Some of it is… Maybe some percentage of it, but the rest goes into a library account with which we buy books as the funds accumulate," Cilla explained.

We agreed it might work, and Rod volunteered himself and Ted to organise and run it once a week – possibly on Friday nights. Maria appeared deep in thought for a moment before becoming excited.

"There's a pizza oven at my place. It hasn't been used since my husband became ill. I was going to include it in the garage sale I'm planning for next weekend."

Maria had barely finished speaking when Cilla responded. "What has a surplus pizza oven got to with bingo or anything else?" But, Rod was way ahead of her.

"Of course… what a great idea, Maria. If we had a pizza oven, Friday nights could be 'pizza and bingo' nights. Residents – and anyone else so inclined – could come and dine out, and then stay on to play bingo, or they could come for just one or the other of the attractions on offer. How does everyone feel about it? And, who would look after the pizza side of things?"

Excited discussion of the proposal lasted quite a while. In the end, a rough plan of how it would happen was drawn up. Some of the people mentioned in the plan still needed to be consulted, but an excited atmosphere pervaded Alice's kitchen… until she raised a further issue.

"Our proposed Friday nights could bring in a little money every week, depending on how much support we get. But, I think we need something to give us a major funds boost to kick-off our fundraising campaign."

"I agree, but I don't suppose you have any bright ideas about how to achieve it, do you, Alice?" Maria asked. "It's taken us ages to come up with the plan we have. Have we got what it takes to come up with some other major event, which is likely to generate a bucket of cash?"

"I think we do," Alice replied. "We could run a fashion parade."

"A fashion parade..." Cilla echoed. "Where are we going to get the clothes to parade?"

"From Vinnie's Op Shop... They have some lovely clothes and accessories in there. I know the woman well who runs it. I think she would be up for a parade featuring her stock. Of course, it would mean a fair bit of work to organise everything, and set it up on the day. ...And, there would need to be models who fitted the clothes in the parade.

People would pay to come in, and their entry fee would pay for morning or afternoon tea, depending on what time of day it was run. I'm sure Vinnie's would help advertise it to all their customers, so we wouldn't be relying on just Village residents to attend."

Longer and more involved discussions ensued, but the excitement continued to develop until it almost was palpable. As a first step, Alice would talk to her friend at Vinnie's Op Shop about the idea. If she wasn't interested, the idea was dead before we expended any further energy on it.

Late in the afternoon, three of us walked back across the park to the Village, while Maria drove to her house in town for the night. Silence reigned until we turned onto our street, and Rod committed to words, the thoughts probably each of us harboured since leaving Alice's place.

"I suppose our first move should be to inform the rest of the mahjong mob of everything we've been scheming and planning all afternoon. We need to work out who will be in charge of the pizzas, and I need to tell Ted he has been volunteered for the bingo nights. As for the fashion parade, if it comes off, that's something which sounds like *women's work* to me." His final comment earned him a heap of derision from Cilla and me.

Rod called a meeting for Saturday morning in the Rec Room. All the mahjong crew were there, including Maria and Alice. As no meeting is complete without morning tea, I supplied a batch of cupcakes to help keep everyone interested. Rod had done his homework, and prepared well for the occasion. We arrived to find a number of sheets of butcher's paper stuck up on the walls. The four females who were involved in the 'scheming and planning session' at Alice's place, sat back in silence, and allowed Rod to address the assembly.

This was the moment of truth. The others would either love it, or hate it – either partially or in total. They loved the concepts – both of them. Then, the hard part began: establishing lists of the required equipment and the tasks associated with each of the plans – and who would do what – to make them happen.

It was a long, arduous morning but, by the time we went home for lunch, those sheets of butcher's paper were filled with notes and lists. Work on implementing the plans would begin next week. And, it included launching the bingo and pizza nights next Friday night – if the pizza oven arrived in time. The hope was Tanya Jellicoe, our director, could be persuaded to allow the Village's maintenance crew to collect it from Maria Lancini's house in town.

Cilla, Rod and I stayed behind to tidy the Rec Room after everyone else left. While obviously assessing the space, Cilla stood, swivelling from the waist, as she surveyed the room. "I'm almost not game to ask this question, but where are all these events we are planning going to happen? This place won't hold many people, not once you set up tables and chairs."

"Good point, Cilla," I said. "I was thinking much the same thought. This is a huge building, but this room occupies less than half of it. What is behind those doors? Rod, do you know?"

"Not exactly but, if this key fits, we'll soon find out." He marched over to try his key, and soon we were pushing the concertina doors open against the side walls.

The place opened up to a huge hall-like space. Several small spaces beyond it occupied part of the area at the other end of the building. One was a substantial storeroom containing a number of trolleys loaded with folding tables, and another held stacks of chairs.

"What do you think all this stuff stacked over here might be for?" Cilla asked.

We went to investigate the 'stuff' in question. It looked like a collection of large wooden crates stacked one on top of the other against one wall of the storeroom. After a cursory inspection, Rod announced, "They go together to form a stage. See how these tags lock them together so they won't move about or separate."

Further investigation of that end of the building revealed a couple of small empty rooms, and a kitchen area running across the width of the very end of the building. Our journey of discovery completed, we returned to the main area. Rod stood, hand on hips, looking down towards the kitchen.

Then, with a decisive nod, he said, "Yes, I think this will do just fine. This building is big enough and has everything we need for all the things we plan to do. All we need to do before next Friday, is install the pizza oven and buy the necessary frozen pizzas."

As we entered our street on our way home, we met Ted coming the other way. "When nobody was home at Rod's place, I guessed you might still be at the Rec Room. Rod, I've had a bit of an idea. How do you feel about a karaoke machine?"

"I don't know how I feel about one. I've never given one a thought. Why would I? They are not my idea of fun."

"No, but other people like them. I thought one might go down well with patrons who stay for pizzas after the fashion parade. If we have the live entertainment we discussed during the parade, people might be in the mood to party-on afterwards."

"Good point... but I don't know anything about such machines, so it will be in your hands to organise and set it up."

"What makes you think I know anything about karaoke machines?"

"You're an engineer."

"Yes, but I don't remember doing Karaoke 101 as part of my studies."

"Well, we will hire one in the first instance, and whoever we hire it from can come and set it up, and show us how to use it. After all, we are only two old codgers who don't understand all this modern technology stuff, and could manage to blow it up because we don't know what we are doing."

"That would work." Cilla quipped. "After such a spiel, I'd be surprised if they didn't insist on coming to man it on the night to ensure the safety of their gear."

By the end of the weekend, the place was buzzing with excitement, and people were attacking their allocated tasks with gusto. My task was to buy a supply of frozen pizzas and store them in my freezer, and then to coordinate the cooking and distribution of them on pizza nights. And, yes, I did seem to escape lightly compared to the tasks others were given. Thanks, Rod.

But then, as an afterthought, I wondered if he considered the task he gave me was the only one I was capable of carrying out.

Chapter 26

The launch of the bingo and pizza nights was deemed a huge success. The maintenance crew had retrieved the oven and installed it in the kitchen of the Rec Room, and the electrician came and tested and tagged it on Thursday, so we were right to go on Friday night. None of us even thought about giving it a test run before the big night. Rod produced a poster to advertise the coming attraction, and copies were spread around the Village, the Senior Citizens' Centre, and various other key places around town.

Our first night saw forty people heads-down playing bingo, and thirty of them wanting pizzas afterwards. It was as well no more stayed for dinner. I had exhausted the supply of pizzas I bought. (Memo to self: look for a bulk wholesale buy before next week.)

A surprising aspect of our inaugural night was the amount of cash in kitty at the end of it. A couple more nights like the first one would ensure we had sufficient funds for everything we needed for the fashion parade – including hiring the karaoke machine.

Marjorie spoke to the school where she does a bit of remedial reading with students. They agreed to have the school choir help entertain those attending the fashion parade. And, one of the other residents, whose granddaughter is a local singer/songwriter, arranged for the girl to come and add to the entertainment.

Although the fashion parade was still a month away, advertising was everywhere, and everything on site was organised, even the hire of the karaoke machine was arranged and paid for. Various residents – both male and female – and a handful from outside the Village had been selected as models.

They covered a range of shapes and sizes, and a good deal of time was being taken up with fittings and alterations to ensure every garment looked 'just right' as it paraded down the 'catwalk'. The local dry cleaners did well out of ensuring all the garments to be paraded looked crisp and spotless on the day.

Ted and Rod had worked out how to set up a tiny stage using some of the plinths in the storeroom, and the remainder of the plinths would to be used to create a catwalk. After the parade was finished, and the event moved to the pizza night part of the evening, the catwalk plinths would be rearranged to provide a larger stage where the karaoke machine would be set up.

My preparations for the fashion parade included baking a mountain of scones and cupcakes for the afternoon tea, and freezing them until the day, when they would be thawed and the cupcakes would be decorated. Judging by the way things were shaping-up, we might need to consider purchasing a small freezer for the Rec Room's kitchen.

Ted's wife, Janet, and a couple of her mates were tasked with making trays of sandwiches on the day. Bookings for tables were rolling in. We all felt confident of a full house. Afternoon tea would be served to each table as its guests arrived. Then, after a suitable interval, and a welcome speech, the parade would kick off.

*****

Now, on looking back, it's amazing to reflect on how the whole event went off without a hitch. My memories are: of the building being a hive of activity from early morning, of streams of people arriving and settling at their tables, of everyone appearing to enjoy the show, of cooking what felt like thousands of pizzas, of terrible karaoke singing until well into the night ... and of being thoroughly exhausted by the time I fell into bed very late that night. The next day was almost as bad, as we needed to clean up and put everything away again.

The week after the fashion parade, we all agreed there was a certain satisfaction in the fact the pizza nights and the fashion parade had achieved their end goals. We had a healthy sum with which to purchase new books for our library. Marjorie was eager to take-up her librarianship, and had already disposed of several of the existing books considered beyond repair.

Our job now was to convince her not to dash out and purchase books on the list she had created, but to consult with the residents first about what they might like to read. She was quite adamant, as a librarian, she knew what people should be reading and didn't need to consult with anyone … particularly those with no knowledge or training in such matters. It was left to Rod and Bernard to convince her otherwise. They had some measure of success when 'consulting with the residents' was reduced to recommendations from a Library Advisory Committee consisting of five residents – of which, Bernard was one.

Over the last couple of months, the Village had come alive. Residents were coming out of their houses and units to mingle and interact. The bingo and pizza nights always attracted a full house. Talk around the place was all the units were either now occupied, or soon would be. People had heard it was a lively place, and had queued up to move in. The new library, with all its books now sporting protective covers, barcodes and Dewey numbers, was a raging success. So much so, Marjorie was forced to source an assistant from amongst the new arrivals.

For me, life had never been so busy since I retired. Our twice-weekly mahjong mornings continued, and a couple of the new residents had joined our ranks to give us three full tables at every session. Bernard's contract with the university had ended at the close of the academic year, and he also became Marjorie's part-time library assistant. I took on more of the responsibility for organising the bingo and pizza nights to take some of the pressure off Rod.

Everything seemed to be running smoothly, until Cilla dropped a bombshell one Thursday as we walked home from mahjong in the Rec Room.

"My *Significant Other* – partner, special male friend, or whatever you want to call him – arrives back in the country next week. I'm not sure how long he will be back, but it probably won't be any more than a month. I will fly down on the weekend to meet and spend time with him while he is here, and we'll also manage to spend some time with my son while we're in and around Sydney. I'll be back before Christmas, so I hope you start planning a Christmas event while I'm away. Just allocate me whatever jobs you think I can do."

A few days later, Cilla explained over drinks at Rod's place how she and her partner had been in a relationship for more than twenty years, but had never sought to formalise the arrangement. He had one of those jobs 'that doesn't exist and can't be talked about', and which necessitated his spending most of his life in strange overseas places. The nature of his job meant a wife, or similar appendage, was a serious liability which would render it impossible for him to continue in his current line of work. So, they maintained a relationship, which exists on an 'occasional' basis, and strived to make the most of whatever time they had together whenever he was back in the country. She said she accepted the arrangement would have to stay that way until such time as he too retired or took on a different role within his organisation.

My reservations about Cilla evaporated after I heard her story. Almost within an instant, she went from being 'competition' to being a solid friend. And, from past performance, one I would want in my corner if the going got rough.

The other major event worth mentioning was the arrival of those parcels Alice sent us before leaving Singapore. I told Alice as soon as mine arrived, and she alerted the Sydney police. It was the day before Cilla left for Sydney, so they instructed her to take charge of the parcels, and they flew her and our parcels to Sydney on a private plane.

Those parcels were the cause of everything Alice endured in Sydney. When she bought them, and while they were being gift-wrapped in the back of the shop, a special 'packing' was inserted. The Asian gentleman who befriended Alice in the shop, and then followed her about all the way back to Sydney was tasked with stealing the packages and delivering them to their 'real' destination – the mob Alice's son, David, was involved with.

When the man and his mates broke into her room at the hotel and discovered Alice didn't have the gift wrapped packages, they assumed, somehow, she had handed them onto David… who just happened to disappear around the same time. When she couldn't give them the parcels, and wouldn't tell them where David was, they abducted her and tried to force the information out of her – information she didn't have. We are still shocked about how that other world, which we only glimpse through media coverage, came so close to home for us here in the Merivale Retirement Village.

So now, with Christmas fast approaching, I can't help but marvel at the change which had occurred over the past year, both in the Village… and in me. I'm feeling more confident and alive than I have in decades. And, it doesn't take a genius to work out why. It probably has a lot to do with the time I am spending with Rod… socialising, working with him, and the frequent intimate dinners we share.

Roll on next year and let's see what else might develop.

The End

Other Books by the Author

An Ancient Solution
A Public Service
Missing!
Connections
A Different Obsession
Shattered Illusions
After The Ball
Unholy Secrets
Fateful Reunion

About the Author

Neive Denis is the creator of the series featuring the Private Investigator, Sonoma (Sonny) Whittington. Neive Denis is the pen name of a writer who was lured from her usual genre to focus on the mystery and excitement that are a part of Sonoma Whittington's world. Neive came into being specifically for this series and, for the moment at least, intends remaining faithful to only stories from Sonny's case files.

This series tells of the intrigue and scrapes – some on occasion life threatening – that are part of the life of Sonoma Whittington, an Australian Private Investigator based in a Central Queensland coastal city. However, Sonny doesn't confine her escapades to Australia, and that provides Neive with an opportunity to weave some of her other areas of interest into Sonny's hair-raising adventures.

This book is the first in what promises to be a new – and different – series set in the Merivale Retirement Village.

See more about Neive Denis and her work at

www.eaglemountbooks.com.au/neivedenis

or contact her at

admin@eaglemountbooks.com.au

www.ingramcontent.com/pod-product-compliance
Lightning Source LLC
Chambersburg PA
CBHW070547120726
47909CB00007B/2269